THE RECONSTRUCTION OF WALTER PIGG

Carl Purdon

Dedication

For my loving wife, Sharon.

Acknowledgements

I would like to thank Pontotoc, Mississippi police officer, Jeff Turner, for taking the time to answer some of my police-related questions, and for giving me a general overview of the hierarchy of investigative agencies in the state of Mississippi. Any mistakes made along such lines within these pages are completely my own.

Also By Carl Purdon

THE NIGHT TRAIN

NORTON ROAD

BLINDERS

RED EYES

TEMPLE'S GHOST

THE DECONSTRUCTION OF WALTER PIGG

CHAPTER 1

Cecil Pigg told his sons to always be men. They had never discussed details. He hadn't sat his sons down and engaged them in how-to conversation on the subject. Always be a man is what he said, and that was all.

"My father would kick me nine ways to Sunday," Walter said, staring down into the coffee cup cradled between his hands on the kitchen table. "First he would say how could you be so stupid, then he would kick me in the seat of the pants."

"Your father never kicked you," Mildred said with a voice tired from not having slept. "And he never called you stupid." She stood at the stove cooking eggs and toast as they conversed back to back. The rattling of pans and the smell of breakfast anchored him in reality. It was Wednesday morning and he was awake. The Hayes Beacon lay rolled up on the lawn somewhere between his mailbox and oblivion, depending on the mood of the paperboy. The headline would be a keeper. All over town people were no doubt rubbing their sleepy eyes in disbelief.

"He liked you," Walter said as he raised the cup to his lips and blew against the hot liquid. Of course she was right about his father. Cecil Pigg had been a disciplinarian but never abusive. His strength came from someplace Walter had never seen. Some secret enclave for men where the weak are not allowed. Sometimes, when his thoughts swirled like leaves in a whirly devil, Walter almost allowed himself to suspect his mother of conceiving him with a substitute. There was no denying he was different from his brothers, and certainly different from his father, though the physical resemblances were too pronounced to dismiss and, of course, there was his mother's virtue to consider. There was no more devoted wife and mother than Mae Pigg, God rest her soul. Walter didn't mean to think such distasteful things about his mother, it was just that he couldn't always control his thoughts.

"Walter?"

"Yes Dear?"

"I said I liked him too," Mildred said. "Your father," she added when he didn't seem to understand. She was too used to his wandering mind to ask if he needed to have his ears checked.

"I should go get the paper before the neighborhood dogs come scrounging."

He heard her switch off the stove eye. They both knew she would be the one to go because his back had flared up again. Since the surgeries, pain had become his new normal, but some days were worse than others and Mildred always seemed to know without asking.

She placed a platter with eggs and toast in the center of the table then started toward the back door. The Hayes Beacon had been in Tipton Palo's camp since the moment he announced for mayor. If there was any satisfaction to be had from winning, it would be watching the editor of that miserable rag eat crow.

Revenge is a weak man's salve, Cecil Pigg would have said at a time such as this, but Cecil Pigg had never been dumb enough to run for mayor.

* * *

Soon the sun would be up and Tipton Palo had not yet loosened his tie. Not so for Rance West, his law partner and so-called campaign manager, who hours ago had sprawled out on the sofa in the lobby of their plush office like a deer hound after an all-day hunt. Tipton had never hunted anything in his life but he knew the lingo. He knew about cover scents and climbing stands and how wives aren't allowed within ten miles of camp not because their husbands are cheating but because they are regressing. Southern men of every profession rush away from their lives on opening day and become savages. Hunting is to the southern man what golf is to the Wall Street financiers who hold the purse strings of the world. Doctors and bankers shuck their coats and ties and pull on camouflage coveralls and orange vests and become indistinguishable among the factory rabble and construction workers and the unemployed. They curse and drink and spit. Lawyers too, and judges. Tipton knew because he listened. A good lawyer absorbs the world around him, and Tipton Palo was more than a good lawyer, he was among the best.

He pushed his fingers through his dark hair and stared down the long table at the empty chairs and the unopened bottles of champagne, at the fancy glasses with long stems and the several bowls of mints and salted nuts. Nothing had been touched except for his personal bottle of scotch and countless empty beer bottles that had followed Rance around the room like breadcrumbs before he finally collapsed onto the sofa and began to snore.

Tuesday night had become Wednesday morning with all the numbers in and a final tally that defied logic. Something was afoot. Pigg had cheated. He had rigged the election and stolen it right out from under Tipton's nose. The election was supposed to have been a formality. Everyone said so. He had already ordered decor for his new office. Paintings signed by dead artists and

2

two lamps that had set him back almost a thousand dollars were ready to be shipped at his command.

The snoring stopped abruptly. Rance lay motionless. Tipton sucked in the dead silence of the room and waited. Five seconds passed, then ten. Rance lived hard and looked it. The wrinkles around his mouth were deep enough to lay a pinky finger in, and his complexion had a two day head start on death. Fifteen seconds, then a gasp that rocked his body from head to toe and his chest began to pump again. Too damned bad. Campaign manager! More like campaign saboteur. Rance twisted and stretched himself but didn't open his eyes. He pushed his feet up over the arm of the sofa so that his dirty socked feet jutted up like some homeless bum sleeping it off on a park bench. Rance was little more than a bum. Sooner or later they would have to renegotiate this equal partner nonsense. They both knew who brought the real money into the firm. Rance was a third-rate divorce attorney and Tipton had just settled a multi-million-dollar lawsuit. Rance consoled jilted lovers while Tipton raided insurance companies.

Tipton scanned the pitiful room them glared at his partner again. "Wake up!" Rance didn't move so he said it again, louder.

"I'm awake," Rance said without opening his eyes. "Who turned the lights on?"

"Go home. You're worthless here."

"I'd be just as worthless at home," Rance said through a yawn. "What time is it anyway?"

"Some campaign manager you are. How much did Haskell pay you?"

"I'll ignore that because you're drunk," Rance said with no hint of offense at being accused.

"I'm not drunk."

"Then get drunk, pal, because you really stunk it up last night. They'll be talking about this fiasco for months. Years maybe." He withdrew a foot from the sofa arm and scratched at the dirty sock. "If you're not drunk you should be."

"I'll demand a recount?"

"And be humiliated twice?" He laughed. "You have to actually get votes before you qualify for a recount."

"This is all your fault you know."

Rance swung his feet to the floor and sat erect, grimacing as the blood rushed to his head. "If that makes you feel better."

"You said I couldn't lose."

"I think you've got that backwards."

"In four years I'll be fifty."

"In four years I'll probably be dead."

Tipton sank his face into his hands and sighed. The thought of being old terrified him. His fourteen-year plan to take the governor's office would have to be recalibrated now. Walter Pigg had ruined everything. "Contest the results."

"Not possible."

"Anything's possible. We're lawyers."

"I think I'll take your advice and go home," Rance said, sniffing at his armpits. "I'm past my expiration date." He searched the floor and found his shoes then pulled them on. "When you call Pigg and congratulate him, pretend you mean it. That kind of stuff has a way of getting out. People remember when you louse it up."

"Ha! I wouldn't call Pigg if you held a gun to my head."

Rance stood. "Suit yourself. It's your funeral." He poked his shirttail into his pants without undoing his belt. "Me, I'm just a caboose who hitched himself to the wrong train. I should've minded my own business."

Tipton seethed as Rance strode out the door without a care in the world. Nothing stuck to him because he had no ambition. No drive. No want for anything beyond what he had. It was different for Tipton. Different because he had a plan. Not a dream or a goal but a plan. Dreams and goals require luck. Plans are the result of action. Tom George resigning halfway through his second term had been the result of action, not luck, but now that plan was out the window and something would have to be done about Pigg.

The door opened again and a newspaper still rolled and banded came flying at him. "Read that," Rance said without coming in. The paper hit the table and rolled through three wine glasses and two American flags anchored in tiny bags of sand wrapped with patriotic ribbon. Two of the glasses shattered against the floor and the third teetered on the edge. Rance was like a bull in a china shop. Like a mutt too ill-bred not to shit on the rug. Tipton moved from one chair to another and rolled the red rubber band off the end of the Hayes Beacon and pressed it out flat against the table, not expecting what he saw: PALO WINS IN LANDSLIDE. His hopes soared then crashed back to earth. It hadn't worked for Dewey, and the Hayes Beacon was a far cry from the Chicago Tribune. He slapped the newspaper away and sent more glasses crashing to the floor, then he shot to his feet and flipped the table.

* * *

Walter met Brant Haskell at a small diner down the street from City Hall. It was a bustling little place that seemed an odd location for a strategy meeting. Half a dozen patrons stopped to congratulate him on his way to the table in the back where Haskell sat waiting, cradling a white coffee cup between his hands at chin level, peering at Walter as he wormed his way through the crowd like a spider waiting for its fly. Walter had the sinking feeling that he was about to learn why Haskell wanted him to be mayor. They weren't friends. Prior to Haskell approaching him with his harebrained scheme, the two men had barely spoken to each other. Once hatched, the scheme outpaced Walter. Haskell paid for everything right down to the bottles of water with *Walter For Mayor* printed on white labels and handed out by high school cheerleaders during the fall festival when the temperature threatened to add a third digit. Dropping his last name was strategy, Haskell had explained, meant to imply familiarity and not because Pigg didn't fit well in a slogan.

"Don't frown so much when you greet your public," Haskell said as Walter seated himself.

"My public!"

Haskell sipped his coffee and motioned for the waitress to come over. "They're your public now, Walter. They chose you to lead them. That's an enormous responsibility."

"They'll regret it soon enough."

"Be that as it may," Haskell said, offering his hand across the table, "congratulations."

Walter viewed the traditional handshake as one of the worst things mankind ever contrived. The human hand is a breeding ground for germs and unthinkable contamination, but to deny the custom is considered offensive, so Walter obliged, then he pulled a small bottle of hand sanitizer from his pocket and squirted a generous amount into his palm.

Haskell's face twisted itself into a question mark.

"Germs," Walter said by way of explanation as he rubbed his hands together and worked the alcohol goo between and around his fingers.

"My hands are clean."

"It's nothing personal," Walter said. "Shaking hands is a barbaric tradition. My first act as mayor would be to outlaw it if I had that power."

Haskell rolled his eyes. "What have I done to the good people of this town?"

"You've saddled them with me," Walter said. "And they may never forgive you for it. They may ride you out on a rail, tarred and feathered with an apple in your mouth."

Haskell smiled. He seemed to be in good spirits and why not? It wasn't Brant Haskell in the hot seat. It wasn't Brant Haskell's reputation on the line.

"Well in the future, when you do shake hands, try to be a little more firm about it."

"Was I not firm?"

"Like a limp noodle," Haskell said. "At least it was dry. You're not nervous and that's a good sign."

"I'm petrified," Walter said. "I'm fairly certain you've ruined me."

"You disappoint me, Walter. I thought you'd be grateful."

"I disappoint a lot of people," Walter said. "Ask my wife. She's terribly disappointed in me right now. She's been moping around all morning as though someone has died."

Haskell smiled again.

"Maybe you think it's funny but I'm in a terrible fix," Walter said. "I know absolutely nothing about politics."

Haskell lowered his cup to the table and leaned back. A very lovely young waitress appeared at their table and asked Walter if he would like to order. He waved her off, then as she turned he asked for coffee.

"Are you always so indecisive?"

"Don't goad me," Walter said. "I don't want this title so you'd better do something to get me out of it."

"It's not a title, Walter, it's a job, and there's nothing I can do to get you out of it."

"Something tells me you wouldn't if you could."

Haskell peered. The spider could smell his fly. His brain was probably churning out all sorts of quid pro quo scenarios. Tit for tat. Tat for tit. You scratch my back and I'll scratch yours. He leaned toward Walter so no one could hear what he was about to say. "We beat Tipton Palo," he said. "That's quite an accomplishment."

The spider was speaking in the collective, confirming Walter's suspicion that Haskell thought he had bought himself a mayor. Well, he had another thing coming and the sooner he understood the better. "I'm an honest man," Walter said, realizing how many times he had proven that statement false. "If you think I'm going to slip you something under the table —."

"I wouldn't dream of it," Haskell said. "My reward is seeing Tipton Palo suffer." He sipped his coffee again then pushed the cup aside. "As a matter of fact, I think you'll be good for this town. We need new blood. Fresh ideas."

"More like ineptitude and brain freeze," Walter said. "I'm an engineer, not a politician. Besides, the Hayes Beacon says I lost. Maybe they know something we don't."

"Dexter Mann is a sniveling little nobody who thinks he's important," Haskell said. "Everything he writes in the Beacon has Tipton Palo's thumbprint on it. Remember that because next week's headline will probably be a doozy. You'll need a thick skin to survive that duo."

"But of course you'll be here to guide me every step of the way."

"Nope. My job is done." He leaned back and peered again. "You really don't believe that I want nothing from you do you?"

Walter didn't, but he was willing to delay the conversation. Procrastination was something he excelled at. "I'll probably be run out of town by next week."

"You'll do fine," Haskell said. "Listen to your wife. She probably knows the ropes better than anyone. Has Palo called yet?"

"An hour ago. I'm not sure if he conceded or threatened me."

"Nothing he can do to you now except smear. If you've got any skeletons in your closet you'd better lock the door. He's a vindictive bastard."

Walter felt the acid churn his stomach. There were things Haskell didn't know. Important things. Things Walter would have told him had he thought the campaign a serious effort. Things Tipton Palo would have dug up if he had considered Walter a threat. He wouldn't really have to dig. Most of it came out while he was lying flat of his back in the hospital but it didn't take root. All anyone cared about back then was Walter the hero, not Walter the gambler. They cared that he threw himself at a man twice his size and saved his family from certain death, not that he had put his family in the poorhouse with illegal bets on everything from horses to football. Hero, what an ugly word to hang around an ordinary man's neck.

"Are you okay? You look like you've seen a ghost."

"I can't take this job," Walter said. "It's not fair to Mildred. I won't have people laughing at her because of things I've done." He watched Haskell's face transform from amusement to concern. Walter honestly didn't know how much people knew about that incident. Polite people don't talk about such things to a man's face. "How much do you know about Perry Stubbs?"

"You're not mixed up with him are you?"

"He does more than run a pawn shop, you know," Walter said. "He makes book in the back."

"I know."

"He almost wiped me out. I hid it from Mildred until it was too late." Walter lowered his eyes and took a deep breath before continuing. "If all that business with my son-in-law hadn't happened we wouldn't be sitting here."

"So the abduction was Stubbs?"

"No, but the timing of it saved my life. Stubbs was about to break my kneecaps or worse." He left out the part about him trying to hang himself. It wasn't something he talked about.

Haskell whistled. "I never would've made you for a gambler."

"Stubbs keeps a book," Walter said. "Names and dollar amounts. Some of the names you'd recognize."

"Such as?"

"It's not for me to say."

"Tom Sherman?"

"What makes you say him?"

"Something made him resign," Haskell said.

Walter didn't know how much he could divulge without being unethical. "Not him specifically."

"Someone he wanted to protect?"

"Something like that."

"How would his resigning protect anybody?"

"Maybe it wouldn't, but Stubbs showed me the book to intimidate me when I couldn't pay. To make me understand he had some powerful people under his thumb. I'm thinking Stubbs blackmailed Tom Sherman into resigning."

"Why?"

"I don't know," Walter said. "I may be completely off base. Mildred said Sherman was as straight as they come. There was a time when she thought the same thing about me."

"Everybody makes mistakes."

"I just wanted you to know it may come out on me, in case you want to distance yourself."

The waitress brought Walter's coffee and warmed Haskell's cup. Walter waited for her to leave before telling Haskell he understood if he wanted to dive for cover.

"I'm a big boy," Haskell said. "Besides, a thing like that might bolster your reputation."

"What's wrong with my reputation?"

"Nothing. Not one thing," Haskell said. "I was making a joke."

Walter had been pondering something all morning but he didn't know whether to share it or not. He certainly couldn't tell Mildred. Not yet. "I don't know how long I'll last in this job, but I've been thinking about doing something."

"Such as?"

"I've been wondering if I can make things hard on Stubbs."

"Hard as in what?"

"Put him out of business if I can. Be a thorn in his side if I can't."

"That's asking for trouble you don't need."

"I may as well do something useful."

"You're the mayor, Walter, not the police chief."

Walter hesitated, then dropped the police chief's name. W.A. Benson's name was in the book. Stubbs had bragged about it.

Haskell whistled again. "If you're asking my advice —."

"I'm not."

"Nobody expects you to risk your neck."

"Perry Stubbs destroys people."

Haskell shrugged. "People destroy themselves, Walter. Keep your mouth shut and your head down. Trust me." He stood and dropped a five on the table for the waitress. Walter watched him weave his way through the crowd until he was gone, then he finished his coffee. Haskell wanted something but wasn't ready to say what it was, and not knowing made Walter uneasy.

CHAPTER 2

Dull gray clouds rolled in from the southeast after church Sunday morning and gave Walter a sense of foreboding as he climbed one painful step after another toward the wide courthouse doors. Mildred throttled herself to his pace while Jackson darted up then down and up again in a grand display of youthful exuberance. Halfway up, Mildred repeated her suggestion that they should have parked around back and taken the ramp, though to go back down would have been folly. Walter was about to be sworn in, and for the next two years he expected to be sworn at, and he was not about to kick off his term by sneaking in through the back door and give Dexter Mann fodder for that rag he called a newspaper.

The streets around the court square were empty except for four cars parked in a row at the bottom of the courthouse steps — five, including Walter's antiquated Town Car. The black Ford Expedition belonged to Judge Bishop, he deduced, because other than Walter's Lincoln, it was the only vehicle large enough to absorb the man. The circuit clerk either drove the Toyota Camry or the Volkswagen Jetta. Certainly not the Jeep Wrangler. Sybil Wentz was built too low to the ground to make the climb.

Mildred took hold of his elbow and forced him to take a breather.

"I'm fine," he said, lying. The pain across his lower back had increased with each step and was beginning to stab down into his left thigh.

"We should've taken the ramp."

"We should've taken the quickest road out of town."

"You'll be a fine mayor." She wore the countenance of a wife accompanying her husband to his hanging, telling him it would be over quickly and he would hardly feel a thing. This particular hanging had been bumped up to Sunday because Monday was Veterans Day.

They made it up the steps and through the wide doors and into the courthouse where Jackson's darting footsteps echoed back as a stampede of children. Mildred shushed him and he giggled. Walter looked at the stairs leading up to the courtroom on the second floor and asked if there wasn't an elevator. There was, otherwise he might have resigned on the spot because his lower back burned with pain.

"You're late," Sybil Wentz said as Walter entered the courtroom to receive his sentence. The scowl on her face stirred something inside him and caused him to quip that they should have started without him. Judge Bishop laughed and said let's get on with it. He was a giant of a man with hands the size of dinner plates. The perfect Santa Claus, given the proper suit and a beard to match his white hair. He seemed jovial enough for a judge who had been dragged out on a Sunday afternoon to hang a man.

The entire ceremony took less than a minute. Walter raised his right hand and repeated the oath with his left hand on his father's Bible. Mildred stood on one side and Jackson on the other, holding the Bible for his grandfather and being very still about it probably because Mildred had threatened him. A man about Walter's age, but balding, stood off to the side snapping pictures with a large camera. Judge Bishop declared Walter mayor then congratulated him with a slap on the back and a good-natured warning not to let the naysayers get him down. Sybil Wentz glared at him as though he had snatched her purse, causing him to remember how nice and polite she had been two years ago when she came to his door campaigning. Shadowing her was a taller woman who looked thoroughly unimpressed. Wentz barked an order to her and she robotically passed a document to the judge, who signed it and passed it back unread. Important people don't read most of what they sign, and Harvey Bishop was one of the most important men Hayes had ever known.

Wentz told the cameraman to take one more, then she ordered everyone back into position and flashed a campaign smile at the exact moment the camera clicked. Perfect timing, Walter thought, then he wondered if his eyes would be cut leftward in the picture because he had been curious enough to look. Leering, might be a word Dexter Mann would use. It occurred to Walter that he may have sexually assaulted the woman without meaning to and he whispered his thoughts into Mildred's ear. She squeezed his hand and elbowed him in the ribs.

"Use that one," she said to the cameraman, who dipped his chin and said yes ma'am.

"I think I was looking off," Walter said, but they ignored him and the assembly broke up and everyone disappeared except for the Piggs and the tall woman. With the thing official, Walter felt a great sense of relief. He inhaled the room, then winked at Mildred and patted Jackson on the head. He was mayor of Hayes, Mississippi, population seven thousand and twelve at the last census. A small town with one big problem — Perry Stubbs.

"I need to lock the room," the tall woman said.

"You can lock it after we leave," Mildred said curtly, then she told Walter to take his time. It was his moment.

"It's our moment," he replied. "But let's not keep this nice lady waiting."

They took the elevator down, then the steps again because Walter insisted on looking out across the court square with the title of mayor in his pocket. It felt different, somehow. Less ominous, as though a veil had been lifted now that he felt he had a purpose. The people had given him a mandate to rid the town of a blight whether they meant to or not.

Mildred stopped beside him at the top of the steps and took his hand. "What are you thinking?"

"That I was right about the Jetta," Walter said. The only two cars remaining were the Camry and his Lincoln. In a few minutes the tall woman would dart past them and leave in the Camry. They would be halfway down the steps by then, stopped again so Walter could rest.

"Who was the man with the camera?"

"Carter Holiday," Mildred said. "He's a general flunky for the Beacon."

"Dexter Mann couldn't stomach it?"

She squeezed his hand. "We don't care about Dexter Mann or what he can stomach."

"And the tall woman?"

"She works for Wentz. I forget her name."

"Does Wentz work for me?"

"No, she's county."

"Good for her."

* * *

Too bad Tipton Palo hadn't bothered to investigate Walter Pigg during the campaign. There was more to the hero than met the eye. "The man assaulted a minor," he bellowed, waving the arrest record at his wife as she came into his study carrying a tray of finger sandwiches. She had changed into yoga pants and a white pullover that hung loose enough to hide the fact that she was not wearing a bra until she leaned forward to deposit the tray on the coffee table.

"What man, dear?" She held her stooped pose to make sure he noticed.

"Pigg! Don't ask me what man when you know what man. What other man would I be talking about?"

She straightened herself with a frown, then retrieved a bottle of wine from the bar he kept inside an innocuous looking cabinet their church friends might mistake for a shuttered bookcase. Church was very important to the Palos, though for different reasons. For Autumn, it was a pathway to salvation, but for Tipton it was a place to rub elbows with the correct people. On that particular Sunday, for him, it had proved to be one of the most awkward mornings of his life.

"What minor did he assault?"

"Some little black boy," Tipton said. "A minority *and* a minor. I'll have Rance's hide for this."

"How is it Rance's fault?"

He glared at her. She was goading him on purpose. "I'm not in the mood for you to act stupid." She tilted the wine bottle to fill his glass but he slapped the glass away and sent it shattering against the floor. "Bring my scotch."

"Get it yourself!" She slammed the wine bottle down beside the platter and dropped back into a nearby chair to sulk. She had become quite good at sulking lately.

Tipton rose and fetched his bottle from the liquor cabinet. "They mocked me this morning, you know. Did you defend me? No, you hammed it up with that little circle of bitches you hang with and pretended not to know me," he said as he poured two fingers into a glass.

She glared at him with piercing eyes but didn't dare challenge him because what he said was true. Every Sunday it was the same with her. She didn't know how to behave and people noticed. How could they not? No telling how many votes her behavior cost him.

"Dan Easterling practically laughed when I walked in."

"My friends aren't bitches," she said, ignoring his point entirely. It was a tactic she employed when they argued. "Unless you're calling me one too."

He dropped two cubes of ice into his glass. The cabinet concealed a small refrigerator stocked with imported beer and two trays of ice. There was a tiny stainless steel sink, not much more than a bowl with a faucet stuck above it, for rinsing glasses and refilling trays. The cabinet had been a gift from a wealthy client he had walked through a messy divorce. "I think it's time we find another church."

"I like our church."

"Life's not always about you, Autumn." He drained his glass then rattled the ice. "The only thing Pigg ever did in his entire miserable life was save his family from that maniac. Saved his own skin, if you ask me. The family came along for the ride. CNN took a nobody and made him a household name around here." He moved to the sofa and sat. "This town has elected itself a racist who beats children and they don't even know it." He rattled his ice again. "Well, they'll soon know it. He'll be gone in a week." He picked a square from the platter and shoved it into his mouth. It was ham and cheese with too much horseradish sauce but he let it pass. She never had been much in the kitchen.

"Don't you think people might take it wrong if you —?"

"What the hell do you know about it? You been talking to Rance again?"

"You know I don't like Rance."

He eyed her with suspicion. She had gone downhill a lot since they got married but Rance had a mind-boggling way about him with women. Autumn mistook his staring and switched from sulk to flirt like flipping a switch. She leaned forward toward the platter and took an incredibly long time picking through the little squares until she settled for one that looked exactly like all the others.

"Stop doing that," he said.

"Doing what?"

He rattled his ice again. "I'm not in the mood."

She sank back into the chair and pulled her knees into her chest. "You're never in the mood anymore! I may as well be married to a monk."

He got up and poured himself another drink. The study was an elaborate room with a wall of books he hadn't read and a very large desk he used only on occasion. He didn't love the law the way some men do, so he didn't bring his work home with him. To him the law was a way to make a living. He had no scruples about using it to take from the rich and give to himself. Damn the poor. What right did they have to anything? Justice was a commodity the same as coffee, except it had value, like gold. Justice cost money. Lots of money, and he only accepted clients who could pay, or clients with a good personal injury case against a Walmart or, better yet, a trucking company. Juries love a good fiery crash. Autumn didn't understand because she didn't share his dream. She wasn't dumb, just indifferent. Indifference is what had propelled Walter Pigg into power. Indifference and fake news. News without vetted sources. Without context. Information spooned out to a society dumbed down by public schools and social media. Sensational stories of how a man who is a nobody does something desperate to save his own skin and in the process saves others. Throw in a broken back and overlook the fact that he had once been arrested for assaulting a child and you have yourself a hero. Pretty soon you have yourself a mayor unfit for the job while the man who deserves the office sits on a three-thousand-dollar sofa in his study sipping cognac.

It crossed his mind to apologize, but he poured himself another drink instead. They had been married such a long time. Since before he made his fortune suing insurance companies, corporations, and one time a church. If it had money, he'd sue it. Suing the church had caused him some grief in certain circles, but when a person slips and falls and has medical bills, they deserve compensation. Autumn was tall and thin and somewhat attractive. Back then she was a catch for a man with no money. Women don't throw themselves at men because of money they *might* someday have. His mistake was not kicking her to the curb before it was too late. A divorce now would cost him a fortune, but he didn't really want a divorce. He simply wanted to be left alone when he wasn't in the mood.

He hesitated at the coffee table and looked down at her puffy face and dripping eyes. The longer it went on the harder it would be to pull her out of it so he relented. "I'm sorry," he said, though he was anything but. It was her fault, not his, but he could be the better person when it mattered. "I've been under a lot of stress, and now this."

She sniffed and wiped her nose with the back of her hand. "When did we become boring?"

"I've never cheated on you," he said. "Not once in twenty years."

"Okay."

"I'm not saying I haven't had opportunities."

She narrowed her eyes. "We're married you know," she said. "Not cheating comes with the license. You don't get extra points for being faithful."

"Well, anyway, I haven't. Cheated, I mean."

"I believe you."

"We're not getting any younger you know."

"We're not old yet."

"I'm staring down the barrel at fifty," he said. "And you're not far behind."

"You're only as old as you feel," she said, repeating some drivel people say when they're too old to be useful but too young to give up completely. Her mindless optimism frustrated him. Just once he'd like to see her break down and cry because she was getting wrinkles around her eyes, or because the skin on her neck wasn't tight the way it used to be, but she didn't seem to notice those things.

"Do you enjoy teaching math?"

"As opposed to teaching something important like, oh, I don't know, English?"

"Teaching," he said. "Do you enjoy your damned job?"

"I love my damned job."

"Being around all those high school kids every day doesn't make you feel old?"

She stood and pressed the flat of her hand against his chest and pushed three fingers between the buttons. "Take me upstairs and I'll show you how old I feel."

He looked into her eyes and for a moment he saw the sparkle of youth. Why not take her upstairs? Anything was better than thinking about Walter Pigg.

* * *

The Piggs stopped off at Sonic for milkshakes after leaving the courthouse. Sitting there waiting for the girl to deliver the shakes, Mildred reflected aloud what a good thing it was for Walter to let Jackson hold the Bible during the ceremony.

"He's my grandson," Walter said. Some might accuse him of pulling a publicity stunt — the boy being of mixed race — but in Walter's heart it wasn't that way at all. His sentiments toward the boy had changed since they first met two years ago. When he looked at Jackson now, he saw his grandson. Nothing more. Nothing less. Not even Mildred believed it completely, else she wouldn't have dropped such a comment on him.

"Well it was nice of you to do," she said.

The girl delivered their milkshakes on roller skates, totally unaware she was serving the newly sworn mayor. Walter joked about it after she skated away, saying he was glad he could still get a milkshake in this town without being hounded for favors, or lambasted for offenses. All that would soon change, he supposed. A lot of things were about to change. His brain had been building toward that conclusion for the past few days.

"When did they start wearing skates again?"

"Probably a new manager," Mildred said. "Their shorts are shorter too."

Walter wasn't about to admit noticing the shorts. "You still haven't given me a firm commitment on staying on as my office manager."

Mildred frowned. "Trying to ply me with milkshakes?"

"Milkshake," Walter said. "You only get one. Of course I could find some attractive young woman with large breasts to fill the position."

"Walter! Your grandson's in the back seat."

Walter laughed. "I don't think he heard me."

"If you'd rather have some attractive young woman with large breasts I won't stand in your way."

"I'd rather have my wife," he said, and he meant it. Mildred was his port in the storm. His safe haven, and he feared the winds would begin to howl soon enough.

She smiled. How could she not? Between the compliment and the strawberry milkshake, he knew he had her hooked. Now to reel her in. He took her hand. "I need you, Mildred. I trust you. You probably know more about what it takes to be mayor than Tom Sherman ever knew. Certainly more than I'll ever know."

"Tom's a good man," she said. "And he was a good mayor. It's awful what they did to him. Now they're going to do it to you."

"They'll probably try."

"Did you see the way Sybil Wentz looked at you?"

"You mean the eye daggers?"

"Don't make light, Walter. They put that poor man through the ringer. When I first started working for him he smiled all the time. This past year I don't think I saw him smile once."

"And he never said anything?"

"Not one word," she said. "But I knew something was wrong."

"Did you ask him?"

"Several times. At first he said it was nothing, then that it was personal."

"Problems at home?"

"She was in and out of the office a lot," Mildred said. "I don't think it was that kind of problem."

"You think I'll fall flat on my face, don't you?"

"Did I say that?"

"No, not with words."

She slipped her hand free of his and stared intently out the windshield, as though they were at a drive-in movie and the villain was about to push the red button and end the world. "I'm sorry if I made you feel that way." Tears crept into her eyes. "You're the smartest man I know, Walter, and you've got a heart as big as Texas, but you don't know one single thing about running a town. There's more to it than cutting ribbons with giant scissors."

Walter reclaimed her hand. "I think I can learn to be good at it," he said. "With your help."

She forced a smile. "Of course I'll keep the job." She dabbed at her eyes with the back of her hand. "Just don't forget that it was your idea when you get tired of me."

* * *

Evening service at Saint Paul's was more scant than usual. Tipton wondered aloud during the ride home how much his being Methodist played into getting trounced by Pigg. The Baptists ran just about everything in Hayes. In the entire South, for that matter. Thick as thieves, and he said so.

"You don't believe that," Autumn said. She had been a Baptist when they met, but he had cured her of it with an engagement ring. Or had it been romance and sex? She hadn't been hard to convince in either regard, now that he thought about it.

"Hypocrites," he said. "Six days a week and double on Sunday."

"Unlike you Methodists?"

"Us Methodists," he corrected her. "Twenty years and counting."

"I've been going to your church for twenty years," she said. "I am what I am." She glared at him. "Oh don't you dare pretend you care what I believe."

"I care what you say in public."

"Don't worry, I won't besmirch your church, though you have no trouble besmirching mine."

"Saint Paul's *is* your church," he said. "And you'd better not forget it."

She folded her hands in her lap. "Yes, master. Anything else I'd better not forget?"

He pressed the accelerator over the speed limit, not worried about getting a ticket because no cop in town was dumb enough to pull him over. Autumn was being combative. "What's gotten into you?"

"Nothing," she said with her eyes glued to the windshield and a terrible look on her face. "It's just the Baptist in me coming out."

They were in her Land Rover because she refused to go to church in his Porsche. People might think they were boasting, as though success was something he should apologize for. "Organized religions are like football teams," he said. "When a player switches teams he's either all in or he's not. It's not enough just to wear the jersey."

"You should write that on a meme," she said. "I bet the jocks would eat it up."

"All I'm saying is, Baptists stick with Baptists, and Pigg is a Baptist. It had nothing to do with who was the better man."

"You didn't lose because of your religion," she said. "Nobody cares about that stuff anymore."

"Why then?" He looked at her and the car veered to the shoulder. She grabbed the dash and told him to watch the road. He corrected course but refused to give up on the question. "I mean it," he said. "You know so much, tell me why I lost."

"I don't know why you lost," she said. "What difference does it make now?"

"It makes all the difference in the world," he said, glaring at her with a fury burning in his chest. "Did you vote for me?"

"What the hell, Tipton?"

The Land Rover dropped off the pavement again. "Did you vote for me or not?"

"Yes, I voted for you. What kind of wife do you think I am?"

"If you weren't my wife who would you have voted for? Tell me!"

"Slow down! You're scaring me!"

"Tell me who you would've voted for if we weren't married," he said, gripping the steering wheel for all he was worth. He was doing eighty in a forty-five, overdriving his headlights but he didn't care because he knew the road and scaring her made him feel powerful. "I'm not slowing down until you tell me."

"You!" she said. "I would've voted for you! Now slow down!"

He lifted his foot off the accelerator and watched the speedometer plummet. "See, that wasn't so hard now was it?" She made no reply and it was too dark to see her features. "I'll destroy him," he said, calmer now. Pigg was a nobody. A nothing. "Total annihilation."

CHAPTER 3

The plan was to continue in his position at H&G in a part-time capacity, continuing with his current projects then taking on new assignments as time allowed. Nothing had been discussed because no one expected him to win, but things had been assumed. At least they had been assumed by Walter.

"I've been fired," he said to Mildred. It was middle of the morning Tuesday, his first day in his new office at City Hall, and the bosses he had loyally served for so many years had fired him in the most humiliating way possible. "By a junior engineer." He carefully placed his cell phone on his desk when he so badly wanted to throw it against the wall. "Last week I was giving him orders and now he's firing me."

"Can he do that?"

"He can't but they can," Walter said. "And they just did. They didn't have the guts to do it in person so they had an underling call me and do it over the phone."

"But why?"

Good question. Being mayor didn't have to be a full time occupation. Nothing in the law said he couldn't work another job. His hours weren't defined by any statute that he knew of, and he had called his boss yesterday and told him he wanted to spend a day or two getting settled.

"He said they'll send my personal belongings here."

Mildred's face grew red. Her eyelids twitched and quivered. Warning signs, Walter knew. Precursors to an explosion if he didn't head it off. What good did it do for her to worry? He reached across the desk and squeezed her hand and told her everything would be all right. He probably wouldn't have time to work on projects anyway.

"They probably think they're doing me a favor not making me lug the boxes myself," he said, knowing it wasn't true. They didn't want to face him because they were ashamed of themselves. A short time later a man showed up at City Hall with two boxes. Walter didn't see him because Mildred stopped him at the door and refused to let him in. He was young, she said. Randy Calloway, probably, though it wasn't important. Fired is fired, regardless who delivers the remnants of a man's career packed into two cardboard boxes.

"Stop pacing," Mildred said. Walter had started without realizing it. Back and forth, forth and back. Pacing and worrying. Calculating payments and bills against his reduced salary. Engineers, good ones, make more than mayors of small towns. A lot more.

He returned to his desk and called his old boss but the secretary said he wasn't in. A lie, probably. She transferred him to HR and he stayed on the line just long enough to hear his firing confirmed by someone in an official capacity. Let go, she had said, then some gibberish about how the firm does business with the city and it would be a conflict of interest. She had been prepped.

"*Did* business with the city," Walter said with a firm voice. "Did!" He hung up without waiting for a reply. Let that soak in a while, he thought, knowing she was probably already in the boss's ear.

Mildred stuck her head in the door. "Is something wrong?"

"Yes," he said. "I won a job I didn't want and lost the one I did."

Her pretty face looked suddenly older. "Well should I go or stay?"

"Suit yourself," he said. He stood and rounded the desk and walked to the wall, pacing again, because when he was upset he paced. Mildred watched him, shaking her head. "You may as well go," he said. "And close the door. I may kick something."

She closed the door a bit too hard not to be angry with him. Mildred wasn't one for theatrics. If she slammed a door she meant it, unlike Walter who sometimes milked a thing for dramatic effect. He turned from the door and kicked an ottoman that had no business being in an office. Offices are for work, not relaxation. Perhaps Tom Sherman wasn't the superhero Mildred had made him out to be.

It hurt his foot — kicking the ottoman. He hadn't meant to kick it so hard. What a boneheaded move. Now he had a sore foot and pain radiating from his lower back in every direction, especially down his left thigh all the way to the knee. Sciatica, the doctor had called it. Unrelated to his injury but somehow it never bothered him before he broke his back. Press a doctor for details and they start muttering about how complex the human body is, disregarding the fact that understanding the complexity of it is exactly why they get paid such ridiculous fees. Medicine is the only profession in the world where you get paid the same for failure as for success. Doctors should try engineering. They should try designing an assembly line for millennials!

As the throbbing in his foot began to subside, he supposed there was an ottoman in the office because there was a matching armchair, and there was an armchair because there was a sofa. Why a sofa? Ask Tom Sherman, or don't, because he suddenly wasn't one for answering questions. Perhaps the sofa and the matching chair-ottoman combo played into his sudden resignation. Perhaps the spunky young clerical with the purple streaks in her hair could answer that. Perhaps it had nothing to do with his father and his brothers' names being in Stubbs's book. Getting caught on a sofa with your purple-haired young assistant might make a man resign suddenly, without explanation. Of course Mildred didn't know. He could never suspect her of knowing a thing such as that. Were she privy to those details, even if she suspected, Kelsey French and her purple hair would have been packed up and shipped out with Tom Sherman's other belongings.

Were it true, that is. Walter had no evidence of it, other than a man's unexplained departure from a job he had worked so hard to get. A job that now hung over Walter's head like a block of concrete suspended by a thread. The same couldn't be said of him if he resigned because he hadn't worked hard at all. The job practically landed in his lap, but how could he resign now and be completely unemployed? They were barely back on their feet after his gambling almost ruined them. He summoned Mildred and apologized. She gave him a peck on the cheek and told him everything would be all right, and under different circumstances he may well have believed her.

* * *

Candice Bey glanced up when her boss strode through the front door feeling satisfied with himself for getting the new mayor sacked from his job. His real job — the one he would wish he still had before the week was up. Politics is about more than winning elections. It's about having connections with the right people. Voters as a group are useful idiots who cast their ballots for purely selfish reasons. The trick to winning is convincing enough people they stand to gain if you win, or that they stand to lose less. Tipton's biggest mistake was entrusting his campaign to his incompetent partner.

"Where's Rance?"

"Lunch," Candice said, totally engrossed with her computer screen. Probably on Facebook, or watching a YouTube video with the volume turned down. Standing as he was, Tipton could almost see her navel. Her cleavage pulled the eyes in and guided them in that general direction.

"It's two o'clock," he said. "Lunch ended an hour ago."

She glanced up and gathered her shirt. "All I know is he left for lunch and hasn't come back yet."

Getting caught with his eyes in her shirt embarrassed him. "Well when he does — IF he does, send him to my office. And button your shirt. This is an office, not a brothel."

She looked more amused than angry. "It doesn't have any more buttons."

"Then don't wear it again. My wife might come in."

"I'm sure she has no reason to be jealous," she said, "but if it bothers you I'll only wear it outside the office. Your wife won't mind that will she?"

Insolence. Another thing he could blame on Rance. Hiring and firing took unanimous consent, and Rance had been banging Candice for months. The man was fifty-five and still couldn't keep it in his pants. Married and divorced three times. Why he went for Candice was easy to see, but why she went for him remained a mystery. It couldn't be money because wife number three had cleaned his clock.

Half an hour later Rance strode into Tipton's office reeking of cheap perfume. "Next time take the afternoon," Tipton said.

"In case you haven't seen the sign out front, my name's on this place too."

"At least straighten your hair. It looks ridiculous."

That knocked the smile off his face. Rance straightened his toupee and plopped down in the chair across the desk from his partner and hooked his right leg over the arm. "Why you gotta be so combative all the time, Tip?"

"Call me that again and I'll punch you in the face."

"Touchy," Rance said. "Candice said you've got your ass on your shoulders. What's up?"

"Is that how she said it?"

"Word for word, except for the what's up part. I came up with that on my own."

"She'll do good to keep her mouth shut and her tits in," Tipton said. "Did you see how she's dressed?"

"How could I not?"

"It's unprofessional."

"Business is good," Rance said. "Maybe she's the reason." He winked. "Most of our clients are men, and most men like that sort of thing. You'd like it too if you weren't so uptight."

"*I'm* the reason business is good," Tipton said, and he meant it. "You don't think I hear about her enough from my wife without her flaunting herself like that?"

"Show me a wife who isn't jealous. Besides, her clock's ticking. Candice, not Autumn." He grinned. "Nothing wrong with putting your best foot forward."

"It's not her foot she's putting forward," Tipton said, "and she can let her clock tick some place other than this office."

Rance shrugged. "Give it a rest, Tip. You like tits don't you? She said you stared hard enough."

"Stop calling me Tip!" He paused to compose himself. Rance liked to rattle his cage and letting him hear the rattle only made him shake the bars harder. "Autumn may not have a big rack but she's got brains."

"Sure she does. She married you, didn't she?"

"That's not what I meant and you know it. She's intelligent."

"Seems a fair trade."

"She's capable of carrying on a conversation about something other than

Candy Crush."

Rance adjusted himself. "You want me for something other than breaking my balls, because if not, I've got Harvey Chapman coming in and you know what a joyride he is."

"I thought you settled that case."

"I did. I got his child support cut in half. Half, mind you, and it was no easy trick considering he's loaded. I almost feel guilty about it. Poor woman. Of course you don't see it that way because you hate kids."

"I don't hate kids."

"How come you don't have any then?"

"We decided —."

"Ha! You decided. Your wife's a schoolteacher, and schoolteachers like kids or they wouldn't be schoolteachers."

Tipton bristled. "That's right, and she's my wife, not yours, and the kids we don't have are our business, not yours."

"Don't be so touchy."

"What have you dug up on Pigg?"

"Nothing," he said, dropping his foot to the floor to stand. "You know why I got nothing? Because the election's over and I didn't dig. We lost. Time to focus on the firm again."

"Like you've been doing for the last three hours? You smell like a whorehouse."

Rance stood and turned to leave, then he turned back. Tipton hated the way his partner sailed through life without bumping against the rocks. Nothing fazed him because he didn't care about anything. He had no ambition other than his next lay. "What I smell like, Tip, is two hours of euphoria after which I get to go my merry way and not spend the rest of the day listening to somebody bitch. That includes you." He stopped again at the door. "Open or closed?"

"Closed," Tipton said. He had an important phone call to make.

* * *

"Yesterday was peaches and cream," Walter said to Mildred over supper after spending his first day in his new office. "Yesterday I had the title but no responsibility. Today I wish I were back at H&G."

"You did fine for your first day," she said. "First days are always the worst."

"I don't see it getting better."

"I'm sure you said that about your first day at H&G. In fact, I'm certain I remember it."

Walter looked at Jackson, who was busy cleaning his plate. "You could have done what I did today, young man. Probably better."

Jackson grinned with bits of white meat on his teeth.

"Your grandfather did fine," Mildred said. "Eat your chicken."

"Your grandmother's trying to cheer me up."

"And it's working wonderfully," she said.

Walter devoured a chicken leg, just then realizing how hungry he was. Even an unaccomplished man has to eat. "I'll make those ingrates sorry they ever fired me." He shook the naked bone at her. "Fire me because they do business with the city, well, I'll show them how this city does business from now on. They're not the only engineering firm in town."

"But they're the best," Mildred said. "You've said it yourself."

"Were the best. Without me they're only mediocre."

"Your grandfather's upset because he's not an engineer anymore," Mildred said to Jackson. The boy barely glanced up.

"They took my job, Mildred, not my degree."

"You'll have more time to focus on being mayor now."

"I'll focus all right. I'll focus on making sure this town only does business with reputable firms."

"Don't be vindictive, Walter."

"In two years I'll be out of a job and we'll be on food stamps."

"You'll get another job."

"Not in this town," he said. "Do you have any idea how much baggage a failed politician carries?"

"Then don't fail."

Walter stared at her with his jaw unhinged. Don't fail? When did that become an option? He knew absolutely nothing about politics and he had two years to prove it, and based on the phone calls he'd gotten all day, the only thing anyone in Hayes cared about was how many potholes were on their street. Come to think of it, maybe he could spend the next two years fixing potholes and win re-election in a landslide.

"Do you know how this town awards bids, Mildred? People think it's a fair process because the lowest bidder always wins. Well, no, the lowest bidder doesn't always win. No bidder wins without greasing the right palms." He had seen enough of the process at H&G to know how it worked. The lowest bid could always be rejected, and there were ways to make certain the right people know exactly when to bid and how much. "It's no accident that the same people always do the work."

"And you're going to fix it I suppose?"

"As a matter of fact, yes. I may fix a lot of things."

"Before or after you punish your old bosses?"

"Instead of," Walter said. "It's been so long since they've had to play fair, they'll be gut-punched before they know what hit them. And when they figure out *what* hit them, they'll realize *who*."

He finished another chicken leg. "The last time we had fried chicken, Amy was home."

"Walter!"

Walter looked at his grandson, who gave no indication of connecting the name Amy to the word momma, then back at his wife. "I'll make a lot of enemies."

"Just remember you're the mayor, Walter, not the police chief."

"Speaking of which, I think it's high time this town had a police chief who's honest."

"You can't say things like that anymore."

"I can and I will. W.A. Benson is a crook and everybody needs to know it. If the mayor can't say it, who can?"

"The mayor can't go around saying things he can't prove."

"Then this town made a mistake electing me." He stripped away the last morsel of chicken with his teeth and peered at Mildred over the bone. "Because I intend to clean up a few things." He dropped the bone into his plate and wiped his mouth with his napkin, realizing he had just added one more goal to his list of one. Or had he? Stubbs and Benson might be a team. Bringing down one might necessarily bring down the other.

"Please be careful."

"Hayes hasn't elected anything except a Democrat to local office since Reconstruction, and I'm the first independent ever. If that's not a mandate for change, I don't know what is."

"People don't like change."

"Shakespeare was a prophet," Walter said.

"He most certainly was not!"

"Not of God, Mildred, of humanity. Of civilization. Of course civilization may have always been this way. Perhaps he was an historian and we remember him all wrong. People may have schemed against one another since Adam and Eve, which I suppose is true because look what she did to him with the apple."

"The Bible doesn't say it was an apple."

"I think it does," he said.

"I'm certain it doesn't."

Walter pondered the possibility of being wrong about such a basic thing all his life. It would be just like humanity to get it wrong. Someone put a name to an unnamed fruit and everyone else fell in line. No one questioned it, except Mildred, and he wasn't about to question her when it came to Scripture. She could find a Bible verse quicker than Google.

"Why are you smiling?"

"No reason," he said. "I retract what I said."

"About the apple or about Shakespeare?"

"Both. Shakespeare wasn't a prophet at all. He was a magnifying glass. A microscope. Most writers are, you know, though only the really good ones pull it off. The rest are merely windows. I may write a book myself someday. I'm sure I could do it. It can't be that hard."

"I wish you'd stop," Mildred said. "You're worked up."

Nervous is what she meant, or agitated. Walter tended to babble when he grew nervous or agitated, even in his thoughts. The octopus inks, the skunk stinks, and Walter Pigg thinks. Overthinks, and when he vocalizes those thoughts, it drives Mildred up the wall.

"Rex Andrews could have won had I not siphoned off so many votes. It would have been quite a feat — the first Republican since Reconstruction, but I won. Me, the independent. That's historic. This town chose me and we'll all suffer the consequences together." The entirety of Walter's thoughts came crashing down around him and he felt suddenly and completely overwhelmed. "The question is, what do I do now?"

"You learn."

"One upheaval after another," he said. "That's what my life has been these past few years. Yours too, thanks to me. I'm the common denominator in every bad thing that's happened to this family." He looked at Jackson and thought of Amy. The boy had her nose. Mildred said chin, but Walter couldn't see it. Everyone sees what they see.

"That's not true," she said. "You had nothing to do with the California matter." She glanced at their grandson as though California were a word the boy didn't comprehend. Jackson looked up at her, chewing, but said nothing. Walter appreciated her effort, but it didn't alter his outlook.

"I should resign."

"A moment ago you were going to change the world."

"A moment ago I was high on fried chicken," he said. "All that grease got my mouth working." The truth was, Walter's life had been one continuous battle with depression. Short bursts of optimism followed by long, agonizing bouts of self-doubt and foreboding.

"You can't put the town through another election. Don't you dare."

"Well then, with that overwhelming vote of confidence, I'll serve out my sentence, but don't say I didn't warn you."

* * *

Dexter Mann had played one role or another at the Hayes Beacon for most of a generation. For the past thirteen years he filled the position of general manager through highs and lows in readership, the highs being low enough to put most newspapers out of business, but the Beacon was a weekly and most people in Hayes couldn't read about their neighbors anywhere else other than Facebook, so the subscriptions held.

"I turned sixty-five in June," Mann said over his tumbler, "and this is the first time I've drank scotch."

"And?"

"I prefer bourbon. Or vodka."

"Ask and ye shall receive," Tipton said, rising from his plush chair. "I have the best vodka money can buy." He winked and added, "On a lawyer's budget, of course." He rarely drank the stuff himself but kept it on hand because it was so versatile. Autumn could be plied with it on occasion, not that she needed alcohol to get her in the mood. She was a better lay when she'd had a few. Whether it was true of most women, he couldn't say, because college girls didn't count and he had been married a long time.

"I've drank my quota," the newspaperman said.

"Nonsense. Alcohol frees the soul." He went to the bar and pulled the bottle from the middle shelf. "Name your mixer."

"Nothing, really. I shouldn't. My soul is free enough."

Tipton laughed as he poured the clear liquid into a fresh glass then dropped in two cubes of ice. "Newspapermen don't have souls," he said. "It's common knowledge." He mixed in two fingers of club soda and delivered it to Mann. "Drink up and tell me that's not the best vodka you've ever had."

Dexter Mann took a sip and shrugged. What good did it do to waste quality booze on a lout?

"I really should be going."

"We haven't finished our conversation," Tipton said. He preferred to say what he had to say with the man well oiled. He settled himself back into his seat and watched Mann take a gulp. The trouble with making your own fortune is that you don't have fathers and grandfathers to throw at the older generation when you need a favor. Sure, Tipton had a father, and a grandfather, but they were nobodies. A real estate salesman and a farmer. His father had sold real estate to the upper class but he couldn't play golf with them now that he had retired. He couldn't call them up and talk about the grandkids. His usefulness vanished with his business card.

Dexter Mann had stopped squirming.

"Let's talk about this week's headline," Tipton said. "You've probably got pictures from Pigg's swearing-in."

"Of course."

"You'll write something cheesy about him. Show him with his family. Especially the grandson. You'll let him use that poor kid as a prop. Shame on you."

Mann's face collapsed. He took another drink. Confused.

"What the people want is news," Tipton said. "Something positive. The election was last week's news. Give them something they haven't already read on Facebook."

"I'm still getting calls about that headline. My lead story this week is an explanation of how deadlines —."

"Forget the headline," Tipton said. "That was last week. Print a retraction on page two. Treat it like it was no big deal and people will forget it happened."

"It's too late to change the lead story. We go to print in a few hours."

Tipton pulled a folded piece of paper from his pocket. "I don't want you to change it," he said. "I want you to replace it."

CHAPTER 4

It was still dark when Walter lumbered down the driveway in hopes of beating the neighborhood dogs to his rolled and banded copy of the Hayes Beacon. Most weeks Mildred made the trip but today the pain in his lower back was minor so he insisted. As he neared the street, he saw it lying in the grass still intact. If not for wanting to see how they covered his swearing-in he might've thought it too much trouble to stoop down and pick it up. Swearings-in always made the front page.

Mildred was putting biscuits on the table when he reentered the kitchen through the back door. Walter loved the smell of fresh biscuits in the morning, canned though they were. From a bag, she corrected him every time he used that word on her. Pre-made, he would counter, then she'd say something along the lines of, *if you made enough money so I could stay home you might get scratch biscuits.*

They didn't joke about money anymore, though. Too much negativity attached.

He flattened the paper on the table as she filled two coffee cups. They liked to get up early so they could have their time together before she went upstairs and woke their grandson. Walter liked that they still enjoyed each other's company after twenty-seven years. Almost three decades of putting each other first, except for that short stretch when Walter let the devil pull him down. Satan had dull blue eyes, bushy eyebrows, and was missing the tip of his left pinky finger. And he kept an unlit cigar clamped between his jaw teeth as he reaped souls in that dingy little office in the back of his pawnshop.

"I can't believe it," Mildred said at exactly the moment Walter saw the headline.

PALO AND WEST DONATE DECORATIONS

Hot acid hit Walter's stomach and made a splash that set his chest afire. "They couldn't be more obvious about it! I'm ashamed to admit it surprises me. It's not even Thanksgiving and the top story in Hayes is Christmas decorations."

"There must be something you can do," Mildred said. "Newspapers are supposed to be honest."

"Ha! They're only as honest as their most dishonest reporter." He flipped the page and saw an editorial about people setting their garbage bags out the night before collection day so the raccoons and stray dogs could scatter trash up and down the streets. "That's some top-notch investigative journalism right there. Dogs and raccoons ripping through the trash. At least they blamed the animals instead of me."

"Don't work yourself up," Mildred said. "People know you were sworn in. It was all they talked about at church Sunday."

He turned another page, then another, all the way through the first section and to the end of the second, past the sports and community news and the classifieds. Buried down in the bottom right corner of the obituary page was a tiny picture that, had it not been for the caption underneath, even he couldn't have made out the people in it. "There we are," he said with a heavy sigh. "Dammit, Mildred, I'll make them sorry for this!"

"Walter!"

Vulgarity wasn't a staple in Walter's vocabulary, but sometimes when a man gets his belly full he lets one slip, and unfortunately this time it slipped in front of Mildred.

"Forgive me," he said.

"It's not me you need to ask forgiveness from."

"I'll take it up with Him later," Walter said. "Right now I'd like to go down to that newspaper office and punch the editor in the nose."

"You've never punched anyone in the nose," Mildred said, and she was right, but he didn't say he was going to go, he said he'd like to.

He flipped back to the front page and read the article underneath the headline. Tipton Palo's law firm was donating Christmas decorations to adorn the lampposts along Main Street. To read the article one might think they were buying shoes for all the Tiny Tims of the world, or donating parents to orphans.

"They'll hang those decorations over my dead body."

"You can't fight Christmas," Mildred said.

"Not only is Dexter Mann a sleaze ball, but his grammar is atrocious. It should be donates, not donate."

Mildred read the headline aloud. "Sounds right to me. Palo and West donate."

"Palo and West is a firm," Walter said. "A single entity, not two people, unless they intend to buy the decorations out of their own pockets, and there's fat chance of that."

"You're probably the only one who caught that," she said.

"I'm smarter than they think I am."

"If you're smart you'll let them hang the decorations," she said. "Or you'll make the front page in a way you'll regret."

Knowing she was right didn't lessen the sting. The Hayes Beacon had all but campaigned for Palo, now it was helping him pout. A short time later Brant Haskell called, mad as a wet hen and cursing like a sailor. Walter got up and went out onto the back porch to keep Mildred from overhearing the salty language.

"Don't give that paper a damned thing," Haskell said. "Nothing."

Walter felt pretty sure that wasn't going to be a problem because the paper clearly didn't want anything he had. "I wonder how they'll cover the board meetings?"

"You be careful what you say," Haskell said. "Say as little as possible. Let the aldermen do the talking."

"They'll say I don't know what I'm doing."

"Then knock their socks off. Just don't embarrass me."

"Not embarrassing you is at the top of my list," Walter said.

"Everybody in town knows I backed you," Haskell said. "Make a fool of yourself and they'll laugh me out of town."

"Second on my list is not getting you laughed out of town."

"Ha ha. You're a laugh a minute, Pigg. I almost wish I hadn't voted for you." He hung up before Walter had a chance to respond, which was fine because the conversation had worn thin. Brant Haskell cared about Brant Haskell, and so went the world. Walter remembered reading someplace that the best revenge is success, but saying is easier than doing. He'd read that someplace too.

* * *

Tipton laughed out loud when he saw the tiny picture of Walter's swearing-in ceremony tucked away on the obituary page. Buried, he thought, with an inner contentment that worked like salve on his sore ego. Buried like all the other stiffs on the page. Dead, that's what Walter Pigg's political career was. Dead.

Rance stormed into Tipton's office and threw down his own copy of the Beacon, covering Tipton's obituary page with his front page. "Care to explain this?" He leaned against the desk with one hand and stabbed the headline with the index finger of the other.

"It's Christmas decorations," Tipton said "What of it?"

"What gives you the right to commit this firm to decorate Main Street without asking me?"

"It was a snap decision," Tipton said. "You weren't there and I didn't think you'd mind. You're the one always saying the firm needs to do more to help the community."

"No, Tipton, I'm not always saying that! I've never said that!" He stood straight and blew his lungs empty. "What were you thinking?"

Tipton decided to come clean. Rance was a pragmatic guy. "I had to give Dexter a story."

"Since when are you responsible for writing the newspaper?"

"He was leading with the Pigg story," Tipton said, then he laughed. "I wish I could've seen Pigg's face when he opened it." He swept Tipton's paper aside and tapped his finger on the tiny photo below the obituary for Martin Barlow.

"You should've seen mine," Rance said, throwing his copy into Tipton's chest. Tipton flinched because he thought Rance had struck him, then he cleared the desk with a broad sweep of his arm. Both newspapers and a stapler hit the floor and scattered.

"It's a few Christmas decorations!"

"That's not the point! If you ever do anything like this again I'll —." Rance stopped mid-sentence and plopped down in the chair used by clients. When he spoke again his voice was calm and tired. "This obsession with Walter Pigg needs to stop."

"Obsession?"

"Obsession. Blind, unadulterated obsession," Rance said. "It's not healthy, for you *or* the firm."

"He stole the election," Tipton said. "I don't know how he did it but Haskell was behind it."

"Maybe the Russians helped him."

"Don't do that," Tipton said. "I'm not a conspiracy nut. People steal elections all the time."

"Democrats," Rance said, "and that's your party. Pigg ran as an independent and they can't steal anything because they don't control anything. That's what independent means."

"Too bad you weren't so politically astute while you were running my campaign."

"How much are we on the hook for?"

"We decorate a few lampposts around the courthouse then down to First Street," Tipton said. "A couple thousand bucks and we'll probably get some kind of citizenship award. It'll be good PR."

Rance threw up his hands and stood. "It's coming out of your pocket." Tipton opened his mouth to protest but Rance cut him off. "Next time ask. It'll go a lot smoother."

"There wasn't time to call a meeting," Tipton said, "You don't hate Christmas do you?"

"You know I don't hate Christmas."

"Do you hate Jesus?"

"I'm not paying your bribe."

Tipton let it drop because he knew Rance would see it his way after he slept on it. If not, Tipton would write the check anyway and there wasn't much Rance could do about it except kick his heels against the floor. He could dissolve the partnership, but they both knew who attracted the wealthy clients. On his own, Rance would starve. He'd be an ambulance-chasing hack.

Halfway to the door Rance said without breaking his stride, "You really need to let this thing go."

* * *

Board meetings in Hayes took place every third Monday of the month, during the day when average people were working and couldn't attend. On purpose, Walter deduced, so he changed the time. People have a right to be heard, and to be answered. Aldermen and mayors have a duty to listen. It was an unpopular decision with the board. The first of many if Walter had to guess.

It was the Monday before Thanksgiving and Walter arrived at City Hall at a quarter to six with butterflies in his stomach and Mildred at his side. Throughout the day and during the ride over she had schooled him on his duties, admonishing him not to make a mockery of the parliamentary procedures he held in such low regard, then cautioning him one final time not to let Alderman Stovall make a mockery of him. She remembered aloud how Mayor Sherman called him being a bully. "Tom called him a grand A-S-S," she said, spelling instead of saying the word.

"I'm sure I can be a grander one," Walter replied, then he laughed and she didn't. Many of their conversations broke that way.

City hall was a modest building that housed the mayor's office, the boardroom, and half a dozen other city offices. From outside it was a blond brick flat in need of a facelift, but inside it had been redone with new tile and paint.

Five aldermen joined Walter behind the bench that spanned the front wall on an elevated stage, curved forward at the ends so the mayor could see all their faces without much effort. Walter had met them individually in his office over the past week, favoring Gordy Kilfiche over the others. Kilfiche had been a circuit judge for thirty years before retiring, then he served Ward 1 as alderman until Brad Stovall unseated him. Since then Kilfiche had served as Alderman At Large. Stovall was the type of man one can read at first glance. A grand ass indeed. He had unnaturally dark hair and a white beard. Walter guessed him to be about his age or slightly older, trying hard to look younger. Vanity and arrogance often travel the same road. Stovall owned a trucking company that hauled dirt and gravel under questionable contracts for the state highway department, according to the retired judge. Speculation, the judge had said. Innocent until proven guilty, but guilty nonetheless.

Kilfiche was eighty-two and still agile. He sat to Walter's far left, then there was Wayne Toms and Lyle Townsend. To Walter's right sat Stovall, then Terrell Sharp. Sharp was pastor of Bryant Hill Baptist Church and the only African American member of the board. The youngest member, Lyle Townsend, was forty years younger than the oldest member, Gordy Kilfiche.

32

Wayne Toms owned a supermarket and had a head like a cue ball with no eyebrows. No facial hair either, but he did have eyelashes and arm hair, which derailed Walter's suspicion that he might have a medical condition.

At six on the dot Walter called the meeting to order with Stovall not yet in his seat. "Meetings will commence on time," he said. "I place great value on punctuality."

The few rows of chairs out front were mostly empty, which suited Stovall based on a comment Walter overheard him make to Toms. It was hard not to overhear Stovall when he spoke.

"Every meeting will begin with the Pledge of Allegiance and a Christian prayer," Walter said. "If either of those two things offends you, step out into the hallway until both have concluded. I'll broker no disrespect of God or country in this building while I'm mayor." He scanned their faces and counted to ten inside his head. No one left the room. "Now please stand and remove your hats and we'll get started." The room stood as one and faced the flag. The city attorney led the pledge. Larry Pace had missed Vietnam by two years, but he was a veteran all the same and he had asked Walter beforehand for the honor. Afterwards, Alderman Sharp led them in prayer because he had been called to preach long before being called to politics.

Over the course of the next hour, Stovall proved to be a real son-of-a-bitch. Every motion set forward met with his disapproval in some form or fashion. Near the end, Walter had a burn in his gut that forced him to action. "I make a motion that this board recognize the seventh day of every week as Saturday,"

The wind escaped Gordy Kilfiche in a loud fashion. All eyes turned to Walter. Mouths hung agape. Carter Holiday with the Hayes Beacon looked up from the notepad on his lap and stopped doodling. Mildred frowned. Walter turned right then left, surveying the aldermen one by one, consuming the looks on their faces. Sympathy on some, amusement on others. Not a man among them understood what was about to happen. His eyes rested on Stovall for what seemed a very long time. "Any objections, Mister Stovall?"

The room erupted with laughter.

Stovall stammered, then emitted a painful laugh. His face turned three shades of red while Walter sat waiting, then the large man set his jaw and squeezed his eyes half shut. His lower lip and the muscles in his chin quivered. For a moment Walter thought Stovall might take a swing at him, but he was too proud of his moment to succumb to fear. Feeling wise like Abraham Lincoln, or better yet, King Solomon, Walter glanced at Mildred, who now sat content, then he stared directly into the eyes of the Beacon reporter and said, "I withdraw the motion."

* * *

Tipton got the blow-by-blow in person from Dexter Mann, who got it firsthand from Carter Holiday, who read from his notes when necessary but otherwise related the events of the meeting from memory, especially Pigg's closing salvo at Brad Stovall's argumentative nature.

"His weakness foretold by a cliche," Tipton said, barely audible.

"I don't follow," Mann said.

"Of course you don't. *Patience is a virtue*," Tipton said. "And Pigg has none."

Dexter Mann sat dumbfounded. Tipton visualized the cogs slowly grinding his brain into pulp. Let him figure it out for himself, he decided, rather than explain. The man was saddled with an unimpressive intellect. His rise through the ranks at the Beacon to become its head spoke more against the talents of the staff in general than for his talents in particular. Perhaps it was because he looked the part more than the others. Gained his rank thanks to visual perception of what a small-town editor should look like, perhaps. Heavyset and dour, with little round glasses not much bigger than the orbs they serviced. Fingertips that begged of the ink of bygone days when he would have set each letter by hand because his would have been a one-man shop. It wasn't important for Tipton to like him as long as he could be of some occasional use.

"You sit on a great throne," Tipton said.

"Me?"

Tipton sighed. Ignorance. A man of intelligence with a newspaper at his disposal could run a town the size of Hayes, yet here sat an idiot letting the town run him. Tipton rose from his plush leather chair and walked to the bar. Autumn was somewhere upstairs with a bottle of wine, making herself scarce because it was late and she had already slipped into something too revealing for company. Something without anything underneath. "Name your poison," he said. "Whiskey? Vodka?"

"Nothing for me," Mann said.

"I've got rum."

"It's late and I should be going."

"But you just got here," Tipton said. "Don't be rude and leave without at least one drink. Vodka, isn't it?"

"Bourbon," Mann said. "Whatever you have."

Tipton lifted a bottle of Wild Turkey from the queue and poured two fingers. "I see a headline in all this," Tipton said. "MAYOR PIGG INVENTS THE WEEK. Or, perhaps, MAYOR PIGG MAKES ASS OF SELF."

"If I print the word ass I'll lose half my subscribers." He took the glass from Tipton's hand and adjusted himself in his chair. "Next month I'll cover the meeting myself. No telling what he'll say." He sampled the whiskey then smacked his lips. "He'll be a boon for my newspaper, I'll tell you that right now." He laughed, then took a sip. "A real boon. I may have to add a third section."

"Do your job and there may not be a next month," Tipton said.

"My job is to sell newspapers."

"Expose Pigg for what he is. Let the people know they've made a terrible mistake electing this, this, rube to be their mayor." Tipton sat and crossed his legs ankle to knee. "They'll force him to resign."

Mann frowned. "I'm afraid you're right," he said, then he chugged his glass without flinching. "And cheat me out of two years of historic readership."

"Forget that," Tipton said. "Once I'm mayor you'll have plenty to write about."

"Yes, but who'll read it?"

Dexter Mann scrambled to his feet, excusing himself with practiced urgency. Tomorrow was an early day and he had a headline to write and yada, yada, yada. Tipton feigned disappointment then showed him to the door with an open invitation he didn't mean. As soon as the door closed again he called Rance and shared his stroke of luck at Pigg harpooning himself. "You can't make this stuff up."

"Sounds like he shut Stovall up," Rance said. "Wish I'd been there to see it."

Tipton had sued Brad Stovall twice in the last three years. Personal injury lawsuits, both, during which he found Stovall to be a loudmouthed bully with no regard for how his gravel trucks ripped and roared up and down the roads endangering other motorists. How he garnered enough votes to unseat old Judge Kilfiche was a riddle yet unsolved, though rumor put money changing hands throughout the ward.

"The enemy of my enemy is my friend," Tipton said. "I'd like to put Stovall's head in a vice and squeeze it until he shits his pants, but right now we need him."

"You keep saying *we* like I'm still part of this," Rance said. "My part ended on election night, remember? No clinging."

"Water under the bridge," Tipton said. "We both live to fight another day."

"You're drunk."

"I'm optimistic," Tipton said, though he could feel the liquor in his face. Rance could be pushed but not forced. Managing him took a certain finesse, like with a child, or a woman. "Your advice is invaluable to me. I need it now more than ever."

Silence. Then, "That sounds better. Not saying I believe you, but it sounds better. Okay, my advice is that you accept the election results and get back to doing what you're good at — practicing law."

"Too bad the Beacon doesn't have a cartoonist," Tipton said. "I have some really good ideas."

"Practice law," Rance said. "Let Pigg harpoon himself."

"Draw him with a big snout, sitting in front of a calendar with the days mixed up.”

"I seem to recall an insurance case you keep putting off.”

"The ideas are endless.”

"The firm could use the cash infusion.”

"The firm's fine,” Tipton said. "Unless you've got a set of books I haven't seen. Maybe we can dig up someone who can draw. They don't have to be good.”

"That *we* keeps popping up out of your pocket,” Rance said. "Be careful what you wish for or you might get a cartoonist who'll draw you with your fists in your eyes crying because you lost an election.”

Tipton stabbed the red circle with his finger and ended the call. Rance could be a real pain when he wanted to be. Autumn appeared in the doorway wearing a see-through negligee, busting out all over.

"You coming to bed?”

"Go drink your damned wine!”

CHAPTER 5

The aftermath of Walter's first board meeting wasn't nearly as painful as the stabbing sensation in his lower back. The meeting was fourteen hours in the books and he had received only two calls berating him for wanting to reorganize the days of the week. He didn't do social media so he didn't fully understand Mildred's concerns in that regard, but by mid-morning she wore an easier face. In her words, the storm seemed to have passed. In Walter's mind, what storm?

At lunch he bumped into Ted Funderburk from the old job and offered to spring for an extra sandwich if his old co-worker would join him. Ted looked about himself like a married man about to slide into a car with his mistress, then ducked into the booth opposite Walter and scooted all the way to the wall.

"How you been, Walter? We sure do miss you at the office."

"Missed me enough to fire me," Walter said. Ted was going to pretend not to know anything but he knew. Walter knew he knew.

"Now you know I don't attend those kinds of meetings," Ted said, already starting to twitch. "We were all as shocked as you were."

"Who's we?"

"Everybody," Ted said, then he dropped his eyes and said he guessed a few people saw it coming.

"Why'd they do it, Ted?"

"Now Walter I told you —."

"Why, Ted?"

Ted exhaled, then he looked around to make sure no one was listening, then he said it was because the boss was afraid of being blackballed when it came to future contracts with the city. "You didn't hear this from me, but there was a phone call."

"What kind of phone call?"

"The kind that sucks all the managers into the conference room and locks the door. When they came out I swear Walter it was like the stock market had crashed."

"Who called?"

Ted swore he didn't know and Walter believed him. He was one of the original engineers and had been with the company two years longer than Walter had, but he wasn't a manager and he didn't usually get invited to high level meetings.

"Remember that time Alvin's wife got caught naked with that cop out at the lake? It's like that," Ted said, "Maybe worse."

"Meaning you've been warned not to tell me?"

"We all have," Ted said. He glanced over his shoulder again. Walter knew there was something he wanted to say but he was scared. Men their age don't bounce back from being fired the way younger men do. Walter had the same fear of being unemployable in two years.

"Nothing you tell me will leave this table," Walter said. "But I understand you not wanting to say anything so I won't press you."

"I did hear something else but it's just a rumor."

"I'm listening."

"A little bird told me Sonora threatened to pull their business."

Walter felt nauseated. Sonora Enterprises made bumpers for Toyota and Nissan and was H&G's biggest customer. They were Walter's biggest account, and until that moment he had thought they had a good working relationship based on mutual respect. Ted must have realized he had dealt Walter a blow because he tried to crawfish his way out of breaking the news by saying he may have heard it wrong, and that rumors can't be relied on, but now that Walter thought about it, the thing made sense. Not sense as to why Sonora did what they did, but sense as to why H&G let him go.

"I've been mad at the wrong people," he said, then no, come to think of it he was still mad at H&G. A loyal employee should be more important to them than a loyal client.

Ted gulped down his sandwich and drained his Coke then said he'd better be getting back. "Please don't say anything, Walter. I've got a wife and three kids to feed."

Walter frowned and waved him off, then he finished his sandwich and paid the tab. The waitress addressed him as mayor, and not in a menacing tone, either. As soon as he returned to the office he told Mildred about his conversation with Ted, but she was more concerned with the way he grimaced when he walked than about why Sonora Enterprises had stabbed him in the back. "My back's fine," he said, "except for the knife sticking out of it." It was a lie because his back would never be fine again. Better some days than others, but never fine. Pain was the price he paid for being able to walk, and he would take that over a wheelchair any day.

"I wish you'd take it easy," Mildred said. "You know what the doctor said about overdoing it."

"The same doctors who told me I'd never walk again. Doctors don't like being wrong." He started toward his office.

"Your doctors are very proud of you," Mildred called after him. Proud was an overstatement. Two of them had tried to claim credit and the third told him it was a fluke. Brutal physical therapy and his refusal to be beaten was his miracle. He had deconstructed himself and now it was up to him to reconstruct himself. He walked because he refused to remain seated.

* * *

Alderman Sharp swooped into Walter's office wearing his battle face. Mildred tried to hold him off but he was so adamant that Walter intervened. It wouldn't do to turn away the town's only black alderman. Terrell Sharp had a reputation, but he began the meeting with a handshake. "Thank you for seeing me without an appointment, Mayor," he said. "I'll be brief, I promise."

"If this is about that thing I said at the meeting, it was a joke on Stovall."

"It's not," Sharp said. He inhaled the way a man does when he's about to say something uncomfortable, or unpleasant. Something he'd rather not say but feels he must, such as we aldermen have met and we think it best that you resign, but that's not what he said. "As you know, I represent the black community."

"I thought you represented the fourth ward," Walter said. "Black, white, and other."

"I represent the people who put me here. I probably didn't get two white votes."

"Aren't we supposed to work for the people who voted against us the same as the ones who voted for us? Isn't that how it works?"

"You have that privilege," Sharp said. "I don't."

"I see."

"Do you? Do you think Stovall represents the black men and women who live in his ward? Do you think Toms and Townsend represent the black men and women who live in their wards? No, they don't. I represent those people. *I do.* It falls on me."

"If that's the way you feel."

"It pains me, Walter. It pains me because I believe deep down inside you're a decent man."

"But not on the surface?"

"A charge has been leveled at you, Walter. A serious charge that quite frankly I didn't believe until I was shown the police report."

Walter knew immediately what had the alderman in a knot and he was surprised it hadn't surfaced during the campaign. "Those charges were dropped," he said. "Nothing came of it because it was a silly misunderstanding."

"The boy's mother tells me you were very nasty about it."

Walter sighed. "You've been busy. Well, if we must rehash this, the boy threw a baseball through my living room window. Three windows in three months."

"That's no reason to assault the boy."

"Did the mother tell you how nasty she was to me?"

"She was a mother defending her child."

"And I was a man defending his house."

"It's not the same thing and you know it."

"She was purposefully rude while I was more than fair. I asked her to pay for a pane of glass that I installed myself. Glass her son broke. The same son who interrupted a family meal and demanded his ball back. What I should've done was turned him over my knee the way my father would've done me."

"Don't you mean you should've tied him to a tree and did what your grandfathers did to my grandfathers?"

Walter stood abruptly. "Good day, Mister Sharp!"

Sharp stood too. "This doesn't go away just because you're angry."

"This has already gone away," Walter said. "If you came to wave votes in my face don't waste your time because I have no intention of running for re-election. Votes mean nothing to me."

"I didn't come to wave votes in your face. Please, can we sit down and be civil?"

"I'm not sure you know the meaning of the word," Walter said.

The Alderman sat. The change in his demeanor was both compete and immediate, and it had a disarming effect on Walter. How could he yell at a man who refused to yell back? Begrudgingly, Walter sat back down. "Looking back, I wish I had handled things differently," he said, "but my actions had absolutely nothing to do with the color of the boy's skin. My grandson is black."

"I believe you *think* it had nothing to do with skin color," Sharp said. "That's the problem with racism. White people don't see anything wrong with what they do because they've been doing things that way all their lives."

"And black people see racism in everything because they've been looking for it all their lives."

"Not looking for it, Walter. Seeing it. There's a difference. Racism is real. Black people are born at the bottom of a hill."

"We just had a black president," Walter said. "Elected and re-elected."

"Just because a few climb to the top of the hill doesn't make it less steep," Sharp said. "Like I said, I believe you didn't have malice in your heart when you assaulted that child, but my people don't know you. All they see is another powerful white man."

"Powerful my eye! I won a job I didn't want and got fired from the one I did want. And please be honest and stop using the word assault."

Sharp smiled. "I apologize for my comment about our grandfathers. I was speaking in general terms — the way things were during that time."

"It was probably true," Walter said. "I don't deny history. My grandfathers were probably as guilty as any, but I'm not my grandfathers and I've never assaulted anyone in my life."

"Should I tell my people it's resolved?"

"Would it make any difference?"

"As long as they trust me, yes, I think so. You should come to my church some Sunday. Get to know some of us in our element."

"Wouldn't that seem contrived?"

"All good deeds seem contrived to some people." He switched gears. "You mentioned the board meeting so I suppose you know you made an enemy last night."

"Only one?"

"Well, three, considering. Brad Stovall is a vengeful man, and Townsend and Toms tote his water. That's three votes against you every single time from now until you quit or get voted out."

"And the other two votes?"

"I vote the issues," Sharp said. "Straight down the line. So does Judge Kilfiche."

"So the best I can hope for is a stalemate," Walter said. He had feared as much, though until the alderman said it, he hadn't been certain. "Just as well, I suppose, since I came in without an agenda." Not true, but he wasn't ready to show his hand just yet.

"Agendas have a way of finding a man in your position," Sharp said.

"So what's Stovall's deal?"

"Inquiring minds have wondered that since the voters in his ward elected him."

"And Toms?"

"Wayne Toms is Stovall's right hand. Don't ask me why because I don't know. All I know is that he is. He's never voted against him. Not once. Lyle Townsend is one of these people who loves turmoil. He voted against Stovall one, no, two times, I think, in the beginning, and they had quite a falling out over it, but that's been resolved and now they're thick as thieves."

"What was the vote?"

"Don't recall. Something trivial. Somebody wanted a property rezoned, or an ordinance waved probably. Most of what we do is mundane."

Walter stood and extended his hand. "I look forward to working with you, Terrell."

Sharp stood and clasped Walter's hand in return. They shook. "Don't get too comfortable. My people expect a certain consternation from me."

"Meaning?"

"Meaning that if I go along too quietly, they'll think I've sold them out."

"I thought they trusted you."

"Once you've been kicked by the mule, you tend to make a wider circle around the barn," Sharp said. "I'll tell the boy's mother you send your apologies."

Walter bristled but didn't protest. If giving that vile woman the satisfaction of an apology would put the sorry business to bed, then so be it.

* * *

Frost glimmered across Tipton's lawn as he slid out of his warm car and plucked the Hayes Beacon from the grass ten steps off his concrete driveway. The paperboy had a good arm but a bad attitude, perfectly capable of lobbing the newspaper over the gate and within reach of the driveway, yet week after week he threw to a different spot. Complaining did no good. Complaining only weakened his throw so that it landed outside the gate where the neighborhood dogs got to it first. Hayes had neither a leash law nor an animal shelter, so dogs both stray and claimed ran together in packs without consequence except to those they terrorized.

Tipton hated dogs. Even as a small boy he disliked them licking his face and jumping on his legs. As he marched to retrieve his newspaper, trying in vain not to sully his immaculate black shoes in the frosty grass, watching his breath puff from his face like smoke from a coal-fired train, he added a leash law to the long list of things he would have accomplished had the people elected him mayor instead of that malcontent Pigg. A leash law and an animal control officer, because what good does it do to restrain some dogs while letting others run?

He reached the newspaper and snatched it from the wet grass. At least the boy had bothered to wrap it in plastic so it wouldn't dissolve. On the upswing from stooping, last night's alcohol sloshed against the inside of his skull and floated his brain, making his first step back toward the car unsteady. The Wednesday before Thanksgiving was always a slow day but Candice had wanted the day off and he had felt the need to assert his authority so now he felt he had to at least make an appearance, hung over or not. He took being a boss very seriously. Left to Rance, Candice would come and go as she pleased.

Candice was all smiles when he strode through the door. He had expected the opposite. Something was up and he didn't like it. As he passed her desk he glanced down and stole an eyeful of cleavage. She could be very attractive when she tried. Hopefully Autumn wouldn't drop by and see the tit show or he would spend the rest of the day defending himself.

"Bring me a cup of coffee," he said without breaking his stride.

When he reached his desk he immediately unrolled the paper and devoured the headline. PIGG'S FIRST MOTION. Pigg, not Mayor Pigg. He liked it already. The article was basically an accurate representation of the meeting as Tipton understood it, with the exception of Walter's soon to be famous motion to make Saturday the seventh day of the week. The last sentence wrapped it all up with a nice bow: *For those who may not know, the week begins on Sunday, then progresses with Monday, Tuesday, Wednesday, Thursday, Friday, then ends, every week the same, regardless of the month or year, on SATURDAY. Would someone please inform the mayor?*

Candice brought coffee. Her good mood had waned but her display of cleavage had not, especially when she leaned forward to deposit the cup. He looked up from the article and allowed his eyes to hover a moment too long.

"See something you like?"

Her delivery implied impudence. He lifted his eyes to her face as she gathered her collar. If she didn't want him to look then why wear it, and why bend so low when bringing his coffee? For Rance, he supposed, though he couldn't fathom why. Rance was old and broken down and wore fake hair while she was, well —. The word delicious came to mind but he forced it away and inserted the word attractive in its place. Attractive beyond measure, actually. More so than he had ever realized before that moment. Violently attractive, like the centerfolds he had coveted as a teen. She gave him those same feelings, too. Those same yearnings. So close yet so out of reach. He became suddenly angry at his embarrassment.

She straightened herself. The forward lean had lasted no more than two seconds, yet in that brief snatch of time she had managed to completely humiliate him.

"When Rance comes in tell him I want to see him," he said, seething but trying desperately not to give her the satisfaction of knowing she had rattled him.

"He took the day off," she said.

His eyes bounced back to her face. "Did you know that when you got dressed this morning?" The question popped out without permission.

"Meaning what exactly?"

"Nothing," he said. "Never mind."

"No, tell me," she said. "Is there something wrong with the way I'm dressed?"

"Go back to your desk."

"Because you were looking hard enough."

"What do you expect when you dress like a whore?"

She stood for a moment glaring down at him. Her face turned red as a blister and her body trembled. "How dare you," she said, then she turned on the heels of her black pumps and stormed out of his office.

He watched her through the door. Instead of returning to her desk she disappeared leftward toward Rance's office, or the break room, or the bathroom. Probably the bathroom so she could cry. Women always cry when they get their feelings hurt. Men don't have that luxury. Men have to wear their troubles like an undershirt.

He knew he should apologize, not because he was sorry but because they lived in a climate where the mere accusation of sexual misconduct is enough to ruin a man's career. Even if she said nothing now she might trot the incident out later and pull the political rug out from under him.

He swallowed his pride and went after her. The bathroom door was closed and he saw light through the crack at the bottom so he tapped lightly with a knuckle and told her through the door that he was sorry. "I've been under a lot of stress and I acted badly," he said when she didn't reply.

"You're only saying that because you're afraid I'll sue you," she said.

He rolled his eyes and shook his head and expelled an audible sigh. She was being ridiculous. Her aroma lingered outside the door like fresh flowers. He breathed it in and savored it, then couldn't resist asking her to pick up a bottle of whatever perfume she was wearing when she went out for lunch so he could give it to his wife.

"I don't wear perfume," she said. "You can't splash me on your wife."

He mumbled another apology then returned to his desk with his brain processing the image of him splashing Candice on his wife. The phone rang and there was no one to answer it but himself, so he did. It was Rance, and he sounded indignant. "What the hell's wrong with you?"

"I don't know what —."

"Don't play dumb, Tip. You'll be lucky if she doesn't sue your pants off."

"You know I don't like being called —."

"I don't care what you don't like being called! How do you think Candice likes being called a whore?"

"I didn't call her a whore," Tipton said. "I said she was dressed like one, and she is. If you were here instead of goldbricking you'd agree that —."

"It doesn't matter what she's wearing, Your Majesty, you can't call her a whore."

Just then Candice appeared in Tipton's doorway wearing a white tube top with no bra and a black skirt cut so high it barely covered the essentials. His mouth dropped open and he felt the tug of his eyeballs being pulled from their sockets.

"These are my whore clothes," she said, planting both hands firmly on her hips. Fire flashed from her eyes and threatened to burn the place to the ground. Tipton tried to speak but nothing intelligible came out. "I keep a pair in my car in case I get lucky," she said, seething, then she smiled but it wasn't a friendly smile. It was the kind of smile that sends a chill up your spine because you know the thoughts behind it are lethal. She pushed herself to her full height and struck a pose. "Try getting this out of your head, you bastard."

* * *

The neighborhood dogs beat Walter to his paper so Mildred sent Kelsey to the gas station on the corner to pluck one from the machine. Mildred delivered it to his office and slapped it down. "You've done it this time," she said. "Everyone in town's probably laughing at you." Mildred wasn't one to slap things down so Walter didn't look up at first, then when he did he tried to laugh the headline off as ridiculous. Only an idiot would believe it. Dexter Mann was exposing himself as a Tipton Palo stooge, and sooner or later things had to break in Walter's favor.

"I warned you they're a dirty bunch," Mildred said. Slapping things down and calling people a dirty bunch all in the same moment was so out of place for her that Walter wanted to reach up and feel her forehead to see if she had a fever, but he didn't want to be the next thing slapped down so he resisted the urge, telling her instead that they were playing right into his hands.

"Absurdity can never beat honesty, Mildred."

"You can't ignore this."

"If you worry about everything those jackals say about me you'll give yourself a stroke. You'll give us both strokes, because seeing you stressed stresses me." He took her hand. "Whatever bothers you bothers me."

She pulled her hand away. "Stop with that nonsense and read what they've said about you."

"They've already called me a racist child abuser. What else can they say?"

He read the article then laughed. "So now I'm a dunce."

"Our friends know you're none of those things," Mildred said. By *our friends* she meant her friends, of course, because on his own Walter had no one he could count on. It was his own fault. He would be the first to admit that. At H&G he had associates, and sometimes they laughed and joked together, but he had never been one to form lasting bonds. Not once had he been invited to a party, or out for drinks, not that he minded. He could socialize when forced to, and he was more than capable of intelligent conversation, but he preferred solitude, and he always needed time to recharge afterwards. Being around people exhausted him.

"You know what this means don't you? They're afraid of me. Why else would they try so hard to get rid of me?"

"Because Tipton Palo wants your job."

"He can have it in two years. I may even let him put a sign up in our yard."

"Walter!"

He laughed at the thought of Tipton Palo planting a sign on his front lawn, like Buzz Aldrin planting the United States flag on the moon. The blast from the lunar capsule during liftoff blew the flag over but the symbolism remained. A new frontier had been conquered.

"I wonder how many of our friends who voted for me have already changed their minds."

"People know who you are," Mildred said. "People voted for Walter Pigg because they're tired of what's been going on in this town. They want change."

"Then change they shall have," he said with flare and a fist to the table.

He winked at her and enjoyed the smile she tried so hard to repress. "That is if you think I can."

"*You* think you can," she said. "And I've known you long enough to know how stubborn you can be once you set your mind to something."

CHAPTER 6

Autumn pulled out all the stops when it came to entertaining, especially with both sets of parents attending. Her father was chief loan officer at a local bank and her mother had been the public relations liaison for a local hospice since its inception. Good people both, as was her sister Kara, who was younger and had the looks of the family. Kara's husband Mark was a talker, and his favorite subject was himself, so Tipton was glad when Autumn told him they had declined the invitation, as had her brother Randal, the recluse.

Tipton sat at the head of the long rectangular table as was his right as head of the household. Autumn anchored the opposite end, with her parents to her left and his to her right. They had turkey with stuffing and sliced ham adorned with pineapple and beets. Tipton didn't care for beets but he wasn't so finicky that he couldn't rake them aside without complaining. Complementing the meats were corn on the cob, dressing, potato salad, egg salad, mashed potatoes with gravy, dumplings, green beans, baked beans, yeast rolls as big as your hand, and several other dishes with the lids not yet removed. On a side table were pies and cupcakes and bowls of fruit. More food than they could possibly eat.

"So how's the banking business?" Tipton asked his father-in-law after the initial passing of dishes had abated.

"Money's flowing again," Anderson Goff said. "Now that we have a president who understands economics."

Tipton's father bristled. "Too bad he doesn't understand anything else."

"I'm surprised at you, Carlton," Goff said. "Being a real estate man and all."

"Retired real estate man," Tipton's father said. "And never so much of one that it blinded me to the overall good of humanity."

Goff emitted some guttural noise. A groan, or a moan. Tipton raised his eyes and saw Autumn wince. He hadn't meant to launch a discussion of politics with his off-the-cuff question, though in hindsight he should have remembered how the two men almost came to blows two Thanksgivings ago when the election was all anyone could talk about.

"No politics on Thanksgiving," Tipton said, eyeing both male parents, one then the other. "At least not at the dinner table." He tossed a disarming wink to Autumn's father.

"My daughter's policy, no doubt," Goff said. "And a good one." He cast a frown-turned-smile at his daughter and tacked on, "Just like her mother."

"This time he means that as a compliment, dear," Mrs. Goff said with an eye roll. "At least I think he does."

"He does indeed," Goff said. "A woman should run her dinner table. Let the men run everything else."

"Understandable you not wanting to discuss politics," Carlton Palo said to his son. "Considering the beating you took at the hands of that … what was he again? An engineer?" The parents all laughed.

"It's the mood of the country," Goff said. "Out with the establishment and in with the outsiders. Kick over the table. Shake things up."

"Sounds like you're describing the French Revolution," Carlton said. "Tale of Two Cities. Dangerous, don't you think?"

Autumn cleared her throat.

"Boys will be boys," her mother said.

"Interesting that you say French Revolution and not American," Goff said. "We threw off our oppressors too, you know."

"I'm hardly establishment," Tipton said. "This was my first run at political office."

"Yet you aimed for the highest seat in town," his father said, "instead of wetting your feet as an alderman first."

"You encouraged me."

"Yes, well, so I did," Carlton said. "But in my defense, I thought you would be a better candidate. You're a lawyer for goodness sake. You've got a sharp mind, yet you ran your campaign like a complete amateur."

"Which is exactly what he was," Anderson Goff said. "You're right, Carlton, he should've become an alderman first." He looked at his son-in-law. "You put your horse before the carriage."

"Horses are supposed to go before the carriage," Carlton said. "I think you mean it the other way."

Anderson Goff looked distant for a split second then a grand smile spread across his face. "By George you're right! I've been saying it wrong all these years." He looked at his wife, Autumn's mother, and asked her why she hadn't corrected him.

"You don't like being corrected," she said. The two mothers exchanged a knowing smile, then Mrs. Palo said Carlton was the same way.

"I am not," Tipton's father said. "I take correction as well as any man."

"Any *man*," his wife said, and the three women laughed.

Tipton felt relieved that his father-in-law's gaffe sidetracked the conversation, but his relief was short-lived as his father soon renewed his observation that Tipton should have stood for alderman first.

"My ward wasn't open," Tipton said, "and old Judge Kilfiche won the at-large seat with double digits."

"The average voter doesn't see you as one of them," Goff said. "Hardly a week goes by without your name in the paper for something or another." He laughed to show his good nature. "My daughter can't plant roses in her back yard without the entire town having to read about it in the paper." He leveled his gaze at Tipton across a forked hunk of white meat and said, "You think that's because she teaches high school math? No it's not. It's because she's your wife. An establishment wife."

"Tipton's important to this town," Mrs. Palo said. "Why shouldn't they write about him and his wife? People are interested or they would write about something else."

Tipton blew his mother a kiss.

"I hate when they write about me," Autumn said. Tipton knew it to be a lie, but it was her lie, and she was entitled to it. Everyone is entitled to his or her own lies. It keeps civilization from eating itself.

But Goff wasn't finished. "All I'm saying, is that to the average Joe on the street, he represents the establishment. The average Joe has to die to get his name in the paper. Literally." He looked around the table for agreement. "Am I right or am I right?"

"Or commit a crime," Tipton's mother said. "There's so much crime nowadays." She frowned at her son. "I wish you wouldn't spend so much time around those people."

"If crime suddenly disappeared I'd be out of a job," Tipton said. "Autumn and I would starve on what she makes." He looked at his wife and watched her absorb the comment. Salary was a sore subject with Autumn.

"We don't pay our teachers nearly enough," Carlton said.

"Nonsense," Goff said. "My daughter knew very well what teachers make before she went to college. No one forced her to teach school."

Autumn's mother elbowed her husband in the ribs and made him grunt, but she didn't make him retract his statement. Tipton agreed with his father-in-law but he tried hard to conceal it.

"The average Joe doesn't commit crimes," Goff said, steering the conversation back toward the rise of populism.

"Ha!" Carlton said, aborting the sip of tea he was about to take. "That may be the most ridiculous thing you've said yet, Goff, and you've set yourself a pretty high bar in that regard." He laughed. The mood was jovial on the surface but Tipton felt the tug of a nasty undercurrent forming.

"Perhaps real estate is more rambunctious than banking," Goff said. "We bankers go to prison if we commit crimes."

"Only when you get caught."

"Are you insinuating —."

"He's not insinuating anything," Tipton said, then with a stern look, "are you father?"

Carlton Palo dabbed at his mouth with his napkin and cleared his throat. "All I'm saying is that everyone takes liberties with the law."

"Speak for yourself."

"You speed don't you?"

"Good grief, man, is that where your head is tonight?"

"Stop," Autumn said.

"They're just being men," her mother said. "In a few hours they'll be drunk watching football."

"Which is not a crime," her father said.

"We were talking about my son getting his ass kicked at the polls," Carlton said. "Then Anderson turned it into a conversation about speeding tickets."

"You turned it into speeding tickets," Goff said. "I simply said the average Joe doesn't commit crimes, and they don't get their names in the paper until they die. Even the Hayes Beacon doesn't print the names of speeders. Yet. Though I bet if this new mayor of ours gets caught speeding it'll be a front-page story. They seem to really have it in for the poor guy."

"This new mayor of ours is a rube," Tipton said.

"A rube who whipped your ass," his father said.

Autumn banged the table with her spoon until everyone stopped talking and looked at her. The room fell silent except for the back and forth rhythm of the grandfather clock keeping time in the living room. "Mother, I hear the sales this year are going to be fantastic."

"I'm too old to get hit over the head for a set of bed sheets," her mother said.

"All I was saying," Goff continued after eyeing the females in turn, "is that when people aren't happy with the way their town's being run, they blame the people running it."

"But my son doesn't run anything," Carlton said.

"I bet if you stopped twenty people on the street and asked them to name the people running this town his name would come up half a dozen times, maybe more, and he can thank the Hayes Beacon for that."

Carlton looked at the ceiling and shook his head. "It's finally happened. Anderson Goff has officially lost his mind."

"People on the streets vote," Goff said. "That's my point. Perception is reality."

"I didn't realize they taught psychology in banking school," Carlton said.

"Laugh if you will," Goff said, "but a good banker had better know some psychology. I rose through the ranks because I knew how to read people. I knew what they were thinking before they thought it."

"Ridiculous!"

"What I mean is, I knew what they would think when the new wore off the loan they were begging for. When times got tough. I can look at a man and tell if he's got metal."

"Look at my son then," Carlton said. "Does he have metal?"

"Of course he does."

"So a loan being the mayoral seat, you would have approved his application?"

"Without question," Goff said.

"And you would have been wrong."

"I've been wrong before."

"So you can't read men's minds."

"His mind wasn't the problem," Goff said. "It was all those other minds — the people who voted — that I couldn't read. I liken them to a tornado, or some other natural disaster that's out of any one man's control. That's why we have insurance."

"But there's no such thing as election insurance."

"True."

"Yet you gave my son his loan."

"You two stop it right now," Tipton's mother said. "There's no shame in losing an election. Lots of great men and women have lost elections."

"The shame is in how he lost," Carlton said, his tone suddenly heavy with disapproval. He turned to his son. "You behaved like a spoiled child."

"Because you spoiled him as a child," Tipton's mother said, then to the room, "Carlton gave him everything he ever asked for."

"I don't think I was spoiled," Tipton said. A general laughter erupted around the table. Even Autumn chuckled.

Carlton Palo pushed back his plate and suppressed a belch. "I think it's time we men retire to the living room and watch our Bulldogs eat shark." He turned to Anderson Goff and said, "It is land shark this year isn't it? Not bears, or rebels. It's hard for us real estate men to keep track."

"Don't blame my father," Tipton said, still reeling from the insult of being called a bad loser. "My grandfather forced him to go to that cow college."

"Tell me, Carlton," Goff said quickly, "had they built the dorms back then or did you still sleep in bunkhouses?"

"Where ever we slept," he said, "it was with females."

"Yes, regardless the number of legs she had," Goff said, slapping the table ahead of the thunderous laughter he unleashed. The room erupted, and Carlton laughed with them. He wasn't one not to laugh at his own expense if the joke was good enough. Autumn rose and shooed the men from the room, telling them to go drink themselves to sleep. Tipton led them into the living room still laughing, thinking how good it was that their parents got along so well. Autumn had a mini bar awaiting them on the coffee table so they could drink without stumbling around breaking things.

"Let's try and stay sober until kickoff," Tipton said as he poured the first round.

"I bumped into our coach at a party the other night," Anderson Goff said. "He said our boys have a foolproof strategy this year." He paused to allow the anticipation to build. "All we have to do is bide our time, then slip into the end zone when your dogs stop to lick their nuts." He and Tipton each pressed a thumb to their foreheads and waved their fingers in the air in true landshark tradition while they bellowed with laughter, then Goff reached over and gave Carlton's shoulder a squeeze. "How's that for a play?"

Without cracking a smile, Tipton's father waited for the laughter to stop, then, "at least the nuts we lick are our own." There was a moment of total silence, then all three men laughed in unison and the liquor began to flow.

* * *

Jackson trotted halfway down the stairs then stopped and peered through the banister at his grandfather. The boy had changed a lot in two years. It pained Walter to think what his grandson had endured at the hands of his stepfather. His only regret at the scoundrel being dead was that Amy had killed him. Society still refused to admit that abused women sometimes have only one recourse. Killing isn't always murder. Taking a life isn't always an act of aggression. Had she not tried to cover it up she might not have gone to prison at all, but manslaughter seemed an awfully harsh punishment for a few moments of panic. What really broke against her was that she threw in with that no-account bum who, last he heard, was a homeless drunk.

He and Mildred visited as often as they could, taking turns to cut expenses because airline tickets weren't cheap. Jackson always went, and they were careful not to say anything negative in front of him. Amy put up a good front when they visited, but a father knows when his daughter is pretending, and Mildred always came back with a melancholy that clung to her for days like the sour smell of an August sweat.

"Come down and let's watch a movie together," Walter called up to the boy. With no money on the line the football game meant nothing to him — that grand rivalry between his alma mater and Ole Miss. It would be all the talk tomorrow, whichever way it broke. He never had been one for sports.

"I'll let you pick," Walter said as the boy climbed up into his lap and wiggled himself into the crook of Walter's left elbow. The boy picked SpongeBob Squarepants over Toy Story and Ice Age, but a deal was a deal, so Walter set the remote aside and called Mildred from the kitchen to order popcorn.

"You know how I feel about SpongeBob," she said when she delivered the large bowl of microwave popcorn and two sodas. She thought the humor too gaudy for children.

"The boy likes it," he said. The humor she objected to went over Jackson's head and did no harm. Cartoons when they were kids were rife with violence and buffoonery and they turned out all right.

"You see ok?"

He felt the boy's head nod against his shoulder.

"I wish Amy could see the two of you getting along so well," Mildred said. She trotted off to grab her phone, then rushed back and captured the scene for eternity, or for as long as digital pictures could be read by devices and displayed. He missed the days when a photograph was printed and one had to wait until the roll was developed to know if the shot was good.

"You can print it and send it to her," Walter said. "She'd like that."

"When's Momma coming home?"

"Very soon," Walter said, but it was a lie. Unless she got parole he would be in high school before he saw his mother free. Someday they would have to tell him the truth, but they saw no need to tell him now.

* * *

Sue Palo and Allison Goff pushed and tugged their husbands out the door and toward their cars with Tipton's father boasting how *we* whipped *y'all* with thick pronunciation and an inaccurate retelling of which side behaved worse than the other. Autumn's father mumbled something about cheating. Tipton was certain the referees had been bought off.

"Men and their football," Autumn's mother said. "Your father will pout for days."

Her father stopped abruptly and straightened himself, patting his crotch with an exaggerated show of concern. "I think Carlton stole my nuts!"

"No, just handed them to you," Carlton shot back.

Sue Palo gave her husband another tug. "You'd think they played the game themselves," she said.

Tipton stepped out onto the cold concrete in his socked feet and shuddered. The temperature had dropped by double digits. Autumn pushed leftovers one last time with both mothers vehemently refusing. The biggest drawback to hosting a holiday gathering was having to eat leftovers for the next several days. As soon as their parents were safely through the gate, he said aloud it was too bad they didn't know any homeless people to give all that food to. Autumn ignored him and went back inside, leaving him standing with his feet freezing to the patio.

He went back inside and found her in the kitchen putting away dishes from the dishwasher. "I thought we'd never get rid of them," he said. He loved them, but enough of anything was enough. His head pounded from too much drink.

"I hope they're okay to drive," Autumn said.

"All the cops know their cars," he said. "They'll be fine."

"I meant I hope they don't crash into something and kill themselves. Or someone else. You'd think they'd let our mothers drive."

Tipton didn't bother to explain. It was a guy thing and he didn't expect her to understand. "You should have seen his face when he talked about the election."

"Your father or mine?"

"Mine."

"I'm sure he didn't mean anything," she said. "He's proud of you."

"He tries to be."

"You're drunk," Autumn said. "Go to bed. I'll clean up." He followed her from the kitchen, which was spotless, into the living room where it looked as though a food truck had exploded and knocked over half a dozen empty liquor bottles.

"He never wanted me to be a lawyer. A judge, now, that's something he could respect, but a lawyer, no. I may as well be digging ditches or laying tile."

"That's not true."

"Doesn't matter how many years a judge has to be a lawyer first."

"I'm sure you're overreacting. Why don't you go to bed?"

It was too early to go to bed so he found a clean glass and filled it with Scotch. "You always take his side."

"If you don't go to bed now you won't be able to get up the stairs," she said. She was sweeping the floor with short brisk strokes. The more agitated she got, the sexier she looked, and she was looking pretty damned sexy.

"How about we go up together?"

She stopped sweeping and glared at him, then swept again. It never failed that when he was in the mood, she wasn't.

CHAPTER 7

Mildred left before sunup with her credit card and a handful of Black Friday sale papers. Fighting the crazies to save a few dollars was a yearly tradition for her, as was pretending to hate it. Black Friday is the opening day of deer season for women. It's the Super Bowl and World Series rolled into one elbow-slinging day. Telling Mildred to be careful as she left the house was a formality. She would be what she would be.

Walter waited a few hours, then telephoned the police chief and asked if he would meet him for breakfast at Shakey's Diner. Chief Benson was on his second cup of coffee by the time Walter arrived.

"You're late. This is my second cup." He noticed the cane. "One of those days, huh?"

Walter hooked his cane over the back of his chair and shook hands across the table. Benson's hand squished like a wet sponge and his hair was two shades blacker than ash. Walter sat, then fished the bottle of hand sanitizer from his pants pocket and washed his hands underneath the table.

"Haven't seen the cane in a while," Benson said. "Temporary setback I hope."

"There was a time when I thought walking with a cane was an impossible dream," Walter said, and it was true. A man takes the simple things for granted until they're taken away.

"And look at you now. You walked right into the best seat in town. Congratulations."

Walter recognized brown-nosing when he saw it. Give Benson the chance and he would pick a Tipton Palo over a Walter Pigg every day of the week. "I'm not sure if it's the best seat in town or the worst," he said. "So far it's been more curse than blessing."

Benson laughed and said he knew how Walter felt, then the waitress came and Walter ordered eggs and bacon with biscuits and gravy on the side. Chief Benson ordered grits and sliced fruit and told Walter he'd better start taking care of his ticker if he wanted to see his grandson grow up.

"I was lucky to survive my heart attack," the chief said. "Woke me up to what's important in life."

"Which is?"

For a split second he looked lost, then he recovered himself and shrugged. "Every man has to answer that for himself."

"I need your help with something," Walter said. "Something really important."

"I'm listening."

"Help me rid this town of a terrible blight."

"We're doing everything we can on that front," Benson said. "This synthetic stuff they're bringing up from Mexico is the worst I've ever seen."

"I'm not talking about drugs."

"Yeah? Well if you're not talking about drugs then I don't know because this is a peaceful little town we've got ourselves." He spooned grits into his mouth and began to chew.

"Perry Stubbs," Walter said.

The chief froze in mid swallow.

"I want you to help me get rid of Perry Stubbs."

Benson looked both ways then leaned in. "You mean kill him?"

"No, not kill him," Walter said, though the idea did have merit. "Arrest him. Charge him. Send him to prison."

"Prison? Stubbs? Are you out of your mind?"

"I realize what I'm asking is —."

"No," Benson said. "I don't think you do realize what you're asking."

"I was into him for a lot of money myself," Walter said, "and he showed me your name in his book."

"He showed you *my* name?"

"Yes, your name, and don't pretend you don't know what I'm talking about because he made a point of telling me he had you in his pocket."

Benson shot to his feet. "I don't have to sit here and take this from you!"

Every head in the place turned. "Oh sit down and stop acting like a baby," Walter said. Had he known the chief couldn't control himself he would have conducted the meeting in his office.

Benson looked around himself and growled at the onlookers to mind their own business, then he dropped back into his chair and crossed his forearms on the table. When he spoke again his voice was low and his tone measured. "If he gets wind of this he'll bury both of us."

"He's not a bear," Walter said.

"Worse than a bear. Why I've seen —." The chief stopped himself.

"You've seen what?"

"Nothing."

"You've seen what he does to people who don't pay and what did you do about it? Nothing, that's what you did about it. Not one thing, because either you're scared of him or you're still on his payroll."

"Now you look here!"

"No, you look here," Walter said. "You took an oath to uphold the law in this town and by George you'll do it or —."

"Or what?"

"Or I'll fire you."

"You can't fire me."

Walter didn't know if he had the authority to fire the police chief or not, but he felt certain the board did and he couldn't imagine the aldermen not acting once he told them what a coward Benson was. "Consider yourself fired at the next board meeting," Walter said. "If not sooner."

Benson leaned in close. "You're dumber than they said you were," he said, then he left, leaving Walter to wonder who *they* were.

* * *

Autumn looked good asleep. Without all the makeup and fuss. Maybe if his head didn't hurt so much he might do something to show her how good she looked, but it throbbed with the rhythm of his heart beating and he thought if he moved too far or too fast he might turn himself inside out, so he relaxed back into his pillow and stared up at the ceiling, not quite at that stage of recovery where one has to put a foot on the floor to keep the room from spinning. That part might come or it might not, his hangovers weren't always the same. They didn't adhere to any pattern, which was one reason he dismissed Autumn's nagging that he was an alcoholic. Wives are supposed to nag.

"Headache?" Her voice was soft as kitten fur and without a trace of anger.

"Did I make a fool of myself?"

"Our fathers were too drunk to notice if you did, and I kept our mothers as far away as I could. It wasn't hard to do. I think if I hadn't been so busy keeping them away they might have kept me away." She laughed the little schoolgirl laugh that had survived her childhood. "You're not working today?"

"How did I get upstairs?"

"Three grown men," she said, ignoring his question as completely as he had ignored hers. "Respected and looked up to and whenever you get together you drink yourselves stupid." Her voiced seemed a muddle all of a sudden, as though it came from somewhere far away instead of from the next pillow. They had a king bed and very seldom used the middle for sleep. Sex had become something of a wrestling match. Go at each other until the bell rings then retreat to your corner.

"I don't remember coming to bed," he said. "Did you bring me up?"

"For the life of me I can't see what reason any of you have to drink. Do you know how many people would kill to be in your shoes? I'm not talking about with me, though I could be. I don't think I'm hard to look at." She raised herself onto her elbow. He felt her looking at him. "Am I hard to look at?"

"Of course not."

"Then why don't you look at me?"

"I'm afraid if I turn my head I'll puke."

"I don't mean now," she said. "I mean ever. You never look at me anymore."

He closed his eyes. "Do we have to do this now?" The bed moved.

"No," she said. There was resignation in her voice. Defeat. When he opened his eyes again she had retreated back into her pillow.

"I was looking at you while you were sleeping," he said. "Thinking how beautiful you still are."

The bed moved again and her head slipped onto his bare chest as though she were listening to his heart beat. Her hand touched his stomach, then moved lower.

"Not now," he said. "Please."

She sighed, then rolled off him. "I don't know what to do anymore."

He knew by the tone it was going to be *that* conversation again. Age hadn't decreased her desire the way it had his.

"You used to be romantic," she said.

"I used to be young."

"You always say that."

"How did I get up here? I know you didn't carry me."

"You staggered up with one hand on the rail and your arm around my neck," she said. "Like a college frat boy who can't hold his liquor."

"Nobody can hold the amount of liquor I drank."

"We'll have to restock the bar before our first Christmas party."

"Did my father see?"

She raised herself onto her elbow again and looked into his eyes. "You seriously don't remember?"

"If I remembered I wouldn't ask."

"You walked them to the door," she said. "We both did. Then you and I actually had a coherent conversation, then you drank yourself to sleep while I cleaned the kitchen."

"I don't remember."

"It's getting out of hand."

"It was a special occasion."

"Your mother's not happy, you know."

"She'll get over it," he said. "I'm a grown man."

"I mean with your father. She's not happy."

"Of course she's happy. What'd she say?"

"She didn't say anything. A woman can tell."

"Sure you can, because you're all fortune tellers and psychics."

She sank into her pillow again. "Fine. We won't talk about it."

"There's nothing to talk about," he said. "My parents are fine."

She didn't say anything for a while, then, "Are they us in twenty years?"

He dropped a foot off the bed and felt the coolness of the floor, not to keep the room from spinning, but close. With some effort he pushed up onto his elbow and swung his other leg over the side and sat.

"Where are you going?"

Anywhere, he thought. Some place far away, but for the moment the bathroom seemed a reachable destination.

* * *

Twice during lunch Mildred asked Walter what was bothering him. It was their second go at the leftovers and from the looks of the containers she hustled back and forth there would be a third, perhaps a fourth. Twice was fine. Thrice was tolerable, but four times?

"We should get a dog," he said.

"You hate dogs."

"I don't *hate* dogs," he said. "I reject the concept of pets altogether."

"Surely you had a pet when you were little."

"I did," Walter said. "A dog. A really big dog that loved to lick faces. My face in particular. Do you have any idea the places a dog's tongue goes?"

Mildred laughed. It was Friday, the day after Thanksgiving, and City Hall was open for business but unoccupied except for a skeleton crew. All the department heads had taken the extra day. Kelsey French was Walter's skeleton crew and he thought her perfectly capable of handling things on her own, and if not, he had a cell phone.

"How come you're home so early anyway? Did Walmart run out of TVs and beds-in-a-bag?"

"It's so chaotic these days," she said. "It's downright dangerous, and you wouldn't believe how many women I saw with children. Babies even."

"Organized chaos," Walter said. "Capitalism run amuck."

"It's not capitalism, it's greed."

"That's what I meant."

She looked at him for a long time, then put down her fork. "I'm not going to stop asking until you tell me what's wrong."

"I believe you," he said.

"And don't think you can dodge the question by being cute."

"I can't help it if I'm cute," he said, flashing a controlled smile to throw her off the trail.

She pushed back her plate and folded her hands. "If it's the job, I think you're doing better than anyone expected."

"Well that's a resounding vote of confidence."

"You may as well get it off your chest because I'm not going anywhere."

"It's nothing."

"Don't tell me it's nothing. You've been moping around here all morning."

"You weren't here all morning," he said. "You've been out elbowing crazed women out of your way hoping to get — what did you hope to get anyway? You brought in one little bag."

"Never you mind what I was hoping to get, or got for all you know. Tell me what's wrong or I'll make you eat leftovers for a week. You were moping when I left and you were moping when I came home, so don't tell me I don't know you've been moping all morning."

He shrugged. The truth was he didn't know exactly why he felt particularly down that morning. It was something he woke up with. A feeling. That heavy blanket of foreboding that came over him on occasion, sometimes without the slightest provocation. Something he dreamed, he supposed. Some hidden memory too awful to confront with his eyes open. It wasn't his brother Mark he was thinking about. It wasn't anything at all. Mildred couldn't understand because she'd never experienced it.

"Depression," he said, breaking eye contact. His almost-empty plate seemed to be the thing needing looked at all of a sudden. "Doctors don't know how to cure it so how am I supposed to know?" Just saying the word aloud made him feel ashamed.

"Well I don't see what you have to be depressed about."

"I feel guilty enough already," he said. "My daughter's in prison, my back hurts all the time, and we're broke."

Mildred would not be dissuaded. "She's my daughter too, at least you can walk, and whose fault is it we're broke?"

"Exactly my point."

Mildred's grabbed his hand across the table. "I didn't mean that," she said, but she had meant it. Why shouldn't she mean it? They were broke because he gambled away everything they had and then some. She had no fault in it. "I don't care that we're broke."

"I don't care that I'm broke," he said, "but I do care that you are."

She smiled the way a woman does when her man says something sappy and melts her heart. "We still have the house."

"Thanks to Amy."

"We have Jackson," she said, squeezing his hand. "And each other."

Walter clasped his hand on top of hers, making it a sandwich. Without Mildred he would be lost, or dead. Possibly both because he believed in the Afterlife. Good or bad. Reward or punishment, and what reward did he deserve? What had he done in his entire miserable life that wasn't selfish? Even his one burst of heroism had been a selfish act. Sure, he wanted to save his wife and grandson, but he also wanted to save himself. Had they not been there he would have done the exact same thing. Behaved the same way. Heroes are people who rush toward danger, not away from it. His exit from that RV had been a rush away from danger. A mad dash of desperation, yet it had made him temporarily famous. His fifteen minutes of fame. Now his fame was local, what remained of it. People forget. People go back to their lives. Their real lives at home and their pretend lives on social media. The attention had all but stopped until he threw his hat into the ring to be mayor, not thinking he had a chance and by all rights he shouldn't have won. Had he not messed things up, Tipton Palo would be mayor now, and the town might be better off because people hate the status quo until someone tries to change it.

"How did Tom Sherman get along with Benson?"

"Is that what's bothering you?"

Saying yes seemed the easy way to derail her probe into his psyche, so he did.

"Fine, I suppose," she said. "Tom had a deep respect for police."

"They never argued about how Benson did his job? Or didn't do it?" He focused on her face, especially around the eyes, and knew she was calibrating her answer. Mildred wasn't capable of an outright lie but she could paint the truth gray as well as anyone.

"As far as I know he didn't interfere."

"Ever hear them argue?"

"Why are you asking me this? Did you have a run in with him?"

They uncoupled their hands. Walter didn't know which one of them moved first. It was consensual, like spontaneous sex except the opposite. Anti-sex. He leaned back against the wooden splines of his chair and felt certain there was something she wasn't telling him. She had a great admiration for her former boss. Plutonic, for sure, but deep and meaningful. There had been a time when he thought it might be more, but he forced such thoughts from his mind. Jealousy is the most aggressive cancer known to man. It destroys everything it touches. Depression's first cousin. Funny how he could defeat the one but not the other.

"Something like that," he said.

"Don't forget he's been at this a lot longer than you have."

"That doesn't make him right."

"I didn't say it makes him right."

"You're saying I should choose my battles wisely?"

"Or choose not to battle at all," she said. "No one expects you to move mountains."

"Is Benson why your mayor resigned?"

"You're my mayor."

"I didn't mean it that way."

"Then don't say it that way. Tom Sherman is a fine man, and he was a good mayor. If you're asking me why he resigned I've already told you I don't know."

"He didn't confide in his trusted ally?"

"Asking someone the same question over and over is the same as calling them a liar," she said, then she stood abruptly and began clearing the table. Walter believed her when she said she didn't know, but his gut told him she had a theory and he wanted to hear it. "You can't fire the police chief without the board's support," she said. "Just in case you don't know."

"I only need three aldermen," he said. "Kilfiche and Sharp should be easy. I don't know about a third."

"Why should those two be easy?"

"Kilfiche is a retired judge," Walter said, "and he seems honest. The Reverend could score some major points with his flock by taking down a police chief."

"Why, because he's black and Benson's white?"

"No, because he's black and Benson's a cop," Walter said. "Being white is icing on the cake."

"You'll think icing if you say something like that in public. You shouldn't be saying it in private either. You shouldn't be thinking it at all."

He almost took the bait. Almost entered into a terribly long discussion with her on race. A discussion he couldn't win because he refused to toss logic out the window and pretend tribal feuding wasn't as old as humanity itself. It's human nature to gravitate toward sameness. Birds of a feather flock together. People have feathers, too, and they flock. All they need is a common goal. A bond. It's why flags were invented. Every tribe needs an enemy. Without enemies we couldn't have friends. Take away man's instinct to flock and society would collapse under its own laziness. People need something to resist. Something to fight. Some evil to extinguish, otherwise they stop competing and the world devolves into one giant Woodstock. Competition keeps society moving forward. Sometimes it boils over and mankind takes a step backward, then it roars back stronger and better, the way a city rebuilds itself anew after a disaster. If not for hurricanes, coastal regions would become old and dilapidated. Without tornadoes and earthquakes and floods, the world's infrastructure would crumble from neglect. Without the evil of Hitler, the genius of Churchill would have gone unnoticed. Walter didn't consider himself a racist. How could he be when he loved his grandson as much as one human can love another? Trying to explain it was as hopeless as digging oneself out of a hole. "I'm well aware of today's climate," he said.

"I would hope so." She stacked the dishes in the sink and returned to wipe the table with a damp rag. "Even if you do convince those two, you still don't have a third."

"Momentum of public opinion, Mildred. Don't underestimate it."

"That's what I'm afraid of," she said. "Nothing rallies people around a scoundrel like someone trying to take him down."

* * *

Tipton sat on his balcony overlooking the golf course. It was cold out, but the house blocked the wind, hence the light jacket instead of his heavy coat. Bourbon warmed his insides. Autumn sat with him until she didn't. One minute she was there, the next minute she was gone.

"The police chief is at the gate," she said from the sliding door behind him.

"Tell him to go away."

"I've already buzzed him in."

A minute later he heard the doorbell chime so he went downstairs. Autumn stayed upstairs without having to be told.

He opened the door with a half-finished drink in his hand. "Something wrong with your phone?"

"Stop being a smartass and let me in," Benson said. His shirt was half tucked and his eyes were bloodshot. Tipton led him into the study and watched him plop down on the sofa without being invited.

"By all means," Tipton said, "make yourself at home."

The chief sat hunched forward with his palms pressed together between his knees, dressed in black slacks and his half-tucked white shirt too wrinkled to have felt the heat of an iron. Benson was a bachelor and looked the part. A man needs a woman to tell him he's being a slob, otherwise he struts around not knowing.

The chief rocked back and forth the way a child does when either he's bursting to tell something or afraid to. From above, as Tipton moved from the door to a matching armchair, the pink of the man's scalp made the unnatural shade of black dye look all the more ridiculous — something else a wife might tell him.

Tipton sat. "Well?"

"I had lunch with the sonofabitching mayor today."

"Good for you."

"He thinks he can tell me how to run my police department."

"Can he?"

Benson bristled. "You know better than that."

"Do I? He's the mayor. He has power."

"I run my department my way."

"Yet here you are, bitching to me. I don't control Pigg."

"I wouldn't be in this fix if it wasn't for you. He wants me to arrest Stubbs."

Tipton left his chair and freshened his glass, then he poured some bourbon over ice for the chief, using the distraction to formulate a reaction. Arresting Stubbs had its advantages but saying so to Benson could be dangerous, so instead he handed him the glass and sat again.

Benson tilted his glass then licked his lips. Good whiskey always finds the drunk. "He could cause a lot of trouble for us, you know."

"We don't have to worry about Stubbs," Tipton said. "Unless you arrest him."

"I meant the mayor."

Tipton scoffed. "What can the mayor do to me?"

"You're in it same as me," Benson said, his eyes danced with fear, or agitation, it was hard to tell which. Benson was the textbook definition of a bully. Preying on the weak, strutting around ready to take on all comers until someone comes.

"Strike first," Tipton said. "Take him down a peg or two, or all the way. Problem solved."

The chief's face brightened. "You got something in mind?"

"It's not me he's after." He watched Benson's face absorb the declaration and knew the man was a liability. Put the screws to him and he might say anything to save his skin. Maybe he thought they were in it together as equals. Compared to his cut, Benson's was chump change, only he didn't know. Stubbs took the lion's share and then some, and maybe he thought he was pulling one over on his lawyer friend, but Tipton knew everything. He made it his business to know. The only reason he let Stubbs get away with cheating was because something was better than nothing, and Stubbs wasn't the kind of man who took correction well. "Keep your head," Tipton said, realizing he had to say something to buy time. "Pigg can't touch you without three aldermen, and he'll never get more than two."

"What if he runs his mouth and whips the public into a frenzy?"

"He won't."

"I don't trust politicians," Benson said. "People start complaining and they'll turn on their own mothers."

"Not Brad Stovall," Tipton said. "He's tough as a tombstone and he hates Pigg almost as much as we do."

"He's one man."

"Toms and Townsend make it three," Tipton said. He didn't know what Stovall had on them and he didn't care. Three for the price of one. "And don't ask me if I'm sure because I am."

"I wasn't going to," he said, lying. Tipton could read liars like a book. Sniffing out weaklings was part of his job description. Put a man on the stand and you'd better know if he'll hold up.

"Go home," he said. "Sober up before you talk to anyone. Better yet, don't talk to anyone sober *or* drunk."

Benson wrestled himself to his feet. "Don't worry about me talking," he said. "I'm not stupid."

Tipton followed him to the door, then locked it behind him. None of that southerly charm business. Good riddance. He turned from the door and saw Autumn halfway up the staircase looking down at him. "Get back upstairs," he said, then he waited until she was gone. She knew better than to eavesdrop on his conversations. He'd never hit her because he'd never had to, but maybe she didn't know that. Maybe she thought he was one of those pushovers who lets his wife keep his nuts in a lockbox. He eyed the staircase, thinking maybe he'd go up and teach her a lesson, then he decided to call Stubbs instead.

"I'm telling you he's become a problem," he said after Stubbs refused to listen to reason.

"You're drunk," Stubbs said. "You can barely talk without slobbering on yourself."

"Drunk or not, I know when a man's losing his nerve."

"Sounds like you're losing yours."

The call ended without a resolution. Stubbs could be a real pain in the ass when he wanted to be, which was most of the time. A two-bit bookie who fancied himself a John Gotti. More like Boss Hogg without the flab. The Burt Reynolds version.

"Are you coming to bed?"

"What?" He opened and closed his eyes a few times and realized he'd been asleep on the couch. Autumn was wearing a white cotton shirt he could see through. No bra. So that's what she came down for. "Help me up."

She reached for his arm and pulled him by the wrist. He jerked away. "Leave me alone! I can get up by myself."

CHAPTER 8

Walter had some very detailed ideas to pitch to the board regarding the Palo-West Main Street Christmas donation but he wasn't ready to reveal them to anyone just yet, not even to Mildred, lest she object and force him to oppose her.

It was Monday morning and he was eager to roll up his sleeves and get to work. Having a plan of action, if not an outright mandate, invigorated him to the point of feeling brave. If Tipton Palo and Rance West thought they could steal the front page and relegate him to the obituary section on the cheap, they had another thing coming. They promised decorations without specifics, and as lawyers they should know better. Walter intended to school them.

He buzzed Kelsey and told her to call the superintendent of Water and Light and get an exact count on lampposts along Main, end to end. For years the town had neglected the southern end of Main when it came to Christmas, but this year would be different. This year it would be all or nothing, and it would come out of Tipton Palo's pocket.

Next he called Gordy Kilfiche. The next board meeting was three weeks away and he didn't want to wait. He knew about special sessions but he didn't know how to call one. Mildred probably knew, but she would demand to know why. Alderman Kilfiche demanded to know, too, but he didn't press so hard for details.

"We don't normally discuss Christmas during official meetings, Walter."

"Then how does the town get decorated?"

"There's usually a committee to make those decisions."

"Is there a legal reason why the board can't discuss it?"

"Depends on who you ask."

"I'm asking you."

"In my opinion, no, there's no reason the board can't discuss it, but I'm not the board attorney."

"I won't be cowed by a bunch of atheist lawyers," Walter said. "Christmas is an American tradition. The board won't discuss it because it's afraid of the ACLU."

"Among other groups."

"And a citizens committee insulates the town from a lawsuit?"

"No, but it gives the board a degree of separation."

"Who picks the citizens?"

"Well, uh, I don't exactly know to be honest," the old judge said. "They just sort of pick themselves."

"In other words, the same unelected people run it year after year?"

"For the most part … yes … but you have to understand the nature of civic-mindedness. It takes a special breed of —."

"We need new blood," Walter said. "Fresh ideas."

"Nobody's ever complained."

"How do you know?"

"Well, they haven't complained to the board."

"How can they? The board has washed its hands of it."

"You're being unfair, Walter. Those ladies do the best they can with what they have, and they're all volunteers so it doesn't cost the town a penny. I hear Palo's ponying up for new decorations this year, too, so they should be happy about that."

"Precisely why I want to call a meeting," Walter said. "Such a generous offer deserves official recognition, don't you think?"

"Not really. I think they did it for the publicity."

"Regardless why they did it, it's done. They can't very well back out now, can they? Not with that front-page advertisement in the Hayes Beacon."

"I think I'm beginning to see where you're going with this and I'm not sure it's a good idea."

"So how do I go about calling a special session?"

"Ask your wife. She'll know."

"I'd like to have the meeting tomorrow night."

"Too soon. You have to announce it in the newspaper so the public can attend, unless you mean to have an executive session."

"Thursday then," Walter said. "The more people who show up the better. I wouldn't dare handle this bit of business behind closed doors. I can count on you being there, can't I?"

"I'm an alderman," he said. "I'm obligated."

* * *

Brad Stovall telephoned Tipton and told him the mayor had something up his sleeve that he probably wasn't going to like. "How should I know what," he said when pressed for details. "I've told you all I know. He's calling a special session to discuss the decorations you donated."

"And you didn't think it important to ask why?"

"I didn't talk to the man. His girl called my girl," Stovall said. "Who knows, maybe he's one of these ACLU types who hate Christmas. Could be he wants to shut the whole thing down."

Tipton hung up while Stovall was still talking. If the man didn't know anything there was no reason to listen to him babble. He had a two o'clock with a client who was getting cold feet waiting for his insurance company to blink and write a big check, the bulk of which would go into Tipton's pocket. The firm's pocket, to be more precise, unfairly enriching his partner for a case he didn't lift a finger on.

What was Pigg up to? The ACLU angle was too good to be true, but it was an interesting idea. Pigg certainly was an odd duck, and Tipton knew so very little about him. Nothing at all about his politics. Pigg had no social media presence but his wife did, and she seemed staunchly conservative. He had them both pegged as Trumpers but maybe that was just her. Husbands and wives don't always vote the same way.

He leaned way back in his chair and put his feet on the desk, careful not to mark it with his shoes. If Pigg came out against Christmas the headlines would write themselves. The people would drive him from office. Of course it could be that he called the special session out of ignorance, thinking he could micromanage how the town decorated itself. Even that, played the right way, would give Dexter Mann plenty of fodder. Practically any scenario he could think of would break in his favor, given the right nudging.

Rance popped through the door as if on cue, looking ridiculous with the part in his toupee twisted toward his right eyebrow instead of following the natural contour of his head, but slipshod was Rance's way. It was expected of him.

"I was just about to buzz you," Tipton said, dropping his feet from the desk and righting himself.

Rance plopped down into the client chair and hooked his left leg over the arm.

"Must you destroy all the furniture?"

"Says the man who just had his feet on a two thousand dollar desk. And why is it you never come into my office when you need something?"

"I don't need anything," Tipton said, leaning forward to rub the invisible spot where his feet had been, "but I do have something you need to hear."

Rance frowned.

"The new mayor's calling a special session Thursday to discuss Christmas decorations."

"Probably wants to hit us up for more money," Rance said.

"Or he may refuse our offer in its entirety."

"Your offer," Rance said. "I wasn't consulted, remember?"

"The firm's offer," Tipton said. "Half the credit went to you."

"Since when do politicians refuse free money?"

"True, but Pigg's not a politician. He's a rube in over his head and everyone knows it but him." Tipton laughed. "He's too dumb to know the board doesn't involve itself in religious celebrations. Mark my words, his mayoral days are numbered."

"And I suppose you think you'll replace him?"

"Who else?"

"After the last election? Almost anyone whose name isn't Palo."

"Let me worry about that," Tipton said. "For one thing I'll have a better campaign manager."

Rance unhooked his leg from the chair and stood. "Are we done here?"

"You came to me," Tipton said. "Did you want something or were you just loafing?"

Rance glared at him, then he sank back into the chair. "Nothing other than to tell you for the hundredth time you need to end this feud with Pigg, but I see now that's not going to happen. You're too blind to see when you're licked."

"Don't lecture me."

"People are laughing at you."

"What people? Tell me who they are and they won't laugh. Tell me!"

Rance blinked. "I haven't *heard* anything," he said. "I don't have to."

"So when you say people are laughing at me, you mean you're laughing at me. Good. Laugh. When I'm mayor you'll be on your own and you'll —." He stopped. "That's why you sabotaged my campaign. You knew if I won you'd have to actually do a little work for a change."

"Now you look here!"

"No, you look," Tipton said. "It's all coming together now. Motive and intent. Pigg won because you made sure I didn't."

"You've lost your mind," Rance said. Instead of being mad he seemed amused. When he stood to leave Tipton stopped him.

"Forget I said that. I'm sure you tried your best."

Rance nodded. "Sure, Tip, I tried my best. We both did, but we lost. Get over it."

* * *

Walter had a habit of going through the house checking lights before leaving for work because Mildred had a habit of leaving them on, and she had passed that awful habit on to their grandson. That particular morning it was the living room light, and just as he flipped it off, he heard Mildred scream. It was more than the typical *I see a spider* scream. Worse even than the occasional *there's a snake* scream. This scream reached deep into Walter's store of Mildred screams, all the way back to the one he heard that day on the RV as he lunged for the demon and rode him out the door like a bucking bull. It was her death scream, and the only thing he could think of was Jackson.

He ran as best he could, out of the living room and through the kitchen with his heart racing almost as fast as his brain, to the back door, which stood open, then out. The instant he stepped through the door and onto the porch he saw it, whatever *it* was.

Mildred and Jackson stood frozen, holding hands and staring at the thing hanging by a rope from the roof of the porch. It was Tuesday morning, not that it mattered what day of the week it was, but that was the odd thought that popped into Walter's head and momentarily pushed everything else aside. Sometimes when the brain receives a shock, it tries to mask it with something mundane. Walter may have spoken the thought, he wasn't sure. Mildred and Jackson took no notice if he did, staring as they were. Frozen. Walter saw only the backs of their heads, but he felt the terror in their faces.

"What is that thing?" Mildred finally said, barely audible, as though she had spoken from somewhere far away. The smell was awful, and it looked to Walter to be the severed head of a horse. Blood stained the boards of the porch beneath the head, having dripped for a while before congealing so that it hung in long clotted strings that almost reached the wooden boards but didn't. Flies gorged themselves, making the scene that much more grotesque. Walter tugged at Mildred's arm to pull her back but she was unmovable.

"Take him inside," Walter said, meaning their grandson. It seemed the manly thing to say.

Mildred didn't move. "Who would do such a thing?"

Perry Stubbs would do such a thing, or have it done, he thought but didn't say. Have his man slaughter a horse, saw off the head, and hang it from the mayor's porch because the mayor had told certain people he was coming for him. No one else had the depravity to do something so grotesque and vile.

Jackson had not spoken a word. He stood frozen like his grandmother, jaw dropped and eyes wide while the image tattooed itself onto his future. Someday he would recall it as a harmless *remember when*, but between then and now it would torment him in his dreams.

"Go to your room," Walter said. He pulled at Mildred's elbow again. "Take him upstairs." His voice was firm, letting her know he meant business. Mildred took orders no better than Walter gave them, but this was not your ordinary household decision. "Go!"

She jumped, then turned with abject horror in her face and almost jerked poor Jackson out of his shoes.

"He won't get away with it," Walter said to their backs. Fear became anger. A moment ago he had trembled in fear, now he shook with rage. In his mind he stormed into the tiny back office where Stubbs kept his lair and ripped him apart with his bare hands. Man against man, beast against beast, then he recovered his senses and dialed 9-1-1.

Mildred reappeared as the first siren began to wail in the distance. As a citizen Walter had called the police many times and not once had they come with sirens. He would look back on this moment later as a turning point. He *was* the mayor.

"I told him to stay in his room," Mildred said, her voice pulled down by the gravity of the situation. "Do you think it was Palo?" Walter turned and looked at her as though she had said the moon was square, then he didn't know. Palo had taken defeat hard but what kind of man was he?

The siren grew in intensity and he soon saw flashes of blue against the morning hue, like grayscale coming alive. The noise would arouse the neighborhood and soon his lawn would be teeming with gawkers. For a brief period of time he would be the center of attention, and in some odd way he enjoyed it.

"You should go back inside," he said, but instead she grasped his elbow with both hands and he felt the rush of adrenaline a man feels when he stands between his woman and danger. Every man needs to be his woman's protector sometimes, if for no other reason than to bolster his own self-esteem. The siren fell silent and a patrol car wheeled into their driveway. "How much authority do I have over the police?"

"Don't badger them," Mildred said.

The interior light popped on, then the door slammed. Walter watched the young officer's face become visible as he drew near, then saw his eyes fly wide. "What the hell is that thing?" he asked, then he saw Mildred and apologized for his language. Walter had seen the officer before but didn't know his name — a failing he would correct. A mayor should know his cops by name.

"Call your chief," Walter said. "Tell him to get his ass down here." The squeeze on his arm intensified then relaxed. Mildred didn't scold him. Walter felt her hand move up the inside of his arm to his bicep then back down. She approved. She was proud of him for taking charge and it steadied him.

The young officer keyed the mike on his left shoulder, tilted his head toward it, and relayed the mayor's request to his dispatcher, all without taking his eyes off the gruesome thing hanging between them. "I've never seen anything like this," he said aloud, then he tore his eyes from it and looked up at Walter, who stood beside it like a statue.

By the time Benson arrived, every cop in Hayes was milling about Walter's yard, in uniform or not, on duty or off. Everyone wanted to see the horse head swinging from the mayor's porch. Crime fighting came to a standstill so everyone could gawk. Both constables were there, as well as reserve officers, and Old Pete who was retired but still worked the school crossing. Neighbors had gathered on the outskirts, held at bay by officers barking at them to stay back.

Benson stood on the porch with his hands clasped behind his back looking like a barnyard chicken. A hen, not a rooster. "I've seen this sort of thing before," he said to Walter after a long time saying nothing.

"In Hayes?"

"No, on TV. The Godfather. You know the scene where the Hollywood mogul refuses to cast the Don's —."

"Not funny," Walter said, then he grabbed the chief by the elbow and pulled him into the kitchen with everyone watching. "You told Stubbs about our conversation."

Benson jerked free. "Don't grab me in front of my men. You may be the mayor but —."

"You're in his pocket so deep you can smell his balls!"

"Walter!"

"Upstairs Mildred!"

Benson's face turned three shades of red. His body trembled and he looked ready to explode but he wouldn't dare lay hands on the mayor in front of the entire police force. At that moment Walter hoped he would, but the moment quickly passed and Walter's temper cooled. He knew Benson had told Stubbs about their conversation but he couldn't prove it. He had to keep his head. The town was watching.

"I want this investigated," he said. "This isn't a broken window."

"Now look here, Walter, I —."

"Mayor," Walter said. "You'll address me by my office."

"You can't tell me how to run my department!"

"Buck me on this and it won't be your department," Walter said, careful to keep his voice down. Embarrassing him in front of his men would only force him to resist. It was Stubbs he wanted, not the chief. "Now get out there and do your job. Your men are watching."

Benson hitched his pants and looked through the doorway at the suspended head. The color slowly returned to his face. "Looks like they used some type of saw," he said. "We'll do what we can."

CHAPTER 9

Front page above the fold of the Hayes Beacon Wednesday morning was a simple headline: HEAD FOUND ON MAYOR'S PORCH.

Two long and discombobulated sentences into the article, the reader learned that while the head could have easily been human, it in fact, belonged to a horse. Dexter Mann followed with this:

Like Jack Woltz in The Godfather, *Mayor Pigg awoke to a bloody surprise, leading some to question whether or not our mayor has mafia ties. Could Don Corleone be his campaign manager, Brant Haskell, and if so, what favor did candidate Pigg make that Mayor Pigg denied? And how is this related to the rumblings that Mayor Pigg is gunning for Police Chief Benson's job?*

Walter wadded the front section into a ball. "They're all in cahoots!"

Mildred stood at the stove pouring brown gravy from an iron skillet into a bowl. The aroma of fresh biscuits controlled the room, which meant no bacon or sausage. She turned at Walter's outburst. He knew by the confused look on her face that she had not yet connected the dots. He was sitting at the table nursing his second cup of coffee.

"Benson mentioned The Godfather when he was here yesterday and now it's in a newspaper article. What are the odds?"

"It's not Saturday but I made gravy," Mildred said, as though gravy on a weekday might undo the media ambush. She placed the bowl and plate on the table in front of him then turned back for silverware.

"Mafia," Walter said, "That's what they're saying I'm part of you know. I'm Jack Woltz. Haskell is Don Corleone. Benson's the deserving actor Haskell screwed out of a movie role by putting a horse head in my bed."

"It was on our porch," she said, planting herself in the chair opposite him at the table. "And all this Godfather nonsense is ridiculous."

"Porch, bed, what's the difference, Mildred?"

"I don't watch movies like that so I have no idea who these people are."

"We watched it together."

"Then I don't remember it."

"Who's Jack Wolf?"

Mildred looked past Walter to their grandson who had entered the kitchen unannounced. "Never mind who Jack Wolf is," she said. "Come and eat your breakfast."

"Woltz," Walter said as the boy rounded into view, "not Wolf."

Mildred's look terminated the conversation. Walter thought her overprotective of the boy but what was he to do? Mothers and grandmothers play a different role than fathers and grandfathers. One protects while the other exposes. Her job was to keep him from seeing the ugliness of the world while Walter's was to prepare him for whatever life may throw at him. Parenting is a balancing act, and more often than not Walter felt like the skinny kid on a seesaw.

Jackson searched the table with his eyes. "No bacon?"

"My thoughts exactly," Walter said. "We're having a meatless Wednesday."

"It won't hurt you to do without meat every now and then," Mildred said to Walter. "The way your stomach is."

"My stomach's fine."

"All that gas."

"Vegetables cause gas."

"My stomach's fine too," Jackson said.

"Your grandmother tries to hide her gas," Walter said with a wink to his wife. She frowned but she wasn't angry. He meant to tell her the biscuits and gravy were so good they didn't need bacon, but his phone rang in his pocket and interrupted him. "Haskell," he said to Mildred after seeing the display. Normally he didn't take calls during meals but the week had been anything but normal. "I'll take it on the back porch."

He answered as he rose from his chair. Haskell didn't give him time to say hello. "Where the hell does he get off calling me Corleone?"

"I wondered where you got all your money."

"Stop being funny," Haskell said. "You're not funny. You know that don't you? You're not funny? I'll sue the bastard. I'll sue the entire miserable newspaper."

"I don't blame you," Walter said. "I might sue too if I could afford an attorney."

"You're a public official," Haskell said. "You can't sue."

"I should sue you for getting me into this mess," Walter said. "I was perfectly happy being insignificant."

"What's all that guff about you gunning for Benson?"

"He's a blight on humanity," Walter said. He heard an audible sigh. "Stubbs has him in his pocket."

"Take my advice and forget about Stubbs or you'll be ruined. And whatever you do, leave Benson alone, especially now. He's been chief forever and Dexter Mann just poisoned the well. Any action you take now will be — ."

"Dexter Mann doesn't dictate my actions," Walter said. "He reacts to them."

"And voters react to him."

"The voters have done all the damage they can do to me."

"You may decide you like being mayor."

"Ha! I'd rather be stung in the face by bees."

"You say that now, but what about two years from now when you're staring unemployment in the face?"

"I still have my engineering degree."

"So do a lot of younger men," Haskell said. "Nobody wants to hire a man your age when they can hire someone a lot younger."

"I have experience."

"You'll also be retiring in ten years. Trust me on this, Walter. Don't burn your bridges. Play your cards right and you could ride this job until you die."

"Or have it ride me."

"It's your funeral."

"Thanks for the encouragement," Walter said, knowing what Haskell said was true. Business is business, and there's no mathematical symbol for loyalty. He felt himself at a crossroads. To the left the road was paved and smooth and had a great big rainbow at the end. To the right the road was gravel, and through the dust he saw Dexter Mann and Tipton Palo and a host of other bad actors throwing out roofing nails to pop his tires. At the end was Perry Stubbs, chomping his wet cigar, grinning because the odds were in his favor.

* * *

Rance barged into Tipton's office and demanded he disavow the horse incident at the mayor's house. Tipton looked up from his work, more annoyed than surprised. Of course Rance would think he had something to do with it.

"Lower your voice and stop being ridiculous," Tipton said.

"Did you do it or not?"

"Not."

Rance moved toward the desk and put both hands on the back of the guest chair. "Let me rephrase the question," he said, "since I know how you are. Did you have anything to do with the horse head Mayor Pigg found hanging from his back porch?"

"Asked and answered," Tipton said. "Where have you been all day?"

"Answer the question."

Tipton told Rance he had nothing to do with the incident, then he went further and swore he had no prior knowledge of it. He was sincere because it was true, unfortunately. Stubbs was his own entity and didn't clear his actions with anyone. Hanging the head had been a brilliant idea. The only risk had been getting caught in the act, and that part was safely over. Benson would do his job and make sure the investigation went nowhere. Even Dexter Mann had come through. His headline and article made Pigg look foolish. It was impossible to read the article and not picture a buffoonish mayor standing on his back porch staring helplessly at a bloody skull.

Deflated by his partner's denial, Rance plopped down in the chair and stared.

"Well?"

"I'm trying to decide whether or not to believe you."

"Believe whatever you want," Tipton said. "Now if you don't mind I've got work to do, and I assume you do too since it's almost one o'clock and you're just now dragging yourself in."

"I clear my cases."

"That's the attitude," Tipton said. "Mediocrity."

"Keep up this ridiculous feud with Pigg and there won't be any cases to clear," Rance said.

"My caseload hasn't suffered." He remembered something. "In fact, there was a wreck last night out near the old gravel pit." He moved some papers and found a sticky note with a name on it. "Since you have nothing to do, how about running down to the hospital and accidentally bumping into Mrs. Lopez." He passed the note to Rance. "A certain nurse told me she'll either be a widow or the wife of a vegetable."

Rance turned the note over in his fingers. "Do you ever get tired of chasing ambulances?"

"No."

"A woman loses her husband and we swoop in like two buzzards to feed on the carcass."

"If we don't swoop some other buzzard will," Tipton said. Rance was being childish again. Dragging his feet. "We may be too late already so get going."

"Don't tell me what to do, Tip. I'm a partner —."

"Stop calling me Tip or you'll be flat of your back on the rug."

Rance shot to his feet and threw the wadded note at Tipton's face. Tipton recoiled, thinking Rance was coming across the desk. The paper ricocheted off his lip and into the floor. The back of Tipton's chair struck the wall. He could take Rance in a fair fight, maybe in an unfair one, but the damage to the firm would be irreparable. He didn't even know what Rance was so upset about.

He collected himself. "Was that necessary?"

Rance glared at him like some wounded animal. "I'm not your law clerk," he said. "You don't send me on errands."

"I gave you a lead," Tipton said. "I'd do it myself but I'm swamped. Don't get so bent out of shape."

"The way you do when I call you Tip?" Rance's fists were balled at his sides and he still had the fight or flight look in his eyes.

Candice rushed in and closed the door. "Your one o'clock is here," she said, glaring at Tipton hard enough to make him think he might have to fight them both.

"The phone would have been sufficient."

"We could hear the two of you arguing," she said. "It's pretty hard to pretend I work for professionals when you fight like children." She turned on her heels and left them both staring after her.

"I don't know about you," Rance said, "but I'm a little turned on by that."

Tipton wasn't. Quite the opposite, in fact. Insolence held no sex appeal for him. Were it his decision alone, Candice would be standing in the unemployment line wondering how she was going to pay for Christmas.

* * *

Turnout for the special meeting was low. Other than the aldermen and support staff, there was Tipton Palo, Rance West, and about half a dozen concerned citizens, only a few of which Walter recognized by sight. Dexter Mann, editor of the Beacon and writer of grand headlines, was late in finding his seat. At precisely the moment the big clock on the wall struck six, Walter swung his gavel and called the meeting to order. They faced the flag as a group and recited the Pledge, then Alderman Sharp led them in prayer. No one kneeled or raised a fist. Hayes hadn't devolved into anarchy like so many of the larger cities.

"I called this session to discuss Christmas decorations," the mayor said half a second after Sharp uttered the word *Amen*, catching those assembled off guard as they scrambled to reclaim their seats. He spotted Palo and West in the second row and paused. "First I'd like to thank misters West and Palo for their generosity." He paused again, enjoying himself very much, watching the muscles in Palo's face twitch. A splattering of applause gained traction, so Walter put his hands together and led them to a thunderous conclusion. When the room fell silent again, he continued. "Our current decorations, I'm told, are still in good condition, so I'd like to see them used in other areas of the city. Along Second, or Fourth?" He looked left then right, inviting feedback from the aldermen. Brad Stovall seemed perplexed, as though he needed to object to something but didn't know what. Walter gave them time, then, satisfied, continued. "I see no sense in discarding them."

"Perhaps we could donate them to a smaller town," Sharp said. "Within our county of course."

"I was thinking we could string them along Barker Street? Or Jackson," Walter said, singling out two predominately black neighborhoods virtually ignored by the city. Sharp nodded his approval. "Yes, I like that idea. We don't do enough in those areas." Barker Street ran through his ward and Jackson ran through Stovall's. Walter had picked those streets to entice Sharp and to hamstring Stovall.

Stovall objected. Walter suppressed a smile. All eyes shifted to Stovall as he sat squirming, looking as uncomfortable as a monk in a strip club. He glanced at Tipton for instruction but what could Palo do?

"You bit it off," Walter said to the alderman. "Now chew."

The room erupted with raucous laugher. Stovall's face glowed red as he sat staring at the mayor and biting his upper lip. After a noticeable duration Walter pounded his gavel and called for order. "Let the gentleman speak," he said, then to Stovall, "to what does the alderman object?"

Stovall stammered, then he said he objected to the meeting.

"Isn't Jackson Street in your ward?"

"No," Stovall said, then Sharp whispered something into his ear and he corrected himself. The idiot didn't even know his ward. The old Walter would have called attention to it but the new and improved Walter left it to the audience to absorb according to each member's ability. In a just world, Dexter Mann would jot a note and skewer him in the next edition but that would never happen. Mann and Stovall wore the same team jerseys.

Walter rapped his gavel and the spattering of laughter died away. "Since you object to Barker and Jackson," he said to Stovall, "perhaps you have another street in mind?"

"Stop trying to twist my words!"

"Your timing is troubling," Walter said. "Objecting to the meeting *after* I mention the minority part of town. Someone in want of a nefarious headline might find fodder in that." He looked at Dexter Mann just long enough for everyone in the room to notice, then back to the alderman. "But I'm sure you're immune to that sort of treatment."

"This meeting is illegal," Stovall said with no force of conviction.

"Illegal in what way?"

"Separation of church and state," the alderman said. "Or have you never heard of the Bill of Rights?"

Walter smiled. He made a point of it — smiling. The alderman's grasp of the law, and the First Amendment, mimicked an all too common misconception. He turned to the board attorney, Larry Pace, and asked for his legal opinion.

Pace cleared his throat and stiffened his spine. "Certain groups look for small southern towns to overstep the bounds of church versus state," he said.

"The question is whether or not it's illegal for this board to meet and discuss Christmas decorations."

The attorney squirmed again. "Well, illegal … no, not technically."

"So in your legal opinion, Mr. Pace, as the attorney for this board, we are entirely within our legal rights to meet in this manner, for this purpose?"

"Technically speaking, yes."

"Speak legally, Mister Pace."

"He's saying it's a stupid thing to do," Stovall said. "And I agree."

"So do I," said Alderman Townsend. Wayne Toms chimed in to make it a trio.

"And what about you, Alderman Sharp?"

"I'd like to hear your ideas," Sharp said.

"Alderman Kilfiche?"

"There's nothing illegal about it," the retired judge said with an admonishing tone. "Fear is a poor substitute for legal opinion."

Pace cleared his throat again. "I only meant that —."

"We all know what you meant," Kilfiche said. "The ACLU might not like it, but we have the right to decorate our streets the way we see fit."

"Can you guarantee we won't get sued?" Stovall asked.

"There's a good chance we will get sued," Kilfiche said. "At the very least threatened. That's how bullies operate."

"It could bankrupt the town."

"Yes it could," the judge said. "They have money and we don't." He looked toward Tipton and West and suggested some of the town's more prominent attorneys might donate their time if it came to a lawsuit.

Palo cleared his throat. "I'm afraid with our caseload —."

"Fear only works against cowards," Walter said. He was an expert on the subject. Ask Mildred. Ask anyone not swayed by that one single incident with the RV. Stovall would have crowed from the rafters had he known the truth about his mayor. The words almost stuck in Walter's throat, but they needed saying so he spat them out.

"Say that when the ACLU sues us and we have to find the money to fight them," Toms said.

"No one can sue us for having a meeting," Walter said. "Not even the ACLU. Am I right, Mr. Pace?"

Larry Pace shrugged.

"Close enough," Walter said before the attorney could prop up the gesture with words. "Now, if we're in agreement that our old decorations will be used in some other part of town, I'd like to address Main Street." He turned his attention to Tipton Palo, who looked somewhat less eager than he had a moment ago. "According to a very bold front-page headline in the Hayes Beacon, Mr. Palo, your firm — you and Mr. West — has generously agreed to supply the decorations for the lampposts along Main. Is that still your intention?"

"Within reason," Palo said.

"You mean you have a budget," Walter said. "Of course. The town isn't here to pick your pockets. Perhaps if you gave us a figure ... say a per-pole best guess of what your firm is willing to spend."

"This should be handled by a civilian committee," Stovall said.

Kilfiche disagreed, saying he saw no reason why the board shouldn't be involved. Walter felt a moment of triumph, then the judge knocked the wind out of his sails by saying the committee would surely welcome the board's suggestions.

"This is our decision to make," Walter said with force. "The good people of this town elected us, not a committee selected based on their last names."

Heads nodded throughout the room. Tipton Palo rolled his eyes. Dexter Mann jotted into his notebook.

"Minus a motion," Walter said, "I took the liberty of looking at a few options." He pulled a small stack of flyers from his briefcase and passed them left and right, then offered them over the bench for those who wanted to step up and take one. Dexter Mann was first in that capacity, and he was kind enough to hand one to Tipton Palo on his way back to his seat.

"There are five hundred and thirteen lampposts on Main Street," Walter said. "The odd one lost its mate a while back when one of our senior ladies missed her turn at Dr. White's office." Almost everyone laughed, including Walter. "They tell me it probably won't be replaced until mid-January."

"We've never decorated south of the courthouse," Stovall said.

"An oversight of the civilian committee I suppose," Walter said.

"That area's mostly residential."

"All the more reason it should be highlighted," Walter said. "Hayes is more than banks and law offices. Christmas is about people — families, not storefront displays."

Walter had kept an eye on Palo as he tended Stovall, watching him sort through the glossy printouts of Christmas ornaments and garnish suitable for a churchgoing town. Rance West sat red-faced, barely looking as his partner passed each flier to him. When they reached the bottom of the pile, Walter put the question of budget to Tipton again.

Stovall rallied to Palo's defense. "If they're forking out the money, then shouldn't they pick the decorations without the mayor dictating the choices?"

"Absolutely," Walter said before anyone else had the opportunity to chime in. "I offer these examples only as a means of settling the budget question. Of course … we can't have just anything going up. If the voters don't like the decorations, it won't be Palo and West they call at all hours of the day and night." A ripple of laughter sent Walter's spirits soaring. He was enjoying himself very much.

"Again," Stovall said, "we've always left this sort of thing to the civilian committee."

"You'll find I'm not a fan of continuing a practice for the sake of continuing it," Walter said. "Now if you have a legitimate reason why this board should not take this matter up, then by all means spit it out. Otherwise we'll be here all night."

"Those ladies on the committee do a fine job," Stovall said. Laughter rippled again. The alderman was getting creamed.

"I'm sure they do," Walter said, "but Misters Palo and West have been generous enough to donate decorations and I think they deserve the right to select them."

Palo, who had been huddled with his partner, snapped his attention back to the discussion and said he had no problem letting a committee decide. "It's a waste of this board's time to get bogged down picking out Christmas decorations," he added.

"Nonsense," Walter said. "There's nothing good on TV on Thursdays anyway." More laughter. Walter could barely contain his enthusiasm, but a glance at Mildred brought him back to earth. Husbands and wives can exchange an enormous amount of information in a single glance, and Mildred was warning him not to get carried away with himself as he tended to do. He could practically hear her voice speaking the words inside his head.

The two law partners huddled again.

"While Misters Palo and West are in executive session," Walter said, eliciting another laugh from those assembled, "I further propose we upgrade the nativity scene on the courthouse lawn to include the third Wise Man who was stolen, I'm told, three years ago. A thorough search has been made and a suitable match wasn't found, so I propose we replace it entirely … and donate the old one to one of our several churches, or perhaps the children's home in Tupelo." He looked at Palo, who came out of his huddle to say the nativity scene was not part of the offer.

"Of course not," Walter said, then, "Let the record show that the city, not Palo-West, will fund replacement of the nativity scene."

"I think replacing the nativity scene would draw unwanted attention," Pace said, in his legal opinion, clarifying when Walter inquired that yes, he meant the ACLU.

"Why should this town … any town for that matter … care very much whether the ACLU approves of our Christmas spirit?"

"The laws are very clear," Pace said. "Regarding public funds."

"Are they, Mr. Pace? Are the laws very clear?"

"Well, I —."

"Because it seems to me that the ACLU is able to bully towns such as ours into submission precisely because the laws are so very vague. Didn't we cover that a few minutes ago?"

"This is different," Pace said. "We're talking the difference in displaying decorations donated with private funds and those purchased by the city itself. It's been the consensus opinion for some time now that —."

"I'm not interested in consensus opinion, Mr. Pace," Walter said. "I'm interested, and I hope this board is interested, in your legal opinion based on what the law states, not what a consensus of like minds agrees it *should* state.

Is it legal or not legal for this town to replace the nativity scene using city funds?"

"In my legal opinion, no, it's not."

"So in your legal opinion, can the town continue to display the one we have?"

"I, uh, think as long as new monies aren't spent —."

"So it's perfectly fine for the town to display an old nativity scene with a Wise Man missing, but not a new one intact?"

"The cost of a lawsuit to the town would be devastating," Pace said.

Walter nodded. Made a show of it, holding his words until he knew all eyes were glued to him, then said, "Again, isn't that precisely how the ACLU wins? The mere threat of a lawsuit sends mayors and aldermen scrambling for cover at the behest of their skittish attorneys? Isn't that why the law is so vague even after all these years of fighting over Christmas, Mr. Pace? Because towns like ours — men like us — refuse to fight?"

"The town can't afford to fight," Pace said. "The ACLU can."

"So we give in to a bully who hasn't even threatened us yet, and pretend our third Wise Man is on a sabbatical." Another laugh rippled the room. "We allow a small few to hold the majority hostage to heathen ideas. That's what we should do in your legal opinion?"

"You can't call them heathens," Toms said.

"Why can't I call them heathens? Has the First Amendment been nullified too?"

"It's simple economics," Kilfiche said, disappointing Walter because he thought he had found an ally in the judge.

"I bet if we sent it to the ballot box the support would be overwhelming," Walter said.

"I've always felt we should stand our ground more than we have in the past," Terrell Sharp said. "God is watching us every minute of every day."

"God doesn't work on those people," Stovall said. "They don't believe he exists."

"All the more reason for us to pray for them," Sharp said. "God works on us whether we believe in him or not. He doesn't need our permission."

"Save your sermons for church," Stovall said. An audible groan from the audience painted his face red again, either from anger or embarrassment — Walter suspected the former but gave him credit for the latter.

"Avoiding the conflict seems to be the logical path," Wayne Toms said. "It costs us nothing." Toms was a little stump of a man with a cue ball head and suspicious eyes. The kind of man Walter wouldn't leave his grandson in a room alone with because he had *that look* about him.

Walter felt his dander rising. "Doesn't it cost us something, Mister Toms? Doesn't our self-respect ... our integrity ... have some value?" Walter of all people understood the cost of backing down as a matter of habit.

"Maybe the churches can raise the money," Sharp said.

"Would that keep us out of the crosshairs of the liberal mafia, Mister Pace?"

"I suppose."

"And it would be okay to display it on city property?"

"Unless someone objects."

"Either it's legal or it isn't," Walter said. "The law doesn't change simply because someone objects to it."

"If someone were to come forward with a display of their own," Pace said. "Non-Christian, I mean, the town would be obliged to allow it given that we've opened that door."

"As long as it's in keeping with the Christmas tradition," Walter said, "I see no harm in it. Of course we can't have the entire lawn covered."

"It could be anything," Pace said. "Some pagan display most likely. That's the trend these days. How would you like a statue of Satan on the courthouse lawn?"

"Do we have pagans in Hayes? Brother Sharp?"

"None that I know of," the pastor said. "Hard to tell what the devil's got up his sleeve these days."

A general laughter followed the comment, then Walter made a motion that the board resolve to require all Christmas displays on city property to be Christian in nature.

"That's absurd!" Stovall said.

"Impossible!" said Lyle Townsend.

"May as well poke a bear," Wayne Toms said.

Walter looked at Kilfiche, who shook his head, killing any chance the motion might pass. Politics was a gutless business. He turned to Palo with the room thinking he had been knocked back on his heels. "My fear now is that this board, in its current mood, will insist you foot the bill for installing your lamppost decorations, Mister Palo."

Palo opened his mouth but didn't speak. West chewed at his bottom lip. The room fell deathly silent. "What about it, Mr. Pace," Walter said. "Would it disturb the ACLU if we use Water and Light employees to hang Christmas decorations donated by Palo and West on city lampposts?"

"Uh, um, it's never been a problem before," the attorney said.

"Does it offend the sensibilities of Mr. Stovall?"

Stovall shifted his large frame and cleared his throat before saying no, he had no objections to using city employees in that capacity.

"So we're back to the budget," Walter said, looking again at the duo of Palo-West. "Have you gentlemen made a decision?"

"Fifty dollars per pole," Tipton said. "North of and including the courthouse."

"Let the record reflect that Mr. Palo has amended his offer to provide decorations for Main Street to exclude that portion of Main Street south of the courthouse," Walter said. "Unless I misunderstood your intent?"

Palo shook his head. Walter suppressed a smile, then said, "On that note I move the board reject the offer as discriminatory."

Stovall hit the table with his fist. "Discriminatory against who!"

"Minorities, Mister Stovall," Walter said. "They outnumber whites two to one south of the courthouse. Am I correct, Mister Sharp?" Sharp nodded his agreement.

"That's how we've always done the Christmas lights!"

"We've never decorated south of the courthouse," Toms said.

"Past discriminations hardly justify new ones," Walter said. "Does anyone second my motion to reject the offer as discriminatory?"

"I second the motion," Sharp said.

Stovall looked ready to explode. "Race has nothing to do with it!" He suddenly seemed aware he was being stared at so he took a breath and calmed himself. "North of the courthouse is our business district. The purpose of Christmas decorations is to make the downtown area more inviting to shoppers."

"The purpose of Christmas decorations *should* be to glorify Jesus Christ," Walter said. He turned to Palo again. "What's your answer?"

Palo glared at Stovall, then he quietly said his firm would pay for the entire street. Walter pretended not to hear him. "We have a motion to reject the offer from Tipton Palo and Rance West. What says the board?"

Terrell Sharp's hand went up first, then Kilfiche. Lyle Townsend looked ready to bolt. Stovall and Toms both sat with their arms folded across their chests. Nothing would move them, but Townsend served a wide mix of clientele at his feed store and it was a volatile time.

"My office is in the process of setting up an official Facebook page for the mayor's office," Walter said. "To clear up some of the confusion caused by certain recent articles in the Hayes Beacon. Tonight's meeting will lay a good foundation."

Townsend's hand shot up.

"The motion —."

"Wait!"

Walter stopped short of declaring the motion passed. "Does Mister Palo have something to add?"

"I said we'll pay for the entire street."

Rance West shot to his feet and stormed out of the room.

"Motion withdrawn," Walter said, then he gaveled the meeting closed.

* * *

Tipton poured himself a drink and told Autumn to beat it. She sulked away in slow motion, probably thinking if she hung around long enough she might overhear something important. Either that or she was intentionally trying to be difficult because Rance was there and she hated his guts. Why, Tipton didn't know. Every time he asked she denied it, so he stopped asking. Rance was no help either. His stock response was that some women are funny that way.

Rance sat slouched on the sofa nursing beer from a half-empty bottle until Autumn was out of earshot. "Pigg worked you like a schoolboy tonight."

Tipton capped the bottle and resisted the urge to punch his partner in the face. The only reason he had let Rance through the front gate was because he kept buzzing and refused to leave. His behavior was predictable in every regard, failing to see the forest for the trees. Trying to explain would be a wasted effort. Rance West lacked the mental capacity to navigate complex issues, which was one of the reasons Tipton had kept his association with Stubbs private. That relationship was extremely complex.

Rance tilted the bottle again as he continued to pout. "Played you and that board of yahoos like a fiddle. Made a complete fool out of Stovall. And Pace — how did he get to be city attorney? He ignored the most important part of his legal opinion — the legal part."

"Are you through?"

"I'm beginning to see how he beat you."

"I had a lousy campaign manager."

"No argument from me," Rance said. "I never saw him coming, that's for sure. I don't think anyone did." His alcohol-soaked eyes flashed a moment of clarity then faded. Whatever thought had crossed his mind was gone. "He sure played that board," he said again. "Haskell probably planned it ... or maybe not. Maybe Pigg's some kind of political genius. He sure played us."

"He got lucky," Tipton said, moving toward the plush armchair that flanked the sofa. He sat. Rance would be lucky to get home without plowing into a tree, or into some unfortunate family of five. The tree might be a godsend. The family of five would sink the firm. For the first time since they hung their shingle together Tipton realized what a liability Rance was. "Pigg's an idiot, just like the people who elected him."

"This town's got an awful lot of idiots if that's the case," Rance said. He raised his eyes from his bottle. "Too bad you didn't have Haskell running your campaign." His eyes fell again. "Or maybe not. You'd of made a shitty mayor."

"You're drunk."

"Maybe so, but I know you. Everything's got to be your way. Your way or the highway, as they say. Politicians have to know how to compromise."

"I'll let that pass because you're drunk," Tipton said, "but you're walking on thin ice. Now say what you came to say and get out."

Rance tilted his head sideways and searched a spot on the ceiling for whatever it was he had come to say, then his eyebrows raised and the corners of his mouth drooped. "I came to say this Facebook thing the mayor's planning could be dangerous."

Tipton laughed. Pigg had zero presence on social media. "I look forward to it. Grandpa Pigg trying to look hip."

"Grandpa Pigg made a fool out of you and that board tonight."

"You've said that half a dozen times already."

"I would include myself but since I wasn't involved in the decision to make that wonderful donation to the city —."

"The only person Pigg made a fool out of tonight was himself," Tipton said. "By the time Dexter gets through shredding him in the paper he'll wish he had stuck to engineering."

"He's got a week to put his spin on it. By next week the whole town'll think we're a couple of racists." He drained his bottle and exchanged it for a full one from the plastic bag at his feet. He had brought his own. "He'll drive us into the poorhouse if you keep going to board meetings."

Tipton checked at his watch. Dexter Mann was due any minute now and Rance had overstayed his welcome. "Speaking of driving, maybe I should call you an Uber."

"Uber my ass," Rance said, scooting forward as though he intended to stand. "I ain't trusting myself to some teenage kid with a learner's permit." He gathered his sack of empty and full bottles and stood. "And I can take a hint, too. If you wanted me to go, all you had to do was say so." He took a step toward the door then stopped and turned with an inquisitive look on his face. "How much do you know about that dead horse they found on Pigg's porch?"

"Don't be ridiculous."

Rance eyed him for a long moment then grinned. "I thought so."

"Shut up about that," Tipton said. "Don't even joke about it."

"Touchy."

"I had nothing to do with it."

Tipton followed Rance to the door and watched him stumble to his car then idle down the driveway and turn into the street without stopping to check for traffic. He closed the door and returned to the bar to mix himself another drink. As he uncapped the bottle, Dexter Mann buzzed from the gate.

CHAPTER 10

Walter's phone rang off the hook all morning. Normal ordinary citizens who had heard about last night's meeting and wanted to thank him personally for sticking up for the little guy. He told them to be on the lookout for his Facebook page and they promised to help make it a success. He felt like Mr. Smith gone to Washington, but he knew all too well how quickly euphoria can turn to despair.

Mildred brought coffee. "I told Kelsey to start screening your calls so you can get some work done."

"This *is* work," he told her. "Good work. The best kind."

She planted her hands on her hips and studied the giant picture on the wall behind him. It was a black and white of the town square in its heyday, after the Great Depression when the nation was picking itself up off its knees. Almost all of the buildings still stood, though most had modern facelifts. "It's crooked," she said, then she stepped behind him and began to straighten it.

"Don't bring the town down on my head," he said. "I'll do that by myself." He laughed as he twisted in his chair to watch her. The frame was real wood and probably weighed enough to knock him unconscious if it fell. "Here, let me help you."

"Keep your hands to yourself," she said as he leaned forward to unseat himself. "The last time you straightened a picture we had to buy a new frame."

"I can't be blamed for a faulty nail," he said. "You straighten yesterday's town and I'll straighten today's." She didn't laugh at his witty remark so he told her he was hungry and suggested they gorge themselves on sausage biscuits from the diner. A celebration, so to speak. He had finally hit one out of the park and he wanted to mark the occasion. Before Mildred could object, he buzzed Kelsey and summoned her.

The young assistant appeared in the doorway at the exact moment Mildred stepped back to inspect her work. Walter produced a twenty from his wallet.

"I'm in the mood for pork this morning and would consider it a personal favor if you would make a trip to the diner and pick up breakfast for three."

Kelsey said she had already had breakfast but she would be happy to go.

"The mayor's ordering us to eat brunch," Mildred told her.

Kelsey took the money and turned to leave.

"Before you go," Walter said, "summon Chief Benson for me. Tell him it's important he come right away." He cut his eyes up toward Mildred and grinned. "Watch me hold that lout's feet to the fire." Mildred's eyes swung toward the doorway and her face told him she wasn't looking at Kelsey.

"The lout is here," Benson said. Walter recognized the voice before he turned to see the chief filling the doorway. He stepped in and allowed Kelsey to slip out. Mildred quickly followed, leaving the two men alone.

Walter felt his face growing warm. "I guess that makes me the lout," he said. "I'm sorry."

"Sorry you said it or sorry I heard?"

"Both," Walter said, expressing a half-truth. His opinion of Benson wouldn't be swayed by temporary embarrassment. He gestured for the chief to sit and waited until he did. "I hope this means you've reconsidered your position on Stubbs."

"No, my feet were cold and I wanted you to hold them to the fire for me, Mister Pigg."

Walter frowned. The man was a bully. Either his badge had gone to his head or he had been that way all his life. Learned behavior from parents who yell and scream instead of discipline. Bullies beget bullies, and Walter had dealt with them in some form or fashion all his life. Logic is wasted on them. They only respond to overwhelming force. "You'll address me as Mayor," he said. "The last name is optional but the title is not. Understood?"

Conflicting paths forward played out on the chief's face while Walter wondered what he would do if Benson bucked him. Luckily he didn't have to find out. "We've investigated Stubbs and didn't find any headless horses in his back yard, *Mayor*."

"Don't be sardonic," Walter said, using a word he felt certain his adversary would google as soon as he left the building. "Stubbs isn't stupid. Of course he didn't kill the animal himself."

"This ain't television," Benson said. "We can't spray imaginary chemicals on your back porch and recreate the crime in HD." He adjusted himself and broke eye contact. "If you want my honest opinion, I think neighborhood kids did it. Probably the same kids who used to break your windows."

"I haven't had a broken window in two years."

"Kids don't forget."

"Kids don't saw the heads off of horses," Walter said. "Are we having a serious conversation or are you recording me for a good laugh back at the station?"

"It was a prank, Mayor. It happens."

"This conversation is a prank," Walter said. "You being in charge of this town's police force is a prank!" Walter caught himself and lowered his voice. Benson wanted to rankle him. He wanted to get under his saddle like a burr. "How much is Stubbs paying you?"

Benson didn't flinch. "I'm paid by the city same as you."

Walter knew at that moment he was dirty. The question now was how many cops were on the take with him.

* * *

Rance strode into Tipton's office and plopped down in the client chair and threw his right leg over the arm in his usual brusque manner, raising Tipton's hackles before the first word left his mouth. "You seen it yet?"

"It?"

"Obviously not," Rance said, grinning while trying to frown. "Your nemesis launched his page."

Tipton grabbed his mouse and launched his browser. Rance told him to search for the official mayoral website of Hayes, Mississippi. He held his breath and typed the phrase, then saw the mayoral seal and an uncommonly good profile picture. Despite being a rube, the page looked professionally done.

"Probably that hot little number with the purple hair," Rance said. Tipton had thought the same thing, except for the hot little number part. Rance had an eclectic taste in women. Eighteen to eighty, blind, crippled, or crazy.

"Two dozen followers," Tipton laughed. "That's probably his ceiling."

"Read the comments," Rance said. "One guy called him a champion of the people."

Tipton scrolled and found it. "Tate Mason," he said, trying to remember where he had heard the name. "Isn't he that man who sued the school district for making his daughter fat?"

"Unhealthy lunches," Rance said. "Nutrition's a thing now. Look down the list and you'll see another name."

Tipton searched then shrugged. He wasn't in the mood for games.

"Beverly Jordan," Rance said. "Doesn't ring a bell? She was a client of yours a few years ago."

"I never forget a client."

"She was Beverly Chambers then."

Tipton remembered. "I walked her through a messy divorce." All divorces are messy but hers carried it to the extreme. Her husband broke into her apartment five times before the cops enforced the restraining order.

"And she voted for Pigg," Rance said. "Small world."

"People have short memories."

"Populism's a drug," Rance said. "Little against big."

"I'll get an injunction against him using the official seal."

"He's the mayor. It's his seal."

"It's the city's seal."

"Go ahead," Rance said. "That's exactly the sort of thing populism feeds on."

"I can't believe these idiots are falling for this stuff."

"People like transparency."

"Until they get it," Tipton said. "Then they cry and whine about how unfair government is. The less the people know the better. That's how government's supposed to function."

"Like making sausage?"

Tipton frowned. Rance enjoyed being difficult. "I need your help with something."

Rance looked at his watch. "Aren't you supposed to be in court?"

"I've got a few minutes."

"It's Judge Bishop."

"I said I've got a few minutes."

"It's your funeral."

"I'd like to use Clarence on something if you can spare him." Clarence Fine was a private investigator kept on retainer by Palo-West because of the high number of insurance fraud cases they handled. His specialty was patience.

"He's working the Hildebrand case for me," Rance said.

"I only need him to do one little thing."

"We go to trial next week and so far the old broad hasn't left her house," Rance said. "I can't spare him."

"This is important."

"More important than ten million dollars?"

"I need him to dig up something on Pigg."

Rance threw up his hands. "By all means then. Let's pull Clarence off a ten-million-dollar industrial accident case so he can help you throw your tantrum because you lost a damned election!"

"Never mind."

"You know you really should get some counseling. Maybe there's a group for people who lose elections and can't go back to living their normal lives. You might even get to meet Hillary Clinton."

Tipton gathered his papers and dumped them into his briefcase and slammed it shut. Rance was still there, glaring at him with righteous indignation. The rooster wanted to crow from his lofty perch of not ever having aspired to leave the coop. Let him. Tipton knocked his chair against the wall when he stood. "Keep Clarence," he said. "I'll find another way."

* * *

Walter heeded Mildred's advice and kept his Facebook page simple and upbeat. His first post was a photo of his swearing-in ceremony and a couple of paragraphs on how much he appreciated everyone who voted for him. Not posted were his thoughts on how the Hayes Beacon had treated him since election night because Mildred had told him not to be the *poor me* guy. In a nutshell, it was a *get to know your mayor* page, and by Monday morning — over the span of a single weekend — he had built something of a following.

He had resisted her efforts to put Kelsey in charge with a made up title: Social Media Liaison. How were people supposed to get to know their mayor if he farmed out his social media to someone who barely knew him?

He posed the question to Brant Haskell when they met for lunch. It was their second meeting since Walter took office and sooner or later the businessman was bound to get down to business.

"Let the girl handle the page," Haskell said. "Or better yet take it down. It's too easy to offend people these days. Why take the chance?"

"And let Dexter Mann define me?"

Haskell pursed his lips and raised his eyebrows as he pondered Walter's point. "Just be careful and don't embarrass yourself."

"Or you?"

"Everyone knows I backed you."

"I'll put a disclaimer at the bottom saying the opinions expressed are my own and in no way reflect those of Brant Haskell."

The semi-private corner booth Haskell had chosen allowed them to talk at a normal tone without being overheard, as long as they didn't forget the waitress when she came. Both flanking booths were empty, as was the nearest table. The post-Christmas doldrums held the town in a state of suspended animation. Most businesses were open for the sake of being open. Schools and factories were closed. People had overeaten and overspent. In a few days they would drink too much and shoot fireworks and start the process anew.

"You never told me why you wanted me to run."

They had their drinks. Soda for Walter, unsweet tea for Haskell. The waitress had addressed Walter as Mayor when she took his order and now she was busy at other tables taking orders, filling tea glasses, and smiling as though she had the best low-wage job in the world.

"Sure I did," Haskell said. "The town needed new blood."

"But you knew I couldn't win."

"Did I?"

The waitress glanced toward the kitchen as though she had heard a dog whistle and disappeared.

"Are you saying you thought I *would* win?"

"There's a movement afoot, Walter. Not just here in Hayes, but across the country. Soon it'll spread to other countries. People are tired of politicians."

The waitress brought their plates. A BLT and fries for Walter and some kind of wrap for Haskell. Mildred would disapprove but she wasn't there.

The only reason men live past fifty is because women force them to stop eating bacon.

Walter checked his phone. "Two new followers since I left the office."

Haskell frowned. The waitress told Walter she thought the page was a very good idea and promised to tell everyone who came in about it.

"That's the movement I'm talking about," Haskell said. "You harness that and there'll be no stopping you."

Walter noticed he said *you* and not *us*. Had he underestimated the man? Either way, he wished he would get on with whatever it was he wanted. "You didn't call this meeting to talk about political movements."

"Maybe I wanted to be seen having lunch with the mayor."

Walter nibbled an overhanging piece of bacon from his sandwich and studied Haskell's face for some hint of conflict. Businessmen and poker players share the art of bluff and bluster if they're good, and too many fuel trucks bore Haskell's name for him not to be good. "If what you say is true, this page idea of mine should be exactly what the public wants."

"The idea, yes, but the execution of that idea is where you'll get yourself into trouble. As soon as you take a position on anything controversial you'll alienated half your public."

"I see no way to avoid —."

"You avoid it by not taking a position," Haskell said. "There's a reason politicians speak in generalities."

"Which leads us right back to this movement you were talking about."

Haskell shoved his wrap into his mouth and barely swallowed before saying being a politician is like skydiving with a bedsheet. The trick is to always be seen in the plane but never jumping.

"But you're forgetting I'm not a politician," Walter said.

"Of course you are, Walter. You're just not very good at it."

As much as Walter didn't want the job, being told he wasn't doing it right rankled him. "Whenever I set my mind to something I'm quite stubborn."

"Like bucking the police chief?" Haskell's face went from calm and pleasant to hard and angry like dropping an anvil. "Did you think I wouldn't find out?"

That he found out didn't bother Walter as much as how he found out. "Who told you?"

"A little bird."

"You shouldn't trust little birds."

"It's how lies and innuendo made the rounds before social media," Haskell said. "Is it true? You've got nothing to fall back on if you screw this up, you know."

"I'm still an engineer."

"An engineer pushing sixty. Take it from a businessman who hires and fires, you're past your sell by date, Walter."

"I've got plenty to offer."

"Yes, experience, but put yourself on the other side of the decision, Walter. You've got experience but you're set in your ways. You cost too much. In ten years you'll retire and draw a pension."

"Don't discount the relationship I have with my clients."

"You mean H&G's clients. They never were your clients, Walter. Trust me, that relationship you thought you had was nothing more than one professional trying to squeeze everything he can out of another."

Walter scoffed.

"Those clients … how many of them do you consider to be friends?"

"Well, I —."

"How many of them have called to tell you how much they miss you?"

Walter felt his insides begin to churn.

"How many have you called now that they're not your clients anymore?" He leaned in and hammered the tablecloth with his fingertip. "Two years, Walter. Two years of not stepping on any toes and you run again." He leaned back into his chair. "Win and this job's yours as long as you want it. That's how politics works."

Walter sulked for a moment, filtering what he wanted to say through the screen of what he should say. Already he was behaving like a politician. The old Walter would have let fly whatever thought popped into his head. "This movement you were talking about. Maybe people elected me to step on some toes. Maybe if I bid my time they'll throw me out. Then what?"

Haskell wore the expression of a man trying to explain quantum physics to a hotdog vendor. "Biding your time doesn't mean doing nothing. The economy's turning around. If the town succeeds, you succeed. If you must step on a few toes then find smaller toes to step on than Benson's. The man's practically a legend in this town."

"Maybe he's surpassed his sell by date too."

"It's not the same."

"Why not?"

"You can't equate cops with engineers," Haskell said. His frustration showed as much in his tone as it did in his jerky mannerisms. "Hayes is a patriotic town. We don't burn flags and we don't protest our cops. We don't protest anything." He leaned in again. "I'm telling you this flat out, Walter, if you go after Benson you'll be lucky to last two years." He finished off his wrap and washed it down with a huge gulp of tea. "Maybe you'd better start with a smaller giant, David. The man upstairs might not load your slingshot with magic rocks."

Everything he said was true. Much could be said of caution. Haskell hadn't invited him to lunch to squeeze him for favors, he had invited him to scold him for stepping out of bounds. He folded his napkin across his half-eaten sandwich. "I've been careful all my life," he said. "I think I'd like to try the other way just once."

* * *

Tipton cut the check for the Christmas decorations. Five hundred and thirteen lampposts at fifty bucks a pop. Just shy of twenty-six grand. One very expensive headline. Rance signed the check because it was firm money and anything over two thousand dollars required both signatures. Not even lawyers trust each other. Whatever goodwill the headline garnered had been erased by the pounding the firm was taking on social media. Pigg had launched his page and dangled the bait, and out came the kooks. One poster who claimed to have been at the meeting said the mayor handed Palo his ass. Ridiculous.

"Society went to hell when they invented the internet," Tipton said.

"Free porn for everybody," Rance said, winking at Candice as she took the check from Tipton's desk then left the room smiling.

"Can't you act your age?" Tipton said. "You're old enough to be her father."

"I don't know when it stops, my friend, but I can tell you it's not fifty-five."

Tipton was nine years shy of that and it had already slowed to a trickle. Throw Candice into the mix and it might be different, but he was smart enough to know the difference in fantasy and reality. "Our Founding Fathers never imagined the internet," he said. "They never envisioned every man, woman, and child having their own printing press. Maybe it's time to rethink the First Amendment."

"You don't mean that."

Tipton wrung his hands. Of course he didn't mean it. How could he? It was Pigg that had him all twisted. Walter Pigg. Mayor. The man was unhinged. A ship without a rudder. Lobbing Molotov cocktails, betting against one someday catching wind and blowing back in his face. Perry Stubbs might be the one to blow back, with the right amount of prodding.

"What's so funny?"

"Nothing," Tipton said. "I was just thinking how Pigg's face must've looked when he saw that horse head hanging on his porch."

"That was pretty sick," Rance said.

"Disgusting," Candice said, suddenly back in his office for some unknown reason. She was always butting in where she didn't belong. "That poor animal."

"Why are you still here?"

"To remind Rance he has a one o'clock," she said.

"Rance has a calendar."

"And you have a one-thirty," she said, then she strode out with an extra something in her walk. Rance couldn't keep his eyes off her.

"A few days of unpaid leave might do her some good," Tipton said.

Rance swung his attention back to his partner. "About that horse —."

"Asked and answered," Tipton said. "I had nothing to do with it. Ask again and I may have to deck you."

CHAPTER 11

Benson telephoned the mayor and announced the discovery of the headless horse as though it were some grand achievement in policing. No stone had been left unturned. No avenue untraveled. No pasture untrod. Then came the letdown.

No one had actually seen the carcass. No one except the rancher who claimed it as one of his stock and buried it where it lay.

"What do you mean buried?"

"Coyotes and buzzards —."

"We don't have buzzards," Walter shot back. "We have vultures. Coyotes and vultures don't eat bones."

Butch Pardue owned a large spread near Sherman in the northeastern corner of the County. He raised beef for consumption and horses for purchase. Due to a sharp decline in the number of people self-identifying as cowboys and cowgirls over the past decade, horses were sometimes abandoned the way one drops off an unwanted dog or cat, rendering Pardue's equestrian herd more of a liability than an asset. Walter knew of him vaguely, having seen numerous business highlights (ads disguised as news articles) about him in the Hayes Beacon over the years.

"I took a personal interest because it makes the town look bad having our mayor embarrassed this way."

"Embarrassed?"

"Put out, I mean."

"Try threatened," Walter said. "You took such a personal interest that you didn't bother to go see the remains."

"It was late yesterday and —."

"Nor did you think it important enough to send a patrolman."

"It's outside our jurisdiction."

"And I suppose the sheriff refused to send a deputy?"

"Since this was a city case I didn't —."

"Impossible!"

Walter felt the chief smiling through the telephone. Instead of sounding contrite, he was being intentionally ignorant of having done anything wrong. "I want him charged with destroying evidence."

"You can't be serious."

"I'm deadly serious."

"I've got no authority outside the city limits."

"Who gave him permission to bury the animal?"

"I suppose I did."

"You suppose? Either you did or you didn't."

"Now you see here —."

"No, *you* see here," Walter said. "You had no authority to tell him anything. Why wasn't the sheriff involved in this?" Before Benson answered, Walter remembered something — a name. "How did Butch Pardue report this — this *discovery*?"

"By telephone, I think."

"By telephone to what person?"

"One of my officers, I believe."

"Which one of your officers?"

"I'd have to check the log to —."

"Could his last name have been Pardue?"

"What difference does it make?"

Walter had his answer. Immediately after the incident in question, Mayor Pigg had made a point of learning the name of every police officer and firefighter in the city's employ. The name Chester Pardue lurked within that memory.

"I don't discount coincidence," Walter said, "but with Pardue being an uncommon name around here, well, I suspect the convenience of it. Don't you?"

"Convenience of what? Chester Pardue didn't take the call. He's a reserve. We only use him for parades and ball games."

"How are they related?"

"I don't know that they are."

"It's an easy enough thing to find out."

"And why should I find out? So what if they're related? It's not a crime."

"No, but if it were it would be in nobody's jurisdiction because Butch lives in the county and Chester lives in town. It's awfully convenient, though."

"Convenient for who?"

"You."

"What are you implying?"

"I'm not implying anything," Walter said. "I'm saying it outright. I think Butch Pardue knows exactly what happened to his horse — if he actually buried a horse."

* * *

They met at a dingy little bar on the outskirts of Tupelo. Tipton wore jeans and a red flannel shirt he had found in a plastic storage tote in the attic. He had worn the shirt exactly once, on a fishing trip with Judge Bishop the year after he and Rance started their firm. The trip proved futile because he lost his next three cases in a row.

Stubbs looked authentic. Perfectly natural, sitting at the bar chomping his unlit cigar while drinking domestic beer from a bottle. The place reeked of sour mash and cigarette smoke. A football game played out in silence on a television on the wall above an expanse of liquor bottles in various stages of empty.

Tipton slid onto the barstool beside Stubbs with neither man looking at the other. The bartender came immediately. He was a large man, burly, with a dingy white towel slung over his shoulder and a cigarette dangling from one corner of his mouth. A wisp of blond hair near the crown of his head kept him from being completely bald. Dark stubble covered his face and throat.

"What'll it be?" The voice matched his gruff appearance, warning Tipton not to say scotch or he might get knocked off his stool, so he answered whiskey — whatever you have. He had Jim Beam, which he promptly dumped into a tumbler freshly wiped with the towel slung across his shoulder.

"I wonder if he sneezes into that towel," Tipton mumbled as the bartender turned away.

"Ask louder and you might find out," Stubbs said.

"Someone should tell him it's against the law to smoke in public buildings."

Stubbs called the man by name and turned him. The hair on Tipton's neck stood up as the big man walked back. "My lawyer friend wants to tell you something."

A clump of ash fell from the tip as the bartender turned to Tipton and grunted *yeah?*

"Nothing," Tipton said. His palms had already begun to sweat.

Stubbs laughed and waved the man away. The bartender obliged and Tipton's fear turned to anger. "What the hell's wrong with you?"

"I don't like talking behind a man's back," Stubbs said. "It's cowardly."

"Why'd you tell him I'm a lawyer? Now he can link us —."

"I picked this place because he won't link us," Stubbs said. "You stick out like a sore thumb in that getup."

Tipton glanced down at his attire. "I see a lot of men dressed this way."

"Men," Stubbs said. "Not lawyers."

Tipton gripped his tumbler and suppressed the urge to retaliate. Self-preservation, mostly. Stubbs was the textbook definition of a sociopath. Had he known that going in he might not have associated himself, but the die was

98

cast and cutting ties was not an option. Stubbs was a gang of one.

"Walter Pigg is becoming a threat."

Stubbs removed his soggy cigar from his mouth and took a swig from the brown bottle. "Pigg's no threat. He's a nuisance."

"If we don't deal with him now he'll get stronger."

"Then deal with him."

Stubbs was being difficult. Tipton gulped his drink and wiped a bead of sweat from his forehead. The bartender had moved to the opposite end of the bar and was talking to a man wearing a wrinkled white shirt with a brown tie. Probably an insurance salesman who hadn't made a sale in weeks and didn't know how to tell the wife they were broke, or a vacuum cleaner salesman lost in a sea of hardwood floors. He looked unsuspicious enough to be suspicious.

"That guy down there," he said to Stubbs without turning.

"What about him?"

"Ever seen him before?"

"Stop jumping at shadows," Stubbs said.

"I've caught him looking this way twice."

"Which means you were looking his way twice." He drummed his fingers on the counter. Anxious, or annoyed. "You were jumping out of your skin to meet so let's meet," he said. "Say what you came to say and get outta here."

"I don't like being stared at."

"Then stop wearing flannel. You look like John Kerry trying to buy a hunt'n license."

John Kerry was the Democrat nominee for president who wondered aloud in front of a national news camera where he could 'git me a hunt'n license' and secured George Bush his second term. Michael Dukakis did the same thing for Ronald Reagan when he stuck his head up out of a tank wearing a combat helmet two sizes too big. Tipton looked down at himself again and failed to see the comparison.

"He's declared war on Benson."

"Benson can take care of himself."

"But what if he can't?"

Stubbs drummed his fingers on the bar again. "What's he got on him?"

"This business with the horse could backfire," Tipton said. "It's got the public in an uproar."

"Let the public roar," Stubbs said. "I cover my tracks. Just see to it you do the same."

"What's that supposed to mean?"

Stubbs turned and looked him in the eyes for the first time. His eyes were cold and hard and they sent a chill down Tipton's spine. "You're supposed to have the board in your pocket. Pigg can't touch Benson without the board. Problem solved."

"You make it sound easy. Pigg's not as dumb as we thought."

"You thought," Stubbs said. "I never said Pigg was dumb. In fact he's right the opposite, and if you push him up against the wall he'll fight."

"So you're saying leave him alone?"

"I'm saying don't push him against the wall. You have to come at a man like Pigg from behind."

Tipton adjusted himself on the stool. "Suppose your man talks?"

"I'm more worried about you talking," Stubbs said, looking at his beer again. The bottle was empty except for a swallow. He pulled the cigar from his mouth and turned it in his fingers. "You're weak, Palo. Someday you'll come at me wearing a wire and I'll have to kill you." He stood and dropped the clammy cigar into Tipton's bourbon, then left without paying his tab. Tipton sat frozen, unable to think. He turned in time to see the door close behind Stubbs, then he turned back and saw the bartender with his hand out.

"Nineteen fifty," he said. Still rattled, Tipton fumbled for his wallet and gave the man a twenty and told him to keep the change.

* * *

Brad Stovall strode into the diner with his chest puffed out and that know-something-you-don't grin plastered across his face. Walter had a table in the back away from the handful of other diners. It was Wednesday morning and the Hayes Beacon had failed to draw blood. Mayor Pigg had tried to cancel Christmas but failed thanks to a generous donation by Tipton Palo. Rance West wasn't mentioned. In Walter's mind, the article exposed Dexter Mann as being Tipton Palo's lackey. If anyone harbored any doubts, Mann had finally cleared the air.

Stovall stopped twice to slap backs and shake hands before reaching the mayor's table then saying in his booming voice that when Walter asked him to brunch he thought it was some kind of wrestling match. A spattering of laughter told Walter their table wasn't as private as he had thought. Walter pretended to be amused. Buffoonery ranked high on his list of dislikes.

The wooden chair creaked against the alderman's weight as he sat, then groaned as he adjusted himself and put both elbows on the table as a further display of his ill manners. "I had to google it," he said, loud again, provoking another admiring response from his buddies. Men like Stovall have lots of buddies and pals but very few friends. People who laugh at clowns rarely see beyond the makeup.

"I'd like us to bury the hatchet," Walter said. "For the good of the town."

The braggadocios oaf grinned. "You believe in coming right out with it don't you?"

"Indeed I do," Walter said. "Politics is new to me and I'm guilty of not knowing how the game is played. We've gotten off on the wrong foot and I'd like us to start over. If I've stepped on your toes I apologize."

The waitress brought coffee. Stovall winked at her, as though she only brought coffee to him, because he was Brad. "Thanks hun," he said in his easy drawl. "Bring me two eggs over easy and a buttered biscuit." Her face flushed red and Walter suspected there was more to the exchange than a food order. She was half his age and quite attractive.

"Just coffee for me," Walter said when asked. Mildred had foisted a fruit bowl on him for breakfast and to his surprise he wasn't hungry.

"This brunch thing could become a habit," Stovall said, "though not with you," he said to Walter, causing the waitress to glance back and smile as she made her retreat. "No offense."

"None taken," Walter said. To be offended, one had to place stock in the offender, and his use for Brad Stovall began and ended in the boardroom. "You're in the dirt and gravel business and I've noticed your trucks coming from that bridge they're replacing in District Four. Cooper's Crossing, I believe."

"Not responsible for busted windshields," Stovall said. "Says so right on the back of all my trailers."

Walter suppressed a smile. Stickers don't absolve one of responsibility when they run trucks on the highways with uncovered loads, but broken windshields weren't Walter's immediate concern so he resisted the urge to correct him. "Be that as it may," Walter said, "you do a certain amount of business with the county, don't you?"

"My business with the county's my business."

"I agree," Walter said, "and when I hear people say you've got an unfair advantage, I wonder how they expect you to make a living on an alderman's salary if you shut down your business."

"Who said something about shutting down my business?

"Never mind that," Walter said. "People say all sorts of things when they're angry." He paused to let the idea saturate the alderman's thick skull. "Now, I was looking over some budgets for previous years and —."

"What are you trying to pull?"

"Nothing," Walter said. "I've never had to do a budget this size before and I was looking at the last few years hoping to gain some insight."

"The next budget's not due until September," Stovall said. He grinned again. "You probably won't be around that long."

"In case I'm not, I was noticing how much money the city pays out to the fourth district."

"The city pays out money to every district," Stovall said. "Every district has a part of the city."

"The lines intersect at the courthouse," Walter said. "Yes, I know, but the disbursement is so uneven. District Four gets a much larger slice of the pie than any other district. Almost double what the others get."

The alderman's face began to glow red. "Maybe the fourth district has a bigger slice of the city."

"I assumed that," Walter said, "but in fact the opposite is true. Hayes has grown more into the first and second districts."

"Just what are you driving at?"

"Nothing. I was hoping you could help me understand the formula."

"Why me?"

"I didn't want to step on any toes," Walter said. "I've done enough of that already. I was afraid if I started asking around you'd get the wrong idea since that new bridge I mentioned is in the fourth district. Maybe you'd think I was questioning why it is that the district you do the most business with gets the most money."

"I do an equal business with every district."

"That's not true," Walter said. "I checked. In fact, the amount of business you do in the fourth district is more than all the other districts combined."

The muscles around the alderman's eyes began to twitch. Tiny spasms of rage danced around the eyelids and down into his cheeks. "You'd better step light if you come after me," he said. "I'm not soft like Palo. You won't make a fool out of me and get away with it."

"You misunderstand me completely," Walter said. "To the contrary, I was hoping we could reach an agreement that might increase your business with the county. *All* of the county."

The twitching intensified, then slowed. Stovall didn't know whether to reach for the bait or slap it away. "Meaning what exactly?"

"Meaning I was wondering what if the city spread the money more evenly across the districts? Seems to me the other supervisors would appreciate it, and you being an alderman and partly responsible — you might even propose the change yourself at the next meeting — might make them *appreciate* you more. The Hayes Beacon would probably jump at the chance to do a big story about how you led the charge to even things up." It surprised Walter how much he found the back and forth invigorating. "Better to have all the supervisors grateful instead of just one, right? And if voters think you've stood up for their interests, well, surely you can see where this might benefit you."

"Yeah," the alderman said, "but how exactly does it benefit you?"

Walter suppressed a smile. Finally the question he had been fishing for. "I'm not opposed to a man making a profit. The county uses a tremendous amount of dirt and gravel and you're in the dirt and gravel business. If they don't buy from you they'll buy from someone else. It's not as though you're selling them something they don't need."

"Maybe they won't see it that way," Stovall said. "Maybe instead of increasing my business with the other three, I decrease it with Boyd."

"Boyd's what? Seventy?"

"Not quite that, but yeah, he's old. So what?"

"From what I've heard he won't run again," Walter said. He'd heard nothing of the sort. Boyd Clayton came from logging stock and would probably outlive them all. "Better you don't keep all your eggs in one basket. I'd be willing to talk to the supervisors. Explain things."

"Why exactly would you do that for me?"

"Because you're going to support a motion I intend to make at the next meeting," Walter said. "And you're going to tell Townsend and Toms to support it too."

Stovall opened his mouth to say something then stopped and tilted his head, thinking, wondering, then, "What's the motion?"

"I want to fire the police chief."

Stovall's jaw dropped. He tilted his chair back on its hind legs and peered down his nose at Walter with his head cocked to one side, then he grinned. "Well I'll be damned. Look at you go."

"Do we have a deal?"

"What about the other two?"

"Doesn't matter about them," Walter said. "Your three votes and my one make four."

"Can you guarantee me more business with the county?"

"No, but I'll do my best."

"Make your motion," Stovall said. "It'll pass."

* * *

Stovall walked into Tipton's office as though he owned the place with Candice at his heels like a Chihuahua trying to turn a Pitbull. Tipton looked up from his brief and recoiled at the intrusion.

"The mayor's going after the chief and he wants my help," Stovall said, then he sat.

Candice looked absolutely helpless. "I told him you were busy."

Tipton ushered her out with an order to close the door behind her, then, waiting, asked Stovall had he lost his mind. "I've got a working telephone you know."

"This seemed like a face-to-face talk since I told him I'd go along," Stovall said.

"Like hell you will."

"Business is business," Stovall said, "and you ain't exactly been loading my pockets lately."

Tipton felt certain the man had lost his mind. "What sort of business?"

"Hauling dirt," the alderman said. "What other kind is there?" He laid out the generalities of the understanding he and Pigg had reached over brunch. "And if you think I came here asking for your blessing you're wrong. I came as a courtesy because I don't want any trouble out of your devil twin."

"You're insane!"

"No, just good old American greed," Stovall said. "Besides, that stunt you and Stubbs pulled with the horse crossed the line with me. A dog I can see.

Maybe even a human, given the right pigmentation." He grinned. "Hell, Palo, don't look so broken down about it. Could be I'm doing you a favor."

Tipton struggled to control his anger. He was no physical match for Stovall and the things he wanted to say might push him over the edge. "You're not thinking this thing all the way through, Brad. If we let Pigg take Benson down then none of us are safe."

"I feel safe."

"Benson knows too much."

"That's Benson's problem." He crossed and uncrossed his legs. "The way I see it, if Benson's that much of a threat to you and Stubbs then problem solved. If you can kill a horse then you can kill a police chief."

"I had nothing to do with that."

"Sure you didn't. Jack Ruby didn't kill Oswald either, huh?" He winked. "My point is, Benson don't mean shit to me but increasing my county business by three districts means a lot."

"Do this and you won't move another spoonful of dirt in this county again. Not in the entire state!"

Stovall stood. "Like I said, I don't want any trouble out of your devil twin, but push come to shove I can hit too."

Tipton saw some logic in getting rid of Benson as long as it was handled the right way. The problem was how to sell it to Stubbs. Benson was loyal, and loyalty meant a lot to the old man. "Calm down," he said, almost to himself as much as to Stovall. "Let's all think this thing through."

"You and the evil one think," Tipton said. "And when you come up with a better offer, I'm all ears."

CHAPTER 12

The third Monday of December came on the seventeenth, forty-one days since Walter's swearing in. It was his second time to gavel the board into regular session. Turnout was higher than expected considering the close proximity to Christmas. Everyone came to see the buffoon, is what he had overheard Alderman Toms tell his cohort Townsend a handful of minutes prior. The important thing to Walter was that they came.

Without delay he entered his motion to dismiss Police Chief W. A. Benson for dereliction of duty. The immediate reaction of the crowd was disbelief. Heads turned and voices murmured and feet shuffled against the floor.

Walter turned to Stovall expecting him to second and immediately knew he had been betrayed.

"This is absurd!" Alderman Townsend said.

"Insane!" Said Toms.

Walter's heart sank. Stubbs had gotten to Stovall and the dirty weasel didn't have the backbone to tell him before he made a fool of himself.

"What's the meaning of this, Walter?" Kilfiche asked, forgetting the formality of the setting. He looked truly disturbed, as did the reverend. Walter regretted his decision to blindside his two allies, but leaving them out of the loop had seemed the logical thing to do with three votes in his pocket.

"I withdraw the motion," Walter said. "And I apologize to the two aldermen who didn't know about this in advance." He eyed the other three with contempt. Mildred dropped her eyes and refused to look up.

Dexter Mann coughed into his hand to get Walter's attention. He sat in the front row smiling like a boy with a new bicycle. "I'm sure you'll print the exaggerated version," Walter said, knocking the smile off his face.

Stovall still had not said a word, not that he needed to. The smug look on his face said everything.

Walter had no choice but to explain himself. "I made this motion because the chief is turning a blind eye to some corrupt dealings and letting his personal interests prevent him from doing his job.”

"You’re out of line,” Kilfiche said.

"Am I?”

"If you have proof of what you’re charging then let’s go into executive session and discuss it without dragging the man’s name through the mud.”

"The very idea of an executive session nauseates me,” Walter said. "The people’s business should be done in public, not behind closed doors where certain people will make promises they won’t keep!” He swung his gaze to Stovall and held him fixed until he acknowledged him with a sideward glance.

He turned to the audience again. "I don’t believe Chief Benson to be corrupt. I believe — know — him to be inadequate for the position he fills.”

Kilfiche’s face had by now begun to glow red. "W. A. Benson has been our police chief for twenty years. He’s above reproach.”

"No one’s above reproach,” Walter said. "When we agree to serve we agree to be held accountable.”

Half a dozen heads in the crowd nodded agreement. Walter realized he was no longer talking to the aldermen but to the people. He saw the thoughts churning in their faces so he decided to go for broke. "If my actions against the chief are without merit then hold me accountable, but if he’s half the scoundrel I believe him to be then stand with me and let’s throw him out because one of us has to go!”

A spattering of applause, then thunder. His chest swelled with pride, then Mildred lifted her eyes from the floor and smiled and his moment was complete.

* * *

Dexter Mann wasted no time telephoning Tipton with his breathless account of Pigg’s shenanigans. Tipton muted the television and listened with forced patience because interrupting Mann only caused him to start over, often from the very beginning. Two full minutes passed before he got to the part where the audience applauded.

"I’m telling you he had them eating out of the palm of his hand,” Mann said. "It was awful.”

"A handful of kooks doesn’t represent the entire town,” Tipton said, but he was more worried than he let on. It was the sort of thing that might get out of hand if left unchecked. "Make sure you tell it the right way Wednesday morning and we’ll be all right.” Perhaps now Stubbs would pay attention.

Autumn appeared at the bottom of the stairs wearing a black negligee. It was her go-to attire whenever she was desperate for sex. She struck a saloon girl pose against the banister, then frowned when she saw the phone at his ear. He waved her over and told Mann he had important business to attend.

"Still plotting against the mayor, I see,” she said, joining him on the sofa where he was reclined against the arm with his feet propped on an embroidered pillow.

"Don't ruin the mood," he grumbled. She leaned across his feet and took the tumbler from his hand and finished his last swallow of scotch. "I've got something to show you upstairs," she said with a sultry tone, then she took him by the hand and pulled him to his feet. At the top of the stairs he caught the scent of jasmine.

"New candle?"

"Do you like it?"

He lied and said he did. She had caught him with just the right blood alcohol content to find her flirting sexy. They reached the bedroom and he pulled her into his arms and kissed her on the neck. Her skin tasted like almonds. What an odd way for a woman to taste, he thought as she pushed him onto the bed and began unbuttoning his shirt. Sex had become a game of connect the dots no matter how hard she tried to spice things up, and she did try. He had to give her that.

Afterwards he lay back with his hands clasped behind his head and stared up at a small splash of light on the ceiling. Autumn nestled her head against his shoulder and twirled his little patch of chest hair with a finger. Each time she exhaled he felt the warmth of her breath against his skin, then the rhythm changed and he knew she was about to ruin the moment by speaking.

"You seemed preoccupied," she said.

"Do you have to critique me every time?"

"I'm not critiquing you."

"Every time I roll off you it's like waiting for the judges to flash score cards."

She rolled away and jerked the covers off him but he didn't care because he had worked up a sweat.

He waited until he knew she wasn't going to speak. "Does everything have to be a fight with you?"

She didn't answer so he stared up at the spot of light on the ceiling and ticked off one possible headline after another. MAYOR TAKES SHOT AT POLICE CHIEF. MAYOR STUNS BOARD. MAYOR PIGG GETS DOWN INTO THE MUD.

He laughed. "I wasn't laughing at you," he said. Autumn didn't move. Didn't make a sound. It was too soon for her to be asleep. The light on the ceiling was a reflection from something. Some light source bounced from object to object until it landed on the ceiling above the bed. Funny he'd never noticed it before. "Did you leave a light on downstairs?"

She slipped out of bed and went to the bathroom clutching her sleeping clothes against her breasts. His eyes had adjusted to the darkness enough that he saw her in grayscale. As the bathroom door closed, she flipped on the light and he saw her in color for a split second and Candice popped into his head. He felt a moment of guilt, then he didn't. The spot of light on the ceiling moved and he realized it was the candle. It danced and swayed, and he replayed the last several minutes in his head, substituting Candice for Autumn.

* * *

"No more board meetings for me," Mildred said over breakfast. Walter had expected it. Hiding feelings wasn't Mildred's superpower. He waited, knowing she had more to say. You don't stay married to the same woman most of your adult life and not know when she has more to say. Her coffee cup hovered an inch from her lips, suspended by a wrapped hand above a propped elbow. "You can't behave that way and expect to stay in office," she said. "You have to work with those men."

"Those men have to work with me too," he said. "I'm the mayor." She sipped her coffee without responding. "Did I embarrass you?"

"No."

Mildred didn't lie often. Hardly ever, but Walter knew this was one of those times. A white lie, meant to protect his feelings, so he let it sit. Later, after they dropped Jackson off at school and they had dispensed with all the phone messages and emails that had accumulated overnight, he asked Kelsey to get a copy of last night's meeting transcript in digital form so he could post it to his Facebook page. Of course Mildred objected.

"Why make things worse?"

"People need to know how the aldermen think."

"Don't the aldermen have a right to their opinions?"

"That's why I'm posting the transcript," he said. "The entire transcript. Let the public decide for themselves."

It ended with a stalemate. More disagreement than argument. Feelings weren't hurt. It wasn't something one of them did to the other that required an apology.

"Tomorrow they'll print another lie in the paper and I want the people to know the truth," he said, still hoping to win her approval. "I'll promise to post the transcript of every meeting from now own. How about that? Open government. Even if it embarrasses me instead of them."

"You don't think this embarrasses you?"

Her question stunned him. So that was her perception of the meeting? He's the one who should feel embarrassed? "I — I stood up for the people. Their interests. Why should I feel embarrassed about that? You heard how they reacted at the end."

Instead of answering, she left, which was answer enough. It took several minutes for him to replay the meeting in his head, analyzing the things he said. The responses. The reactions. Under almost every circumstance he trusted Mildred's instincts. Yielded to them more often than not, but this was not one of those times. This time he felt the energy of being right. Absolutely right.

The technology of copying from the file Kelsey emailed him into the white rectangle on his Facebook page was simple enough, but it yielded an ugly result. Spacing was uneven and paragraphs ran together so that he had to do a lot of editing to make it readable. Of course he could delegate the task to Kelsey, but the page was his responsibility. Good, bad, or indifferent, it would be his doing.

In the span of two hours his transcript had a dozen shares and almost one hundred likes. Brant Haskell telephoned with a warning that he was asking for trouble. That transcript isn't as flattering as you think, Haskell told him. Larry Pace, the board attorney, ordered him to take it down before Benson or Stubbs sued the city in general and Walter in particular. Walter understood enough law to be fairly certain the board attorney's role was to advise, not order. Larry Pace didn't have the authority to dictate to the mayor, so Walter told him to go soak his head.

He ate lunch at his desk. Mildred sent Kelsey out for plate lunches from the diner down the street but was unable to tear Walter away from his computer long enough to eat in the break room.

"You know you can get the app on your phone," Kelsey yelled from somewhere outside his office. Mildred, who was standing just inside his office, shot back an over-the-shoulder warning not to make matters worse.

"I don't know what you're so afraid of," he said, keeping his voice down so Kelsey wouldn't hear. "You really should read some of the comments."

Mildred shook her head and walked away.

At thirteen minutes past one, a man named Terrell Gains posted the first defense of Chief Benson. *It seems the mayer [sic] should support the chief not undermine him.* Two minutes later a woman by the name of Jerri Cortez gave the comment a like, then followed it up with a claim that the police chief had been shot in the line of duty and deserved better treatment from the mayor.

The floodgates swung open.

Walter stepped out of his office and into the staring crossfire of his wife and her assistant. The phone rang. Kelsey answered and said the mayor was in a meeting. Walter felt a ball of ice forming in his gut.

"It's the fourth one," the young assistant said with a frown.

"Stop worrying," Walter said. "The vast majority of people support me on this."

"The vast majority hasn't weighed in yet," Mildred said.

Walter felt himself on the precipice of learning a valuable lesson in public relations, he just wasn't sure yet what the lesson would be. He still had the numbers, but momentum had shifted, and within the hour his page was inundated with nasty, hateful comments and one poorly veiled threat on his life.

"At least they're congregating in cyberspace and not outside my door," he said to Mildred without looking away from his screen.

"I have to go pick Jackson up from school," she said.

"Is it that time already?"

"Hopefully I won't get mauled before I get back."

He searched her face for sarcasm and saw nothing. "It's not that bad."

"Did you see where the guy said he was going to put a bullet in the back of your head?"

"He said *someone* should," Walter corrected her.

"Oh, never mind then. I feel safe now." She stood her ground, fists balled against her hips, staring.

"Please, Mildred, you know I don't like it when you do that." He looked back at the screen and saw another message hit his feed. He frowned. "How can people be so ignorant?"

"You should ask them," she said. "Exactly that way."

"Ignorant as in uninformed," he said, clarifying his poor choice of words. "Benson wasn't shot in the line of duty. I checked. He shot himself in the foot hunting quail. Ten bucks says he was drunk."

"Twenty bucks says it doesn't matter," Mildred said.

"The Hayes Beacon probably made the birds out to be Mexican drug lords," Walter said. "Police Chief Benson, hero, single-handedly took them all on and was gravely wounded in the foot." He laughed, not because it was funny, but because it was possible. With Dexter Mann at the helm, the local newspaper was capable of anything. Any partial truth, half-truth, or downright lie. Facts and Dexter Mann mixed like oil and water. The phone continued to ring off the hook.

"Maybe if you issued a public apology."

"Mildred!"

"Oh Walter, do you always have to be so stubborn?"

"Some people call it determined."

"Not on Facebook they don't."

She had a point about people in general, but not about Benson. At best the man was lazy. He deserved no apology. Walter had offered him an easy out but he refused. If his name was being dragged through the mud it was his own fault.

On the way home he floated the idea of her taking Jackson and staying a few days with her aunt in Bruce. She rejected it immediately. Christmas was exactly one week away and she still had shopping to do. A poor excuse, he almost said, before realizing it was her way of standing by her man. There was no one Walter would rather be in a foxhole with than Mildred, but he didn't want their grandson there with them.

"Then we won't let this ruin our Christmas," he said. "We'll hold our heads high and ignore it. Who knows, by this time tomorrow, things might swing my way again. That's the way with mobs, you know. They run toward the brightest torch."

An idea struck him as he turned into their driveway but he kept it to himself until they were inside and Mildred was busy cooking supper, then he slipped into the living room and posted a grotesque picture of the horse head hanging from his porch rafters, with the comment: *I don't want this to happen to you. We need a police chief who will enforce the law.*

The doorbell rang, as though the submit button were tied directly into the doorbell circuitry. He jerked his eyes up from his keyboard and questioned the coincidence of the two things happening at exactly the same instant.

"Was that the doorbell?"

"Yes," he yelled back, already halfway to the door. "I'll get it." It could be anyone. Not friends, certainly, because no friend of theirs would dare show up unannounced. They all knew how much Walter disliked intrusions.

"Be careful."

What a thing for her to say in their own home. They weren't living in Afghanistan, or Chicago. Hayes hadn't yet devolved into anarchy where it wasn't safe to answer one's own front door. One social media mishap hadn't turned his town into Dodge City, or Memphis. Still, the thing that crossed his mind was that if he opened the door and saw a flaming bag of dog poop on his porch he wasn't going to stomp.

Before opening the door he peered through the keyhole and saw a police uniform. So Benson had sent one of his goons to scare him, huh? Typical jackboot thuggery. Walter swung the door open. "If Benson sent you here to scare me, you can go back and tell him it failed!"

The officer looked temporarily confused, then he told Walter they had caught the man who hung the horse head on his porch. Walter felt suddenly foolish. He probably blushed. "Come in," he said, then he called for Mildred to come from the kitchen so she could hear the good news firsthand. When she joined them and they all stood as a trio near the coffee table, Walter told the young officer to start over.

The officer cleared his throat. "We arrested a suspect in your case," he said. "A man by the name of Corey Pickle. Does the name mean anything?"

Walter shook his head, trying to recollect, then said no. Mildred gave the same answer.

"He's a deadbeat hood who works for Perry Stubbs," the officer said. "Makes deliveries and pickups. Pawnshop stuff as far as we know. He's been on our radar for a while but we've never been able to pin anything on him."

"If he works for Stubbs he does more than deliveries and pickups," Walter said. "Did you check his trunk for an iron pipe?"

Mildred touched Walter's elbow, which was usually a signal for him to stop talking. "Are you sure?"

"Pretty sure, ma'am. Your neighbor across the street saw his car in your driveway early that morning."

"Good ole Mrs. Crinch," Walter said. "Eyes like a cat."

"We doubted her story at first, it being dark and all, but the description she gave us matched Pickle's car, and we found traces of blood in his trunk."

"She probably has night-vision binoculars," Walter said.

"Walter!"

"The dear old woman watches us like a hawk," Walter said in a mocking tone. "Bless her heart."

After the officer left and Mildred returned to the kitchen, Walter rushed to his study to post the news on his Facebook page, thinking surely it would turn the tide from negative to positive again. With Stubbs being behind the bloody head, and Benson being behind Stubbs, the public had to see things his way. Before making the post official he read it back to himself twice. Typographical errors rankled him more than poor grammar, especially when the errors were his.

Just then the doorbell rang again. Another revelation, he thought. Perhaps a confession that implicated Stubbs. He hurried to the door and threw it open without checking the peephole first, then he froze. "Roger?"

* * *

Stubbs called at half past nine and told Tipton to get his ass down to the jail and make sure Corey Pickle kept his mouth shut. The old man sounded more angry than concerned, but the concern was real enough. Too real. Tipton had no idea how much Pickle knew about their little enterprise, but apparently he knew plenty about the dead horse.

"I told you this would blow back in your face."

"Shut up and go do your job," Stubbs said.

"Why can't Benson handle it?"

Stubbs grumbled something incoherent about a so and so detective who needed to be brought to heel, then he cursed Benson's mother, then he said he would see to Corey Pickle as soon as he was out of jail.

"You can't say stuff like that over the telephone," Tipton said before realizing he was talking to himself. Stubbs wasn't the kind of man to make idle threats. Corey Pickle was a dead man walking, and he didn't want to be the last man to see him alive so he called Rance.

"Why don't you do it?" Rance said without letting Tipton finish his pitch.

Tipton told him he was in hot water with the wife and couldn't leave the house without sending her over the edge. The truth was she hadn't come home and he had no idea where she was. He hadn't thought it strange until that moment. Unusual, but not strange.

"Let him find another lawyer," Rance said. "I don't like Stubbs."

"His money spends," Tipton said. "Besides, he swore to me he had nothing to do with that horse business. Pigg's trying to get to him by framing his man."

"Of course he is," Rance said. "How could I not know that?"

"I'm just repeating what the man told me," Tipton said, making it up as he went. "What happened to innocent until proven guilty?"

"You owe me for this."

With Rance dispatched, Tipton called Benson and demanded to know who arrested Pickle and why was he still in jail.

"By the time I found out it was too late," the chief said. "He shouldn't have been so sloppy."

"What kind of department are you running?"

"Who the hell do you think you are talking to me that way?"

Judging by the way he slurred his words, Benson was too far into his cups to be rational. He had always answered to Stubbs and until now had pulled his weight. The department only had one detective so it had to be Gant. Tipton had dealt with him plenty of times in court and he struck him as one of those men with the annoying habit of being too honest. He supposed it really was too late to handle it the usual way. Rance would have to earn his money this time.

"Rance is on his way over to get him released. Can you at least see that your detective doesn't get in the way?"

"Tell Rance he's wasting his time," Benson said. "I got no choice but to play this one by the numbers. He'll have to see the judge in the morning. The whole town's in an uproar about that damned horse."

Tipton's next call was to Dexter Mann. "I better not read a word about Corey Pickle in the paper tomorrow morning."

"Why would I write about Corey Pickle?"

"You haven't heard?"

"Heard what?"

"Never mind."

How the Hayes Beacon survived was a mystery for the ages. Tipton had a few ideas for a headline but Mann had already gone to press. Just as well. Pigg's official mayoral page was blowing up in his face. At least something was going right.

CHAPTER 13

Roger Pigg was a ne'er-do-well. A loafer. A bum. He was two years younger than Walter and bore a strong physical resemblance, beyond that they were night and day. The last time Walter saw him was when their mother died. He came for the funeral and stayed two days too long. Walter loved Roger, but he didn't like him.

Walter and Mildred sat at the kitchen table having their pre-breakfast coffee, waiting for Jackson to dress himself and come down. Mildred had fixed extra in case Roger joined them, but there had been no mention of waking him. Her face carried the extra weight of wondering what trouble Roger had brought with him this time. Last night's conversation had not touched the finer points of Roger's sudden appearance. To call it a visit would be wishful thinking.

Walter peered at Mildred over his cup. "I suppose it's too late to cancel Christmas," he said, then he waited for her to rebuke him. Instead she frowned and said nothing. "He'll ride out the year here, you know."

"It's Christmas," she said. "Let's not forget the reason for the season."

"We'll have to get him a present."

"He's your brother."

"And of course he'll be broke. No telling how much it'll cost us to get him to leave this time."

Mildred's eyes jerked toward the doorway and Walter felt a presence behind him. How much had he heard? Walter disliked confrontation. When Mildred looked his way again he raised his eyebrows like question marks. She gave her head a very quick and subtle shake. Without a word passing between them he had asked the question and she had answered. Roger lurked behind him but he had appeared too late to overhear their conversation, thus sparing Walter the burden of pretending to be contrite.

"Join us," he said without turning. "We were just talking about you."

Roger took a seat at the head of the table. Mildred sat to his right, Walter to his left. "I didn't get a chance last night to ask you about your accident."

"Incident," Walter said. "There was nothing accidental about it."

"Peggy told me it was all over the news," Roger said. "I don't know how I missed it."

"Walter doesn't like talking about it," Mildred said. "It was a very traumatic time for us, and your brother saved our lives." She passed the food around and wondered aloud what was taking Jackson so long. "He's our grandson," she told Roger. "He was already in bed when you came last night."

"Amy's got a kid? Why last time I saw her she was —."

"It's been a long time," Walter said. "A lot has changed."

Roger grew very somber. "I heard she's in prison."

"We don't like talking about that either," Walter said. If he knew she was in prison then he knew why, so there was no need trotting it out again.

"I didn't mean to bring up bad memories," Roger said. "You know how Peggy gets things twisted sometimes." Walter knew no such thing. Their sister Peggy was their mother made over. She would sooner cut out her own tongue than lie. Roger was the one who twisted things.

"How is Peggy?" Mildred asked.

"Still Peggy," he said. "Last time I saw her, anyway. Her and Ray sure do have a nice place." He caught himself and looked around. "Not knocking this place."

"Never mind that," Walter said. "What about you? You living anyplace or still bouncing around?"

Mildred kicked him in the shin. He winced.

"You know me," Roger said. "Never could stand to be tied down."

Just as Walter suspected. Homeless. He couldn't kick Mildred in the shin but he could slap her with an *I told you so* stare, which he did to no effect.

"She told me you were a cripple," Roger said. "That's why I looked so surprised last night when you answered the door."

"Well he's certainly not a cripple," Mildred said. "And I don't like that word." Her eyes bounced between them as though she expected Roger to apologize, then, "Walter was in a wheelchair for over a year," she said. "He worked very hard to get well. His doctors were amazed."

"Walter always was the doer of the family," Roger said. He winked at Mildred. "He married better than the rest of us."

Mildred twisted her face into a pretend frown but Walter saw the smile bleed through. "I'm sure that's not true," she said. "You could find yourself a good woman if you'd try."

"Doris divorced that preacher she married," Roger said. "Peggy said he was dipping into the choir." He winked at Walter as though Mildred didn't know what he meant but she quickly disabused him of that notion by telling him she would have none of that talk at her table.

Walter sliced off another strip of bologna. "The only time Mildred lets me have bologna is when you come," he said, stretching the truth but not by much. "If you stay long enough I may get bacon."

"Pay no attention to him," Mildred said. "You can tell by looking at him he doesn't starve."

Roger had been married and divorced four times and by Walter's estimation had inflicted enough damage on the female population and the institution of marriage and shouldn't be encouraged to inflict more. Leave it to Mildred and the entire world would be married.

"You'll regret not having someone to take care of you when you get old," she said.

"My last one did it for me," Roger said, starting to eat now. "The first three left *me*, but this one, let me tell ya, I couldn't get away fast enough."

"I'm sure she's all broken up over it," Walter said.

"Walter!"

"Walter don't mean nothing," Roger said, grinning big enough to show bits of egg in his teeth. "Remember that time you smarted off to pop and he knocked you under the kitchen table?"

Walter remembered no such thing. "He raised his hand and I tripped over my own feet," he said.

"I heard the smack," Roger said. "Peggy heard it too." He was talking to Mildred now, defending his exaggeration. "Call her and ask her if she didn't."

"That doesn't sound like the Cecil I knew," Mildred said.

"Pop mellowed by the time you came along," Roger told her.

"Dad didn't mellow," Walter said, frowning at his brother because it was so typical of him to misremember everything. "He never mistreated anyone in his life."

"You went under the table just the same," Roger said. "I'll never forget that. Peggy said you're a mayor now. Everybody always said you'd be the first Pigg to make something of yourself."

The comment rankled Walter because it discredited their father. The measure of a man shouldn't be how high he rises, but how far he rises above his starting point, but explaining anything to Roger was an exercise in futility, so he refrained. "Hayes isn't New York City," he said instead.

"Walter didn't want the job," Mildred said. "But now that he has it, he's obsessed."

"That's ridiculous," Walter said.

"He was that way when we were kids, too" Roger said. "He didn't like nothing until he had it, then you couldn't take it away from him."

"Didn't like anything," Walter corrected him. "And I don't remember being that way at all."

"One time Daddy bought us all new bicycles and Walter pitched a fit because he didn't want to give up his old one, then he rode the new one and you couldn't get him off of it."

Walter looked at Mildred and shook his head. Didn't happen. Roger must have lived a duplicate childhood in another universe, or he was simply lying. It was hard to tell whether Roger believed himself or not.

"I bet you're a fine mayor."

"Apparently you don't do social media," Walter said. "Stick around and you may witness the first mayoral impeachment in Mississippi history. Assuming they don't hang me first."

Roger laughed, then he jerked his head toward the door as though he had seen Bigfoot. "What the hell?"

Walter knew without looking that Jackson had entered the room. "Come on in, son," he said. "Your Uncle Roger barks a lot be he won't bite."

"Is that —?"

"Our grandson," Mildred said. "Jackson, this is your papaw's brother Roger."

Jackson bellied up to the table beside Walter, still rubbing the sleep from his eyes.

"He's a great kid," Walter said. He looked at Jackson and rubbed his head. "Aren't you, son?"

Jackson shrugged.

"He's very smart," Mildred said.

Roger finished his coffee with a gulp. "Well, it ain't none of my business, but —."

"Exactly right," Walter said. "It's not. Why don't you tell Mildred why you left San Antonio?"

"I doubt she's interested."

"Sure she is," Walter said.

"I'm sure he had his reasons, Walter."

"He had some trouble with a clerk in an automotive store," Walter said. "Ask him."

Mildred gave Roger a stern look. "I hope you left whatever trouble it was in Texas." Roger had a way of dragging his troubles with him like the tail of a kite.

"It was nothing," Roger said, glancing at her, then at Walter, then back at the boy.

"Go on. Tell it."

Roger sat straight and brushed the breakfast crumbs from the front of his shirt with the flat of his hand. "Well, you see, I went into an auto parts store for a quart of oil and the clerk recognized me, and one thing led to another and some punches were thrown and —."

"Tell her where he recognized you from."

"I'm sure she's not interested in —."

"She will be," Walter said.

"If you're going to goad your brother into telling the story then let him tell it."

"It's key to the plot," Walter said.

Roger cleared his throat. "He recognized me from outside his house the week before."

"Tell her where."

"Walter!"

"My brother enjoys embarrassing me," Roger said.

"Four wives and four divorces," Walter said to Mildred. "My brother was peeping through the man's bedroom window. Naked"

"Roger!"

Walter laughed, enjoying his brother's discomfort very much. The story had Mildred's attention now and couldn't be stopped. She would pull it out of him by the roots if she had to. Every last detail.

"I — I wasn't peeping. I was looking back … to see how much of my skin I'd left on the windowsill."

Walter watched Mildred closely, wanting to savor the moment when she realized Roger was escaping from a rendezvous. It came. Her eyes flew wide. Roger didn't know because his eyes were sagging toward the gravy bowl.

"A man your age," Mildred said.

"Four wives and four divorces," Walter said again.

"Okay, I lied," Roger said. He looked across the table at Walter with fury in his eyes. The lie was up. It couldn't stand up in the face of Mildred's condemnation. She had that way about her. "There was no bedroom window and no woman. The truth is, I had borrowed a friend's car and I ran over a garbage can that had blown out into the street and I put a tiny scratch on the front fender." He paused and looked at them both. "Okay, so it wasn't so tiny. I went into the parts store for some touchup paint and — and you wouldn't believe how much that stuff costs. It's highway robbery."

Mildred pursed her lips and shook her head. "So you stole it?"

"Tried to steal it," Roger said. He looked at Mildred then to Walter, who actually felt a little sorry for his brother all of a sudden. "I … was strapped for cash, and I —."

"Stealing food is one thing," Mildred said, "but paint?"

"It wasn't my fault. People ought not leave empty trash cans on the curb so they blow out into the street." He dropped his eyes again. "I slipped away while the clerk called the police, and, well, here I am."

Walter believed him. Roger Pigg, petty thief, fit the profile so much better than Roger Pigg the errant lover. "So do they have a warrant for your arrest? Should we expect the US Marshals to kick down our front door in the middle of the night?"

"No, they don't have a warrant for my arrest. It was a ten dollar bottle of paint and I didn't make it out the door so it wasn't even a crime."

"Then why run?" Mildred asked. "Obviously you were afraid of something."

"I was ashamed," Roger said. "And maybe I have a few unpaid parking tickets against my name."

"Without a car?"

"That's why I was without a car. They booted mine while I was ——. They booted it. Then they impounded it, and they may as well have pushed it into the river for all the chance I had at getting it back."

Walter's suspicions were confirmed. "Well you can put your hand back in your pocket because Mildred and I don't have a cent to spare. Being mayor doesn't pay as well as being an engineer."

"We have a few dollars put back," Mildred said.

Roger sighed. "I'm afraid a few dollars wouldn't do me any good."

"How much can a few parking tickets be?"

"Several hundred dollars," Roger said. "Then there's the impound fee, and the fine." His eyes bounced between them. "The main thing is the insurance."

"Let me guess," Walter said.

"I don't have insurance. Can't afford it. Once the government sets its sights on you they put you in a hole you'll never dig out of. It's impossible."

"Nothing's impossible," Mildred said.

"Tell me how if I couldn't afford insurance I'm supposed to pay this enormous fine then buy the insurance I couldn't afford in the first place? Ordinary average people can't stay above water the way they stack the deck against us. It's a conspiracy. The government knocks a man down then kicks him until he gives up."

"The government didn't park your car illegally," Walter said. "Or tell you to drive without insurance."

"A man's gotta drive."

Mildred chimed in. "If you knew you didn't have insurance, why did you illegally park and draw attention to yourself?"

"Because he's stupid," Walter said.

"Walter!"

"Go ahead," Roger said. "Gang up on me. Everyone else has."

"Poor, poor Roger," Walter said. "Millions of people get up every morning and go to work and pay their bills and park in legal places and drive with insurance, but not Roger."

"Spare me the lecture."

"Spare us the violin," Walter said. "It wasn't the government that kept you from getting a job. A man makes his own decisions."

"Don't preach," Mildred told Walter. "You've made a few bad decisions yourself."

Her rebuke stung. It kicked the wind out of his argument. "You're right. Of course you're right. You're always right, Mildred." He folded his napkin and shot up from the table with as much urgency as a man in his physical condition could shoot. How many more years would she throw it back in his face? Forever, he supposed. She had the right, forgiveness and religion and biblical teachings aside. "I'll be in the car." He looked at his brother. "You won't make off with the silverware while we're gone I trust."

"Walter!"

"Walter never could take a scolding," he heard Roger say as he escaped out the back door, not slowing to hear what, if anything, Mildred said in return. Helping Roger was like trying to heat a room without walls. The man was a perpetual screw-up. One handout after another. How or why it happened he couldn't say. They were reared by the same parents, in the same house, under the same rules. Roger had always been Roger. Even as a child he claimed the short end of every stick. Every circumstance had been finely honed against him. In school it was the teachers. At home it was Walter, and Peggy, and Doris. When they went fishing, it was the fish. In baseball it was the coach, or the umpire, or the unfortunate way the wind always seemed to shift when Roger stepped up to bat.

Walter sat in the car with his hands gripping the steering wheel — ten and two — without the car running lest Mildred come out and accuse him of attempting suicide with the garage door closed. When she did come out, Jackson in tow, she simply got in on her side and folded her hands across her lap. Walter pressed a button on the remote clipped to his visor and sent the door rattling upward, then he backed down the driveway and almost ran over his newspaper before he remembered it was Wednesday. Dexter Mann's day to skewer him with sharp headlines and barbed sentences.

* * *

Dexter Mann's headline lacked effort. MAYOR TRIES TO OUST CHIEF. The article barely propped it up with an impotent account of how Pigg's motion to unseat Benson failed with all five aldermen opposing. What it didn't do was connect the dots for the average schmuck who bothered to read the Hayes Beacon. It didn't offer a motive. It didn't say the mayor had a personal vendetta against the chief. For all anyone would know from reading the article, the mayor might have a valid reason for wanting the chief's head. The article cast as much doubt on Benson as it did on Pigg.

The thing that kept Tipton from going into a full-blown rage was the fact that Pigg had inflicted enough damage to himself on social media that the article hardly mattered. The official mayoral page might turn out to be the bullet to Pigg's head.

"Who needs Mann when Pigg does it to himself?" Tipton said, tossing the paper aside without bothering to read below the fold. Rance sat across the desk from him with his leg thrown over the chair arm, cleaning his fingernails with a penknife.

"You're carrying this feud with Pigg too far," Rance said without looking up.

"Can you do your nails in your own office?"

"I'm not *doing*," Rance said. "I'm *cleaning*." He held a finger up for Tipton to see the black dirt underneath. "I had a flat in my driveway this morning and had to change the tire. You wouldn't believe how filthy those little spares get hanging underneath like that. Have you ever changed a tire?"

"Of course I've changed a tire."

"I bet you couldn't do it now," Rance said. "Or wouldn't. You'd call somebody to come do it for you."

"As a matter of fact I would. What of it?"

"Nothing. Some people do their own dirty work while others hire it done." He looked up from the nail he was cleaning. "Like killing a horse because you need its head."

"I told you I had nothing to do with that!"

"So you keep saying."

"I keep saying it because it's true!"

"I hope so … for both our sakes. A thing like that could sink this firm. Neither of us would ever work in this town again. What? You don't believe me? Animals are a big deal now-a-days," he said. "Won't be long until they'll be able to sue in court." He laughed to himself, then focused on his nails again.

"Can you stop doing that? You're getting grease all over my floor."

"I'll stop cleaning my nails if you'll stop feuding with Pigg."

"I didn't start it."

"Sure you did. He won and you pitched a fit. Now you both look dumb."

Tipton bristled. "All he has to do is resign."

"Why should he? He won."

"Because he's a nobody, and nobodies don't get to be mayor."

Rance dug at another fingernail. "So if somebody important beat you … like, oh, let's say, Jesus … you'd be fine with it."

At that exact moment Candice buzzed Tipton's phone to tell Rance that Clarence Fine was waiting for him in his office. Fine was the private investigator the firm kept on retainer. He specialized in insurance fraud cases. Catching cripples doing normal stuff like walking to the mailbox without their crutches, or getting up out of the wheelchair to let the cat out. Things people do when they think no one's looking.

"He's been sitting on Katie Sample's house," Rance said as he folded the knife back into his pocket. Sample was a thirty-three year-old woman who turned in front of a bread truck. Palo-West represented the company that owned the truck. "A much better use of his time than having him spy on the mayor."

Rance didn't know what Rance didn't know.

Half an hour later Fine stuck his head in and asked Tipton if he knew Pigg had a brother. Tipton waved him in and told him to close the door. Fine was tall and slim and extremely fit for a man of forty-six. More importantly he was discrete.

"How is that important?"

"You know how Jimmy Carter had Billy?"

Tipton was too young to remember President Carter's time in office but he knew the story. His brother Billy was a drunken embarrassment but he hadn't been fatal to the campaign.

"Roger Pigg has priors in Texas and New Mexico, but never served any real jail time that I could find."

Tipton shrugged. "You're not telling me anything important."

"He just hit town," Fine said, "and he looks like he just crawled up out of a ditch."

"Keep an eye on him," Tipton said. "And don't tell Rance. He's been in a mood lately." He decided to press his luck. "You know he drew that awful horse case?"

"I heard you drew it and pawned it off on him."

"Regardless, it's pretty airtight." What he really wanted to ask was whether or not Rance had him digging into it, but he couldn't frame the question without making himself seem overly interested in the outcome. Fine was no idiot. "About the only way we win this one is if it happens again while Pickle's in jail."

"Rance said he's guilty."

"All the more reason he needs your help."

"You know me better than that," Fine said. "Besides, he bonded out this morning."

Tipton tried to laugh the suggestion off as a joke. "You're a straight shooter, Clarence. I like you. Anybody ever tell you how much you look like Wesley Snipes?"

"Just you," Fine said. "Every time you want me to do something illegal."

Tipton sent him away. What use was he if he wasn't willing to get his hands dirty? At least he knew now that Pickle was out on bond. He wondered why Rance hadn't told him. He also knew the DA was going to drop the felony animal cruelty charge, but he hadn't told Rance yet. Better to let him find out through the proper channels. Benson had bragged to Tipton about it but Stubbs was the force behind it. Benson didn't have the juice to influence the DA.

The remainder of the morning passed without incident, then Rance barged in with a pizza for lunch and spread the box on Tipton's desk without asking. Tipton hadn't had pizza in ages. Too much cheese for the digestive system, but it looked delicious so he took a slice.

"Clogs your colon and your arteries all at the same time," he said as he chewed his first mouthful.

"Nothing clogs my colon," Rance said. "My plumbing's clean as a virgin cheerleader." He grinned, displaying cheese and peppers in his teeth. "Doctor Tremble told me that."

"Did he use those exact words?"

"Probably not. He said I was clean, though. Say, that reminds me of a joke. You know what a joke is don't you?"

Tipton frowned. Rance could be very annoying when he wanted to be.

"There was this intern who was always spouting off at the mouth. Trying to be a show off to the other interns. Always sucking up." He paused to take a bite, chew, and swallow. "One day they were examining this patient, you see, and the old doc, he pulls on his latex gloves and rams his finger up the patient's ass, both knuckles, then he puts his finger in his mouth and takes a pull on it. This man's diabetic, the doc says, then he looks around at the group of soon-to-be doctors and asks if anybody wants to give a second opinion. This young suck-up of an intern snatches on his gloves, buries his finger in the guy's ass, jams it in his mouth and sloshes it around, looking dreadful. Pale. About to puke. I concur, he said. This man's definitely diabetic. Amazing, the old doc said. I had to look at his chart." Rance slapped his leg and cackled.

"I don't get it."

"What don't you get?"

"They both stuck a shitty finger in their mouths."

"No, the doctor was left-handed."

"So?"

"So the finger he put in his mouth was on his right hand."

"You didn't say that."

Rance took a moment, contemplating, then he frowned. "Never mind."

"Stick to law," Tipton said.

"By the way, that little outfit Candice modeled for you the other day wasn't hers. One of her friends left it at her place and she was going to drop it off after work." He looked at Tipton and grinned. "That's why it was so small. Her friend's a hot little number. I almost —."

"I don't care what you and Candice do as long as you keep it out of the office," Tipton said.

An incredible amusement swept Rance's face. "You think —." He laughed. "Me and Candice?"

"Don't deny it."

"Deny it? Hell, I'd claim it if I could. I'd brag about it. I'd make it my Facebook profile picture. Me and Candice?"

"I notice how the two of you act around each other," Tipton said. "Rampant flirtation."

"Rampant flirtation? We're friends. It does happen, you know, though I like your version better. I wonder if I could talk her into it. Her and the friend with the outfit you saw."

"Get out," Tipton said. "And take your pizza with you." After Rance left, Tipton called his wife and invited her to lunch. She countered by inviting him to come eat with her and her nineteen students in the school cafeteria. No thanks. Then he heard laughter from outside his office. Candice and Rance.

* * *

Wednesday afternoon a reporter for the Associated Press called Walter's office and badgered him to justify the charges he had made against Chief Benson. Why did the Associated Press care about a backwater police chief? Walter suspected him of being a fraud — a pretender hired by Stubbs to intimidate him, so he hung up on him three times.

"Why would Stubbs care?" Mildred said after Walter floated the idea to her over their nine o'clock coffee. "The town council already dropped it for you."

She had a point. Misguided, but a point nonetheless. The aldermen could overrule him, but they couldn't silence him. He could still beat the drum, and no one beat a drum like Walter.

Stubborn — that's the word Mildred used. Harsh, Walter thought, because he believed he had right on his side. Right makes might, but it doesn't always sway aldermen, so he resolved himself to beat the drum.

"I don't want another head hanging from my back porch," Mildred said.

"It's our porch," he said, "and I didn't hang the thing." His coffee had cooled below the point of being tolerable. Coffee should be hot, or aggressively warm, otherwise it tastes like cigarettes. He pushed the cup away. "I may as well take up smoking."

"You'll find another wife if you do."

"Is that all it takes? Start smoking and potential wives show up at the door?"

"That's not what I meant and you know it." She reached for his cup to refill it but he waved her off. He'd had enough caffeine. Too much and his skin would start to crawl across his bones.

"One day they say it kills you, the next day they say it cures you," he said. She stared blankly. "Coffee," he said, clarifying. "First they browbeat us into drinking decaf, then they sing the praises of caffeine. It's the same thing with liquor."

"And who would *they* be?"

"You know very well who *they* be," he said. "They. The ultimate authority on everything that can be bought, sold, or consumed. Doctors and scientists who've sold their souls to the highest bidders. Professional studiers, with the conclusion predetermined by whoever signs the check."

Mildred rolled her eyes — she had perfected eye rolling. If Walter rolled his eyes at her it might trigger a third world war, but when she did it, oh well. That's how it is with husbands and wives — with men and women in general — uneven. Women demand equal rights without realizing they have the

124

advantage already. Why saddle themselves with male equality when they rule the world outright? It was an argument he didn't dare raise with Mildred again. He wouldn't make that mistake twice.

"I wish you'd take down that ridiculous Facebook page," she said. "Have you looked at it this morning? You're losing the war, you know. They'll be throwing rotten tomatoes at us before the week's out."

It wasn't as bad as that. Sure, some of the comments were against him, but it was early in the campaign and the natural instinct of people is to take a dump on everything. One person posts something and gets a few likes and suddenly everyone is jumping on the bandwagon, thinking the same way because they don't want to be the odd duck. Humans are by nature herd animals. Break from the herd and they peck you to death.

"It's only a small group," he said. "The page hasn't taken off yet."

"Good thing for you it hasn't."

She was playing devil's advocate, at least he thought she was. Sometimes it was hard to tell. Usually she smiled and gave herself away but not this time. Perhaps she meant it. The comments on the page were decisively negative. There had been a time when such a thing might have plunged him into a deep depression, but his near-death experience two years previous had cured him of the gnawing need to exterminate himself. Death defeats death. No one wants to live more than the man in the foxhole. Or had it been the months of narcotic painkilling drugs the doctors pumped into his bloodstream? What a ride that had been. At one point he felt certain he had traded one addiction for another. Instead of slinking off to fork over his money to Stubbs, he feared he might troll the streets looking for narcotics like some common drug addict. Walter Pigg, junkie, but Mildred and his paralysis saved him. They worked as a team. Mildred prevented anything from entering his system without her permission, and his paralysis prevented him from slipping away. By the time he was physically able to transport himself, the cravings had subsided. Crisis averted. The memory of feeling helpless gave him a much greater compassion for human suffering. Somewhat. The further a man gets from a thing, the less it steers him. There were still days when the depression came, but it hadn't been so heavy as before. Instead of covering him like a thick blanket wet with some unidentifiable sticky ooze, pushing him down until he could barely breathe, it came on as a manageable sadness. Even with all the negative pressure against him on social media and in the press, the calls to his office Mildred tried to shield him from, the sideward looks when he came and went, even with that he could manage. It wasn't faith. Walter had always believed in God. Nothing had changed on that front. No grand revelations sent to him in a dream, tapping him on the shoulder saying everything is going to be okay now, Walter, go back to life. It was the experience. The experience of almost dying, or was it the experience of being heroic? Not a hero — he wasn't that — but heroic. A one-time thing.

"Earth to Walter."

"I was counting how many days until Christmas."

"And?"

"And what?"

"How many days?"

He glanced at the calendar near the corner of his desk. "Six."

"You don't have to lie to me, Walter. I'm your wife. If it bothers you what people are saying, then take down the page and stop giving them a platform."

"I was thinking about something else." He realized she was waiting for him to explain himself, and he had already lied to her once. "I was thinking about two years ago."

"Oh." She reached across the desk and took his hand.

"For the life of me I don't know if I acted on your behalf or mine."

"It doesn't matter," she said. "The important thing is you acted."

"I was in as much danger as you were," he said. "And Jackson."

"And you saved us. All of us."

"But was I saving you or saving myself?"

"What did you think would happen to you when you went out that door?"

Walter pondered the question. "I don't remember thinking about it."

"That's what heroes do," she said. "They act without considering the consequences to themselves."

She was right. He had to have known they would both go out the door. In fact, he planned it that way because he lunged and threw his arms around the demon. He didn't lunge and push. He didn't shove the demon out the door and get pulled along by accident. That simple parsing of logic made him feel better. "I *was* heroic, wasn't I?"

"Very much so."

All his life he had backed down in the face of physical threats, telling himself each and every time that if he ever found himself in a position to save someone else he wouldn't hesitate to sacrifice himself, which is what he did, only he survived. Surviving didn't make him less brave.

"What I'm doing now is heroic too," he said, just then making the connection. Sometimes a man looks at a thing so hard he can't see the obvious. Taking on Perry Stubbs was a brave act even if a small part of the reason was his own need for vengeance.

"It's suicide," she said, then her face sank because she had used the forbidden word.

"I'm sacrificing my political life to save people from Stubbs, and from a corrupt police chief. If that's not heroic, then what is? If anything, it's more heroic than jumping out of an RV because unlike then, I've had time to think this one through. Opposing Stubbs is the right thing to do, and doing so is a conscious decision on my part. Heroic, even if it is suicidal."

"Such a stubborn man," she said with a sigh, almost to herself but loud enough on purpose for him to hear.

"Determined, Mildred. The word is determined, and yes I am. If Perry Stubbs is not a demon from hell then I'm a Canadian goose."

"I never said he wasn't."

"And if the chief of police is protecting him, well, what am I supposed to do?" She didn't answer with words but her face told him she understood in some regretful kind of way. "People are beginning to react to that article in the Beacon," he said. "It's not entirely hopeless yet."

"Two comments is not a movement," she said.

"Three comments, and if it gains traction, who knows?" he hesitated before saying the other thing he had been thinking. "I was thinking I might create a fake profile and —."

"Don't you dare!"

"Half the profiles on Facebook are probably fake," he said, grabbing a percentage out of thin air. "For all I know Tipton Palo could be the one posting all those comments."

"If you get caught doing that they'll laugh us out of town."

"They're practically doing that now," he said. "Besides, how could I get caught?"

"Don't you do it, Walter. I know you well enough to know that if there's a way to get caught, you'll find it."

"I could force myself to use bad grammar."

"No."

"I could type every message in all caps. Wouldn't that be a —."

"No! I mean it, Walter, if you do I'll never speak to you again."

She meant it. Creating fake accounts was officially off the table.

* * *

Autumn buzzed the police chief through the front gate without asking. By the time Benson rang the doorbell, Tipton had scolded her and ordered her upstairs. She went with resistance, but she went. Their relationship had not yet devolved to the point of outright defiance.

"Pour me whatever you're having," Benson said as he blew by Tipton and plopped down on the sofa.

Tipton looked at the glass of brandy in his hand, then at the rumpled man who looked to have had a few too many already, then he disappeared into his study and poured a shot of bourbon over ice with two shots of water and returned to the living room.

"Dexter Mann needs his ass kicked," Benson said as he snatched the glass from Tipton's hand, splashing the leather sofa with whiskey.

"Try not to pee on the rug," Tipton said, glaring down at him. "And keep your voice down." He threw his eyes to the top of the staircase and considered moving the conversation to the study in case Autumn was angry enough to eavesdrop.

"Don't talk down to me," the chief said. "I'm not *that* drunk."

"Debatable," Tipton said under his breath, thinking the sofa probably cost more than his uninvited guest made in a month. "What's Dexter done now?"

Benson drained the glass then clanked the ice. "What is this stuff?"

"You were complaining about Dexter," Tipton said. He glanced upstairs again then dropped into the armchair that sat perpendicular to the sofa. "What's he done now?"

"Don't pretend you didn't read the paper this morning," Benson said. He rattled the ice in his empty glass, then leaned forward and banged it down onto the coffee table two inches from a coaster. Tipton eyed it, then glanced again toward the top of the stairs, half expecting his wife to swoop down and save her precious antique from the dreaded ring, but Autumn was probably already in bed with her nose buried in a book, or in the tub half asleep. Her existence revolved around reading and soaking.

Tipton leaned forward and moved the glass. "I'll admit he could've done a better job defending you, but —."

"But nothing! He didn't defend me at all. He skewered me!"

"It wasn't as bad as that."

"I've devoted my life to this town."

"No one questions your character."

"Everybody questions my character," Benson said. "Have you seen his *official* Facebook page?"

Tipton laughed. "Is that thing still up?"

"Oh it's up," Benson said. "Take a look if you don't believe me."

Tipton checked his phone and saw dozens of new comments, most of them supporting Pigg. One comment called the chief a Stubbs crony. Another questioned how he managed to build a mansion on a cop's salary. Combined, they had almost a hundred likes. "So the pendulum swings."

"Damned right the pendulum swings," Benson said. "And right now it's swinging up my ass."

The turn of events concerned Tipton, but the public was nothing more than a very large jury, and nobody worked a jury the way he did. There was still time. Plenty of time. "Ignore it," he said. "Whoever wrote that probably lives in a doublewide. He's jealous."

"Easy for you to say. They're not coming after you yet."

Tipton's analytical brain hung on the word yet. What a loaded word, yet, used by a man with crosshairs on his forehead. It implied something inevitable. "I don't like the way you said that."

"Don't listen then," the chief said. "I'm probably jealous."

"Let's not turn on each other."

"Why should I be the only one ruined?"

Benson snatched up his glass and rattled the ice again. "Pour me another drink," he said. "Without the water this time."

"You've had enough."

"I'll say when I've had enough."

"And I'll say when a man's drank enough of my booze," Tipton said. "And I'll tell him when it's time to get out of my house."

Benson shot to his feet and teetered. "We'll see who gets ruined," he said, steadying himself with a wobble.

Tipton stood too. "Nobody's getting ruined. All we have to do is —."

"Stick together? Keep our heads? Ride it out?"

"Something like that."

"You and Stubbs think I'm stupid," Benson said. "You think I'll take the fall for you like a good soldier."

Tipton checked the stairs again. "Keep your voice down."

Benson glanced over his shoulder and up, then he grinned. "Afraid the wife'll find out what you've been up to?" He sneered. "Keep your whiskey. You're right. I've had enough."

Tipton reached for his elbow but the chief jerked away. "You'll probably call the highway patrol as soon as I leave. You think they'll arrest me? Maybe the sheriff'll do your dirty work for you."

"Stop acting childish."

"You think the sheriff's nose is clean? You and Stubbs ain't the only game in town you know. I can take a lot of people down. You better remember that. Stubbs better remember too."

"Nobody's taking anybody down," Tipton said, reaching for Benson's arm again.

"Don't put your hands on me."

"You're drunk. Sit down and I'll get you some coffee."

Benson started for the door and bumped his shin on the coffee table. He cursed, then he started again.

Tipton grabbed him by the shoulder and turned him. "Pigg's easy to take care of," he said. He glanced at the staircase again. Autumn was either unaware or too smart to show herself. He leaned into the chief's face and lowered his voice to a whisper. "You've got drugs in your evidence locker don't you? Well, Pigg has a back problem. All that pain, and doctors can't prescribe painkillers the way they used to. Not the good stuff."

"You want me to frame the mayor?"

"All I'm saying is, suppose one of your men stopped Pigg for a traffic violation and found a bottle of opioids in his console?"

"He's never had a ticket in his life. I checked."

"Well there's always a first time," Tipton said. "Be creative."

Benson's brain went somewhere, then he snapped back. "Everything's tracked by computers now. It ain't as easy as it used to be. I'm the boss and even I can't get in the evidence room without the computer logging it."

"Never mind that," Tipton said, thinking. He was nothing if not resourceful. A good attorney has to be able to think on his feet. "The world is full of drugs," he said. "No need taking unnecessary risks." He slapped the chief on the back. "Go home."

"What about Pigg?"

"Leave him to me," Tipton said. "And forget this conversation ever happened."

CHAPTER 14

Roger exhausted the week with no mention of leaving. Not one word that betrayed a plan of action. Every time Walter tried to broach the subject, Roger evaded him, or Mildred interceded, but now even she was growing restless. A guest is a guest until he isn't, then he's a short hop away from being a nuisance, though Mildred would never call him that. Not to Walter, regardless how many times he used the word himself.

Saturday morning they went fishing — Walter and Roger. Going was Roger's idea. He remembered a pond they used to frequent when they were kids, and to Walter's surprise it still looked exactly the way he remembered, but of course memories have a way of melding with the reality of the moment. Roger agreed that it hadn't changed, except for the house visible in the distance and the almost complete deterioration of a nearby barn.

"I don't remember all that timber we drove through," Roger said, sitting on his upturned bucket with his cane pole arched over the murky water.

"I don't remember it being this cold," Walter said. Fishing was a warm weather pastime and here it was three days before Christmas.

"Who owns this place now?"

Walter admitted he didn't know, then they both agreed they were technically trespassing, though there had been no signs warning them to keep out, then Roger thought he had a bite but didn't.

"I suppose it don't matter, you being mayor and all," Roger said.

"That might work against us," Walter said. They were in the county so he didn't have to worry about the chief arresting him, though he didn't know the sheriff at all. Cops tend to stick together. "It would be quite a write-up in the Beacon."

"What's that guy got against you anyway?"

Assuming his brother meant Dexter Mann, Walter said he had spent considerable time pondering that very question.

"And?"

"And I don't know, except that he was pulling for the other man."

"I thought newspapers were supposed to be unbiased."

Walter laughed.

The pond was small. Little more than a watering hole for the cattle that had grazed the pasture back in the day. Now there were no cows. No bulls to lower their heads and paw the ground and send two young boys scurrying back under the fence, or into the barn and up into the loft where they would stretch back on the hay and dream of all the things they would do when they grew up.

"What was it you wanted to be?" Walter asked, trying to squeeze the memories into focus. "An astronaut?"

"Air Force pilot," Roger said.

"What happened?"

"Found out I'm afraid of heights," Roger said. "Remember that time dad dragged me up onto the roof with him to install that little whirly-jig?"

"You mean the turbine vent?"

"That thing that spun when the wind blew," Roger said. "It was supposed to cut the light bill and all it did was leak every time it came a hard rain."

"I remember you crying your eyes out until mom made him let you come down," Walter said. "That's what turned you against the Air Force?"

"That's when I figured out I was afraid of heights," Roger said. "Terrified. I never told anyone but I wet my pants that day."

"No secret there," Walter said with a big laugh. "Mom threatened to pull our ears off if we teased you about it."

"She was the best," Roger said, his voice tapered off into some distant place.

"So was dad."

"Yeah, but mom was really the best. Sometimes I think I hear her calling me. Telling me not to forget my toboggan."

"I wanted to be Glen Campbell," Walter said.

"You never could sing."

"He was from Arkansas, you know."

"I remember when they bought you that guitar for Christmas."

"I never could get the hang of it," Walter said. "I tried though. I bought every instructional book Chet Atkins and Roy Clark ever wrote."

"You almost drove us all crazy."

They sat without talking for a while. Each lost, Walter supposed, in his own version of childhood. The morning gloom seemed the perfect incubator for remembering. Neither of them had mentioned Mark, but how does one sit at water's edge without thinking about the brother who drowned?

"Do you blame me for Mark?"

"Nobody ever blamed you for Mark but you," Roger said. Walter wished he could believe him. Everything changed that day. Everyone changed. The way they looked at him. Talked to him.

"Thank you."

"You called Peggy about me," Roger said.

"She didn't waste any time telling you."

"I heard you." He looked a bit sheepish. "I was eavesdropping in the hall."

It made Walter feel better knowing his sister didn't rat him out. Eavesdropping was expected of Roger, but Peggy was supposed to be above reproach. "I was concerned," Walter said.

"Can I not visit my brother?"

"We're not a visiting family."

"Should I leave?"

"No."

Roger's face betrayed no emotion, as though leaving or staying didn't matter. "So what did she say?"

"Does it matter?"

Roger shrugged. "Not really."

"She said Ray helped you out of a jam in New Mexico."

"What else?"

"Just that."

Roger smiled. "She married good."

"*Well*," Walter said. "She married well." Roger bristled at the correction. He was a lost cause when it came to self-betterment. Even as a kid he resisted correction, hence his life as a functioning vagrant. He was right about Ray, though, as far as Walter knew. Peggy had always dated above her station. Lucky her. Not so for Mildred.

"What's funny?"

Walter realized he had laughed. "I told myself a joke," he said.

"Tell me."

"It wasn't that funny."

They both laughed.

"How was Peggy when you saw her?"

"Peggy was Peggy," Roger said, meaning he didn't know because he was more interested in himself than in his sister's wellbeing. "What did she tell you about New Mexico?"

"Just that you got into some trouble," Walter said. "You know how she is."

"Somebody must've fished this hole dry," Roger said, meaning he didn't want to talk about New Mexico any more than Walter wanted to listen. Roger's problems were Roger's problems, unless they followed him to Hayes and became Walter's.

"Snapping turtles probably ate all the fish," Walter said.

"Remember that time dad caught that snapping turtle and it wouldn't turn loose of his hook? He sawed his head off with that dull Case knife he carried."

Walter remembered. Their father said he needed to sharpen his knife, and Mark said he bet the turtle wished he would. They all laughed their heads off. "I sure do miss that old man."

"And Mark."

Walter nodded. And Mark.

They were back home by noon. As they turned into the driveway, Roger asked to borrow the car later.

"This old tank?"

"I'll be careful with it."

Walter thought of every excuse in the world to say no, then he shelved them all and said it would be okay. They were brothers, and Walter had insurance.

* * *

Autumn agreed to entertain despite the chill between them. It was Saturday night. Three days before Christmas. It was expected of them, and if she were honest, she would admit she enjoyed it as much as he did. More, perhaps, because it was her time to shine. Her opportunity to prove to the Hayes upper crust that she was more than a high school math teacher.

Rance was there. Being a bachelor, he wasn't expected to throw Christmas parties. Other parties, yes, but none the wives were invited to. He sidled up to Tipton and remarked that it wasn't as big a turnout as last year. Last December they were gearing up to launch Tipton's campaign for mayor even though it was not yet public knowledge that Mayor Sherman would resign. Tom Sherman may not have known it himself, but Tipton knew, and Rance knew. Tom Sherman was one of those men who put duty above self. Honor above glory. His father and brothers had sealed his political fate by placing bets they couldn't pay with Stubbs, and there was nothing for a man of honor to do but protect their reputations. How ironic that names in a book undid one mayor and made another. Pigg had no honor. Cared nothing for it. Some men rise from nothing to become something, but Pigg brought nothingness with him. Soon he would be a laughing stock, then he would step down. Walter Pigg would learn his place.

Judge Harvey Bishop was there, as were three assistant district attorneys. Bishop was above reproach. Incorruptible, if there was such a thing. Rance insisted he was. Tipton believed in his heart that every man has his price. Stubbs had a way of probing a man. Finding his price. Benson had been a cheap buy. Pocket change. He wasn't at the party because he hadn't been invited. Pigg hadn't been invited either, for reasons no one in attendance questioned. It was the first Christmas party in memory not attended by the sitting mayor. Even Tom Sherman came last year. Perhaps he thought it might save him, but more than likely he did it out of duty, like attending a ribbon cutting or handing out a community service award. Sherman was a reasonable man, and reasonable men know how the game is played. Tipton liked him personally, but politics is a contact sport.

"Lesley brought the girls tonight," Rance said under his breath as he brushed past Tipton again, nudging him in the ribs. Lesley Branch was one of the three assistant district attorneys and the only female. All female. The girls, as Rance called them, were on grand display, ready to pop out of the low-cut black evening gown should she make a wrong move, or a right move, depending on one's point of view. Her husband was around someplace, glad-handing all the important people he only saw when he served as her plus one. Tipton spotted him near the bar, chatting up the chancery clerk as though they were equals.

"Control yourself," Tipton said to Rance. "Her husband's twice your size and Autumn's moody enough already."

"He ditched her the second they hit the door. If she was mine I'd —."

"She's not. She's his. Stay away from her."

"Yes, Mother," Rance said, then he slapped his partner on the back and slinked away. Half a minute later Tipton saw him near the kitchen door chatting up Autumn. She looked annoyed, but at least she was occupied, freeing Tipton to work the room without the ball and chain.

Trevor Harland sang the first verse of Silent Night before his wife corralled him into the kitchen. It was an awkward rendition fueled by too much alcohol too soon. Later they would sing as a group, and no one would care how they sounded because they would all be well lubricated.

Tipton mingled toward the bar, mindful of the disappearing brandy in his glass. The host can't be seen with an empty glass. Lesley Branch had caught up with her husband at the bar and had a firm grip on his elbow, probably to ward off a certain bank president who had forgotten his manners. He was old enough to be her father, and rich enough to be her sugar daddy. Tipton introduced himself to her husband. They had met, but not officially.

"My husband is in real estate," Lesley said. "He was telling me as we came through the gate how much he admires your home."

Tipton knew she was lying but didn't care. She was covering for him because he was clearly out of his element. Tipton had spent years rendering Autumn that very service until she found her footing in his world.

He felt a familiar hand press against the small of his back. "Lesley, I'd like you to meet my wife," he said, then he turned slightly rightward and put his arm around Autumn. "Autumn, Lesley Branch. She's our newest assistant DA." The women exchanged pleasantries, then, almost as an afterthought, Lesley introduced her husband to Autumn. Tipton detected a hint of jealousy in his wife's voice. Understandable, considering, but it was completely unfounded. He barely knew the young attorney. Every woman in the room had looked at her with some degree of disapproval when she arrived, just as every man had looked at her and thought what if. It was her own fault for dressing so provocatively. A little cleavage is seductive. Too much is a distraction. Lesley was proving to be an interruption.

Autumn said she needed help in the kitchen, which meant she was pissed. He followed her and waited while she dismissed the two ladies who had been helping her prepare hors d'oeuvres.

"Care to explain *that*?"

"I told you," he said. "She's the new assistant DA. I told you about her months ago."

"You told me she was a woman," Autumn said. "You didn't tell me what kind."

"Frankly I'm as surprised as you are," he said. "Until tonight I've only seen her in pantsuits."

"What kind of man lets his wife dress like that?"

Tipton laughed, trying to defuse the situation. "Something tells me it's not up to him."

"You think it's funny?"

"No," he said. "I was just trying to —.""

"Tell her to leave."

"What? I can't do that."

"Then I will." She started toward the door but he grabbed her arm. "Let go of me!"

"I won't let you go out there and make a fool of yourself in front of our friends."

"They're your friends," she said. "Not mine. I don't get to invite my friends to your parties."

"Don't do this now," he said, still gripping her arm. "I'm sorry if you don't make friends with people who aren't schoolteachers. You could if you tried, you know."

She jerked away but didn't move. "Maybe I'll go upstairs and change into something more revealing so you won't have to be ashamed of your schoolteacher wife."

"Don't embarrass yourself."

"Don't embarrass you, you mean."

"Take it however you like," he said, "but behave yourself."

"Or what?"

His method wasn't working. He grabbed her hand and pulled her into his chest and put his arms around her. "You're being silly," he said, then he tried to kiss her but she turned away. He kissed her anyway — on the cheek. "You know I love you."

She pushed away. "Do you?" Before he could answer, she escaped. He closed his eyes and waited for the yelling to start, then it didn't so he steeled himself and followed her back to their guests. Rance intercepted him near the sofa.

"We were all waiting for dishes to break," he said, then he was too far away for Tipton to respond without everyone hearing. Rance glanced back, proud of himself for being clever. The world was full of clever people. Too full. Tipton saw Lesley across the room surrounded by men. Her husband was at the bar. Autumn was near the Christmas tree pretending to straighten an ornament.

"Nice ornaments," a voice said from behind him. Tipton recognized the judge and turned.

"My wife has an eye for it," Tipton said, turning. He saw the judge looking in another direction, toward the assistant DA. Was that his price? Women? He laughed. "Oh, those ornaments. Yes, very nice. Where's she been hiding those?"

"I'm already looking forward to your next party."

Lesley's husband drifted toward the tree and struck up a conversation with Autumn. They looked friendly enough. Had they met? Tipton felt the temperature of his blood rising and it surprised him. Jealousy was foreign to him where Autumn was concerned. The judge drifted into the crowd and Rance returned.

"They look chummy."

"Shut up."

"Now, now," Rance said. "Maybe she wants to swing."

If not for the caliber of people around them, he would punch his partner in the nose. He wasn't sharing Autumn with any man. Woman either, for that matter. She wasn't built like Lesley Branch, but she was his. "Get lost," he said to Rance, then he strode over and interrupted Autumn's private party. Mister Branch walked away.

"How do you know him?"

"I don't," she said.

"What were you laughing at?"

"He said something funny."

"Well stay away from him."

"You stay away from his wife," she said. "And stop staring at her breasts. You're making a fool of yourself."

They went back and forth that way as the evening wore on, then, when everyone was sufficiently drunk, Tipton called them all to the tree and led them in song. They were a boisterous bunch. More noise than note. Judge Bishop sang the loudest, then left first. One by one they trickled away until it was just Autumn and Tipton and Rance. Tipton felt his phone vibrate in his pocket and slipped into the hallway to check it. It was Benson. Tipton had put a plan into motion a few hours earlier and hoped it had paid off.

"We got Pigg," Benson said, then hung up. Tipton smiled. It was going to be a good Christmas.

* * *

The desk sergeant called Walter shortly before midnight and broke the news.

He rushed upstairs and woke Mildred. "They've impounded my car! Get up!"

Mildred sat up in the dark. "Impounded your car? Why?"

"Cocaine," Walter said. "I'll be lucky to get it back." He flipped on the light. "I'll break his neck when I get my hands on him."

"Is he arrested?"

"Yes, and he'd better hope they keep him," Walter said. "Cocaine. What was he thinking?"

Mildred flew from the bed and snatched her robe from the chair at the dresser and pulled it on, then she went to the closet and started pulling out clothes.

"When the phone rang I thought he was dead," Walter said, watching his wife pulling clothes from the closet then putting them back. "Then when Benson said he was arrested I thought DUI. Never in a million years would I think cocaine. Why are you getting dressed?"

Mildred turned and looked at him as though he had grown a second head. "Your brother's in jail. We have to go get him out."

"We're afoot, remember?"

"Then call a cab."

"I'll be the laughing stock of the town now."

"Stop thinking about yourself and think about your brother."

Walter felt suddenly selfish. "You're right. I'll go down to the station and find out what's going on. They won't release him, you know. Not tonight. I bet Benson's loving this."

"I don't understand you sometimes," Mildred said, jerking yet another blouse from the closet then discarding it. Family was everything to her. His or hers, it didn't matter. Family was family. Perhaps if her side had a Roger, she wouldn't be so quick to judge Walter's lack of enthusiasm.

"I said I'll go," he said. "You stay here with Jackson."

They all went. There had never really been any doubt about it. Mildred wasn't the kind to sit on the sidelines. In less than half an hour a cab dropped them off at the police station. Being mayor gave Walter certain privileges, such as being allowed to talk to his brother before arraignment, but instead of finding him sorrowful and contrite, Walter found him angry. Seething. He demanded Walter fix what Walter didn't break.

"Why should I?"

Roger's hands were cuffed to a bar that ran down the center of the table. Totally unnecessary, Walter knew, but perhaps the indignity might do his brother some good. He looked ready to explode. "How could you do this to me?"

"You're insane," Walter said. "Terminally insane. I should have you transferred to the loony bin."

"Be a man for once, Walter. Don't do this to me."

Walter stood and glared down at his brother, thinking what a fix he'd be in if Roger had left the stuff in his car and he'd been stopped himself. Or Mildred. Did he not care about the people he hurt? He was glad their parents weren't alive to see how far Roger had sunk. Even Peggy's husband wouldn't be able to get him out of this one, not with Benson running the show.

"You've really fixed yourself this time," Walter said. "And me. They'll probably take my car over this."

"I'm facing prison and you're worried about a car?"

"It's not the car's fault," Walter said.

"I swear to you the drugs aren't mine," Roger said. "If they're not yours, then they must belong to Mildred."

Walter lunged forward and slapped his brother hard enough to leave the outline of his fingers on his cheek. "How dare you!" He stomped to the door and pounded, yelling for the guard to let him out. Roger yelled something incoherent at him as the door closed again, then Walter followed the guard up the hallway back to the sergeant's desk. Mildred left her seat against the wall, pulling Jackson in her wake, and met him at the sergeant's desk.

"When do I get my car?"

The sergeant turned up his palms. "Ain't up to me."

"I'm the mayor," Walter said.

"The law's the law."

"Tell your boss the gloves are off."

* * *

Midnight loomed as Rance left the Palo estate. Exactly two minutes and twelve seconds later Chief Benson called Tipton and told him he had bad news. Something had gone wrong with the arrest. His idiot cop had arrested the wrong Pigg. Tipton pulled at his hair and kicked a table and sent half a dozen tiny figurines dancing in the air, bouncing off the wall, then breaking against the floor. Autumn heard the breakage and ran from the kitchen with a dishrag swinging from her hand.

"Get back in the kitchen!"

She stared at the shattered pieces on the floor, then at her husband. "Those belonged to my grandmother!"

"I'll buy your grandmother another set!"

"She's dead!"

Tipton stormed into his study and slammed the door. "How could you be so stupid?"

Benson's ho-hum tone angered him almost as much as his lame excuses. He didn't make the arrest, a uniform did, as though that erased the mistake.

"I want the arresting officer fired," Tipton said.

"Fire your guy," Benson said. "He's the one who planted drugs on the mayor's brother. My cop acted on a tip." He was right, Tipton knew, but it didn't make it any easier to absorb.

"When did you geniuses figure out you had the wrong man?"

139

"My cop recognized that tank the mayor drives and called his sergeant for instructions. The sergeant called me. I told him to play it by the book. That was the plan. Your guy messed up, not mine."

Both men stopped talking. Tipton heard Benson breathing through the phone. They had both said too much already. Tipton took a deep breath to clear his head. Pigg's brother was in jail. Maybe it was something he could use.

"How many people know?"

"The entire department," Benson said. "You can't keep a thing like this quiet."

"Not about the arrest you idiot! About the plan!"

"A concerned citizen called in an anonymous tip as far as anyone knows but us."

Tipton grilled him for details of the aftermath. Benson told him the mayor seemed more upset about the prospect of losing that big tub he drove than he was about his brother going to prison, and the brother was making a lot of noise about the drugs not being his. He said Roger was despondent one minute, then yelling at the top of his lungs the next. Tipton thought about how to play it. Dexter Mann could have a field day with it if he got his head on straight. Pigg didn't need to go to jail for the plan to work, he only needed to resign. Spin it right and people would think the drugs belonged to the mayor since they were found in his car.

"Has he asked for a lawyer yet?"

Benson laughed. "Not that he can prove."

"I want it."

"He ain't got two nickels to rub together."

"Make sure I get called."

"It's not your turn."

"Let me worry about whose turn it is."

"It's your nickel," Benson said.

CHAPTER 15

Walter endured a mixed reaction from the congregation before and after Sunday morning services. It was the averted glances that angered him most. No one was base enough to mention anything directly, not at church. No doubt they talked plenty about it in their cars on the way home, especially after seeing the Piggs leave the way they came — in a cab.

Alderman Kilfiche had called out to Walter as he was getting into the cab and asked why he wasn't driving his city-issued car. He wasn't driving it because he didn't know he was entitled to one. Mildred admitted knowing when he pressed her. Mayor Sherman had driven a city vehicle, as had every other mayor in modern history. Before that, mayors had probably ridden city horses. Her defense was that she knew how Walter was about those things — whatever that meant — so she had decided not to tell him unless he asked.

It seemed a misuse of city funds, but since the city seemed hell-bent on misusing his Town Car, he thought it more than fair.

"Any other perks I'm entitled to?"

She folded her hands in her lap and pretended not to hear him. The cab reeked of vomit, making the ride a most unpleasant experience.

"Well, do I have to call someone in order to get this car?" She told him the key had been in his desk the entire time. He redirected the cabbie to City Hall then paid him the exact fare, no tip. "You should swing by a carwash and pressure wash the back seat," he said. "I think you've ruined my best suit." The cabbie sped away, almost running over Walter's foot.

Mildred pulled Jackson toward the front door. "Would it hurt you to be nice to people?"

"Yes," Walter said, then he unlocked the door and asked her if she would please retrieve the key since she knew where it was.

The car was a white Chevrolet Impala parked in the back lot. Mildred showed him the gas card in the console and told him his PIN. A city car and city gas. No wonder the town had a budget shortfall. As they left the parking lot he asked if the aldermen had city-issued vehicles and was glad to hear they did not. The thought of Brad Stovall knocking around town burning city gas would have been too much for Walter to bear.

"There's a chatter in the left front," he said as they turned into their driveway. "Did you hear it?"

"No."

"Well it's there. More *tap tap tap* than chatter. Like a small hammer against a skillet." He parked in front of their garage and got out and pushed against the top of the wheel with his foot. "I suppose it'll be all right if I'm careful," he said, but Mildred was already mounting the back steps.

When he went inside she asked if he was going to bring Roger home. The question was loaded with suggestion, meaning he *should* bring him home.

"He dug his hole."

"He's your brother."

"He dug his hole, Mildred."

Jackson's attention bounced between them. Mildred told him to go upstairs and change, then she told Walter he was setting a fine example, meaning he was setting a terrible example. Instead of arguing his point, he retreated upstairs and changed out of his suit, then he showered because the suit smelled like the cab. When he came downstairs again, he saw a man standing in the middle of his living room talking to Mildred. Walter recognized him as a detective but they had never officially met. He had short hair and a clean-shaven face and no visible tattoos.

He introduced himself as Detective Gant. Walter's father would have approved of his manly handshake. They chatted briefly about the department, then Walter insisted he sit, then he broke the ice. "How much trouble is my brother in?"

Gant seemed uncomfortable with the question. "It's a serious charge." There was something else he wanted to say, or ask. Something he would have come right out with had Walter not been the mayor.

"Spit it out, detective. This is your visit, not mine."

"He's adamant the drugs aren't his," Gant said.

"I would be too if I were in his shoes," Walter said. He didn't like implicating his brother but the alternative was to implicate himself. "My brother isn't always on speaking terms with the truth, detective. I hate to say it but you should probably check his record."

"I did," the detective said. "No drug arrests."

"There's something else, isn't there?"

"He tested negative for cocaine."

Suddenly Walter felt his neck on the chopping block. "Are you here to test me?"

"Not without your permission."

"Because I'm the mayor?"

"No, because I'd need a court order and I don't have just cause." He shrugged. "Even if you tested positive it wouldn't help your brother. He was driving the car."

"But his lack of priors and the negative test should help him?"

"He's charged with felony possession with intent."

"Intent?"

"To sell."

"A drug dealer? Roger? That's impossible." Walter looked around for Mildred but she had left the room. "My brother can't be a drug dealer. He has no business sense. No determination. He's the most unorganized person you'll ever meet. Besides that, he's lazy." Walter was up now, pacing a narrow strip of hardwood between his recliner and the thrice-broken window. "Who would he sell to here? Mildred and I are the only connections he has in Hayes." He stopped and glared at the detective. "You've got my brother all wrong. He's a ne'er-do-well on his best day, but what you're suggesting would take brains he doesn't have."

"You'd be surprised."

"If not brains then money, and my brother is a perpetual vagrant. He left our sister's house to come here. She lives in Wyoming. Her husband's a lawyer. A good one, too, from what I've heard. They have money, but she wouldn't give it to Roger. Not serious money. He probably pumped her for everything he could get, then he left right before her husband threw him out — he has a knack for knowing exactly when he's about to be asked to leave, you know. I was about to ask him myself, then he suggested we go fishing and he snookered me into loaning him my car. *My* car — the one you have locked up in your impound yard. This thing I have in my garage belongs to the city, and it has a tapping in the left front wheel when I turn."

"For what it's worth, he's got the best lawyer in town," Gant said.

"Roger can't afford a lawyer and if he's got one on credit I can't afford him either so you'd better tell him before he runs up a bill."

"The court appointed Tipton Palo."

The name hit Walter like a backhanded slap. Suddenly everything fell into place. "They're setting me up," he said to no one in particular. He looked at the detective. Studied him. Was he in on it? "I asked you when you came in if you were here to test me."

"I can't force you."

"But you'd like to."

"A charge *has* been made."

"Give me a cup," Walter said. "I need to pee anyway."

"It's a blood test," the detective said. "Completely voluntary. They can do it at the hospital."

Walter rubbed the inside of his left elbow without realizing it, then told the detective to lead the way.

"You'll have to sign a waiver."

"Let's go before I change my mind!"

* * *

Roger Pigg looked a mess. The innocent ones always take it hardest. "Not your first time in jail," Tipton said as he perused the sparse file he had collected on his client, pretending to read from one document then the other, consuming dates and details he could already recite verbatim. "No drug history," he said without looking up.

"That's good right? No drug history? It means I'm innocent?"

Tipton looked up at his client with his best *you poor dumb bastard* look and said, "what it means is you've never been caught ... until now."

"Whose side are you own?"

"I'm being pragmatic ... that means practical ... about it."

"I know what it means," Roger said. Clearly he didn't, or hadn't.

"Of course you do," Tipton said, allowing himself the tiniest of smiles. "I didn't mean to insult you." He examined the paper he had been reading again. "How many times have you been arrested for drunk and disorderly?"

"A few," his client said. "Six. Eight. You've got the report. How many does it say?"

"I count twelve," Tipton said, flipping a page then another as though he were making a tally. "An even dozen. Shoplifting. Trespassing?"

"It was a bar," Roger said forcefully, then his voice tapered off and he looked at his hands folded on the table in front of him. "I forgot I was banned." He looked up and made eye contact. Tipton waited patiently for an elaboration. Pigg's brother was a godsend. Too bad he hadn't stumbled into town before the election instead of after. "I had too much to drink and I slapped this waitress on the ass ... except she wasn't no waitress. It was a simple case of mistaken identity."

Tipton's grin was genuine this time. He'd known a few ass-slappers back in his college days. Rich kids whose parents never taught them to respect women. If one wants to succeed in life he should surround himself with successful people. In college that meant spoiled rich kids with bad manners and a ridiculous appetite for alcohol and sex. "Never mind that," he said. He put his finger on a particular part of the page. "It says here you were arrested for felony evasion six years ago."

"Arrested. Not convicted. The judge laughed it out of court. These friends of mine threw a party, and things got a little too loud for the neighbors so they called the cops. I ran upstairs and crawled under the bed." He chuckled. "But I was too drunk to realize my legs were sticking out."

"That's hardly felony evasion," Tipton said, dubious of the story. He'd known cops to pad charges but there had to be more to the story than hiding under a bed.

"The only reason he arrested me was because I was making pig noises."

He frowned. "Don't say it, I know. A man named Pigg oinking at a cop."

Tipton shuffled the papers back into the folder and closed it then looked his client in the eye. "Of course I'll do everything I can for you."

"What's that supposed to mean?"

"It means I'll talk to the prosecutor and get you the best deal I can."

"Deal? I don't want a deal. I'm innocent."

"Possession with intent to distribute is a serious charge."

"Now you look here! I may drink and get too loud sometimes but I ain't no crack head. I didn't intend to distribute nothing!"

"Regardless what your intentions were, legal intent is based on weight. Now I may be able to get it knocked down to simple possession, but —."

"Simple possession my ass! You get it knocked down to me not knowing a damned thing about what was under the seat of my brother's car!"

Tipton folded his hands atop the tiny file on Roger Pigg and stared into his client's eyes until he had his undivided attention. "The only way that's going to happen is if your brother steps up and claims the drugs."

"They have to be his," Roger said. "It's his car."

"Then he needs to say so. Your brother's the only one who can keep you out of prison."

"Prison? They can't send me to prison for something I didn't do!"

"They can and they will," Tipton said. "Unless your brother comes forward." He paused to let the gravity of the situation sink in. His client's eyes danced side to side and all around as though he were watching some maniacal game of tennis play out on the table between them. "When you take the wheel of a motor vehicle you assume responsibility for that vehicle and everything in it, regardless who holds the title."

"What kind of stupid law is that?"

"The kind of stupid law that's going to send you to prison … unless your brother claims his drugs."

"Walter won't let me go to prison."

Tipton stood. "He's letting you sit in jail."

"Maybe he's telling the truth."

"It's either him or you … unless —."

His client looked up, hopeful. "Unless what?"

"It's a longshot … and I don't think a jury would buy it in a million years … but there's one more person with access to the car."

Roger Pigg struggled to understand, then he did. His eyes flew wide. "Not Mildred."

"It's one or the other," Tipton said. "Or it's you. Somebody has to face the jury."

"Not Mildred," Roger said. "You don't know her. Not Walter either. You don't know any of us."

"Neither will the jury."

A light came on in his client's eyes. An idea. "Maybe somebody planted it." He looked up at Tipton, searching for some hope that his new idea might save him. Tipton had expected it sooner. Had practically led him into it. It needed to be explored so it could be dismissed.

"Who?"

Roger's eyes danced again. The little fan inside his head probably kicked on to cool his brain from so much thinking. "Maybe the cop planted it."

Tipton shook his head. It was a calibrated reaction to an expected charge. The only surprising thing about it was that it took his client so long to think of it. "If that's your defense you're dead. You don't need me. Call the prosecutor and tell her you're ready to do the full stretch." He moved toward the door.

"Hold up. Where are you going?"

"I have other clients, Mister Pigg. Clients who want to help themselves."

"Tell me what to do."

Tipton stepped back to the table but didn't sit. "Get your brother to take responsibility."

Roger dropped his eyes and shook his head. "Walter can't be a drug addict. He's as straight as they come."

"He broke his back didn't he? I've seen the way he walks. Doctors can't hand out opioids like candy the way they used to. I've seen it happen."

"Not my brother."

"Addiction doesn't care how good a person is." He paused again. "Of course there's another possibility."

His client perked up.

"It's not your brother's first bout with addiction. You know about his gambling. No? He didn't tell you?" He had Pigg's attention now. "He got in over his head with a local bookie. The way I heard it he was about to lose everything, then all of a sudden he was solvent again. Desperate people do desperate things."

Tipton left his client to stew. Halfway to his car his phone rang. It was Benson. He wanted to talk. Tipton told him to meet him in the high school parking lot in five minutes. Better they be seen talking in public than on some back street. There were a ton of legitimate reasons a defense attorney might meet with the police chief.

"I don't like where this is headed," Benson said. They were parked door-to-door, windows down, in plain sight for anyone to see. Nothing suspicious about it. "If you'll question the legality of the stop in the arraignment hearing tomorrow, I'll handle the fallout on my end."

"I question the legality of every stop," Tipton said. "That's my job. You know how many times it works? Zero. Judge Bishop says motion denied before I get the words out."

"I wish I knew which prosecutor he'll get," Benson said. "This Lesley

Branch girl seems pretty green. She might be easy to intimidate."

"She's ambitious," Tipton said. "You should've seen the dress she wore to my Christmas party last night. Tits spilling out all over the place. All over the judge, too."

"I wasn't invited."

"Yeah, well, my wife handles the invitations. Lots of people weren't invited. Don't take it personal."

"I had better things to do anyway," the chief said. He was probably used to not being invited to parties. "So how do we get out of this?"

"By seeing it through to the end," Tipton said. "I've got the poor bastard ready to throw his brother under the bus."

"So what if he does? We can't charge the mayor with anything."

"No, but we can drag it out and force him to resign."

"What if he don't?"

"He will," Tipton said. "When I get through with him he'll hunt Brant Haskell down and put a bullet in his head for getting him into this mess." They both laughed. "Now go home and don't drink. When you drink you run your mouth too much." It was a problem he had been meaning to discuss with Stubbs — Benson's mouth.

* * *

Walter's blood test came back negative. Big surprise. His doctor hadn't prescribed anything stronger than ibuprofen in over a year. When the pain in his back flared up, he gritted his teeth and dealt with it.

Mildred begged him not to go back to the jail until he calmed down but she wasn't as persuasive over the phone as she was in person. Besides, he passed right by the jail on the way home from the hospital so why not stop and get the thing over with?

"Visiting hours ended fifteen minutes ago," the desk sergeant told him when he asked to see his brother.

"Is that really what you want to lose your job over?" Walter was in no mood for guff. He was mayor, damn it, and either it stood for something or it didn't. He was tired of getting kicked around.

The sergeant looked perplexed. "Uh, er, I, uh —."

"Stop stammering and take me to my brother."

The man picked up the phone and spoke in a hushed voice, eyeing the mayor with disdain. Perhaps he misinterpreted. Mildred often told him he found insult where none existed. It was her way of sparing his feelings when he'd been insulted.

"Be a few minutes," the sergeant said. He was a short man with a soccer ball head and eyes that looked punched back in their sockets by tiny fists. Childhood must have been hellish for him. "What's so funny?"

"Nothing," Walter said. "Nothing at all."

A few minutes turned into half an hour. Walter sat in an ill-built chair against a dirty wall and tried to ignore the pain in his lower back. The jailer was dragging his feet, probably at the behest of the sergeant. Eventually a door opened and an old man stuck his head out and motioned for Walter to come. They had Roger sitting behind a thick sheet of glass that ran the width of the room. There were five stations on each side of the glass, each with a chair and a telephone handset so visitors and prisoners could talk without shouting.

Walter sat and waited for the jailer to leave the room. The counter in front of him had just enough space to prop his elbows but he didn't touch it. He touched as little as possible because he didn't have his hand sanitizer in his pocket. Across the glass, Roger picked up his telephone handset and put it to his ear. Walter looked at its mate on his piece of counter and imagined all the ears and mouths and hands it had touched. The jailer was gone now and the door behind him was closed. He glanced around for some antiseptic wipes, or any wipe at all. Something. Anything.

Roger tapped on the glass with a finger. *Pick it up* he mouthed. Of course he had to pick it up. Walter was no dummy. He understood the principle of communicating but couldn't they be sanitary about it?

Pick up the damned phone, Roger mouthed, a bit more animated. Perhaps they could mouth their conversation and not go home with hoof and mouth disease, or hepatitis, or the dreaded common cold.

Walter picked up the phone and wiped the cups of both earpiece and mouthpiece on his sleeve while his brother shook his head from beyond the glass like a disappointed father. Roger was in jail for possession of cocaine and it was him passing judgment on Walter. The world had gone upside down.

He raised the handset, careful not to let it touch his skin. "I passed a drug screening this afternoon."

"I passed mine this morning," Roger said. "What of it?"

Walter sighed. Roger was going to be difficult. "This isn't a bottle of paint at Auto Zone. They've got you on a felony charge."

"Damned right it's a felony charge," Roger said. "You need to step up, Walter. For once in your life be a man about something."

Walter squeezed the handset and bumped the earpiece against his ear. Roger stared at him through the glass like some trapped animal snarling at anything that moved, ready to snap at any hand that reached toward him, friend or foe. Walter wanted to be angry, but he remembered how it felt to be desperate. Not that long ago he was in a cage of his own making. A man who traps himself is still trapped. Still cornered. Still helpless to save himself.

"You did this to yourself," Walter said, measuring his words. "Denying it only prolongs the agony. Trust me, I know —."

"You know what? Go ahead, Walter, tell me about how you gambled away everything. Tell me how you were about to lose everything then all of a sudden you were free and clear."

Walter felt suddenly violated. He felt his internal organs squeezing themselves into tiny balls. A million thoughts hit his brain at once like pellets from a scattergun.

"What's the matter? Didn't think I knew about that?"

"How — who —?"

"Does Mildred know you're selling drugs to pay off your bookie?" Roger's face looked evil through the glass now. Before his very eyes his brother had transformed himself into a monster. A madman. He had lost his soul.

"Damn you," Walter said. "Damn you to hell!"

"Sure, Walter, damn me. Why not damn me? I'm the Pigg who never amounted to anything. Call Peggy and Doris and Betty and tell them what a rotten snake I am. Tell them how I borrowed your car and put cocaine under the seat then tried to frame you. Tell them! They'll probably believe you. Peggy will. And Doris. They think you're really something, did you know that? They're proud of you, Walter. You're their hero." He spat a noise that sounded like a laugh wrapped in barbed wire. "Not Betty though. Betty thinks you're a complete ass. Know what she told me? She told me Walter thinks he's all high and mighty but he ain't no better than the rest of us. That's what she told me, Walter. You ain't no better than the rest of us."

"I never —."

"Sure you did. You still do. Mister Mayor. Your Honor."

"That's not true. Nothing you said it true."

"Of course not," Roger said. "I'm a liar. Roger Pigg the liar. Roger Pigg the bum. Who's that on the phone, Peggy? Roger? How much money does he need this time?"

"Stop feeling sorry for yourself and —."

"And what? Stop telling the truth before they find you out?"

Walter studied him through the glass, trying to make sense of his rambling tirade. How could one brother turn on another and try to ruin him with lies? How could he say something so vile knowing it was a lie? Knowing the damage his lie was doing? Something clicked. A veil lifted and suddenly Walter understood.

"He's framing me."

Roger stared back with his mouth agape.

"It's clear to me now," Walter said. "Of course you don't know anything about the drugs because they're not yours. I don't know anything about them because they're not mine. Neither of us know anything so we blame each other. I know they don't belong to me so they must be yours. You know they don't belong to you so they must be mine." Roger looked as dumbstruck as a first-grader staring at algebra. He didn't even understand enough to be curious. "The drugs were planted."

"I thought so too," Roger said, "but my lawyer shot it down."

"Your lawyer! Don't you know who he is?"

"The best in town so I'm told. Everybody says I got lucky."

"Do you feel lucky?"

"No, but that's not his fault."

"Do you think the man I defeated for mayor just happened to draw your case?"

Roger shrugged. "Maybe not, but I'm glad he did. Everybody says —."

"Everybody who?"

"Everybody," Roger said. "The detectives, the jailers, the inmates. Everybody but you."

"And he's happy to take your case for free," Walter said. More of the picture was becoming clear, though he didn't yet understand how the dots connected.

"He said it landed on him. He had no choice."

"Nonsense. I'm no lawyer but all he has to do is say he can't represent you because he ran against me in the election. It's an ethical conflict."

"Well he seems to be doing his best," Roger said. "I told him maybe the cop planted the drugs and he almost walked out on me. He said if I tell the jury that they'll hang me, and he's right. How many traffic tickets did you ever get out of by saying the cop was wrong?"

"I've never had a traffic ticket," Walter said. "If you'd obey the posted speed limits you wouldn't either."

The conversation was going nowhere and they only had a few minutes. Walter asked him to recount exactly what happened, leaving nothing out. Even the smallest detail might be important. Of course Roger balked. Roger, after all, was Roger. He needed a prod.

"The detective said they received an anonymous call," Walter said. "You were swerving all over the road."

"That's a damned lie. I wasn't swerving over nothing."

"You had just left a bar."

"Pool hall."

"You'd been drinking."

"I wasn't swerving. If I was drunk why didn't they charge me with DUI?"

"They found the drugs under the seat and didn't need to."

"Ha! When has a cop ever not needed to charge something? They tack on every charge they can think of. They make stuff up. If that tank of yours had had a broken taillight I'd be charged with that too."

He was beginning to get the picture — Roger. Some people can't be explained to, they must be shown, and Roger was one of those people. Walter watched as the light came on in his brother's head. His eyes brightened. The corners of his mouth ticked upward.

"That cop stopped me for no reason at all. He —."

"Received an anonymous tip," Walter said.

"He must be a magician. I watched him walk right up to your car and pull out the drugs."

"Was it the first place he looked?"

"No, he made a show of looking everywhere but under the seat. He looked there last."

"Did you give him permission to search the car?"

"Sure I did. I had nothing to hide."

"Where were you standing?"

"Against the front of his car. He made me walk heel-to-toe and touch the tip of my nose with my finger and count backwards from ten. I guess it pissed him off that I did it. I've passed every field sobriety test ever concocted, drunk *and* sober."

"I don't think the officer planted the drugs," Walter said. It was a conclusion he had just reached. Cops weren't magicians, nor did they have any reason to frame Roger.

"But you just said —."

"I said they were planted."

"Who then?"

"The same person who placed the anonymous call. A lackey whose job it was to frame me."

"Nah, I locked the car. Nobody could've done it but that cop."

"Have you ever locked your keys in your car?"

"Sure. Plenty of times."

"And who do you call to unlock it?"

"Nobody. I get a coat hanger and do it myself."

"But suppose you didn't know how to do it yourself? Who would you call?"

"A cop?"

"No," Walter said. "A wrecker service."

"I don't want it towed, I want it unlocked."

"Haven't you ever heard of a slim jim?"

Roger's face lit up again. "Yeah, I forgot. I saw a guy boost a car using one of those things one time."

Walter cautioned his brother not to confess to any new crimes. They were, after all, being recorded. Listened to, at least.

"I think you should get another lawyer," Walter said. "The one you have now will do anything to embarrass me."

"I'm sitting in jail and you're worried about being embarrassed."

"Stop being childish," Walter said. "That's not what I meant and you know it."

The door opened behind Walter and the jailer told him his time was up.

"One more minute," Walter said.

"Thirty seconds and that's it," the man said. Walter waited for the door to close.

"Sit tight and I'll see what I can do."

"What choice do I have?"

"I'll talk to the detective. Maybe there's something he can do."

"Can't you give me a pardon or something?"

"I'm the mayor, not the governor. Besides, you haven't been convicted yet. Sit tight and be careful what you tell that scoundrel you call a lawyer."

CHAPTER 16

Detective Gant stopped by Walter's office first thing Monday morning and joined him in a closed-door meeting. Walter had telephoned him Sunday after leaving the jail and pitched his theory that the drugs were planted. Gant was skeptical, but he promised to look into it, and look into it he had. They dusted Walter's car for prints and hit pay dirt on the floorboard just inches from where Officer Alexander Kirkwood found the drugs. Gant had an eager look on his face, as though he couldn't wait for Walter to ask him who the print belonged to, so he asked.

"Does the name Corey Pickle mean anything to you?"

Walter almost came out of his chair. Corey Pickle worked for Stubbs. He was the lowlife who slaughtered the horse and hung its head on Walter's back porch. If his fingerprint was inside Walter's car then there could be no doubt about Stubbs. "Does this mean my brother goes free?"

"That's up to the DA," Gant said. "I notified his office. I bumped into Tipton Palo and told him, too." He looked a bit sheepish. "I'm probably risking my job not running it by my boss first."

"Let me worry about your boss," Walter said.

"I put out a BOLO on Pickle. That means —."

"Be on the lookout," Walter said. "I'm familiar with the term. I'm also familiar with Perry Stubbs. You might consider dragging all the local lakes."

Gant stood to leave, then he hesitated. Something else was on his mind. Something he wanted to say but didn't know if he should. It might be inside information and it might be criticism of the way Walter was doing his job. The only way to know was to ask, so Walter did.

The detective hesitated. "He's a good chief," he said. "Despite what you might think."

"Despite what I might know firsthand?" He eyed the detective, consuming his discomfort. The young man's face brightened but didn't flush. For the most part he maintained his composure, though Walter felt certain he would like very much to retract his statement. "Don't worry, detective, I won't hold your loyalty against you."

"I mean no disrespect."

"Nor do I," Walter said. He admired the young detective for his loyalty, misplaced as it might be, and he had lived long enough to understand that no man is all good or all bad. People are complex organisms capable of doing good with one hand and bad with the other. In fact, it's expected of them. Leaders especially. Every decision that helps one group hurts another. Giving requires taking. Chief Benson was no exception. "Tell me … what do the men think of me?"

"I can't speak for everyone."

"Every time I walk into your station I feel daggers in my back."

"Not from me."

"No, not from you. From your desk sergeant, though. And most of the other uniforms I walk past."

"We rally around our own."

"How old are you, detective?"

"Thirty-seven."

Walter rubbed his chin, making a show of thinking through a complex problem he had already solved. "Might be a hard sell to the board, but there's a lot to be said for youth."

"Sir?"

"Never mind," Walter said. "We'll talk about it more when the time comes."

* * *

Roger Pigg sat beside his lawyer at the defendant's table bumping the tips of his fingers together, nervous as a whore in church. Every few seconds he glanced back over his shoulder toward the door, searching for the brother who wouldn't come. Tipton had arranged for the mayor to miss the hearing. It was nine fifteen and Tipton had just made a motion asking the judge to dismiss the case with prejudice. Judge Bishop dismissed the motion instead, as Tipton had known he would, with a warning that it was Christmas Eve and he had grandchildren to get home to.

"My client is guilty of borrowing his brother's car," Tipton said. "Nothing more."

"Save it for the trial," the judge said.

His defendant pled not guilty when the proper time came, then Tipton reminded the judge that it was Christmas and his client had no criminal record. He wanted his client in jail but he couldn't make it obvious. A certain effort was expected of him.

Lesley Branch was the prosecutor. She looked nothing like the woman she had been at Tipton's party. She wore dark pants and a matching jacket and a white blouse buttoned to the throat. Her hair was twisted into a bun and pinned at the top like a librarian. Judge Bishop couldn't keep his eyes off of her. "The state has no objections," she said, forcing Tipton to smile while the judge gaveled the matter closed.

Tipton sidled up to her as she arranged her papers for the next case. "Since when does the state let drug dealers walk without bail?"

"You made the motion," she said, flashing white teeth with a gap where it mattered most. Braces would have fixed the defect, meaning she probably came from a poor background. Useful information should he ever need to bribe someone in the DA's office.

"Why'd you do it?"

"To see the look on your face," she said. "Why didn't you mention the fingerprint they found this morning?"

"I don't like firing all my ammo so early in the game."

"He would've thrown it out, you know." she said, tossing her eyes toward the bench.

"You could've withdrawn the charges."

"You'll find I don't give up so easily, counselor."

"Then why didn't you object to no bail?"

She smiled again. "It's Christmas."

Judge Bishop told them to hurry it up so he could hear the next case. Roger Pigg still sat at the defense table like a schoolboy waiting for the bell to ring.

"Go home to your brother," Tipton said. "You're free."

* * *

Walter summoned the aldermen, leaving it to Mildred to set the schedule. He thought it best to make his pitch one-on-one instead of to the group. Brad Stovall came first. Win him over and Frick and Frack would come along for the ride.

"What's so urgent that it can't wait until after Christmas?"

"Sit down," Walter said. Stovall was a bully and easy to read. Beg for mercy and you get stepped on, but punch a bully in the nose and you've got his attention. Sometimes he runs, sometimes he punches back. Stovall was much too big to punch in the nose. "I'll be straight with you, Brad. I don't like you one bit more than you like me, but we're stuck together until one of us leaves office, and I don't plan on going anywhere for two years, do you?"

"Get to it."

"I mean to rid this town of bookmaking," Walter said. "One way or another I'll do it."

Stovall reared his chair back on its hind legs. "What's that got to do with me?"

"It's got plenty to do with you," Walter said. "And don't break my furniture!" He heard the front legs bump the floor. "Either you support law and order or you don't."

155

Stovall grunted. "Stop trying to drag the board into your personal vendetta. Nobody forced you to gamble." He grinned. "Yeah, I know all about it."

"Why did you become an alderman, Brad? Can I call you Brad?"

"You can call me the king of France if you want to, but I don't have to sit here and answer your questions."

"You don't know why you became an alderman?"

"Yeah, I know, but I don't have to tell you."

"What do you care about? What pushes your buttons?"

"If you're trying to make a deal with me you're lousy at it."

"Remember what we talked about a couple weeks ago? The gravel contracts with the county? I thought we had a deal then you stabbed me in the back?"

"That was just politics," Stovall said. "You took it personal."

Walter didn't believe a word Stovall said, but he needed his vote so he let him frame the story to his liking. "Don't you want more business with the county?"

Stovall stopped grinning. "You asked me what I care about. Well I'll tell you. I care about me. I care about Stovall Trucking. I became an alderman to line my pockets. Does that surprise you?"

"Why should it?"

"I don't care about Stubbs or Benson."

"Then why protect them?"

"Sweeten the deal," Stovall said. "Make it worth my while."

"You make a motion to even out the disbursements to the county districts and I'll support it, and I'll personally talk to each of the supervisors on your behalf and tell them it was your idea."

"And you'll steer city contracts to me?"

"No, but I'll recommend," Walter said. "I won't break the law."

Stovall rolled his eyes toward the ceiling, thinking, or giving the impression of trying to think. Walter felt his insides crawl at the prospect of striking a deal with Stovall. He hated bullies, but dealing with him was a necessary evil. Forgivable only if it moved the needle against Stubbs.

"It'll be messy," Stovall said. "Benson won't go easy." He drummed his fingers on his knee. "I'm only one vote."

"You're three votes."

Stovall flashed a knowing grin. Walter didn't know what power he had over Townsend and Toms, but he had it, and if he agreed to Benson's ouster and kept his word, the chief was as good as gone. "I'll only do this if it's unanimous," he said. Walter buzzed Mildred and asked her to summon the other aldermen immediately. When they came, Walter stated his case plainly.

"The police chief is protecting Perry Stubbs," he said, looking each man in the eye one after another. "Instead of being a cop and helping clean up this town, he's helping the man most responsible for corrupting it. If we sit on our hands and do nothing, we're complicit."

Kilfiche, the judge in him coming out, asked Walter what proof he had to back up his charge. Walter related the conversation he had with the chief a month previous, before the board meeting where the board rejected his motion to remove him. The conversation in which the Chief of Police, in his official capacity, told the mayor he was too afraid of Perry Stubbs to bring him to justice.

"A lot of people are afraid of him," Kilfiche said.

"Imagine how much more afraid of him they'll be when they find out the city's top cop is scared of him too," Walter said. "And mark my words, every man, woman, and child in Hayes will know their chief is a coward if you fight me on this."

Kilfiche recoiled. "Like him or not his record of service is impeccable."

"Only because you've taken him at face value," Walter said. "I've offered him every opportunity to go quietly and he laughed in my face." He took a breath to let his words soak. "This is important to me, gentlemen, and if you can't support me on it then you'll force me to take whatever action I can on my own."

"That's not how government works," Kilfiche said. His face glowed red and his lower left eyelid quivered. "We decide issues as a group, and we abide by those decisions. We don't pout when a vote doesn't go our way."

"I called this meeting to do exactly that," Walter said. "To decide as a group."

"Unless we don't decide your way," Wayne Toms said.

"I won't support it," Kilfiche said.

"It's immoral," Sharp said.

"Sounds like we're done here," Lyle Townsend said. He shot to his feet. Wayne Toms followed suit.

Stovall glared at his two lackeys. "Sit down." He waited until they obeyed, then he looked each alderman in the eye one at a time. "Now maybe what the mayor said makes sense."

Wayne Toms opened his mouth but couldn't speak.

Townsend spoke for him. "What's got into you, Brad?"

"He's joking," Kilfiche said. "Cut it out, Stovall. You'll have the mayor thinking this hair-brained idea of his has merit."

"Maybe it does have merit," Stovall said. "I'm not saying it does or it doesn't, but I'm not joking. Let's hear him out."

"There's nothing more to be said," Sharp said. "You can't fire a man with Benson's record without good reason."

"The reason is more than good," Walter said, bolstered by Stovall's coming around. "Benson told me himself he won't lift a finger against Perry Stubbs. What about that don't you understand?"

"Maybe he doesn't have any proof of wrongdoing," Kilfiche said.

Walter looked the judge in the eyes and held his fire. It was a trick he had learned from an old engineer back when he was just coming up at H&G. Stare a man in the eyes and hold him. Make him second-guess himself before you speak. Take your time. The longer the better. "You talk about proof as though it trumps everything. What about common sense? What about when everybody who knows anything at all knows a thing is rotten?"

"Thinking something isn't the same as knowing it," the judge said.

"Do you have any doubt in your mind that Perry Stubbs is a low down rotten snake?"

"That doesn't mean a thing in a court of law."

"We're not in a court of law," Walter said. "You're not a judge anymore and this isn't a trial. We're politicians, and the only thing it takes to make a decision is all of us agreeing on it."

"But we don't agree," Toms said.

"Shut up, Wayne," Stovall said. "The mayor's right. I'm just a dumb ole dirt hauler and I know Stubbs is a snake. Everybody in town knows it."

"But we're not voting on Stubbs," the judge said. "We're voting on our police chief, and his record as a law enforcement officer is ——."

"Impeccable," Walter said. "We know. You'll find I'm not one to care much how long a man has held a position he's no longer fit to hold. A police chief who turns a blind eye to corruption is a blight on the community, and if we support him then we're no better than he is. No better than Stubbs."

The judge's hands trembled as he tried to suppress his rage.

"You of all people surprise me," Walter told him. "You're a judge. You swore an oath to uphold justice, yet here you sit defending injustice."

"You have no right to talk to me this way!"

"He has every right," Stovall said. "Anybody with half a brain knows Benson's been phoning it in for a long time now. Let's sack him and pick somebody new."

Townsend scoffed. "The man's been decorated for bravery." He looked at the judge for support. "You remember, Judge, it was back when ——."

"Back when doesn't matter," Walter said. "This is now. I used to have a peaceful job as an engineer but now I've got a title around my neck and the people of this town deserve to be protected."

"You've let that title go to your head," Toms said.

"Now everybody just calm down," Sharp said. "Fighting amongst ourselves doesn't solve anything."

Walter turned his attention to the pastor. "You've been quiet, Brother Sharp. What do you think of Stubbs?"

"The man donated an organ to my church last year."

Stovall and Toms laughed.

"I'm not saying that affects my decision, mind you."

"In my business we call that tainting the jury, preacher" Kilfiche said, more calm than he had been a moment previous. He sighed. "Maybe I'm too old for this. I see a man who has dedicated his life to this town and, well, maybe I'm too old."

"No one doubts your sincerity," Walter said.

"I hope it's a fine piano," Stovall said to Sharp. "Sounds like it cost you plenty."

Sharp's eyes pierced the group. "It wasn't like that. I went to his pawnshop because one of my members said he had a Baldwin. While I was haggling over the price with the front man, Stubbs came out of the back and donated it."

"So now you owe him," Walter said. "The question is, how much are you willing to pay?"

"I led the entire congregation in prayer for him," Sharp said. "In my book that makes us even."

Walter decided it was time to move. "Are we in agreement or not?" He looked at each of them in turn. Stovall was grinning like a Cheshire cat. Wayne and Toms kept looking at Stovall then at each other, confused. Pastor Sharp dropped his eyes and refused to look up. Kilfiche looked angry.

"I say we can his ass," Stovall said. "But only if it's unanimous."

"I'll vote with the board," Sharp said.

All eyes turned to the judge. "Once upon a time Benson was a fine police chief."

"Once upon a time I wore diapers and shit myself," Stovall said. "Which way are you voting? I've got a business to get back to."

"Sounds like the jury has spoken," the judge said. "But only if we give him the chance to resign with dignity."

Walter felt suddenly generous. "We'll keep this to ourselves until after Christmas."

* * *

Every time Tipton entered the chief's office he felt sorry for the man. No family pictures on the walls. No paintings. Nothing to indicate any cultural maturity whatsoever. The most prominent display was a plaque behind his desk dated 2008 recognizing him for ten years of service. Ten years, and all he had to show for it was a beat up metal desk and a chair that looked like a rat's chew toy. The chair for visitors had an arm missing. The tile on the floor was scuffed and dull. Worse than the furnishings was the dank smell of a man with chronic gas.

"Why don't you hire somebody to clean this place up?"

Benson jumped at the sound of Tipton's voice. "Why don't you knock before you come in a man's office?"

Tipton stepped all the way in but didn't sit, nor did he close the door. The stench overpowered the risk of being overheard. "Why so jumpy?" He leaned forward for a peek at the chief's computer screen but Benson poked a button and turned it off. "I've got a job for you," Tipton said. The place stunk worse than the men's room at the courthouse. He made a show of sniffing the air. "What the hell is that smell?"

"Pinto beans and fried ham," Benson said. His chair popped and groaned as he leaned back. "You've got some nerve coming in here."

The chief's mood caught Tipton off guard. He glanced back to make sure they weren't being listened to. "What's got you in such a pissy mood?"

"You're supposed to have my back," Benson said. He was almost snarling. His top lip quivered and curled. "I've got a good mind to tell everything. How would that suit you?"

It didn't suit Tipton at all, not even as a joke, which he felt certain it wasn't. Whatever had happened had Benson mad enough to be dangerous. Tipton forgot about his expensive suit and sat in the filthy chair and leaned forward so they could talk without being loud. "Lower your voice," he said, glancing back again. With the door open anyone could walk by. On second thought, he got up and closed it then sat again. "Whatever it is that's got you stirred up, I promise I don't know anything about it."

"The hell you don't," Benson said. "You told me you had Stovall in your pocket. Don't worry, you said. Pigg can't do nothing without the board. Well he's done something."

Getting the story was like pulling teeth. Wayne Toms couldn't wait to call Benson and tell him the board had decided to can him after Christmas. He wasn't supposed to know yet but he knew.

"And it was Brad Stovall who put the nails in my coffin."

Tipton couldn't believe what he was hearing. There had to be some kind of mistake. "I'll get to the bottom of this," he said. "Don't worry, you're not going anywhere."

Benson pulled open his upper left drawer and took out a small cedar box and placed it on his desk. It had a fragile brass hasp and a Confederate battle flag emblazoned on its lid. "My sister brought me this from a gift shop in Gatlinburg several years ago," he said. "It's full of business cards now. All these years I've kept it hidden inside this drawer because I was afraid it might offend somebody." He fingered the hasp and flipped open the lid, then he reached in and pulled out an ink pen and read the lettering up its length. "Cardinal Bonding Service. They went belly up year before last." He let the pen fall from his fingers. "Their logo was a red bird flying out of a cage. Ninety percent of those birds ended up right back in that cage because they don't know how to be free. So many people don't know how to be free. Did you know that?" Melancholy replaced the anger in his eyes. "Society keeps throwing the same people in jail over and over and can't figure out why they don't learn, and those same people keep going back wondering why society won't teach them."

Tipton wanted to slap the box off the desk and tell Benson to get hold of himself. The man was a ticking time bomb. He had seen enough clients self-destruct to recognize the signs.

Benson's focus consumed the box. "She was standing there in that gift shop and she saw this box and something made her think of me." A tear glistened in the corner of his right eye.

"Autumn buys souvenirs all the time," Tipton said. "For everyone she knows. It's just a damned box."

"I never married. Did you know that? Most people assume I married and divorced, but I never found a woman who'd have me."

"You're working yourself up over nothing. Stovall's a blowhard. He knew you'd tell me and now he's waiting for me to make him a better offer."

Benson glanced up, hopeful for an instant then sad again. "It's too late for better offers. I wouldn't stay on now if they begged me."

"Sure you would."

"No, I'm finished."

Tipton knew what he had to do.

* * *

Roger spent the afternoon and most of the evening pouting, not coming out of the guest bedroom except to eat, and even then he refused to speak. Mildred made his favorite meal — meatloaf — but he barely touched it. At first Walter tried to console him, but he grew quickly tired of the charade and ended up lecturing Roger on personal responsibility. The lecture targeted Roger's life in general more so than the drug arrest. More shotgun than rifle. Walter stood at the mouth of the guest bedroom with his brother lying on the still-made bed with his hands behind his head and his elbows in the air, staring at the ceiling, not speaking a single word in his own defense.

Frustrating.

Twice Mildred had come up from behind to intervene. Twice Walter had shooed her away. Now was not the time for mollycoddling. Roger had dodged a bullet, yet there he was still pouting because Walter hadn't believed him. Well, Roger hadn't believed Walter either. Roger had been caught with drugs but it was Walter's car. Roger knew they weren't his and so did Walter. Logic dictated that each man think the other guilty. Walter bore his brother no ill will yet there lay Roger, sullen, refusing to interact, giving Walter the silent treatment as though they were married.

Mildred touched Walter between the shoulder blades. In her kind and gentle way she was telling him to let his brother be. Walter wasn't ready to walk away, but he knew from experience that kind and gentle had an expiration date with Mildred. She had other emotions at her disposal.

Walter turned and frowned at the fatigue in her face. The last few days had been hard on her, but it was more than that. They were deep into his second month as mayor and the job had put them both through the wringer.

"Let him sleep. He'll feel better in the morning. We all will." She turned and took a step toward the living room with Walter obediently in tow.

"You're really letting this happen?" Roger's voice rang out loud and clear, like the first strike of a church bell on a Sunday morning, as though he had saved his strength all afternoon and evening for just that moment.

Mildred's face sagged. Walter's blood gushed hot. Roger reminded him of a spoiled child. Their parents hadn't spoiled them. It wasn't their fault. Roger Pigg had taken his spoiling from adulthood. Demanded it. Peggy was as much to blame as anyone. Lovable Peggy, the sister who couldn't say no.

Walter spun, feeling the skin stretch tight across his face. A flood of vulgarities hit his brain and almost tumbled out of his mouth with Mildred only a few feet behind him. Curseful thoughts were new to Walter. Recent. They flew in the face of his upbringing and violated the basic tenets of his life. Mildred would have fainted had they slipped out. Walter might have fainted, too, because thinking them and realizing how easy it would have been to say them made him weak in the knees. *What have I become*, he thought to himself as he stood prepared to unleash justice onto his brother. An overwhelming guilt flushed the anger from his system. In two seconds flat he had gone from frustrated to livid then back again. He stopped two feet from the foot of the bed and stared down at Roger. What would Cecil do? How would their father handle the situation? Cecil Pigg had made being a man look easy. Natural. He wore masculinity like a second skin. "What exactly is it you want from me?"

"I want you to fix your damned mess!"

"Watch your language in my house!" He felt the familiar hand on his back again.

Roger frowned. For a moment Walter thought he might cry. "I'm sorry. It's just that I don't understand why you're letting this happen."

"Walter isn't letting anything happen," Mildred said. "He's done everything he can to help you."

"Please, Mildred," Walter said. "Let me talk to him alone."

"I'll go check on Jackson," she said. "But if I hear yelling I'm coming back with a switch."

Roger smiled, then after she left he told Walter how lucky he was to have her. It was a kind thing to say, but unnecessary. Walter didn't need reminding. On his list of ten best things that had ever happened to him, she comprised the first eight.

"I'm sorry you got caught up in all this," Walter said, "but there's nothing else to fix. It's Christmas Eve. Try to forget about it."

"Forget about it? I'm going to prison and you want me to forget about it?"

Walter was confused. Had Palo not told him about the fingerprint? "You're free," he said. "It's over."

"Nothing's over, Walter. I'm free on my own recognizance because my attorney sweet talked the DA."

"You're free because the detective found evidence to clear you. At my insistence, not that it matters. I asked him to check my car for fingerprints and he did."

"I don't know anything about any fingerprints."

"Then you need a new lawyer. I keep telling you that but you won't listen. He's helping frame you, can't you see that?"

"You're delirious," Roger said. "Nobody said anything in court today about any new evidence."

"Corey Pickle," Walter said. "He's a knee-breaker for Perry Stubbs. They found his fingerprint inches from where they found the drugs. It's over."

Roger sat up in bed. "That son of a bitch."

"And the reason I wasn't in court is because someone from Palo's office called my office and said the hearing had been postponed."

Tears crept into Roger's eyes. "Is it really over?"

"Yes," Walter said. "It's really over."

CHAPTER 17

Jackson tore upstairs and flew into his grandparents' room bursting with excitement because Santa had left a slew of presents underneath the tree. So many presents that they had spilled out onto the floor almost all the way to the coffee table. Walter feared the boy's eyes might burst from their sockets if they didn't get out of bed and follow him downstairs. Halfway down he saw the sea of red and green below and knew Mildred had blown through their Christmas budget like a runaway train. He didn't mind as much as he pretended to. Certain behavior was expected of him.

Roger ambled from the hallway, rubbing at his eyes and yawning. He stopped when he saw the pile of presents, then he looked at Walter and Mildred with a sheepish grin. "I didn't have a chance to go shopping." Big surprise. Mildred told him they didn't expect anything, which was the understatement of the year, then she rummaged the pile and came out with a semi-flat package for him. It was a flannel shirt that had probably been meant for Walter but got repurposed by Mildred at the last minute. Walter didn't mind. Not having to pretend to like red flannel was present enough for him.

As they sat lined across the sofa like three crows on a wire, watching Jackson rip into one present after another with undiminished enthusiasm, Walter remarked aloud that they hadn't suffered a single broken window in the past two years. The thought had come to him because the tree was in front of the window that had been broken three times in three months.

"You scared the poor little things to death," Mildred said. "You should've seen how your brother tormented those little boys," she said to Roger.

"I broke a window once," Roger said. "Dad whipped me good, then made me work it off with extra chores."

"He only threatened to whip you," Walter said. "And you never did half your chores anyway."

"It taught me a lesson though."

Walter rolled his eyes at Mildred and she slapped him on the leg. Jackson held up a video game and said it was exactly the one he had asked for, then he discarded it into the already-opened pile and grabbed another present.

"Just what a boy his age needs," Walter said. "Another reason to stay inside on a sunny day."

"Well it's not sunny today," Mildred said. "It's supposed to snow."

"Supposed to snow my foot," Walter said. The only time it snowed in Mississippi was when the meteorologists *didn't* predict it.

"You wouldn't want snow if you had it all the time," Roger said.

Walter scoffed. "I have coffee every morning and I still want it."

"Yeah, but you've never had to shovel coffee out of your driveway so you could go to work."

Walter laughed, not at the thought of shoveling snow but at the thought of Roger going to work. Mildred went to the kitchen and made coffee for the adults and cocoa for Jackson. After a few sips they all joined hands and said a prayer for Amy. Jackson's eyes teared up but he didn't cry. Mildred told him it was all right to cry if he wanted to. Walter felt his own eyes tearing up but he concealed it with a fake cough.

After Jackson had blown through his pile, Walter gave Mildred a pair of earrings and a sweater. She gave him pants and a coat. When you reach a certain age, gifts should be practical.

Roger promised to carve something for the boy if he could find a stick of cedar. "How about a whistle," he asked his nephew. Jackson said a whistle would be fine.

"Since when do you know how to carve a whistle?"

"Walter!"

"I can do a lot of things," Roger said. "When I put my mind to it."

Walter's phone rang in his pocket. Probably Peggy calling to wish them a Merry Christmas, he said aloud, but it wasn't. It was Detective Gant, and he told Walter that Chief Benson was dead.

* * *

Tipton gave Autumn a diamond bracelet and she gave him a set of golf clubs, then his phone rang.

"It's done."

He felt sick to his stomach. Autumn stopped admiring her new bracelet and asked him what was wrong. Nothing and everything, he wanted to say. He looked at the backs of his hands, then turned them over and looked at the palms. They were covered in blood. Invisible to the naked eye, but covered nonetheless. Dripping.

"Tipton?"

"The police chief shot himself."

Autumn's hand flew to her mouth and she gasped. "Is he dead?"

"Yeah," Tipton said, barely audible. When he rehearsed his reaction in his head it had gone a lot smoother. Autumn was a smart girl and she would eventually ask questions, like who called, and why didn't you ask any questions? Why didn't you say anything at all? Who would call and tell you a thing like that then hang up?

She looked as though she might cry but didn't. Benson was nobody to her. Sure, she had let him into the house a few times but they never invited him to any of their parties. As far as he knew they had never spoken beyond hello and goodbye. Maybe not even goodbye because Tipton always sent her away when he came.

Tipton stood. "I can't believe it," he said. "I talked to him yesterday and he seemed fine." What was he doing? What a stupid thing to say. "I mean … he was upset." Think, man, think! What was he upset about? "Pigg … the mayor."

Autumn flew from the sofa and took his arm and told him he should sit down. "You're pale."

He felt pale. No, not pale, green. And exhausted. He had hardly slept a wink last night anticipating the call. Wishing for it one minute then dreading it the next. Stubbs shouldn't have hung up the way he did. He shouldn't have called at all. Sooner or later Autumn would ask who called. She wasn't stupid. The police might ask who called, too, then the million-dollar question would be *why*? What connection did he have with Stubbs, and how did Stubbs know before they did?

"We should've invited him to our party," Autumn said. "He was all alone and didn't have anyone."

"What are you saying?"

"Sit down," she said, tugging at his arm until he sat. "You look like you've seen a ghost. It's horrible. You knew him pretty well, didn't you?"

"What? No, I —."

"Working together on cases," she said. "On opposite sides, I mean, but still, you knew him. I wish we had invited him."

Tipton felt faint. He had never killed a man before. If they found him out it would destroy his parents. Everything he had built would go down the drain. He wanted to call Stubbs back and demand details. No, the less he knew the better. He knew too much already. "Surely you're not blaming me."

"Of course I'm not blaming you," she said. "Why would you say that?"

"So what if we didn't invite him to our parties? It's not like we were friends. I barely knew the man."

"But he was here the other night and —."

"Stop it!" He shot to his feet again. What was she trying to do to him? Thoughts swirled like a hurricane inside his head. Say one wrong thing and it's over. He needed a drink. "Fix me a drink," he said. "Make it anything. I don't care."

"Do you think you should —?"

"Now!"

She rushed into his study and came back with half a tumbler of scotch. He snatched it from her hand and gulped it down. The alcohol hit his stomach like a tonic. "Pigg drove him to it," he said. "He put the gun in his hand." He put the tumbler to his lips again then realized it was empty. "The poor bastard."

"Lots of people kill themselves on Christmas," she said. "It's a depressing time of year if you're alone. It's nobody's fault."

"It's Pigg's fault! Didn't I just tell you that?"

"Well you don't have to snap at me," she said, then she started crying and rushed upstairs. Good, he needed time to think. To clear his head.

He went into his study and poured more scotch. Suppose Stubbs made a mistake? Suppose he left evidence behind? Hayes didn't have a crime lab, but the state did, and a dead police chief would trigger a state investigation. They probably handle enough suicides to know when it's staged. At least he had been home all night with his wife. Not the best alibi in the world but better than not having one at all. Stubbs had promised to handle it personally. Corey Pickle had bungled his last two jobs.

No details. That was their deal. The less Tipton knew the better, not that anyone ever had any reason to suspect him. He had gone to bat for Benson. If they suspected anyone it would be Pigg. Dexter Mann could push that angle in the paper.

It dawned on him to call Rance. They were partners and it was the sensible thing to do. Their back and forth was natural because Rance truly was surprised. His partner asked the kind of questions he should have asked Stubbs. No one would know unless they had Stubbs under surveillance, but with him anything was possible. How long before someone listened to their one-sentence exchange and put two and two together? It's done? What kind of thing was that to say? If the feds had Stubbs under surveillance he was screwed.

* * *

The last thing Walter expected to be doing on Christmas Day was standing behind a podium outside the police station fielding questions from the press. It was noon, and he and Mildred had hurried their grandson through the opening of gifts so Walter could attend to the duties of his office before someone else stepped in to usurp his authority. That someone, according to a frantic phone call from Brant Haskell, was Assistant Chief Ball, who according to a source Haskell had inside the police department, had called the presser with the intention of making an official statement himself. Ball put Walter in mind of a whippet reared on its hind legs. He was thin and balding and wore too much of something in his hair that gave it an unnatural shine. Walter supposed he would have to fight him for control of the police department because he had already overreached. A man who thinks he's owed doesn't give up easily.

Why did Haskell have a source inside the police department?

The lineup was Walter at the podium, Ball at his left elbow, Sergeant Curtis Snapper with the Mississippi Bureau of Investigations at his right, the sheriff beside Snapper, the coroner beside Ball, and a throng of county and city officials jockeying for positions behind them. Four of the five aldermen were there. Gordy Kilfiche, the octogenarian judge, was said to be home with the flu.

Walter couldn't help but think that a well-placed bomb might wipe out the controlling authority of Hayes in its entirety. Kilfiche would become acting mayor and the fire chief would be his only soldier, and the town would probably be better off. He was tempted to say as much to the press, but the gravity of the situation forbade it.

The police chief might have been proud at the turnout from the media. Television stations from Tupelo and Columbus were there, of course, and Dexter Mann from the Hayes Beacon, but also a female reporter with an Associated Press badge dangling from a lanyard around her neck. Thrown into the mix were at least a half dozen faces Walter didn't recognize, most armed only with cell phones. Bloggers, perhaps, or simply curious. No one had bothered to vet them. One man stood out with his notepad and pen — a relic of a bygone era when journalists attempted to hide their dishonesty.

Walter read a statement he had prepared himself on a single index card. He wasn't one for fancy oratory, but human decency required him to express his condolences to family and friends. Duty required him to mention the chief's long history of service to the community (he omitted the word *dedicated*). The reporters, already knowing the chief was dead, made little pretense of listening to what the mayor said. His part was a mere formality. Seeing them so eager to ask their questions made him regret not having more to say, not because he wanted to say more, but because he dreaded their questions.

They pelted him with questions they had to know he wouldn't answer. Not yet. He stepped aside and introduced Sergeant Snapper as the lead investigator. Snapper came armed with a list of standard responses: *It's too soon to tell, I can't comment on that at this time*, and, Walter's favorite, *we'll see*. Undaunted, the seasoned reporters rephrased and pitched their questions again, over and over, disgusting Walter with their morbid curiosity. Assistant Chief Ball shifted from foot to foot, anxious because he hadn't been asked a single question. There he was, heir apparent, and no one cared a wit what he thought about his boss being suddenly and undeniably dead.

Near the five-minute mark, Dexter Mann raised his voice to an unavoidable level and said, "Mayor Pigg, how much do you blame yourself?"

The press pool, small as it was, fell silent. Walter glanced at Assistant Chief Ball for a split second and saw the makings of a smile grip his face, then he replaced Sergeant Snapper at the podium and locked eyes with Mann, hating him to the very core of his soul. The question was not *if* he blamed himself, but *how much*, as though blame at some level was automatic. Until that moment Walter hadn't considered blaming himself. The thought had not crossed his mind. When a man takes his own life, the reasons why die with him. Reasons, plural, not singular, because suicide is the culmination of sustained hopelessness. Walter felt himself an expert on the subject — as much as anyone still alive could be, and he knew that even if his actions were the last straw for Benson, it wouldn't have amounted to much had not a pile already existed. Chief Benson's reasons were his own. They were private, and perhaps he hadn't understood them himself.

Walter took a deliberate breath. All eyes were on him. Some he saw, some he felt. Mann's eyes were giddy with anticipation and satisfaction of self. Whatever words Walter uttered next would be set in stone, or ink, which is more permanent. "Now is not the time for you to be an ass," he said, his voice steady and firm. The AP reporter giggled. The Channel 9 reporter's mouth fell open. Someone behind Walter groaned. Dexter Mann's face collapsed. "Does anyone have an adult question?"

The reporters eyed each other. What now? No one knew quite what to do until the old man with the notepad and pen raised his hand and waited to be recognized. "Mayor Pigg ... uh ... will the assistant chief assume the duties of ... uh ... the deceased?"

"It's my understanding that's the natural progression," Walter said. He was powerless to leapfrog the assistant chief with the man he already knew he wanted in the position. Nothing against Ball — Walter knew next to nothing about him. "I'll be meeting with the aldermen to discuss a permanent replacement."

Ball leaned toward the podium but Walter refused to yield. He wasn't about to give him a platform from which to spring himself. Being an assistant anything carried with it a certain stigma, deserved or not. Almost being in charge of something is nothing to boast about.

The press conference ended and Walter held the podium just long enough to be certain no follow-ups would erupt, like fires that pop up to complete the task of burning down a house after the fire trucks leave. Ball followed him back into the police station and hovered while he discussed the next phase of the investigation with the primaries.

"The absence of a note strikes me as odd," Walter said to the sergeant after the men with badges stopped talking.

"You'd best leave the investigating to the professionals," Ball said.

"Don't you dare tell me what I best do," Walter said.

Ball's face reddened. He tried to grin it away, but the crimson flowed in and stained him. He puffed out his chest and cleared his throat. "All I meant was," he looked around at the other lawmen, "after you've seen a few suicides, you know what they look like."

"Keep an open mind," Walter said. "Consider the possibility that it was murder." He looked at the sergeant, who asked if he had a suspect in mind. Walter named Stubbs.

Ball half sighed, half laughed. "Stubbs, the bogeyman."

Walter disliked Ball immensely now. The man had sealed his fate. "What about you?" he asked Sergeant Snapper. "Is your mind made up?"

"It's an open investigation."

"I asked if your mind's made up."

"No, but nothing I've seen —."

Walter tossed the question to the sheriff without allowing the sergeant to finish.

"Cut and dry," the sheriff said.

"Detective Gant?"

"It's way too soon for that," Gant said, and Walter believed he meant it.

"Too soon my ass," Ball said. "You've got a single gunshot to the head and no sign of forced entry. No sign of a struggle. What more do you need?"

"A suicide note, for one," Gant said.

"Suicide note to who? The man lived alone. He never married and he had no children. Whatever money he had squirreled away will probably go to some nephew or niece or fourth cousin twice removed."

"He had a son," Gant said. Everyone looked surprised except Sergeant Snapper.

"That's a lie," Ball said. "I've worked with the man for twenty years, the last nine as his assistant chief. You don't think I'd know if he had a son?"

"His life insurance policy lists a son as his sole beneficiary," Gant said. "Donald Wayne Thrasher."

"How the hell do you know? It's Christmas." Ball laughed as though he had just exposed the detective as some grand fool. The sheriff laughed too, though he had the courtesy to do so in silence.

"We all have a life insurance policy through the department," Gant said. "I checked his records this morning."

"We're in the process of tracking him down," Sergeant Snapper said. "His last known address was Dallas, Texas."

"You knew about this?" Ball asked Snapper. "Why wasn't I told?"

"I tried to tell you before the press conference," Gant said. "You told me not to bother you."

Probably busy preparing a speech he didn't get to deliver, Walter thought. He had seen Ball fold a sheet of paper into his shirt pocket as they gathered at the podium. "Is your mind still made up?"

"This Donald Thatcher was obviously the result of a tryst the man had a long time ago."

"Thrasher," Walter corrected him. "At least pay enough attention to get the name right."

Ball glared at the mayor, probably tasing him over and over in his mind. "I know Benson cared about his legacy. He told me last week."

"Told you what?"

"That you were out to get him. He was worried about his reputation."

"Nothing tarnishes a man's reputation like suicide," Walter said. "All I'm asking is that this investigation be thorough."

"It will be," Snapper said.

"But you've already made up your minds," Walter said. "With the exception of the detective."

"It's as plain as the nose on your face," Ball said. "The doors were locked. The windows were locked. Or maybe you think a ghost killed him and escaped through the wall." He laughed, looking around for others to laugh too. The sheriff chuckled, but no one else cracked a smile.

"Maybe the killer locked the door on his way out," Walter said.

"How did he get in?"

Walter couldn't believe how stupid the assistant chief was. "I don't know, maybe he knocked and Benson let him in."

"Why would he do that?"

"Because Benson and Stubbs knew each other," Walter said.

Snapper stepped away to take a call. When he returned, he told the group that Donald Wayne Thrasher denied knowing the deceased. Walter suggested there might be more than one man by that name, but the sergeant said his social security number matched.

Ball tried to redeem himself. "That explains why he didn't leave a note." Ball said.

"Does it?"

"If you were going to kill yourself, would you write a note to a son you had never claimed?"

"He claimed him on his life insurance," Walter said. Again they were making assumptions. Assuming Benson's son didn't know him because of a decision the father made.

"You've raised some valid concerns," Sergeant Snapper said. "I give you my word every avenue will be exhausted."

Walter thanked him, but Ball couldn't leave well enough alone. "You publicly humiliated the man, Mayor Pigg, and now you want us to believe you care about his reputation."

Walter bristled. "I don't care one bit about his reputation, Assistant Chief Ball. I care about making sure Perry Stubbs doesn't get away with another murder in this town."

"Unbelievable," Ball said, scoffing and rolling his eyes. "When you set your sights on somebody you don't stop."

"You'd do well to remember that," Walter said.

"You're making wild accusations without a shred of evidence," Ball said.

"Are you sure you're not trying to clear your conscience?"

"If I pushed him to take his own life, wouldn't he want the world to know? Wouldn't he leave a note and tell everyone how I drove him to it?"

"He's got a point," Gant said.

"Doesn't make him a cop," the sheriff said.

Sheriff Rayburn had been a shift foreman at a tire plant in Tupelo before he ran for sheriff six years ago. Now he was a super sleuth. A real-life Sherlock Holmes. Walter disliked him immediately, but not as much as he disliked Ball.

* * *

Danny Palo was younger than his brother by four years and they bore a striking resemblance, except that Danny's hair was thinning on top and his at-rest expression was a smirk. Tipton took their father's nose while Danny had his high cheekbones. He had always been self-conscious about his nose, thinking it a bit too long and almost too narrow at the bridge for the black-rimmed glasses he sometimes wore.

The two brothers sat on stools in their father's game room watching the old man run the table like a pro, tapping a pocket with the tip of his cue then sinking his ball. He had solids for the third game in a row, and it was Danny he was beating.

"You don't have to call the pocket except for the eight ball, you know," Danny said. "Show off." The brothers laughed, but Carlton was all business as he lined up on the one, then tapped it just left of center and sent it rolling past the eight and into the side pocket. He straightened himself and grinned. Tipton didn't care much for pool, but he did enjoy watching his brother get his ass handed to him by the old man.

"Pool is like golf without all the walking," their father said as he chalked his cue.

Danny scoffed. "Two minutes ago you said it was like chess."

"I think it's like Monopoly," Tipton said. "Dad buys up all the property and puts hotels on them then bankrupts us when we come to visit." They all laughed. It felt good to laugh after the day he'd had. All day long he had jumped at the slightest noise, expecting the cops to rush in and arrest him for accessary to murder. He regretted not cultivating Ball more than he had. Like it or not, he was part of something now.

Carlton stooped forward to take his next shot. The table was littered with stripes and he had two balls left before the eight. "Looks like you get to shoot after all," he said to Danny. "I can't see a pocket for your balls."

Danny grinned. "That's what she said." Tipton eyed his father and rolled his eyes. Carlton frowned. Danny's head bounced between them. He lifted his hands and shrugged. "What?"

"Don't let your mother hear you say something like that."

The wives were in the kitchen erasing the aftermath of Christmas dinner.

Tipton and Autumn had spent the afternoon with her parents eating the exact same meal. Turkey and ham and everything that goes with it. His stomach bulged from overeating and the last thing he wanted to do was perch himself on an uncomfortable stool and watch his father show off.

"She's heard worse," Danny said.

"Not from her sons she hasn't."

"Son," Tipton corrected him. "I'm innocent." Saying the word triggered imagery of the door flying open and the room filling with cops.

"You seem jumpy tonight," his father said. He took his shot and missed his ball. "Something wrong?"

"Nothing's wrong," Tipton said. "What makes you think I'm jumpy?"

"Because you've been acting nervous since you got here." He exchanged places with Danny and sipped his drink. "Is it because of what happened with the police chief?"

Tipton tried to laugh it off but he felt his insides freezing over. If he couldn't withstand an innocent question from his father, how would he stand up to a state investigator? How many times had he seen someone tripped up by an innocuous question? They say something unimportant then forget and answer a different way later, or they offer up an alibi before they're accused. A good detective has a thousand tricks up his sleeve. "I'd rather not talk about that."

"The holidays can be a lonely time for a man without a family," Carlton said. "We're lucky we've got each other."

"Maybe it wasn't a suicide," Danny said. "Maybe he knew something on the Clintons."

"Don't make jokes about the dead," their father said.

Danny laughed, then he leaned over the table and studied his options. Over the next few seconds he sank two balls then scratched. The silence gave Tipton time to collect his thoughts. It was just idle conversation. They didn't suspect him of anything so why couldn't he stop shaking inside?

The two players changed places again. Danny nudged Tipton with his elbow. "I moved a couple of my balls out of his way so he can put me out of my misery." He laughed again. Danny could be terribly annoying.

"Maybe Tip knows something too," Danny said. "Maybe that's why —."

Tipton dropped off his stool and stood ready to fight. "Don't call me that!"

Danny threw up his hands and leaned away. "Whoa big fella. It slipped."

"Well don't let it slip again!"

"Stop it," their father said. "Act like men or I'll cut off your liquor." He sank the eight ball and declared himself the winner.

"I didn't see you call a pocket," Danny said.

"Because you were too busy running your mouth." He returned his cue to the rack on the wall and rolled the remainder of Danny's balls into the pockets so they wouldn't sit overnight and mar the felt. It was his signal that he was tired of playing and it suited Tipton just fine. "What is it with you and that name?"

Danny laughed. "Uh oh. Now you've done it."

"Shut up, Danny," Tipton said. He looked at his father. "I don't like it, that's all."

"That's not all," Danny said.

"How'd you like a punch in the face?"

"Cut that out before you get your mother in here."

Danny couldn't wipe the big stupid grin off his face. "Tell him the reason," he said. He looked at Tipton then at their father with the secret bursting to come out. "He was always the tip of something in school."

"I'm warning you."

"Stop being a baby," his father said.

"The tip of a Marty Harpo's dick was the one I heard most often," Danny said, then he burst out laughing.

"Who is Marty Harpo?"

"A big fat nobody," Tipton said. He had made it a point to keep track of the man who had tormented him in school. Last account he had, Marty Harpo was an auto mechanic working in his father's garage. The Harpos lived in their own private trailer park in the southwestern corner of the county. Marty's trailer was a singlewide with half the underpinning ripped away. He drove a 4x4 with a bumper sticker proclaiming him to be a proud Redneck. Poor, dumb, and proud.

"Don't he live down the road from where that boy drowned in a well when we were kids?"

"I wouldn't know," Tipton said. Danny probably named the wrong part of the county on purpose, thinking he could draw him out.

"Remember that limerick Drew Tracy made up on the playground?"

"It wasn't a limerick," Tipton said. "It was a stupid rhyme."

"It stuck, though," Danny said, still laughing. No power on earth was going to prevent him from sharing it with their father.

Tip be nimble,

Tip be quick.

Tip be the red on Marty Harpo's dick.

Their father laughed, then he caught himself and said kids can be mean but it's all part of growing up.

One of Tipton's recurring dreams had Drew Tracy charged with murder and every lawyer in Hayes had turned him down. He walks into Tipton's office in rags, sobbing, and begs him to take the case. In his dream, Tipton answers him in rhyme:

Drew, Drew puddin' pie,

Killed his girl so now he'll die.

He had kept tabs on Drew Tracy, too. He was selling used cars in

Pontotoc. Cars Marty Harpo probably worked on in his father's garage. Frick and Frack.

Their father asked Danny what childhood traumas he had suffered, to which Danny replied being the brother of Marty Harpo's dick was trauma enough.

"Very funny," Tipton said. "Ha the hell ha!"

Carlton rattled the ice in his glass. "Stop being a baby and refill this."

"Mine too," Danny said, grinning.

Tipton poured vodka for his father but nothing for Danny, who said he was tired of vodka anyway and filled his glass with bourbon, laughing as he poured. Always laughing. Danny was the type of man who could look you in the eye and laugh while he rifles your pockets. He owned a cash-for-title business in a downtown storefront, bilking people who were down on their luck until he bled them dry. Tipton despised him for it but had never told him to his face.

"Why didn't you tell me kids were picking on you?" Carlton asked. His voice was serious now. He had laughed it out and now he wanted to play dad.

"So you could do what?"

"I would've stopped it."

"How? By going down to the school and making it worse?"

"Dad would've punched the principle in the nose," Danny said.

"Shut up, Danny," Carlton said, then he focused on Tipton. "I would have, you know. If that's what it took."

Tipton believed him. Carlton Palo was a take-no-shit kind of guy, not to say he was a roughneck. Exactly the opposite, in fact, until someone crossed him. "You can't punch everybody in the nose who cracks a stupid joke."

"Maybe not," his father said, "but you punch one or two and the rest will figure it out quick enough. I didn't raise you boys to be pansies."

"I'm not a pansy."

Instead of following up with something fatherly, Carlton downed his drink and said they should all go to the kitchen and check on the women. Tipton burned with anger and humiliation as they filed out of the room. Danny would get his someday. Maybe the way Benson did. They can't put the needle in your arm twice.

CHAPTER 18

First thing Wednesday morning — the first business day after Christmas, after Benson's death, suicide or murder or accident, however the coroner ultimately ruled it, Walter assembled the aldermen in his office at the agreed upon time for the purpose of selecting a new police chief. The meeting wasn't official so no formal decision could be made, but it was Walter's hope they could come to a sensible understanding.

Wayne Toms suggested that the board attorney be present. It was the first suggestion Toms had ever made without Brad Stovall's hand up his back, and it was Stovall who told him to shut up and have some sense. Toms folded his arms across his chest and sulked.

Of the two comfortable chairs the mayor had for visitors, Stovall took one and Lyle Townsend took the other, leaving the octogenarian judge to sit in one of the folding chairs Kelsey had set up prior to their arrival. Walter eyed the men as they settled in, one by one, thinking how predictable it was for the man in the best physical condition to take the most comfortable chair. He probably ate the last piece of cake at parties, and took the last roll at the dinner table. Townsend had taken the other comfortable chair because he probably considered himself number two, behind his leader, leaving Wayne Toms to fold his arms and pout.

Walter considered giving up his chair to the judge but the gesture might be misconstrued as weakness. What a shame it was that a simple human kindness could work against a man. Even the judge might interpret it as submission given their dustup at the last board meeting.

Kelsey brought Styrofoam cups and a pot of coffee on a tray. Walter thanked her and waited until she closed the door on her way out. "Everyone had a merry Christmas I hope," he said.

"If a man blowing his brains out is what you consider merry," Stovall said. So that's how it was going to go. Stovall was having his Monday on a Wednesday.

"You know damned well that's not what he meant," Kilfiche said. "Sorry, preacher."

"I was thinking the exact same thing," Sharp said.

Walter frowned and shook his head. "We all hate what happened yesterday." He remembered the judge's flu and inquired. Kilfiche said it had been a false alarm.

Stovall adjusted himself in his comfortable chair. "Can we skip the warm and fuzzy and get on with it?"

"Very well," Walter said. "None of us can change what happened yesterday but we can change the direction of our police department going forward."

"Give it a rest," Stovall said. "The man's dead."

"Dying doesn't make us saints," Walter said. "It only makes us dead."

"It makes us stand before God," Sharp said. "He's the only judge that matters." He looked at Kilfiche with a sly grin. "No offense, Your Honor."

"None taken," Kilfiche said, then he addressed the mayor. "Since you called this meeting I assume you have someone in mind for the job."

"We've got a man already," Stovall said. "That's why chiefs have assistants."

Walter scoffed. "Glenn Ball is a buffoon. Hand over the police department to him and you may as well nail up a For Sale sign on the door."

"That's unfair," Kilfiche said. "Unless you have proof of something you haven't shared with us."

"There's no burden of proof here," Walter said. "We're not in a courtroom." He paused to take a breath, to collect himself. "Look, I don't have any evidence that Glenn Ball is guilty of anything. I'm not making that charge, but I've talked to the man and my gut tells me he's not the one to lead this department."

"Your gut said that about our last chief," Stovall said.

"Yes, Brad, and yesterday proved me right. The man was unstable." It pained him to put it in those terms but he knew more than a little about the subject having contemplated suicide countless times. Of course he kept his reasoning to himself. "And before you say what I see in your face, don't. Stable people don't kill themselves."

"Yesterday you said he was murdered."

"No, yesterday I raised the concern."

"At least you've come to your senses."

"Can we please get on with it?" Toms blurted. Suddenly being the focus of attention made him squirm. "I mean, well, can we?"

Walter didn't want to lose the momentum of having called the meeting so he said he thought Detective Gant might make a good candidate."

The aldermen exchanged curious glances.

"I realize he's young," Walter said, "but he seems to have a very good head on his shoulders and I believe he'll be an honest leader."

"I've heard good things about him," Kilfiche said. "But it seems awfully unfair to promote him over Glenn."

"Being police chief isn't a right," Walter said. "It's our responsibility to appoint the best man for the job."

"Best person," Lyle Townsend said. "It doesn't have to be a man."

"Shut up, Lyle," Stovall said. "We have one female cop and she's your wife's cousin. Nobody's gonna be chief except Glenn Ball." He glared at Walter, daring him to dispute it.

"Does no harm to see who's interested," Sharp said. "Set up some interviews."

"Interview whoever you want," Stovall said. "Interview the whole damned town for all I care, but I'm voting for Glenn Ball."

"Me too," Wayne Toms said.

"And me," said Lyle Townsend.

So the best Walter could do was a tie, which seemed unlikely given what the judge had said already. Kilfiche was a product of a system that prided itself on procedure. On loyalty. On biding one's time. Waiting one's turn. When a man's turn comes, he can't be denied without a good reason, and no reason is ever good enough. Walter loathed such blind allegiance because it gave no consideration to merit.

"So we sit on our hands and show the good people of Hayes that we're all a bunch of fools," Walter said. "We give the job to Ball because it's his turn. Justice be damned."

"Now wait just a minute!"

"I'm sorry, Judge, but that's how I feel about it," Walter said. "If we as a body can't consider other candidates because we're afraid of insulting Glenn Ball then we should all tender our resignations and go back to private life. A group of old hens could do a better job. At least they'd knit a scarf while they twiddled their thumbs!"

"What harm could it do to open this thing up and do some interviews?" Sharp asked.

"Open it up my ass," Stovall said. "The mayor wants his man in the job. Ain't that right, Mayor? You want Gant because why? He did you a favor? He promised to set your brother free?"

"That case is settled," Walter said. "Stubbs tried to frame me and it backfired."

"Stubbs again," Stovall said. "It's a broken record with you. If he's as bad as you say why ain't he in jail?"

"Because this town protects him," Walter said. "Everyone's afraid to touch him because he's got their names in his book." He read their faces and knew what they all were thinking. "And yes, he has my name too."

"Yet you're not protecting him," Stovall said. "Right the opposite, you've made it your personal crusade to take him down. You've just disproved your own logic."

"I don't care what people think of me," Walter said. "I have no intention of seeking re-election, nor do I intend to seek any other office. Ever. Him having my name in his book is of no consequence to me, and he knows it. That's why he sent his man out to butcher a horse and hang its head on my back porch. It's why he sent that same man to plant drugs in my car for the purpose of framing me, but that plan backfired and they framed my brother instead."

"You've got some imagination," Stovall said. "You should write a novel. Besides, it's too late to pick anyone else, or haven't you read the paper this morning?"

"The Hayes Beacon doesn't get to name our police chief," Walter said. "This board does. We do."

"The Hayes Beacon is the pulse of the people," Toms said.

Sharp grunted. "It's not the pulse of my people."

"Let's not drag race into this," Stovall said. "Every time we have a decision to make you have to remind us how black you are."

"Easy thing for a white man to say," Sharp said, "Does the thought of interviewing a black man scare you that much?"

"Why not a black woman then?" Stovall said. "While we're at it, let's see if we can find an oriental. And a Mexican. Let's turn it into an international contest."

"There's no reason to attack each other," the judge said. "Alderman Sharp has every right to make whatever motion he wants to make. Interviewing new prospects won't do any harm."

"I say we form an independent committee," Lyle Townsend said.

"There's no such animal," Walter said. "Any committee would have its own prejudices. Different from our own, perhaps, but prejudices nonetheless."

"I like the idea of a committee," Toms said.

"We've got a list of names," Townsend said.

"The same surnames we've all been reading in the Hayes Beacon for decades," Walter said. "Husbands of the women you proposed for the Christmas decoration committee, no doubt. I'll oppose a committee every step of the way. This decision is ours to make and I won't see it farmed out."

"Sounds like we've reached an impasse," Stovall said. "Makes no difference to me if Ball's chief or acting chief." He stood. "Now if you gentlemen will excuse me, I've got a business to run."

"Not so fast," Kilfiche said. "Seems as though everybody's making assumptions that aren't necessarily true."

All eyes fell on the judge.

"Sit down, Brad," he said. Stovall dropped his big frame back into the padded chair and the judge continued. "It's up to the mayor to appoint an acting chief." Walter's ears perked up. "The board has no say in it until we agree on someone permanent."

"That's nonsense," Stovall said. "You're making it up."

"I wish I were." He looked at Walter. "Think about the consequences to your Detective before you make this official. Leapfrogging him over his boss is bound to put a target on his back. You have to know this board won't keep him."

* * *

Tipton took the news like a kick to the groin. Stovall called him as soon as he left the meeting and told him the old judge had really fouled things up. Pigg could appoint an acting police chief and there wasn't anything anyone could do about it short of the board coming together and appointing someone permanent. Larry Pace was no help. He didn't even know about the statute until he looked it up, then he mumbled something stupid about learning something new every day.

"Just how many other powers does this rube have that we don't know about?"

"I suppose if we don't know then we don't know," Pace said. "Why do you care so much who he appoints?"

Tipton realized he was ranting to the wrong man. Larry Pace was city attorney because a long time ago his father had been an alderman and no one had thought since to change it. Nothing short of death or retirement would dislodge him.

Rance popped his head in the door and invited Tipton to lunch but Tipton had better things to do than eat lunch with Rance, then he called him back. "Say, did you know the mayor has the power to appoint an acting department head without consulting with the board?"

Rance came halfway in, smiling as though he found it amusing. "Let me guess, you're talking about —."

"You know damned well what I'm talking about," Tipton said. "Either you knew or you didn't."

"Didn't."

"No one knew except Kilfiche," Tipton said. "Somebody needs to cave his damned head in."

"That seems extreme."

"I wonder if Judge Bishop knows."

Rance shrugged. "I'm going to lunch now."

"I think I'll file for an injunction."

Rance laughed. "You're off your rocker."

There had been a time when an injunction could be had for the price of a steak dinner, but the state of Mississippi had rounded up a handful of lawyers and judges a decade ago and threw a scare into everyone. Most of Tipton's judges had either retired or died.

Rance left without giving Tipton a chance to respond which was just as well because he had already tired of the exchange. Then, in an act of desperation, he telephoned Dexter Mann. When the law fails, turn to the press.

"I don't see what I can do about it," Mann said before Tipton had finished explaining.

"Quit interrupting and I'll tell you," Tipton said. Mann's problem was that he had begun to believe his own hype. "You've got a week to dig up all the dirt you can on Gant."

"Suppose he doesn't have any dirt?"

"Then make it up! Do I have to write the articles for you?"

The background noise put the newspaperman at the diner, meaning Tipton had to be careful not to goad him into saying something that might be overheard.

"Look, no one knows who Gant is," Tipton said, forcing himself to be calm. "He's young and inexperienced and Pigg probably thinks he can control him. We need a police chief who'll be his own man."

Mann laughed.

"Stop laughing! I was giving you something to build your article on."

"Oh."

"Tear him down without making it look like you're tearing him down, then you build Ball up by highlighting his good qualities."

"That might be harder to dig up than dirt on the kid detective."

"Truth is what people believe," Tipton said. "We have to set the tone now."

"I don't know," Mann said, obviously speaking with his mouth full. "A week's a long time. I'll be talking against a man who's already on the job. What if he hangs onto it? Where does that leave me?"

"Do your job and he can't hang on. Once the public rallies behind Ball the board will have no choice but to act."

* * *

Ball didn't know whether to be aggressive or submissive. Walter watched him from his desk while he sat waiting in the lobby. A basket of nerves one minute, smug and sour the next. It had to be tough being in his spot, not knowing if he was keeping his job or moving up. Even Walter didn't know — wasn't certain — yet. The board had made it clear they intended to install the man regardless of his fitness for duty, and there was much to consider when it came to promoting Detective Gant over his boss. A small part of him hoped Ball would redeem himself and solve the problem for him, but the larger part knew better.

He entered Walter's office with an air of superiority. It very soon became clear to Walter that Ball knew every word that was said in the private meeting he had with the aldermen. That development alone sealed his fate, at least on a temporary basis. The board might promote him over Walter's objections but he would sit on the sidelines in the meantime.

"Tell me why I should appoint you acting chief," Walter said. His answer wouldn't affect the outcome but he hoped to gain some valuable intel that might help him convince Kilfiche and Sharp to oppose him.

Ball recited his record. Nine years as assistant chief with twelve years on the force before that, predating Benson's rise to the top spot by one year. In a surprise move, he said Benson had gone soft. He vowed to take a firm stand against lawlessness, including, he said with emphasis, one Perry Stubbs.

Walter found his sudden change of heart amusing, but unconvincing. Ball was the worst kind of leader — the kind who will say or do anything to climb the ladder. Walter looked him directly in the eyes and very calmly asked a question. "You don't like me very much, do you?"

Ball twisted himself into a less uncomfortable position. "I ... uh ... I like you fine," he said. "We got off on the wrong foot, that's all." He forced a smile. "Yesterday was a lot to take in. I think we both probably regret some of the things we said."

"Such as?"

"Well, uh, I'll be the first to admit I was out of line."

"In what way?"

Ball squirmed again. His forced smile faded, then reappeared. "Do you have to make me say it?"

"Yes," Walter said. "I think I'd like to hear you say it."

"Okay then, I shouldn't have spoken to you in such a disrespectful tone in front of everyone."

"And had we been in private?"

"A mayor and his department heads should be candid with each other in private," Ball said.

"Meaning you meant the things you said ... you just wish you hadn't said them in front of the other officers. Or do you mean you should have waited until I left then said them behind my back?"

A splatter of color hit the assistant chief's face. "I rose up through the ranks," he said curtly. "Nobody pulled any strings for me."

"And now you have an alderman at your disposal," Walter said. "Or is it the other way around? Are you at his?"

"Nobody's at nobody's," Ball said. "I'm my own man." The color in his face spread. "That's why you don't want me." He stood. "I'm wasting my time. You want a man you can cow."

"I don't like your attitude," Walter said. "Were it up to me, you'd be off the force completely."

"But it's not up to you," Ball said, then he started for the door and stopped. "I'll be here long after you're gone." He stormed away, then Mildred came in and said she had heard the entire conversation from her desk. So had Kelsey, and Jackson, who was spending his Christmas break underfoot. She said she hoped he convinced the board to fire him, then she cautioned him not to take the argument to Facebook.

"What a shallow man he is," Walter said. "Rude and shallow. I can't see how Stubbs could want him."

* * *

"I'll sue," Tipton said. "I'll get a restraining order!"

Larry Pace laughed. "Don't make a fool of yourself. The mayor has the right. He's got the balls, too."

"Balls! More like he's got Kilfiche and Sharp on his payroll."

"Some say you've got Stovall on yours," Pace said. Tipton punched the red dot and ended the call. Pace had some nerve. Three years ago it was Tipton who got him out of his DUI with a manufactured cough syrup story. He even had Dexter Mann do a big write-up on the dangers of over-the-counter medications and driving. It didn't matter if the public bought it or not. Let them piss and moan on social media all they wanted. People forget soon enough, and if they don't, so what? Pace, though, he shouldn't forget. Not before repaying his debt.

Next he called Judge Kilfiche. The way Pace framed it, the old judge was their best hope. Kilfiche was a law and order man. Institutionalized from decades on the bench. He bristled when Tipton asked him where he stood on Ball, asking him what business it was of his either way. Tipton quickly realized he had overstepped, so he tried a different tact, saying Ball came to him for legal advice.

"Suppose you were still on the bench and a lawyer filed for an injunction to keep Pigg from replacing Ball?"

"On what grounds?"

"Personal vendetta."

"I'd throw it out," Kilfiche said. "And laugh the fool out of my courtroom."

Tipton bristled. Had he not needed the judge's vote he would've told him to go hang himself. Instead he chuckled, then agreed with the judge and said that was exactly what he had told Ball.

"The mayor can appoint a ham sandwich if he wants to," Kilfiche said. "Tell your client if he attempts some lowball legal maneuver he not only won't be chief, he won't be assistant chief. I'll see to it he never wears a badge in this town again."

"He's not my client," Tipton said, fearing he had unwittingly put a nail in Ball's coffin. "He asked me if there was anything he could do legally to stop Pigg from ruining his career."

"You might try calling him Mayor Pigg."

"I meant no disrespect to the mayor," Tipton said.

"Sure you did. He beat you and you're still sore. My advice to you is to rub some salve on your ego and stop making a fool of yourself."

Tipton backed out of the call with an apology for wasting the judge's time, then he slammed the desk with the side of his fist and bellowed for Rance. Candice appeared in his doorway with her blouse buttoned to the throat and told him Rance had left for the day.

"Cancel my appointments," he said. "Then lock up the damned office and go home. If Rance can take off, so can I!"

Halfway up his driveway he saw Rance's car parked in front of his house and his brain exploded. Every emotion known to man hit him with the force of a cocktail injection directly into his brain stem. His vision dulled then heightened with every beat of his heart until he couldn't tell if he was seeing in color or grayscale. His car dropped off the concrete and into the grass but he didn't have the awareness to pull it back. Something scrubbed against the underbelly, front to rear, but all he could see was Rance's car. All he could think was Rance and Autumn. Damn her. Damn them.

"Autumn!" He yelled his throat dry all the way up the stairs and into the bedroom where he found the room empty and the bed made. He flew from the room and started back down the stairs, then he stopped cold. There she was, standing at the bottom of the stairs looking up at him with eyes big as quarters.

"What's wrong with you?"

He bounded down two steps at a time. "Where is he? I'll kill the son of a bitch!"

Rance stepped out of the study with a drink in his hand. Tipton's study. Tipton's drink. Tipton's wife. She put her hands against his chest at the bottom of the stairs and told him it wasn't what he thought. She was frantic to protect her lover. Wild-eyed and desperate. He flung her aside with a sweep of his arm. She stumbled but didn't fall. Rance stood five feet away, looking concerned but not scared. Not concerned enough to put down his drink — Tipton's drink. The bastard had been sleeping with other men's wives so long he probably didn't know it was wrong.

"Calm down before you make a fool out of yourself," Rance said.

Tipton closed the distance between them and shoved Rance backward with a two-handed push. The back of his right leg hung a table and knocked over a lamp. Autumn screamed. The tumbler Rance had been holding hit the floor but didn't break. Vodka and water splattered the hardwood. The cocky smirk was gone now. He had Rance's attention. He swung and missed. "You better duck you son of a bitch!" He swung and missed again.

"At least let me explain!"

Tipton stopped because Rance was too quick. His brain shifted from offense to defense. Twice he had missed. Push his luck and Rance might swing back. "You've got two seconds," he said, breathing fast and hard. So hard he feared his chest might burst. Let Rance think he was safe then he would pop his nose like an overripe tomato.

"I came to talk to Autumn because you need help," Rance said. "She was just about to throw me out when you came in."

"You're a liar."

"Among other things," Rance said, "but I'm telling you the truth. Think about it. What would she want with an old man like me?"

"How should I know? What do any of them want?"

"I hate to burst your bubble, pal, but my life's not as exciting as you think." He grinned. "I spend most of my lunches getting hammered at that little juke joint out by the feed store."

"You're still lying. It's not feed you reek of when you come back in the afternoons."

Autumn gripped his right elbow. "He's telling the truth about today," she said.

"I get huggy when I drink. Sometimes I pinch a waitress on the ass and don't get my face slapped. They've got a high tolerance for drunks, you know. Plus I tip good. Last week one of them even danced with me. I probably smelled really good that day."

Tipton still didn't believe him. "What about Candice?"

He threw back his head and laughed. A perfect time to land one on the chin but Autumn had a death grip on his arm. He pulled but she pulled back. "Is that what this is about? Candice?"

He felt the grip on his elbow tighten. "What about Candice?"

"Nothing," Tipton said. "Go upstairs."

"No. I'm staying right here," she said. "Are the two of you fighting over me or over that ... secretary!"

Tipton felt the momentum shifting. One mention of Candice and he was suddenly on the defensive. Rance stopped laughing and looked at him with unbridled amusement. "I've never laid a hand on Candice, not that I haven't wanted to. We're friends. Her choice not mine."

"You've never denied it before."

"You've got a short memory."

"I want her gone today," Autumn said.

"Shut up, Autumn," Tipton said. "I don't care what Candice and Rance do on their own time so stop trying to turn this around on me."

Autumn released his arm and moved between the two men so she could glare at each of them in turn. "If you want your secretary then —."

"I don't want my secretary!"

"Everybody calm down," Rance said, suddenly the peacemaker. "I don't want your wife and you don't want Candice. I came here to talk to Autumn about getting you some help and she told me to leave. I figured while I was here I may as well have one for the road."

Tipton glared at him, then he switched to Autumn.

"He's telling the truth," she said. "At least about why he's here. He said you're obsessed with Walter Pigg beating you."

"That's ridiculous!"

"I also said you're drinking too much," Rance said.

"Ha! You drink more than I do."

"I've been doing it longer," Rance said. "I have a high threshold."

"Get out."

"With pleasure."

CHAPTER 19

Walter liked a man who answered his own door. Tom Sherman was shorter than he expected. His build was average, and he was completely gray, including the stubble on his face that may or may not have been the beginning of a beard. Walter believed him to be mid-fifties, mostly because he was certain Mildred had mentioned it. She had strongly opposed the visit, then just as strongly insisted she tag along. Walter quashed the idea for fear Sherman might be less candid with her in the room. He didn't like Mildred being angry with him, but the meeting was too important to compromise over hurt feelings.

The former mayor's home was very well kept, but modest. A three bedroom brick flat with a nice lawn and plenty of Christmas decorations. Nothing gaudy. Traditional in the truest sense. The door hanger said MERRY CHRISTMAS, not HAPPY HOLIDAYS. One is in keeping with the spirit of the season while the other is, well, something else.

Sherman invited Walter in. He wore a white button-up and gray slacks with black shoes. Throw on a tie and a jacket and he could address the garden club, or cut a ribbon. Walter had done neither yet, and he wondered if the Hayes Beacon might cover it if he did. Dexter Mann might turn the ribbon cutting ceremony into some fiendish act of vandalism on Walter's part. Some nice new business put up a very pretty ribbon and up sneaks the mayor with an absurdly large pair of scissors.

The living room was very tidy. It clearly benefited from a woman's touch, though she was nowhere to be seen. Sherman offered coffee and Walter declined, so they sat. The sofa was leather and very comfortable. It practically swallowed Walter when he sat. He made a joke about needing help when it came time to leave. Tom Sherman laughed in an uncomfortable way. Very polite, but not enjoying the visit for whatever reason. Perhaps he didn't like being reminded of the job he had given up.

It's common to refer to a person by the most recent title they've held, sometimes applying the word *former* to avoid confusion. The practice applied to mayors, Walter supposed, so when he spoke again he addressed him in that manner. "Mayor Sherman, I —."

"Call me Tom," he said. "You're the mayor now. Congratulations on your win, by the way. I voted for you because of my admiration for your wife."

"Thank you … Tom." Calling him by his first name felt acutely awkward. "I think. To tell you the truth, I wish so many people hadn't." That was still true, but less so than at first.

"Our town is better off without Tipton Palo," Sherman said. "And I know Mildred wouldn't keep you around unless you had some good qualities." They laughed together. Awkward again. The former mayor was probably wondering what the current mayor wanted, and the current mayor wasn't sure how to state his case without seeming weak.

"I've heard good things about you for so long I feel like I know you," Walter said. "That's why I came. I … have a situation, and I'd like your advice."

Tom Sherman nodded. "My advice would be to take down the page," he said. Assuming a question not asked. "The people who don't like you will vent and the people who do won't defend you. It's human nature."

"It's not that," Walter said. "I'd like your advice on naming an acting police chief."

"Why?"

"Because you know the police department better than me," Walter said. "The easy thing is to allow the assistant chief to move up. That's what the board wants … and it's what they intend to do at our next meeting."

Tom Sherman nodded. Walter knew instantly that he understood the problem.

"What's your impression of Detective Gant?"

"If you're asking me if you should name him chief, I'm afraid that's your decision, not mine."

"But would you recommend it?"

"No."

"No?"

"Nothing against Detective Gant — he's a fine man and an excellent cop, but you said yourself the board doesn't want him."

"It's not that they don't want Gant," Walter said. "There's a natural selection process and they —."

"You can't take the politics out of politics, Walter, no matter how hard you try."

"I was thinking if I appoint Gant he might win them over before the next meeting."

"Not the board I know," Sherman said. "They'll eat you alive."

They went back and forth, then the conversation devolved into chitchat.

Walter hated chitchat. Some men excel at it, but not Walter. More often than not his thoughts drifted and he lost track of what was being said, then he ended up saying something foolishly out of context.

"Why did you resign?"

The question ended the conversation like hitting a tree. Sherman stopped in the middle of a sentence Walter had stopped listening to. He sat there — Tom Sherman — with his jaw unhinged and the oddest look on his face. Walter realized he had overstepped and he felt terribly embarrassed. "Never mind," he said. "It's none of my business. I've only been at this less than two months and already I'd like to resign."

"Dexter Mann had a story ready to go to press," Sherman said. "Resigning was the only way to stop it."

"You don't have to explain to me. I had —."

"You and I share a common enemy, Walter. There's nothing I'd like more than to see Perry Stubbs brought to justice, but I'm afraid he's got his hooks into this town deeper than you realize."

"His book would embarrass a lot of people," Walter said.

"It's more than that. He *owns* certain people. Important people."

"Who?"

Sherman shook his head. Scared or taking the high road, Walter couldn't tell, but he knew something. He knew names. Walter guessed a few — Stovall, Benson, Ball — but got no response. Not so much as an eye blink or facial twitch.

"You should play poker," Walter said. The former mayor smiled.

"At least tell me Detective Gant isn't dirty."

"Not Gant," Sherman said. "At least not that I know of. Gant's a good man, and he'd make a fine chief, but it's not his time."

"If I survive this job long enough, you'll find that I'm not concerned with maintaining the status quo."

Sherman stood, signaling that the visit had concluded. It was a polite man's way of asking a guest to leave. Walter didn't take it personal. They shook hands. Sherman asked Walter about his back. Walter lied and said it was fine. They walked to the door and stood on opposite sides of it, exactly the way the visit had begun.

Walter thanked him for his time and meant it. He now understood why Mildred admired the man so much. Tom Sherman belonged at the head of something. Anything. For a split second Walter considered offering him the position of police chief but knew he would refuse for the same reason he resigned. The forces that sidelined him were still in control of the town.

"Maybe I was a coward," Sherman said, "but I don't regret walking away from public life. It's no kind of work for an honest man."

* * *

Autumn had been on her best behavior since getting caught with Rance.

Tipton no longer believed they were lovers, but he still had a chip on his shoulder that his law partner and wife were discussing him behind his back. The notion that he was too obsessed with Walter Pigg was preposterous. He didn't believe for one second she had told Rance to leave. The drink in his hand disproved it. She had tried to throw Candice into the argument but he shut her down. They had both yelled a lot, then they made love.

She made his lunch and packed it in a brown paper bag the way she did when they were first married. He gave it to Candice and told her to be sure to let him know what it was in case his wife asked when he got home. Brown bagging was for the poor. Autumn should know that. Of course she did.

"On second thought, throw it in the trash" he said. "I don't care what's in it."

"You should be grateful she cares enough to make your lunch."

"You should mind your own business," he said, then he went to his office. People were always telling other people how thankful they should be. Candice should be thankful she still had a job.

Rance dragged himself in at a quarter past nine, saying he had stopped by the courthouse to drop off some papers. The only reason Rance West ever stopped by the courthouse was for court, or to see the redhead who worked in the circuit clerk's office. Missy something. She flirted with everybody but with Rance it probably meant something. He had that way about him regardless what he had said about spending his lunches at a juke joint. Rance was no better at lying than he was at practicing law.

"About yesterday," Rance said.

"Forget about it."

He closed the door and plopped down in the chair and stared at Tipton long enough to be annoying.

"Well?"

"I just wanted to say that," Rance said. "We're cool, right?"

"Is cool still a thing?"

"You know what I mean."

"Didn't I say forget about it?"

"As long as you don't think —."

"You're not her type," Tipton said. "She hates you."

"Hate's a strong word."

"Disgust then. She's used that word more than once."

Rance frowned. Good. Serves him right for meddling.

"Just so you know," Tipton said, "I've had Clarence doing some legwork for me."

"He told me."

"Why would he tell you?"

"Why shouldn't he?"

"He doesn't tell me everything he's doing for you."

"Maybe it's because when he's working for me, he's actually on a case," Rance said.

"Did he tell you what he found?"

"No, and if he'd tried I would've stopped him. This business with Pigg has gone too far, Tipton. I've tried telling you but —.

"Oh stop with the theatrics! I wanted Clarence to check Pigg's background during the campaign but you said no. You said we didn't need to worry about Pigg."

"I think you've got that backwards," Rance said.

"Pigg was arrested two years ago for beating an African American boy," Tipton said. "A child." He had Rance's attention now. The hook was in and all he had to do was reel. It would play that way with the public, too, if he could keep Dexter Mann focused long enough to write the story.

"I don't believe it," Rance said. "A thing like that would've made the news. He'd be in jail."

"Probably would be if he hadn't got himself abducted. By the time all that mess was over the boy's mother had dropped the charges. I wonder how much of the abduction tale was true and how much was fiction."

"You're not immune to being sued for libel," Rance said.

"Are you calling me a liar?"

"No, just reminding you that facts can be tricky little bastards … and the mayor doesn't like you already."

"You're lucky I don't punch you in the nose for yesterday," Tipton said.

"You tried, remember? Don't push your luck." He looked more annoyed than afraid, then he looked curious. "Define beat."

Tipton didn't understand, then he did. "Assault on a minor was the official charge. Grabbed him by the ear. Can't you see Pigg doing that? Grabbing a little boy by the ear like some old woman?"

"But when you said he beat the boy —."

"Pigg's a racist," Tipton said. "People don't tolerate that sort of behavior anymore. The way everybody gets worked up these days he'll have no choice but to resign."

"After you get Dexter Mann to write a salacious article about it in the Beacon, you mean?"

"Creative, not salacious," Tipton said. "He pulled the kid's ear, not his pecker."

"You know what I meant."

"To answer your question, no. I have a better idea."

* * *

Friday morning Walter named Detective Gant acting police chief effective immediately. Assistant Chief Ball took the news better than Walter expected, even promising to do everything in his power to make the transition a smooth one. A lie, but one told with a straight face nonetheless. Walter thanked him then dismissed him. Gant seemed more surprised than anyone. It hadn't occurred to Walter to give him a heads up before gathering the men and making the announcement. So many parts of the job required a nuance Walter still lacked. As he left the station he passed the patrol captain in the hall. The captain gave Walter a thumbs up. It was the first positive reaction to a policy decision since he'd won the election.

Now if only he could make the decision stick.

When he returned to his office, he found Kelsey leaning over Mildred's shoulder looking at her computer screen. He saw the familiar blue-on-white color scheme, then his own mayoral seal. Something on his page had their attention, and he was an old hand at reading Mildred's face.

"What now?"

"They've brought up that boy," Mildred said.

"What boy?"

She turned the screen so he could read the comments. He saw damning words such as racist, child abuser, and bigot. One man wanted him hung and another wanted him castrated. By tomorrow he would be a serial killer, or worse. Such was the nature of social media. To Mildred's credit, she didn't gloat.

* * *

"I'm burying the bastard," Tipton said. He was in a fine mood after seeing the mayor's Facebook page.

"If you don't bury him I will," Stubbs said. Tipton wasn't sure if he meant in the literal sense or not. Stubbs was a scary man. They were sitting in the parking lot of an abandoned warehouse at the edge of Industrial Park. Doubly safe because every factory was closed for the holidays. Empty buildings and empty parking lots. Stubbs was driving an old beater with the left front fender held in place with duct tape and a bungee cord, and there sat Tipton in the same car he drove to work every day. The same car he went everywhere in. Anyone happening by might recognize his car and think he was talking to a client, or a frightened witness, but not Stubbs. No one would see that pile of junk and think Perry Stubbs.

"I don't like being called away from my office," Tipton said, trying his best to sound as intimidating as the man he was meeting.

"Don't tell me what you don't like," Stubbs said. "Tell me what you're doing about our little problem."

Tipton held up his phone. "Have you read this stuff? Oh, I forgot, you're too old school for social media."

"If I need to tell a man something I go tell him, or I send somebody to tell him for me. If they need to tell me something they come to my office, or they keep it to themselves."

"Yet here we are," Tipton said. "Meeting outside an abandoned parking lot like two mafia kingpins."

"Put down that damned phone and act your age."

"Old school beat-downs may work in your circle," Tipton said, "but in mine it takes brains and technology. You send Corey Pickle with a kilo of cocaine and I create a dozen fake profiles on Facebook and ignite a shit storm. Take Latisha, for example. Two years ago Pigg threw a clod of dirt at her young son because he cut across Pigg's front lawn on his way home from school. Hit the boy in the shoulder and left a bruise the size of her hand." He paused to gage his ally's reaction, which proved to be no reaction at all. Nothing. Just that hard, cigar-chomping stare. "I made Latisha up," Tipton said. "I made up the story. The woman's African American." Stubbs was making him nervous. "Since I … she, posted this comment two hours ago, there's been almost three dozen negative reactions. People are outraged."

"That's your plan? Kill Walter Pigg with mean comments from black phantoms?"

"They're not all black women," Tipton said. He forced a little laugh then wished he hadn't because his nerves rubbed through. "Romero is Mexican. He's a fifteen-year-old bag boy at Piggly Wiggly. Pigg gave him a quarter tip and said that was more than enough for a wetback."

"Pigg don't have to make a fool out of you," Stubbs said. "You're doing it for him."

"Nobody knows the profiles are fake."

"Suppose they find out?"

"You're missing the point," Tipton said. "All it takes is one loud noise to stampede a herd."

"People aren't cows."

Tipton laughed. This time his nerves stayed put. "People are the dumbest herd animal of them all. Try reading a history book every now and then."

Stubbs asked him about Corey Pickle. How the case was going and what he thought his chances were at beating the charges. He didn't like the answers, but what did he expect? Pickle had bungled the job from start to finish. How can a so-called professional leave a fingerprint half a foot from where he plants drugs? He may as well have hung a neon sign.

"If he talks we could be in some real trouble," Tipton said.

"He won't talk."

"But if he does —."

"I said he won't."

Tipton believed him. Stubbs was an imposing figure. Seventy, but hard. Tall and lanky with dull gray eyes and bushy eyebrows two shades darker than his graying hair. His left arm lay along the car door where the window went up and down. His hand patted the door, dragging Tipton's attention to the pinky finger with the missing tip.

"Stop looking at my damned finger," Stubbs said. It was a touchy subject with the old man, which drew Tipton's attention to it all the more. Tipton had never found the nerve to ask him how it happened, and he wasn't about to now. Rumor was his father had chopped it off with an axe when Stubbs was a boy, on purpose, but the rumor didn't say why, and Tipton didn't believe in rumors anyway. Not that rumor. What kind of father would do that to his son?

"Maybe you should've waited until after Christmas to kill Benson," Tipton said.

"Maybe you shouldn't run your mouth so much."

"We're alone."

"Are we?"

For a split second Tipton almost panicked. Almost threw his phone out the window and punched the gas, then he forced himself to breathe. It was cold enough that he didn't sweat. "I've got the board in my pocket," he said. "This Gant thing is a temporary setback. In a couple weeks I'll have Ball where he belongs."

"You've got Brad Stovall in your pocket," Stubbs said.

"And he's got Townsend and Toms. That's three. That's enough."

"That's a tie. A tie leaves Gant in charge."

"Not this time. Ole Judge Kilfiche is solid on this."

"You'd better be right."

"I am, but just in case, I've got a plan to make sure Sharp's on board too. You may think all this social media stuff is a waste of time, but you give me a week and I'll have Pigg in a Klan outfit hanging blacks in his back yard. Sharp won't dare support him."

"Don't overplay it," Stubbs said. "People may not be as dumb as you think they are. I'm too old to go to prison and you're too weak."

Stubbs was brash and unlikable. Sometimes Tipton wished he hadn't thrown in with him, but it was too late for second-guessing. Much too late. Disentangling himself from Stubbs would be like leaving a street gang. A gang of one. His palms began to sweat. "You never did tell me," Tipton said, "exactly how it was you got rid of Levi Glusman."

"Why the hell are you bringing that up?"

"Just something I've always wondered," Tipton said. "I kept you out of prison. The least you can do is tell me how you did it."

"You wearing a wire against me?"

"Hell no!"

"You ever wear a wire against me and you'll meet Levi Glusman personal." Stubbs laughed in a dour way. Terribly unsettling. Tipton's hands began to shake but they were out of sight so it didn't matter.

"You know anything you say to me is protected by attorney-client privilege," Tipton said. "You've got me on retainer, you know."

"I don't pay you a retainer."

"My books say you do," Tipton said. "For our mutual protection."

Stubbs started his car.

"You never told me why you called me out here," Tipton said.

"I told you."

"Not really you didn't."

Stubbs drove away. Tipton took a deep breath to steady his nerves, then he pressed the red dot on his phone and turned off the voice recorder. The old man wasn't the only one stockpiling evidence.

CHAPTER 20

Roger came to breakfast wearing his nerves like a hair shirt. Walter beat him to the table by mere seconds. His nose told him sausage and biscuits and coffee, then his eyes tacked on eggs and brown gravy. Not a fruit bowl in sight. Something about Roger being there made Mildred pull out all the stops and feed them real food, which suited Walter just fine. Fruit was for snacks, not breakfast. A side dish at best, or a reward for doing something positive like cleaning your plate. If not for women, men would eat themselves to death. They would clog their arteries and stuff their hearts with fats and flavor until they clutched their chests and fell to the floor dead.

Jackson arrived last but in a hurry. Mildred scolded him for running, then she looked away, trying not to smile, probably thinking the same thing Walter thought. The boy had come a long way in two years. His mother would be proud. Children have an enormous capacity for healing, but Walter still worried because he knew all too well how trauma can tuck itself away inside a person and lay dormant for years, sometimes decades, then string itself across his path like a tripwire.

Roger reached for a biscuit before Walter blessed the food and Mildred scolded him. Her table, her rules. Walter delivered the short version because the smell of sausage tempted him. Satan could lure half of mankind to hell with pork. The thought amused him but he suppressed it because Mildred couldn't stand to hear the devil mentioned except in church when the preacher damned him. To mention him otherwise risked conjuring him from the depths of purgatory. Walter thought her fears foolish, but he respected her wishes and feared her scolding with equal measure.

Dishes went around the table until all plates were full. The adults had their coffee and Jackson had his juice. Everything looked and smelled delicious, which might not necessarily be a good thing where Roger was concerned. He made a snap decision to put the question to his brother plain and simple. "How long do you plan on staying?"

"Walter!"

"It's a simple question, Mildred."

"The judge told me not to leave town."

"You're welcome to stay as long as you like," Mildred said. "Isn't that right, Walter?"

"Within reason," Walter said. "I still don't understand why they haven't dropped the charges against you."

"We like having you here," Mildred said to Roger. "Don't listen to him."

"We like having a Christmas tree too," Walter said. "But there comes a time —."

"Walter!"

"It's okay," Roger said. "I know Walter doesn't mean it."

Walter meant it, but it was a moot point as long as the judge wouldn't let Roger leave town. Corey Pickle's fingerprint on his car floorboard blew the case against his brother to smithereens and he told him so.

They're not dropping the charges," Roger said.

"They have no choice," Walter said. "This is still the United States of America, not Iran. It's not North Korea. If Tipton Palo can't get the case thrown out then get another lawyer."

"Somebody destroyed the evidence."

"What evidence? The fingerprint? What are you talking about? Who told you that?"

"My lawyer."

"Nonsense! Hogwash! That's … horse shit!"

"Walter!"

Walter slammed his fist on the table and rattled the dishes. Jackson jumped. "Stop Waltering me, Mildred!" He left the table and grabbed his phone from the living room and dialed Detective Gant's cell on his way out the front door. The detective answered on the fifth ring and they had a heated conversation with Walter pacing the front porch, back and forth, forth and back. Gant wasn't making sense. The fingerprint was fine and then it wasn't. It was in the computer then it wasn't. How, he couldn't say. Mistakes happen.

"Mistakes happen my ass!"

Walter froze. All of a sudden he understood. Gant had sold him out. Stubbs had got to him. Every man has his price. He almost voiced the charge then Gant spoke again.

"I understand your frustration, Mayor. I'm frustrated too."

"Somebody's losing their job over this," Walter said, surprising himself at how calm he now was.

"If you want me to resign I will."

"Should you?"

"If I've lost your confidence, yes."

"What are you doing about it?"

"There's not much I *can* do at this point," Gant said. "Except to tell you it didn't happen under my watch, not that it matters to your brother."

Walter remembered they still had his car in impound. "Take another sample. You've still got my car."

"We tried," Gant said. "It's wiped clean."

"Wiped clean! And you call that a mistake?"

"Officially, yes. I have to protect the reputation of my department. Unofficially … I think we both know what happened. What I don't know is who."

"One of your cops is on the take," Walter said. "Who had access to the evidence?"

"Several people," Gant said. "I'm looking into it."

"And what happens to my brother?"

"That's out of my hands, I'm afraid. For what it's worth, he's got the best lawyer in town."

"He's got the most corrupt lawyer in town," Walter said. "If you ask me Tipton Palo's behind the missing evidence."

They went back and forth that way for a while, then Walter went back inside and found his brother in the study, standing almost in the exact spot where Walter had almost hanged himself two years prior. Roger was looking at the lamp on the table where Walter had left his note — the note no one ever read. Unaware, of course. Attempted suicide isn't the kind of thing one broadcasts unless they live in Hollywood where it's a rite of passage.

"It's hand-carved," Walter said, meaning the lamp. "A previous owner of the house picked it up in Africa. It's a lion's paw."

"Looks like a dog's foot," Roger said. "Is it valuable?"

Good question. The answer, Walter supposed, depended on one's appreciation of art, or antiques, or whatever combination of the two the lamp represented. "Not at all," he said, hoping to eliminate any temptation his brother might have to make off with it, not to say his brother was a thief, just that he couldn't be sure he wasn't. Desperate people do desperate things. "I'd throw it out but Mildred loves the thing."

"I'm facing real jail time," Roger said. "I … I'm, not blaming you. I know now the drugs weren't yours."

"It was me they were trying to frame."

"That don't make you responsible."

On that they agreed, assuming Roger really meant what he said. Walter still believed Gant was a good cop. Stubbs could have anyone on his payroll. Multiple cops. Civilians. Clerks. Janitors. Police stations aren't as secure as most people think. That's what Gant had said — not as secure as most people think. Police stations. Computers, he meant, because that's what they were talking about. Disappearing evidence. Corey Pickle's fingerprint.

"I feel responsible," Walter said. "I'll fix this somehow."

"How?"

"I don't know. Give me some time," Walter said. "The first thing you have to do is get another lawyer. You can't trust Tipton Palo. For all we know he may be working for Stubbs too."

"He told me you'd say that. You never take responsibility for anything."

"You just said yourself I'm not responsible."

"And you said yourself you were the target, not me. The only way to help me is by claiming the drugs."

"But they're not mine."

"They're not mine either. They were after you, so they're more yours than mine. I've got a record and you don't. All you'd have to do is resign and they won't prosecute you."

"Is that what Palo told you?"

Roger nodded.

Mildred entered the room, stopped and looked at the two of them, then retreated. Walter had shooed her away with a flap of his hand and a horrible look. He felt himself full to the eyeballs with horrible looks. Who was Roger to lecture him? When he looked back at Roger, he thought his brother about to cry. The look disturbed him and he felt suddenly awkward.

"You became a man overnight," Roger said. "I ... I never did."

"Nonsense. What are you babbling about now?"

"Mark," Roger said. "Our brother. Before he died me and you played together. You were my best friend. Afterwards you ... you, I don't know how you did it but you ... grew up. You never had time for me anymore."

A lump hardened in Walter's throat. "I lost my brother."

"And I lost two." He stepped forward and grabbed Walter by the elbow. "I lost both my brothers, Walter. Mark died and you may as well have. I was all alone."

"That's not true."

Walter pulled his elbow free, not with a jerk but with a gentle stepping back until the backs of his knees bumped against a chair. He sat, staring up at his brother with the lump in his throat growing larger by the second. "I .." The words stuck. All those years and he'd never known. Not once had it occurred to him that Roger suffered too. "Do ... do you know how Mark died?"

"He drowned," Roger said.

Walter looked at him. Through him. Through him and into the years they had lived since that day, all the way to that day. "Sit down," Walter said. "There's something you need to hear."

* * *

Alderman Sharp arrived at Tipton's home for Saturday lunch, asking as he stepped through the door what was so all-fired important, then he looked about himself and marveled aloud at the grand style in which the attorney

199

lived. Tipton enjoyed the look on the pastor's face. Tending God's flock didn't pay quite so well as tending the devil's. Often their two flocks overlapped, and the pastor wasn't shy about inserting himself into legal matters when one of his sheep strayed. Thus the invitation.

They went into the game room and sat on barstools at a round table in the corner nearest the pool table. Autumn trotted out cheeseburgers and fries and beer for two, then she politely excused herself and left the men to their business. She was an excellent hostess.

"I suppose I should be curious why I'm here," Sharp said, living up to his reputation as a man who liked to cut to the chase.

"Because I invited you and you came," Tipton said. "I hope you like cheeseburgers."

Sharp was no fool when it came to politics. Religion is politics and politics is religion. The pastor hadn't touched his beer. Hadn't paid it any attention whatsoever beyond the initial glance. He betrayed no annoyance and gave no hint that he would prefer another beverage. He simply ignored it as he might ignore a low-neck blouse.

"You have a very lovely wife."

"I'll be sure to tell her you said so," Tipton said. Could that be his weakness? Women? Every man has one — a weakness. Every woman, too. Every human. Every animal that roams the earth has something it can't resist. "Do you play?" he asked, noticing the pastor's eyes on the pool table for the third time. The table was regulation size, with a one-inch slate playing surface. He had rescued it from a bar and had it modified so it didn't require coins, and the felt was practically new. Sometimes he liked to sit and look at it and wonder about its history. About the lies it had heard and the fights it had seen.

"Back in the day," Sharp said. "I was pretty good, too." He looked around himself and released a nostalgic laugh. "There was this one place — Moe's — that had a slot machine they would roll out of the back when the sheriff was out of town. That's the only time I got to play it. Moe wouldn't let us kids in his back room. That's where he kept his girls. He had two. White girls. Anybody younger than twenty was a kid to Moe." He eyed Tipton as if searching for a reaction. "Ole Moe and them girls didn't care if you was black, white, or Indian. He didn't like Asians, though. Never heard him say why."

Tipton studied him as he talked, waxing nostalgic. Remembering with fondness the days of his youth. Missing those days at least a little bit, he thought. What an odd thing for a preacher to volunteer to a man he barely knew. Still hadn't touched the beer, though. Hadn't acknowledged it existed.

"Sounds like you miss those days."

"Not one bit," the preacher said. "I miss being young, but I don't miss those days. We was poor as dirt. My daddy worked himself into the ground for half the wages they paid a white man to do the same job."

"What'd he do?"

"He died. A lot of black men died."

"No, I meant what kind of work did he do?"

"Anything he could find." He looked up at the ceiling and let the memories wash him with fondness as he spoke. "I remember he worked a spell for Steeple Randolph's daddy. He was proud as a peacock when Mr. Randolph let him drive that big Case tractor of his. Mr. Randolph told me at his funeral that Daddy was the best tractor driver he ever had. Said it was because he loved it so much." His face turned grim. "Daddy quit him when he found out he was paying a white man eighty cents more an hour to drive his other tractor."

"Injustice," Tipton said. "We both fight it, you know. Me in the courtroom and you from the pulpit. We're a lot alike, you and me."

"We're a lot different, too," Sharp said. He puffed himself up with a deep breath. "You still haven't told me why I'm here so I'll guess. You want me to vote a certain way on something at the next board meeting and you think you can charm me into it … or bribe me by donating a large sum of money to my church."

Tipton grinned. "How large a sum are we talking?"

"I won't stain my church with dirty money. The Lord don't need dirty money."

"Couldn't the Lord wash it clean?"

The pastor frowned and Tipton withdrew the question, then he left the table and crossed the room to the bar, then returned with a small stack of papers stapled in the upper left corner. "Offering you money never crossed my mind," he said, sliding the papers onto the table beside Sharp's plate.

"What's this?"

"Police reports," Tipton said, remounting his barstool. "Everything here is public record, in case you're wondering."

Sharp began to browse the papers one by one, reading probably just enough to understand what he had. "Why me?"

"I think that should be obvious enough. You're an alderman. You're black."

"I see."

"Do you?"

Sharp continued to browse the papers, stopping longer to read some parts than others. Tipton watched as the hook sank deeper and deeper into his lip, then he yanked. "Every single incident was our mayor calling the police because black kids from the neighborhood were on his lawn."

"This one says they broke his window," Sharp said. "This one too."

"Read the last page," Tipton said, then he sat back and watched the pastor's face harden as he read the words *assault*, *minor*, and *racial slur*. "The boy's mother filed that one," he said. "Against the mayor."

"This doesn't sound like the man I know."

"Yet there it is," Tipton said. "A police report from twenty-sixteen. Two short years ago. This is the man we've elected to lead our town."

"Bygones," the alderman said. "Seems like the man's trying to do something good for the town now." He looked hard at Tipton. "I guess you aim to stop him."

"The only reason it went away was because of the abduction. The poor woman had to choose between prosecuting a hero or letting it go."

"Seems to me if she let it go, so should you."

"You remember how it was then," Tipton said. "With Pigg in the hospital and all that coverage he got in the news … people calling him a hero. They had him on CNN and Fox News. Hayes had never seen anything like it. What choice did the poor woman have?"

Sharp tried to hand the papers back. "I won't help you."

"I'm going to give this to the press," Tipton said. "Your congregation might wonder why you didn't get out in front of it."

"My congregation knows me."

"What about all the blacks in your ward who aren't part of your congregation? What about all the blacks in the other wards? You represent them too, you know."

Sharp's face flashed with anger. "Does Brad Stovall represent the white people in my district?"

"You know how it works," Tipton said. Sharp might not like what he was saying but he knew it was true. He also knew he had no choice but to act on it. Tipton had him over a barrel. "He didn't deny assaulting the boy."

"If grabbing a boy by the ear was assault they would've sent my momma to Alcatraz." He moved his hand to his left ear. "Still feels like this earlobe is longer than the other one." He chuckled.

"It's different when a white man does it to an African American child."

Sharp frowned. "I've seen racism," he said. "True racism. It's ugly and vicious and it turns my stomach. Wasn't that long ago you didn't have to look for it. You didn't wonder what it was when you saw it."

"People are more subtle about it now," Tipton said. "They've learned how to hide it. They won't call you the n-word to your face but they'll say it behind your back."

"That reveals their character, not mine." He studied Tipton with a piercing stare. "Are you speaking from experience?"

"I've never said that word in my life," Tipton said. "I'll swear it on a stack of bibles. It disgusts me to hear it, but you can bet Pigg says it. I bet he says it all the time. It wouldn't surprise me if he was part of the Klan."

The preacher scoffed, but he wasn't so sure of his mayor now. "You take that with you," Tipton said, meaning the police reports. "I'm sure you'll do the right thing."

* * *

Walter summoned his brother out to the back porch after lunch, with an eye toward Mildred not to intervene. She had spent the better part of the morning trying to talk him out of what he was about to do, arguing that Roger might not be strong enough to take it and might suffer some mental collapse. Nonsense. Walter had carried the truth for forty years and he was no Hercules. No Superman. He couldn't bend steel with his brainwaves. Roger could deal with it the best way he could, good or bad, but it was time he knew. He deserved to know, and Walter deserved to unburden himself of it.

He wouldn't have to tell his sisters because Roger was like a mynah bird, repeating everything he heard.

It was cold out but the house blocked the wind. Walter wore a light jacket and Roger wore the red flannel shirt Mildred had given him for Christmas. They sat opposite each other at the little round table where Walter and Mildred sometimes sat and had coffee. An amorous squirrel chased its mate up and around a tree several yards away. Way up high Walter saw their nest and it triggered a memory. He was sixteen and Roger was two years younger. Mark was six years dead. They were shooting their .22 rifles in the back yard and Roger shot at and missed a squirrel, so he followed it up the tree with his aim, then unloaded into the nest. A momma and two babies fell to the ground. They both got whippings. Roger for shooting and Walter for letting him.

It wouldn't do to mention it because Roger would deny it, or he would reverse their roles, or he would say something unforgivable about their father and Walter would put off doing what had to be done.

"Mark was pulling me down," Walter said. "He had the broken arm, and the gravel he had been standing on suddenly collapsed and he went from standing in knee-deep water to drowning. I tried to save him. I did everything I could."

Roger sat dumbfounded. "Where did that come from?"

"It's time you know some things," Walter said.

"What things?"

"Exactly how Mark died."

Roger rolled his eyes and made a noise. "Nobody blamed you but you."

"I'm trying to tell you what happened," Walter said.

"I already know what happened," Roger said. "Mark drowned and then he was dead, and he's not coming back and it was a long time ago and I'm sure it's been rough on you because you were there, but nobody blames you but you, so stop."

"I killed him," Walter said.

Roger opened his mouth to continue his rant, then he closed it again and stared back at Walter with an unreadable expression.

"He wouldn't let go of me. I would've drowned too if I hadn't —."

"What are you saying?"

"I pushed him under and I held him. Afterwards I tried to pull him to the bank, but he was too heavy and I was exhausted. If I could have gotten him to the bank maybe I could have pushed on his chest and saved him. I remember very clearly thinking that. You have to believe I tried."

"All these years …"

"It couldn't be helped."

"Did Mom and Dad know?"

"I couldn't tell them," Walter said. "I've never told anyone until two years ago when I told Mildred. Now I've told you."

"Peggy know? Doris and Betty?"

"I just said no one knows but you and Mildred."

"You killed him on purpose?"

"No, I didn't kill him on purpose. Don't make it sound like something I planned."

"But you pushed him under."

"It was him or both of us," Walter said. "He was out of his head with fear."

"He had a broken arm."

"He hit me in the head with his cast and I almost blacked out."

Roger had the most incredible look on his face. He looked as though he could see through time, all the way back to when Eve tempted Adam with the unnamed fruit that through the centuries had become an apple. "All this time … you, you let us think it was an accident."

"It *was* an accident."

"All those years I had to listen to *poor Walter*."

"I didn't —."

"*Poor Walter* had to see his brother drown. *Poor Walter* hasn't been the same since. *Poor Walter*. Always *poor Walter*. Never poor Roger, or Doris, or Betty, or Peggy. Always *poor Walter*.

"You're taking this out of context," Walter said. "I never —.

"You never what, Walter? Never what?"

Meant to deceive anyone is what he wanted to say, but anything he said now would only be misconstrued. The truth was he had deceived. He had told a terrible lie, then allowed it to grow and fester into a lifetime of guilt and depression and self-loathing. "I … I tried to hang myself once."

"Yeah? Well you didn't try hard enough, did you?" Roger stood and glared down at his brother. "If you wanted to hang yourself you would've hung yourself. It's not rocket science!"

"A neighborhood kid threw a ball through the window just as I was about to kick the chair."

"How convenient for you," Roger said. "You escaped death twice. First by drowning our brother then by a ball through the window. It doesn't take much for you to save yourself does it?"

Before Walter could formulate an answer his brother was gone. He had turned abruptly and stomped into the house. Mildred appeared through the screen as Walter looked after him. The look on her face left no doubt she had heard enough to say *I told you so*, but she didn't. She was a remarkable woman to be so right so often and never gloat.

She came out onto the porch and stood behind her husband. Walter's eyes were moist and she probably wanted to save him the embarrassment of seeing his tears. "I'll talk to him after he calms down," she said. It wasn't a question, or an offer, but a statement of fact. Roger had always held Mildred in high regard. Everyone who had ever spent five minutes with Mildred held her in high regard.

He sniffed. "You were right. I shouldn't have told him."

Mildred patted his shoulder. He had unburdened himself onto his brother. Now they both carried the weight of what he had done. The full weight, because instead of splitting the burden between them, he had reproduced it onto Roger.

* * *

For the second time in two days Tipton found himself sitting in the same vacant parking lot having a nefarious conversation with a lowlife. Two days ago it was Stubbs, and he had the conversation captured on a micro SD card in his wall safe at home. Today it was Assistant Chief Ball. Tipton had taken great pains to cover his bases. To grease the right cogs. Detective Gant — now Acting Chief Gant — was the fly in the ointment. Tipton didn't even know the man's first name. He was a nobody, like Pigg, and he wasn't about to let him remain chief. Maybe the two of them would go down together. Pigg and Gant. Gant and Pigg. So much depended on Glenn Ball now, and for that Tipton felt partly responsible. Disposing of Benson without a backup plan was sloppy.

"He's busted me back to detective," Ball said. Busted back was a generous summation, from what Tipton knew of Ball's rise in the department. He had been a detective in name only, and even that for a short time. The only reason he was promoted to assistant chief was to get him out of the way. Now Tipton needed him, and it turned his stomach.

"You're still assistant chief," Tipton said.

"Assistant chief working cases like a rookie."

"I wouldn't call taking down the mayor a rookie case," Tipton said. He eyed Ball, waiting for something more than disinterested curiosity. The man had no drive. No ambition. "Didn't you hear me?"

"I heard you."

"I said the mayor, not his brother," Tipton said, assuming he'd been misunderstood. "Do you want the information or not?"

"I'm listening."

Tipton repeated what Roger Pigg had told him about his brothers — both his brothers. About the drowning that was an accident for a lifetime and then it was something else. His client had teared up telling it.

"Impossible to prove either way," Ball said when Tipton had finished and asked him what he intended to do.

"Nobody said you have to prove anything. Just charge Pigg with murder and leave the rest to me." Tipton had a plan. Attack Pigg from every angle. Dare him to survive the onslaught. "Walter, not Roger."

"I'd have to lean on your client pretty hard."

"Fine, but don't get reckless," Tipton said. A reckless man overestimates his worth, then he tries to punch above his weight and gets his nose bloodied. Blood on Ball was blood on Tipton, and Stubbs, who had enough blood on him already to paint a barn. "Squeeze my client all you want, but keep this conversation between us. I could lose my license for this."

"Suppose the new chief asks questions?"

"Lie."

"Suppose he takes me off the case?"

"And gives it to who?"

"He could take it himself," Ball said.

"Acting chief investigating the mayor? The aldermen won't stand for it. *Acting* chief," Tipton repeated. "Don't forget that part. Keep your head until the next board meeting and you'll be chief. Permanently."

Ball smiled. "My first official act will be firing that son-of-a-bitch."

"You're not firing anybody," Tipton said. "Especially not Gant. He'll probably end up being appointed assistant."

"Not if I have anything to say about it."

"You won't."

A car passed and Tipton got nervous. It was an old car. Nothing anybody important would drive, unless they wanted to look unimportant. He asked Ball if he recognized it.

Ball laughed. "Nervous?" He was a complete idiot but it was too late to replace him. The board might bolt and side with Pigg. It was Ball or nothing.

"Now about the other investigation," Tipton said, meaning the investigation into Benson's death. He was tiptoeing into dangerous territory because he didn't yet know the full measure of the man he was pushing into power. "Anything I should know about?"

"What's to know? The man killed himself."

"Is it official?"

"Talk to Sergeant Snapper," Ball said, pronouncing his last name with flourish. "How'd you like to have a name like that? Snapper. Bet he caught hell growing up. I can think of a dozen zingers right off the top of my head."

"Why don't they announce something?"

Ball shrugged. "Why do you care?"

Tipton couldn't say why he cared, so he let the matter drop. They should've announced something, though. It had been four days.

CHAPTER 21

New Year's Eve afternoon was busy for Walter. Twice a year the town paid a pyrotechnics group out of Birmingham to come shoot fireworks over the lake in the park. Fourth of July and New Year's Eve. The current contract had been approved long before Walter took office, so all he had to do was help Mildred stay on top of logistics for the celebration as a whole. She handled her duties with so much confidence that he sometimes felt unnecessary, but in a good way, because a good leader delegates, though in total disclosure, Mildred had taken the task upon herself without being delegated to.

All morning clouds had been building to the north. Rain or snow would be a matter of timing. The temperature would definitely drop below freezing overnight and the moisture would definitely fall. Snow would make tonight's celebration all the more spectacular. Rain might force them to cancel. The best the local meteorologist could do was assure Walter there would be no lightning, so he instructed the pyrotechnics crew to fire everything they had into the air until it was too wet to continue. Earlier in the morning, using time freed up by Mildred's diligence, Walter had read the fine print of the preexisting contract and discovered that in the event of cancellation, the city would receive a credit valued at fifty percent of the cost of the unused fireworks. Why fifty and not one hundred was a question he intended to ask the board at their next meeting.

The phones rang off the hook, keeping Kelsey French on her toes answering questions about time and location and parking. People wanted to know if they could bring their dogs, their children, their concealed firearms, their own fireworks, and beer in coolers. The answers were yes, yes, no, no, and no. One woman asked if fireworks emitted carbon, and if so, wasn't it irresponsible to fire them into the air. Kelsey told her the city had turned off the heat in City Hall to offset the environmental impact, and that she was wearing a heavy coat and gloves, then she hung up and laughed until the phone rang again. A man called and asked how the city could afford fireworks but not new uniforms for the high school band. And so it went, call after call after call, hour after hour, testing the bounds of the young assistant's sanity. Not once did Walter hear her raise her voice or act in a rude manner, and he had never been more proud to have her on his staff, purple hair or not.

There came a point when Walter realized he was in the way. Kelsey was explaining the permit process to someone on line one and she had line two on hold. Mildred had a walk-in who felt the need to express in person her objections to beer being allowed in open containers in a park paid for and kept up by her tax dollars, as though her taxes alone funded the park. Mildred told her three times she was confusing tonight's celebration with the Fourth of July — the only time the city relaxed its strict no-open-container ordinance — before she comprehended.

"Well it shouldn't be allowed then either," the woman said, pushing herself to her full height of Mildred's shoulder. She looked well over the hump of fifty, and Walter vaguely remembered seeing her in church. One of the front row sitters, if memory served. Nothing wrong with sitting in the front row at church. Admirable, perhaps. He had a habit of categorizing people by certain traits and habits.

"Personally I agree," Mildred said, though Walter knew she felt the opposite. "But it's a decision the board made two years ago and it really hasn't caused any problems."

"It sets a horrible example for our young people," the woman said. She wore a blue dress with a yellow flower on the chest and green sneakers with white socks, an ensemble Walter thought set a horrible example for young and old alike, but who was he to judge fashion? Just about everything he owned came from the rack at Walmart.

"Well you won't see any open containers in the park this evening," Mildred said. She had her hand on the woman's shoulder now, trying to gently nudge her toward the door. Had Walter put his hand on her shoulder she probably would have sued the city. She seemed the type.

"It's a shame when decent people can't enjoy a celebration," the woman said. "Shame on the board and the mayor." She threw her eyes toward Walter, who had been standing just outside his office door admiring his wife's diplomatic skills.

"Tom Sherman was mayor then," Mildred said.

"How about you," she asked Walter directly. "Are you going to allow drinking in the park?"

"It's awfully hot in July," he said. "I may bring a small cooler of my own."

His response hit her like a dash of scalding water. She recoiled, owl-eyed and quivering, then called him a vile serpent of the devil. For a split second he thought she might paw the floor with a hoof and charge him, but instead she tossed her head over her shoulder and left.

"Perhaps I should go home and let you ladies handle things," he said.

"You'll get no argument from us," Mildred said.

"I think you should answer the phones," Kelsey said, meaning, he supposed, that she approved of the way he handled the woman's scorn, or she was mocking him. It was impossible to know which. Mildred didn't say anything, which said everything.

"On second thought, we only have the one car," he said to Mildred. "I'm your ride home so I guess you're stuck with me. I'll be in my office if you need me."

A few minutes later Roger called his cell for the third time and for the third time he ignored it. Somehow, like it or not, Roger had to go. Brotherly love has its limits. Even Mildred realized it, though she wasn't ready to say it. Walter knew because she had stopped protesting when he complained. Had Roger picked up after himself he might have kept her in his corner a bit longer, but the man was a slug.

A short time later Mildred stuck her head into his office and told him Roger was on line one and he may as well talk to him.

"Not until he apologizes for calling me a murderer."

"He didn't call you a murderer, and how can he apologize if you won't talk to him?"

She had a point, but he wasn't ready to let his brother off the hook, so instead of taking the call he told her to close the office and send Kelsey home. It was New Year's Eve and the town had practically shut down anyway. To his surprise she didn't object. On the way home he told her Roger could cry all he wanted but he had to go.

Jackson asked from the back seat if Uncle Roger cries. Mildred said he didn't.

"He whines," Walter said, making eye contact with the boy through the rearview mirror.

"What's whine?"

"That's crying without getting your face wet."

Mildred frowned. She had spent half of her married life frowning about one thing or another, but this time Walter's mind was made up. Roger had reached for the low-hanging fruit all his life and it rankled him to see anyone outreach him. He wasn't just lazy, he was jealous. Envious. Covetous. As Walter swung the city-issued Chevy Impala onto their street, Mildred swung the conversation toward another subject. "I hope you won't post anything on Facebook about how much this celebration is costing the city," she said.

"Where did that come from?"

"You know very well where it came from."

The contract with the pyrotechnics company galled him. The terms were ridiculously one-sided. If it rained, the city lost a fortune. Half the cost of the fireworks and all of the labor. The labor he understood, but the fireworks could be used later. At the very least the city should own the fireworks it paid for. "Money changed hands under the table somewhere in that deal," he said.

"Tom didn't like it either," Mildred said.

"He voted for it."

"Tom tried his best to get along with the board. If he knew he didn't have the votes, he voted with them."

"And look what it got him," Walter said. "He should've stood his ground and made them respect him."

"You can't stand your ground every time, Walter, or pretty soon they'll vote against you out of spite. You'll be powerless."

"Powerless, maybe, but I won't be quiet about it," he said. "Maybe they'll shut me down in the boardroom but they won't shut me up on Facebook. I'll shine a light, Mildred. A great big light of truth right up into their nest. Let people see who's got their hands in each other's pockets."

"Maybe people don't want to see."

She had a point again. It was an annoying habit she had of applying logic to his fevered plans. Maybe the people really didn't want to know. People eat sausage but they don't want to see it made. They want their fireworks in the park but they don't want to know how much it costs. It didn't matter that the town had homeless people. Almost half a dozen according to the police department's official count. They could feed them for a year on what it cost to shoot twenty minutes of sparklers and noisemakers. Of course they didn't want to see, and when it came down to it, he didn't blame them. Most people work hard for their money and they pay their taxes, and sometimes they just want to blow something up. Walter wanted to blow something up, too, but in a different way. He wanted to blow up Perry Stubbs. Blow him right out of the ground, roots and all. Limbs, leaves, and branches, and if Gant had half the backbone Walter hoped he had, they might just get it done.

* * *

Roger Pigg was a godsend. Ten minutes with Ball and he dished up his brother on a silver platter. According to Ball it was the easiest interview he had ever conducted. Didn't have to lay a hand on the guy is what he said over the phone. Tipton was growing weary of discussing sensitive matters over the telephone because he didn't trust the feds not to be listening. The target of a warrant is always the last to know. He poured himself a drink then walked out onto the back patio and stood defiant against the cold north wind. He could smell the crisp clean tease of snow that probably wouldn't come. Even the weather guy had admitted it was a remote chance. Slim to none was how he put it. And after teasing it for two whole days. Tipton loved snow. Some of his fondest memories as a child were the snowball fights he had with the neighborhood kids. It snowed more back then he thought, which seemed perfectly natural given the effects of climate change. The next generation might never see it at all, or they might be suffocated with it. It was impossible to know. The only certainty was that it would be different, and extreme, and it was man's fault. Man had no respect for the planet and it was about to bite humankind in the ass.

Pigg didn't believe in climate change. Still called it global warming, which was a neoconservative dog whistle for climate deniers. A willful ignorance still popular in the South. He took another sip of brandy and tried to recall how the subject came up during the campaign. Something from a questionnaire sent out by the Hayes Beacon, if memory served. Not by Dexter Mann. Mann didn't have the imagination to compose a list of questions that forced one to think.

Pigg wasn't as dumb as he had assumed him to be though. Where did he come from? Men don't just wake up one day and decide to run for mayor. Supervisor or constable maybe, but not mayor. To be viable, a candidate has to have connections. They have to belong to the right clubs, and the right jobs. They have to rub the right elbows. Tipton had rubbed the right elbows, and he had the right job, and he belonged to the mandatory clubs, yet something went wrong. The voters betrayed him.

He drained his glass then refilled it from the bottle he had brought out with him. Glenn Ball was dumb. Real dumb. He wanted to arrest the mayor at the New Year's celebration. Make a public spectacle of it. The backlash would be disastrous, especially after the wheels fell off the case against him, and they *would* fall off. True or not, Roger Pigg's cock-and-bull yarn wouldn't make it past a grand jury. Arresting the mayor without an indictment would piss off the judge. The court of public opinion was the place to convict Walter Pigg. His brother's testimony was a vehicle. A means to an end. Turn up the heat enough and Pigg — Mayor Pigg — would have no choice but to resign. Charging Pigg with murder had been his idea, but arresting him was dangerous.

The wind picked up and whipped against Tipton's partially numb face. Walter Pigg, murderer. Brother killer. It had a nice ring to it. Now to dig up people who knew the family back then and prime them with Roger's account of what happened and let human nature do the rest. Mark Pigg, saint. Cut down by a jealous brother. Drowned. Carried down by the weight of a cast on his arm and a wild-eyed brother around his neck like a millstone. Ball couldn't understand that an investigation would serve their purposes better than an arrest. An investigation opened the door to the wildest speculation Dexter Mann could imagine, and all Ball had to do was say no comment. Acting Chief Gant might throw up a roadblock but one good newspaper article accusing him of trying to protect his benefactor would sideline him. The plan couldn't fail.

Something moved behind him, then he felt his wife's arms slip around his waist and squeeze him from behind. There had been a time when it was the other way around — him behind her. In a few hours they would be watching fireworks from the balcony, assuming the weather cooperated.

"Are you trying to bed me?"

"I can remember a time when I didn't have to try," she said. He remembered those times, too, and for the life of him he couldn't recall when it changed.

"I hope it rains," he said, both to change the subject and because he really did hope it rained. As illogical as it was, a certain segment of the population would blame the mayor if the fireworks show had to be canceled. Politics is a fickle business. He had spent July Fourth melting in the brutal heat, shaking hands and kissing babies, listening to endless complaints and making endless promises he had no intention of keeping and for what? So he could lose to a nobody like Pigg? No thanks. He would watch the fireworks from the comfort of his own home, then step into the background and wait for the real fireworks to begin.

* * *

Roger had flown the coop. His shaving kit and toothbrush were gone from the downstairs bathroom, and his suitcase and clothes were gone from his room. No warning. No goodbye. Walter supposed he had jumped bail and was probably on his way to Wyoming to impose on Peggy and her lawyer husband until his legal troubles blew over. Sometimes Walter envied him, having no roots. Nothing to tie him to any one place. Most times, though, he pitied him, and for those same reasons. Humans aren't meant to live alone, and legal troubles rarely blow over. Trouble must be faced head on and dealt with, lest one thing turn into another thing and so on until circumstance decides a man's future without any input from the man himself.

"Should we call the police?" Mildred stood halfway down the stairs after searching the upper rooms.

"No."

"Aren't you concerned?"

"What would you suggest I tell them?"

"Tell them your brother's missing."

"Missing? He packed his things and left," Walter said. "That's called leaving."

"But he didn't say goodbye … or leave a note."

"That's called poor manners, and you know as well as I do that's not unusual for Roger. Remember that time three years ago when he stayed for a week then left in the middle of the night without a word? For two months we didn't know if he was alive or dead."

Mildred came down the stairs with a look of foreboding. Since their ordeal with the demon — learning their abductor's name hadn't changed Walter's term for him — she was quick to see foul play everywhere. It was an easy trap to fall into. Walter had dealt with such thoughts himself. He remembered the time she had stayed too long shopping and her cell phone died and he, being wheelchair bound, had panicked and called the police and was halfway through a tearful plea to the 911 operator when he saw her car through the front window. She didn't know because he never told her. When a man goes through an ordeal and survives, he makes certain adjustments. Walter's adjustment was to be stronger. More manly in outward behavior.

She sent Jackson upstairs to play in his room.

"Won't they charge him with something for leaving like this?"

"Only if he doesn't come back for court," Walter said. "Unless we report him missing and they find out he's skipped town." Walter didn't know the law beyond the common understanding he had gleaned from television cop shows, but he assumed his brother's release from jail had certain conditions attached.

Mildred went into the kitchen and fried some ham slices and washed some lettuce and poured potato chips into a bowl, then called them to supper. Had she not been so distracted, she would have sliced the tomato that was on the counter already washed. They were all seated and the food had been blessed and Walter spotted the tomato. Had tomatoes been in season he would have mentioned it, but it being the last day of December and winter tomatoes being what they were, he smeared mayonnaise onto a slice of white bread and built his sandwich.

"I forgot to slice the tomato," Mildred said abruptly. She sprang from the table and made quick work of it, then delivered it to the table in a saucer. Walter opened his sandwich and applied a slice, saying he hadn't noticed. Husbands sometimes lie to make their wives feel better, and there's not a thing in the world wrong with it.

"Tomorrow we'll have black-eyed peas," she said as the meal commenced. "And cabbage."

"No ham hocks?"

She laughed. "You'll have to settle for ham without the hock."

Jackson turned up his nose at the mention of peas and cabbage.

"You're just like your mother," Mildred told him. "Eating black-eyed peas and cabbage on New Year's is a tradition."

"Superstition," Walter corrected her. "It's supposed to bring good luck in the new year," he said to the boy. "Traditions are what people do without expecting a return on their sacrifice."

"Peas and cabbage are hardly a sacrifice," Mildred said. "This world is full of people who'd love to eat peas and cabbage."

"More full of people who wouldn't," he said, winking at his grandson. Jackson grinned and kept eating.

An hour later they were at the park, mingling. Walter hated to mingle. He hated small talk in all its ugly forms. It didn't take long to notice the cold shoulder given him by certain upstanding citizens. Marlin Baker from the bank barely acknowledged him, and Mercie Gains practically did an about face and went the other way when she saw him. Walter suddenly felt like a fish out of water. He felt embarrassed, as though everyone in the crowd knew he was a fraud. Mildred told him not to let it bother him. They were all jealous. Jealous? No, they were angry. Angry that their man hadn't won. Palo was a name that fit well in headlines and newspaper ads disguised as articles. Palo was one of *them*.

Half an hour into his embarrassment, a man grabbed Walter's hand and thanked him for the Christmas decorations on his part of Main Street. It was high time, the man said, that the town considered the little people, then the man did something very odd. He apologized for bothering him.

Walter stood in the midst of the crowd and watched the man retreat, thinking he had imposed himself on the mayor when in fact he had been the shot in the arm Walter needed. Mildred bobbed in and out of his periphery, tending to Jackson and speaking to this lady or that. More popular than her husband by leaps and bounds.

Walter nudged her with his elbow and pointed. "See that man?"

"Who is he?"

"I don't know," Walter said. "He lives on the residential end of Main, and he just thanked me for the Christmas decorations."

"That was nice of him."

"Then he apologized for bothering me and hurried away."

"He probably thought you were busy."

"That's who I'll fight for, Mildred. That man and all the men like him."

"And women?"

"If it won't make you jealous."

"Walter!"

CHAPTER 22

Three days into the new year and Walter hadn't heard a peep from his brother since New Year's Eve. It was as though Roger had dropped off the face of the earth. Or worse. None of his sisters knew anything either, or if they did they weren't saying. He reminded Mildred not to worry. Roger bounces from place to place. It's what he does. Like a ball. "At least he didn't steal the city car."

"What a terrible thing to say."

"Betty thought you had died when I called," he said. "Do you know how long it's been since I called Betty?"

He tried to recall their last conversation but his memory failed him. Probably she had called him, and probably it was something trivial. Walter had no stomach for triviality. Betty, more than the others, found his distaste of small talk off-putting.

They dropped Jackson off at school without Mildred escorting him to his classroom. He rarely asked about his mother anymore. It was a mixed blessing because trying to explain to a six-year-old why his mother was in prison ranked high on Walter's list of things to avoid, but he didn't want the boy to forget her. She wouldn't be in prison forever. It was a fine line to walk.

Half an hour into his morning, after a quick meeting with the staff, Walter summoned the acting chief to his office and harangued him for not keeping closer tabs on his brother's case. Either Gant didn't know where Roger was or he was a very good liar. Walter liked Gant, and he believed him to be an honest man, which left him facing the likelihood that his brother had fooled them all. Good riddance, he supposed, except for the crummy way it left things between them. They had never been close, but not talking is different than not speaking. As was his nature, Walter grumbled aloud to deflect his anxiety. Deflection was a term he had picked up in a self-help book somewhere between youth and middle age, long before he learned the true meaning of another word: addiction. Gambling, not chemicals, as though that were somehow less damning.

Gant apologized for not being more on top of things in the department (he didn't call it *his* department, which answered for much of the problem) but Ball was the vindictive sort, and being forced to shoulder the detective work galled him. He made no bones about it, especially not to his subordinate-turned-boss. "The quicker the board appoints someone to this position permanently, the better for the department," Gant said. "Everybody's afraid to show any sign of loyalty out of fear the tables may turn and they'll end up on the wrong side."

"And you're afraid to take charge for that same reason," Walter said. Understandable, he supposed, considering the awkward situation he had put the man in. "Never mind. Forget I said that."

"No, it's true," Gant said. "I'll be out of a job if the board appoints him."

"I never should've put you in this situation," Walter said. "I thought if the board could see what a good job you'd do —."

"And here I am not doing such a good job."

"It's not your fault."

"Can you promise me he won't be chief?"

"You know I can't," Walter said. "You know as well as I do what the board will probably do. They've vowed to, you know. It's already decided."

"Then I'm digging my own grave," Gant said. "I may as well start looking for another job."

"You're best chance is to take charge," Walter said. "Make these next two weeks count. Show yourself."

"He'd love for me to interfere with his investigation of your brother."

"We both know he's the one who destroyed the evidence," Walter said. "You can't let him get away with it."

"I'm afraid he already has," Gant said. "He covered his tracks."

"I won't have a man like him running my police department," Walter said. "I won't tolerate another Benson."

Gant frowned.

"Being dead doesn't make the man a saint," Walter said.

"Still."

"Still nothing. Benson was a crooked cop. He admitted as much to my face. If you'd really like to do some detective work, find out what happened to him."

"We already know what happened," Gant said. "And it's not my investigation. The state —."

"I know," Walter said. The state had taken over the investigation and there was nothing Gant or anyone else could do about it. "Tell me something," he said. "What do the men think of me?"

Gant hesitated. The abrupt question percolated below the surface of his young face. Walter meant to take his measure. Test his honesty head on. He already knew he wasn't popular.

"I can't speak for individuals," Gant said.

"Don't."

"But the general opinion —."

"That's what I want."

"They don't like you."

"At all?"

"They blame you for Benson."

"Is it irreversible?"

"Probably. Once people set their minds to something it's hard to get them to change."

"And you?"

Gant smiled. "I'm probably biased."

"Do you blame me for Benson?"

"No."

"Did you at first?"

"No."

"Honest?"

"Benson put the gun in his mouth, not you."

"I'm not convinced he did," Walter said.

"You've made that very clear," Gant said. "Some people interpret that as your way of avoiding guilt."

"Is that what you think?"

"No. I believe you're an honest man. Perhaps too honest for your own good."

"A man can't be too honest."

"Sure he can," Gant said. "Especially if he's a politician."

"But I'm not a politician."

"You ran for office and won," Gant said. "I'd call that a politician."

"The Hayes Beacon has everyone thinking I'm a racist," Walter said. "Do you think I am?"

Gant shrugged. "Impossible for me to say. Some people think all white men are racist."

"My grandson is black."

"Half black," Gant said. "And he's your grandson. Some people call that an exception."

"Some people being you?"

Gant laughed. "Actually, no. I don't think that at all."

"Why?"

He shrugged again, and that was all the answer Walter was going to get.

Gant left and Mildred entered, bringing with her a fresh cup of coffee. She picked up on the pain in Walter's back without him mentioning it. It was the way he sat to one side that gave him away.

"Brad Stovall called a little while ago," she said. "I told him you were busy."

Walter reached for the phone to call him back.

"He left a message."

Walter withdrew his hand and waited. Mildred was being deliberately slow in telling him, which meant she didn't like the message. Understandable, given the source. Any exchange with Brad Stovall was a strain on the senses.

"He told me to tell you he's ready to support Gant."

Walter choked on his coffee. "Did he say why?"

"No. But he said you should call a special meeting of the board as soon as possible."

Walter reached for the phone again, wanting to hear it for himself. Stovall didn't answer, so he called Gant and delivered the good news, then told him to take control and make the department his.

* * *

Tipton stashed Roger Pigg in a hotel in New Albany where his brother couldn't find him. Roger had quite a story to tell, and he was becoming reluctant. Twice he had tried to recant, but both times Tipton had distracted him with a bottle of whiskey and a lecture about doing the right thing. Both times Tipton had explained how telling the truth was the right thing. Right for his brother Mark because it avenged him, and right for Walter because it allowed him to cleanse his soul of the terrible guilt he carried. Roger Pigg was malleable, like putty, and Tipton was a master of manipulation.

Rance injected himself into the situation and demanded to know what Tipton's plans were. They argued, at one point getting rather loud, then Rance threw up his hands and declared himself no part of it. He couldn't make up his mind — in or out.

"Judge Bishop will laugh you out of the courtroom," Rance said on his way out of Tipton's office.

"What courtroom," Tipton said to his back. "I'm not a fool."

Rance kept going. He was shortsighted. Without vision. Too quick to climb up onto his high horse and pretend to be above the fray. Trickery is a tool in any profession. Why should the law be any different? Roger Pigg had a fanciful story that would embarrass his brother and Tipton meant to capitalize on it. So what? There was nothing unethical about it. The prosecutor could take the case to the grand jury or not, it was up to her. Probably she wouldn't. All that mattered to Tipton was that the accusation stick with the voters.

Rance stopped to flirt with Candice, or to gossip. Tipton saw them talking but couldn't hear the conversation, but he could imagine. He was probably telling her about the two little Piggs. One was a vagrant and the other had built himself an office made of straw. Tipton was the big bad wolf, and he meant to huff and puff and blow the office down. Of course Rance wouldn't tell it that way. In his version the wolf would crack up and be carted off to the loony bin.

His blood boiled as he watched them. At one point Candice giggled. What he wouldn't give to have a microphone hidden at her desk.

After Rance left she gathered some papers and brought them to Tipton's office under the guise of needing them signed. "They need to go out this afternoon," she said, transferring them from the crook of her arm to his desk.

Tipton pushed them aside. "I'll get to them when I can."

"They're important."

"Then you should've brought them to me sooner."

"It'll only take a few seconds," she said.

"What was Rance saying to you just now?"

"Nothing that concerns you," she said.

"Don't forget you work for me. Any conversation you have in this office concerns me."

She stiffened her back. "You hired me, Mister Palo. You didn't buy me." There she stood, beautiful in her anger. Straightening her back had increased her chest by a cup size. The buttons on her blouse tugged against the buttonholes. The tan skin between the buttons wicked the moisture from his throat. He imagined his fingers working the buttons, then his hands pushing the blouse back over her shoulders, exposing the soft skin of her neck. He could almost taste her. "I feel sorry for your wife," she said, then she turned and reached the door with three angry strides. Suddenly he felt very small, then angry. For a moment he hated her, then he signed the papers.

* * *

The board met Friday morning in the City Hall conference room two doors down from Walter's office. The room was generally used for meetings with small groups, or with contractors pitching some new way to sop up city money. The clerk and city attorney were the only ones present except for the mayor and the five aldermen.

Walter officially called the executive session to order, then the six men began discussing the only issue on the table — appointing a permanent police chief — without any of the public grandstanding a regular meeting seemed to require. The meeting itself was a formality, but a necessary one. Stovall had capitulated for reasons unimportant to Walter. Walter had made no deals and would be bound by nothing the aldermen may have agreed to behind his back.

"Why not just vote," Lyle Townsend said above the hum of back and forth.

"I second," Stovall said. The room fell silent. All eyes swung to Walter.

"All those in favor of appointing Andrew Gant as our Chief of Police say aye," Walter said, as was his duty.

"Aye," said Gordy Kilfiche, but no one else uttered a peep.

"Aye," Walter said, searching the other four faces for some reason behind their hesitation. Brad Stovall sat with his jaws clamped shut, then his face softened and he smiled. Walter knew he'd been had.

"What dirty trick are you trying to pull?"

"Politics is a blood sport," Stovall said. "Don't take it personal."

Wayne Toms nominated Glenn Ball. Lyle Townsend seconded. Walter had no choice but to call for a vote. The motion carried four to two. Glenn Ball was in and Gant was out. Bushwhacked. Walter looked at Terrell Sharp, but the preacher kept his eyes glued to the table.

The mayor adjourned the meeting, then stood with a great deal of pain in his lower back. More pain than he had brought to the meeting. More pain than he had felt in a long time. He glared at Stovall. "You can forget about those contracts with the county," he said. "After I talk to the supervisors you won't move a shovelful of dirt or gravel."

Stovall threw back his head and filled the room with his booming laughter. Overdone to the point of foolishness, as though he had suddenly become a very bad caricature of himself. At that moment Walter hated him. *Despise* was too mild a word for the deep and complete feeling of disgust that consumed him. He hadn't felt such an overwhelming need to throw himself at another human being since that day in the RV when he popped his cork and saved his family from certain death. Stovall was almost as big as the demon Walter had killed that day. Rode him out the door and through the air and splat against the ground at seventy plus. It was the most terrifying and most exhilarating few moments of his life. The perfect storm of juxtaposed emotions. The impact ripped them apart and cast them bouncing and tumbling toward different fates. Death for one, life for the other. Life with consequences. A broken back but alive. A second chance he might not have had otherwise. God works in mysterious ways, but at that moment, standing across the oblong conference table from Brad Stovall — the grinning hyena, there was no mystery in the outcome should Walter fling himself in that direction. Stovall would bat him down like a fly.

"I'm already filling contracts with four of the five," Stovall said, meaning the county supervisors. "They think you're a joke." He laughed again. Something else seemed to be on his mind. Another card up his sleeve. "That brother of yours sang like a bird," he said. "So I hear. Don't hold me to it." He left the room still laughing.

As the others filed out, the old judge paused to tell Walter he was sorry that it played out the way it did.

"You knew?"

"We all did," Kilfiche said.

"A simple heads up would've been nice."

"This thing had to be settled. The town needs a police chief."

Walter studied him. His old face seemed truly sad. "Why didn't you vote with them? You wanted Ball too."

"Because I hate the way they did it." He clapped Walter on the shoulder then left him standing alone in a room that had handed him his first major defeat as mayor.

* * *

Six months before Walter Pigg was sworn in as mayor, a dump truck loaded with red dirt swerved into the oncoming lane and hit seventy-year-old Millie Guntharp's Nissan Pathfinder six inches behind the driver's door. The truck rolled onto its side and dumped seven yards of dirt onto the highway. Millie Guntharp survived with a broken collarbone, three cracked ribs, and a severed big toe on her left foot. The truck belonged to Brad Stovall. Millie Guntharp's husband hired Tipton Palo to file the lawsuit. Thus began the understanding between Palo and Stovall.

"You've got your police chief," Stovall said to Palo as he pulled out the chair uninvited and interrupted the lawyer's lunch.

"Keep your voice down!"

Stovall dropped into the chair like sack of potatoes. People began to stare. "Now the lawsuit goes away."

Tipton knew the deal but now was not the time. "A phone call would've sufficed," he said. "You don't have to tell the world."

"I'll tell the world more than that if you don't hold up your end of the bargain."

The man was too dumb to be discreet. Worse than a bull in a china shop.

"You've been hanging this thing over my head long enough," Stovall said. "I've done everything you told me to do and then some."

The lawsuit had not been the entirety of their deal. Stovall had been compensated for services rendered, sometimes with cash, other times with favors. One hand washing the other. Tying this favor to the lawsuit had been a last minute demand on Stovall's part because he was impatient.

"I can't just end the lawsuit," he said, trying to keep his voice down. "My client has final say in any offer we accept."

"You've got two days."

"It's Friday. Even if I could get my client to —."

"Two business days then," Stovall said. "And I don't give a fat damn what you have to do to make it happen."

"Millie Guntharp's set on going to trial," Tipton said, lying. Her husband called every week wanting to take whatever deal the insurance company had on the table.

"Then you'd better talk some sense into the old bag or I'll do some talking of my own," Stovall said.

Tipton folded his napkin across his half eaten sandwich already plotting the alderman's demise. Who did he think he was to make threats? "I'll do my best," he said. "In the meantime it's not in your best interest to threaten me."

Stovall bellowed with laughter. He was a brute with powerful lungs and a weak brain and every head in the place was turned now.

"Okay!" Tipton said under his breath. Saying it aloud would be useless unless he screamed so he said it with his eyes and with his face.

Stovall stopped and grinned. "I thought you'd see it my way."

"I'll take care of it," Tipton said, ignoring the room because acknowledging the stares would only make it worse.

"Two business days."

"Okay."

The waitress came to take Stovall's order but he waved her away. "I was just leaving," he said. She left them quickly. Tipton asked for his ticket but she was already out of earshot. He hazarded a quick glance and was relieved to see the people going about their own business again.

"This was completely unnecessary," he said to Stovall as quietly as he could. "You've embarrassed us both for no good reason."

"I'm not embarrassed."

"No, you're probably not," Tipton said, "but you should be. If you had any sense you would be."

"Don't worry," Stovall said. "I won't talk. As long as the lawsuit goes away."

CHAPTER 23

Walter tried to reach Gant by telephone after the board meeting concluded but it went to voice mail both times. The news he needed to deliver wasn't the kind to be left on an answering machine, so he told him to call back as soon as possible. Shortly after noon, a verbal scuffle between Mildred and the detective erupted in the outer office. It was short-lived because Mildred had a low tolerance for disrespect.

"I told him you were busy," she said, squeezing between the doorjamb and the just-replaced acting chief.

Walter waved her away, then told Gant to close the door and sit. He was in no mood to be nice, not even to the man who had every right to feel betrayed. "I'd tell you how the meeting went but something tells me you already know."

Gant closed the door with a thud. "You've ruined me."

"Sit down," Walter said. "I've ruined us both."

Gant moved to the back of the chair and glared across the desk at the mayor. For a moment Walter thought things might get physical, which would be no contest given his crippled back and the detective's superior physical condition.

"The least you could've done was told me."

"Sit down!"

The detective pulled the chair back and sat. The two men glared at each other, sizing each other up. Walter tried his best to explain things. He'd been hoodwinked. Blindsided. His mistake was in trusting Stovall to keep his word, now there was nothing to do but make the best of the situation. Easier said than done, he agreed, then he found it awfully hard to look the detective in the eye because he felt responsible.

"Ball's gunning for you now," Gant said.

"Gunning for both of us I'm sure," Walter said. "Sharp was the turncoat. I've been trying to call him but he won't answer."

"You should've told me there was a meeting."

"Stovall promised me it was a done deal," Walter said. "We had an arrangement … so I thought."

"So they got to you too?"

"Not that kind of arrangement," Walter said. "Simple backscratching. I was going to put in a good word for him with the county supervisors and he was going to deliver three votes for you. Nothing illegal about it. I was duped."

"You should've known better than to trust that snake."

Walter realized that now and he felt like a complete fool. Gant must have read it in his face because his demeanor softened.

"Ball's a known quantity," Gant said. "No one on the board knows me. I don't blame them for voting the way they did."

"The man's a wet noodle," Walter said. "Completely useless."

"He told me I hitched myself to the wrong horse," the detective said. "Meaning you. Does he have something on you?"

"Anything that clown has on me, I'll own," Walter said. Tipton Palo had already thrown his gambling past at him and it didn't stick. He almost had his debts paid off but being broke wasn't against the law. If it was, half the town would be behind bars. An advantage of leading a boring life is that you don't leave much of a trail.

The door opened and Mildred stuck her head in to tell him he should take the call on line three.

"We're fine," Walter said, thinking the interruption was her way of rescuing him from an unwanted visitor. Gant thought so too, judging by the displeasure on his face. He stood and said he would go. Walter told him to sit. "I appreciate what you're trying to do," he said to his wife, "but I don't need rescuing."

Mildred's expression remained the same. "What I'm trying to do is tell you there's a call on line three that you really need to take."

Walter looked at the phone. Line three was blinking red. He looked at the detective and shrugged. Gant took his leave. Mildred waited with doorknob in hand until Walter lifted the handset and punched the button.

"Walter?" It was a female voice, oddly familiar. Very familiar on second thought, though he hadn't heard it in a while. "Is this Walter?"

"Yes," Walter said. "Peggy?"

"Doris," she said. His oldest sister. Older than Mark would have been had he lived, but just barely. Doris never called. Hardly ever. The last time had been — he couldn't recall the last time. Something must be wrong with Peggy. Peggy was the official family notifier. If Doris was calling then Peggy must be dead. That's how Walter's mind worked it out.

"Has something happened to Peggy?"

"What? No. I don't know. I haven't talked to Peggy. Should I call her?"

Roger then. Of course it was Roger. He had probably worn out his welcome with Peggy's husband and cast himself on Doris. Suddenly it occurred to him to ask about her husband. "Nothing's happened to Bill I hope," he said, meaning it at some level. He had nothing against his brother-in-law but they had never been close. More Doris than Bill. A man can't be close to his brother-in-law if he's not close to his sister.

"Bill's fine," she said. "Is it true about you being a mayor? Of course it's true. I called the City Hall and some young woman answered. She has a very nice phone voice, and she was polite. That's important, you know. So many young people are rude these days. She said you were in a meeting and couldn't be disturbed, but I told her I was your sister and that it was urgent. That's when Mildred came on the line. I recognized her voice —."

"Stop babbling," Walter said, suddenly remembering why he disliked talking to Doris on the phone. "What's so urgent that you've interrupted my meeting, Doris?"

Silence. He had insulted her. Doris was the clam-up-and-sulk type. He should've been more patient with her. Let her get to the point in her own way. Now he would have to wait twice as long. He apologized, trying hard to sound contrite. Maybe it worked because he heard a gust of air against the mouthpiece. It sounded more exasperation than sigh.

"A man called," she said.

"Okay."

"He was asking about Mark."

"Mark? Why? What did he ask?"

"It was all very strange," she said. "Why would a police detective ask me about something that happened forty years ago?"

"A police detective?"

"That's what he said."

"From where?"

"He didn't say from where."

"How could he not say from where? Think, Doris. If he said he was a police detective then he said where he was from."

"I took the call, not you," Doris said. "I think I know what the man said." Her pitch was elevated. Doris was an emotional swamp. If he had any hope of getting the details he had to pace himself.

"Of course you do," he said. "I didn't mean it the way it sounded. What questions did he ask you?"

"I hope I didn't do anything wrong by talking to him. Do you think it was one of those phone scams?"

"How would a phone scammer know about Mark? You haven't posted anything about him on Facebook have you?"

"No, of course not. I haven't thought about Mark in years," she said. How could she not think about her dead brother? No, don't ask that. Definitely don't ask her that.

"What did he ask you, Doris?"

"Crazy stuff," she said. "Like how he died, and how you and him got along. He asked me how you acted afterwards."

"Did he mention Roger?"

"No. Just you and Mark. He asked me if I thought you did it on purpose. What did he mean on purpose?"

Walter's blood froze in his veins. Telling Roger had been a mistake. A big mistake. A catastrophic blunder. Had Gant called his sister? Had the Judas just left his office? "This detective who didn't say where he was from," Walter said, "did he give his name?" It seemed a ridiculous question. A detective who won't identify his agency certainly won't leave a name.

"Yes," Doris said, surprising Walter and giving him hope. "He mentioned it several times. Grant, I think it was."

"Gant?"

"Yes! Gant. That's what he said. He mentioned it so many times I can't believe I said it wrong. I was so shocked, though, him calling and asking about Mark that way. Did I do wrong, Walter?"

"No," he said. "You didn't do anything wrong. How long ago did he call?"

"Are you angry with me?"

"No, of course not, Doris. Not with you. How long ago did the detective call you? How many hours has it been?" He didn't want to confuse her with time zone differences by asking her to name the hour.

"About an hour ago," she said. "Are you in some kind of trouble?"

"Why didn't you call me right away?"

"The number I had was out of service."

"We don't have the landline anymore," Walter said.

"I called Betty and she said you were a mayor now, so I looked up the number for City Hall. He called Betty, too," she said. "And Peggy."

"You talked to Peggy?"

"No." Her tone begged him to ask her why, but he didn't. Whatever feud his sisters did or didn't have going on at that moment didn't concern him. Doris and Peggy's relationship had been strained for as long as Walter could remember. Why, he didn't know, and he didn't care. He really didn't. "Betty told me."

"Did Betty tell you when he called them?"

"What difference does it make?"

"Timeline is important," he said. "Think."

"Don't talk down to me, Walter. You always talk down."

"Please, Doris, I'm not talking down to you. I really need an accurate timeline." If Gant called either of his sisters before the board met and replaced him, it meant he had been working against Walter all along. It meant Walter had been duped twice. Doris hem-hawed, saying she couldn't be sure, then she threw out a number only to retract it and throw out something else. Eventually she said the detective called Peggy first, then Betty, so the first call had to be at least four hours old because Peggy had gone to see her doctor immediately afterwards, and doctors take forever. Walter realized he wasn't going to get a definitive answer without calling Peggy, so he thanked her for calling and said he had to get back to his meeting.

"Don't you want to know what I told him?"

"Yes," he said. "Of course."

"I told him Mark drowned and you tried to save him."

"Good."

"That's how it happened isn't it? It was so long ago."

"Yes," Walter said. "That's exactly how it happened. If anyone tells you anything different they're lying." Roger might get around to telling them all, but it would be his word against Walter's, and against what his sisters had believed all their lives. Peggy was the one he needed to convince. She was the stalwart of the family. The anchor. The sane one in the asylum. First, though, he wanted to hear from Gant.

Instead of buzzing Mildred, Walter left his desk to tell her in person to get Gant back and don't take any excuses. As soon as he stepped outside his door he saw the detective chatting up Mildred's young assistant. Kelsey was all smiles, eating up the attention from the young detective.

"Get back in here," Walter barked. Gant turned from Kelsey and stared at the mayor with his mouth agape, deciding not to speak the thought so clearly on his mind. Smart, Walter thought. Now was not the time for Judas to stand on honor. "Now," Walter said. He was angry and it didn't much matter to him how he came across.

Gant flashed an incredulous grin as he left the young lady's desk and followed the mayor back into his office. Walter waited at the door with his hand on the knob, then closed the door and told Gant to sit.

"I think I'll stand until you tell me what this is about," Gant said. Walter saw beyond the calm exterior and knew he was seething at being embarrassed in front of the woman he clearly had an interest in.

"Why did you call my sisters?"

Gant's mouth tightened. His eyes constricted. The reaction was too sudden, too complete, not to be authentic. Walter knew before Gant answered that something sinister was afoot.

"What sisters?"

Walter rounded his desk and eased himself into his chair. His lower back pain prevented him from plopping, which would have befitted the occasion. He sighed. It was an elongated expulsion of air from his lungs. "Please," he said, his voice devoid of hostility now. "Sit."

Walter pondered what to do, then he reached for the phone. "I'm going to ask you to do something," he said. "Humor me. I think this will clear this up. Part of it anyway." He dialed his sister Doris and put the phone on speaker. "When she answers, tell her you have a few more questions."

"What's this about?"

Doris answered. "Hello?"

Walter nodded at the detective. Ask her.

"Uh, I have a few more questions," Gant said.

"Who is this?"

Walter nodded again.

"Detective Gant … from the Hayes Police Department," he said, looking to Walter for confirmation that he had said the right thing.

Doris hung up. Walter redialed the number without the phone on speaker. She didn't answer, so he called her from his cell phone. When she answered he asked her if the man who had just called her was the same man who had called her earlier that morning. She said he wasn't. The other man sounded older. She was certain.

* * *

It was Mildred who tracked Alderman Sharp down. She knew a woman who knew his wife, who apparently didn't know that her husband was in hiding. Walter dropped Mildred and Jackson off at home after picking the boy up from school, then he drove across town to Bryant Hill Baptist Church where the preacher was laying tile in the sanctuary. Compared to Walter's church, Bryant Hill was tiny. It reminded him of the church he had attended as a child, then as a young married man.

Walter let himself in and found the pastor on his knees in the lobby smearing grout on a spot of bare concrete with a trowel. "What kind of church makes its pastor lay tile?"

Sharp jumped at the sound of Walter's voice, then he turned and looked back over his shoulder. "The poor kind," he said, not missing a beat. Being a man of God for so many years had probably inoculated him against almost every kind of shock imaginable. The next three seconds of silence passed like minutes, then the pastor turned back to his work and smeared more grout onto the last remaining spot of bare concrete. "If you're here to lecture me don't bother."

"I was hoping to get some answers," Walter said. "I thought we were on the same page."

Sharp placed the last piece of white tile. There were nine clean tiles in all, forming a 3x3 square just inside the front door. "Your page got too crowded for me. I've got a flock to tend, and in case you haven't figured it out for yourself, this is a black church. My congregation is black. I'm black."

"What's race got to do with it? Your people stood a better chance at a fair shake with Gant than they do with Ball."

Sharp tamped the tile down with the wooden handle of the trowel. "Ain't Gant they're concerned with." He raised himself upright on his knees and twisted at the waist so he could look Walter in the eyes. "It's you."

"Me?"

"You," Sharp said. "All that stuff about you chasing black kids off your lawn, and assaulting that boy. How do you think my people are supposed to feel about that?"

"Surely you don't believe —."

"My people believe," the preacher said. "Phone calls day and night. All hours. Got so I couldn't sleep."

"None of that's Gant's fault."

"Stovall put the word out that I was your lackey."

"And you don't call that racist?"

"Sure," Sharp said. "Makes me angry, too, but it don't change the fact that now I gotta prove him wrong."

"Stovall's a bully."

"And very good at it."

"So you just let him intimidate you? You don't fight back?"

Sharp discarded the trowel into the plastic bucket of grout. "When I took this church it was one room. I baptized people in the creek out back. Hot or cold it didn't matter. When a child of God gets the Holy Ghost they can't wait to get dunked, so I dunked 'em. There's been many a Sunday I stood waist deep in water cold enough to make my teeth chatter." He laughed. "I think some of 'em liked it cold because they were scared of snakes." He grinned. "And that was fine by me because I'm no fan of snakes myself."

"I'm not a racist," Walter said. "Most of the stories about me aren't true, and the ones that are true sound worse than it was."

"I believe you," Sharp said. "Sunday I plan on laying it out to my congregation — the one's who'll listen. You should come."

"Couldn't you have laid it out for them last Sunday and avoided all this?"

Sharp wiped his hands on his pants. "Last Sunday I wasn't getting deluged with phone calls. You can't avert a crisis you don't know's coming."

"All you had to do was call me and explain things and I would have delayed the meeting," Walter said.

Sharp shook his head. "It's a difficult time. Reminds me of the sixties sometimes the way people go at each other. This morning don't change the way I feel about Brad Stovall. If you're worried about me being like Townsend and Toms, don't."

"A lot of good that does Gant."

"The Gants of the world are insignificant in the grand scheme of things," Sharp said.

"No one is insignificant."

"Now that sounds mighty fine, Mayor Pigg, and if I was standing in my pulpit I might say that very same thing, but you and I both know it's not true. Not when it comes to politics. If Ball doesn't do his job, we can remove him.

Gant's a young man. He'll land on his feet. Tell Ball to make him assistant chief."

"Fat chance of that," Walter said. "He'd fire him outright if he could."

Sharp launched a half-hearted defense of the chief, reminding Walter of Ball's many years of service in the number two spot. Walter listened with patience. He really had nowhere he needed to be. The anger he had harbored against the pastor since morning had waned somewhat. He was willing to hear the man out.

Sharp stood and wiped the dust from his knees.

"You should get some of those knee pads the professionals use," Walter said.

"I should get one of those professionals," Sharp said. "The ladies had a bake sale and raised money to repair the floor. Every contractor I talked to wanted to rip out the entire floor, so I did the job myself. Not bad, don't you think?" He wiped his forehead on his sleeve. The floor was spotted now. A handful of new tiles amid a sea of old. Not pretty, but functional. "Keeping Ball was me repairing the rift in my congregation, Walter. It's not the prettiest fix, but maybe it'll keep the foundation from cracking."

* * *

Tipton was up late. Tomorrow was Wednesday and Dexter Mann had promised a sensational headline propped up by a damning account of how the mayor killed his brother. The revelation would knock the town back on its heels. Public outrage would force Pigg to resign. Ball would apply pressure if needed. Arrest him if he had to, though Tipton couldn't imagine it coming to that. Once people heard how their mayor drowned his brother and covered it up for decades, the mayor's political career would be finished. His goose would be cooked.

Thirteen minutes before midnight his phone rang. He didn't recognize the number so he didn't answer, then it called again. The female identified herself as a nurse from the hospital in Tupelo. Rance had had a heart attack and Tipton was his emergency contact. He shot to his feet and yelled for Autumn. Three yells later she appeared at the top of the stairs wearing her sleep shirt. "Get dressed!"

"Why? What's wrong?"

"Rance had a heart attack and I can't drive." The cops in Tupelo might not care who he was if they pulled him over with alcohol on his breath. They had the legal limit so low a man could fail just by sniffing a bottle cap, or by reading the label on a good stiff bourbon.

Autumn rushed back upstairs then took her sweet time coming down again. When he next saw her, she was made up and fresh.

"Rance is dying and you're worried about makeup."

"Don't pretend you care if he dies," Autumn said. She was right, but what a thing to say. He scolded her, then told her she'd better watch her mouth at

231

the hospital. Rance was hard enough to get along with as it was.

When they got to the car she asked him how bad it was.

"You think they tell you something like that over the phone?"

"You don't have to bite my head off."

The drive to the hospital took thirty minutes. Tack on six more to get from the parking garage and through security at the ER entrance, then another two or three to get past the nurse at the front desk. She was a young nurse with pimples on her face and she couldn't find Rance's name in the computer, then she asked Tipton to spell it and she found it right away. He didn't know whether she had trouble with Rance, or West. "Through that door," she said, pointing toward a set of double doors that opened automatically when he and Autumn approached. At the next desk the nurse was polite enough to escort them down the hall and into a small room occupied by a lone female with long brown hair and eyes red from crying. She couldn't have been a day over thirty-five.

After the nurse left them, Tipton asked the woman how Rance was doing. "I'm his partner, by the way. Tipton Palo." Given the social climate, he felt a sudden need to clarify himself. "His law partner," he said. "This is my wife, Autumn." The woman glanced up at him but didn't answer, so he and Autumn sat directly across from her. The chairs all had red vinyl padding in the seat and upper back, and they were not nearly as comfortable as they looked. There were ten chairs in all, placed almost touching around the four walls of the room. Two of the corners had tables, and on the tables were magazines that ranged from Time to Guns and Ammo — an odd choice for a hospital, but then again maybe not.

He tried the woman again with no better result. This time she didn't even look up. Grief affects people in different ways, so he didn't press her. She probably didn't know anything anyway.

Autumn rummaged her purse for a bottle of nail polish and began painting her nails pink. The smell quickly filled the tiny room.

"Some people might be allergic," he said.

Autumn ignored him.

The woman across from them sniffled and dabbed at her nose with a tissue from a box in the chair beside her. Rance didn't have a daughter, so the woman had to be one of his flings.

After a few minutes of silence, Tipton told Autumn to try her luck with the woman.

Autumn cleared her throat. "Have they told you anything yet?"

Nothing. Autumn whispered that she might be in shock. Tipton whispered back that she probably gave Rance the heart attack. Autumn squeezed his arm.

Finally he could take it no more. "Are you here for Rance? Hey! At least look at me when I'm talking to you!"

The door opened and a nurse glared at him. "If you can't keep your voice down you'll have to leave," she said. She looked healthy enough to make good on the threat.

"It's her fault," Tipton said, nodding toward the woman. She looked up. "I'm trying to find out if she knows anything about my partner but she won't answer."

The woman opened her mouth and a strange noise came out. A grunt.

"She's deaf," the nurse said.

Tipton felt his face change colors. "I'm sorry. I didn't know."

The door closed and they were alone again. The woman continued to make grunting noises but he refused to look at her. Her handicap made him feel uncomfortable. Autumn asked her if she could read lips, then she asked if she was there for Rance. Tipton raised his eyes and saw the woman nod, then Autumn asked her if she knew his condition. She didn't.

"Leave her alone," Tipton said, trying not to move his lips, speaking low even though it didn't matter.

"I'm talking to her."

"I know you are, stop."

Autumn ignored him and kept talking to the woman who couldn't talk back. He bristled. Lately she was becoming difficult for no good reason. Early menopause, he suspected. It had hit his mother early and he remembered how much trouble his father had with her. It was years before she was normal again.

He pulled out his phone and exhausted Facebook, then spent half an hour looking at memes on Reddit. Finally the doctor came with a young woman in tow who repeated everything he said with her hands. Tipton found it terribly distracting.

Rance's heart attack was serious but not life threatening. In the morning he would have three stents inserted and go home with a new diet, blood thinners, and a prescription for exercise. A month from now he'd probably be saying he never felt better, like Tipton's uncle Roy had done, right up until the day he dropped dead with heart attack number two.

Tipton made a mental note to have Candice double-check Rance's life insurance policy to make sure it was paid up. They each had a million-dollar policy paid by the firm, with the surviving partner as the beneficiary. "Can I see him?"

"Not tonight," the doctor said. He was short and dark-skinned and spoke with an accent that sounded more German than Asian. He wore pale green scrubs with a white lab coat emblazoned with an unpronounceable name above the left pocket. If Rance died he would be sure to verify his medical license. "You're welcome to stay, but you might be more comfortable going home and coming back in the morning."

Tipton and Autumn left. Doctor's orders, almost. Doctor's suggestion, which was excuse enough. The deaf woman stayed behind, either out of loyalty or desperation. He remarked on it during the ride home and Autumn told him he should be ashamed of himself. He wasn't. When they got home he was tired and sober, so he went to bed. As his eyelids grew heavy, he thought about the life insurance policy, and how nice it would be to have a million dollars.

CHAPTER 24

MAYOR PIGG INVESTIGATED FOR MURDER.

Walter expected a headline. He even expected a story, but he didn't expect to be taken to with a verbal hatchet. Investigated was a strong word. Too strong, considering the investigator misrepresented his identity to Walter's sisters. Of course it was Ball. Who else? It certainly wasn't Gant.

The dishonesty of the story lay in what it didn't say more than in what it said. Yes, he held his brother under until he drowned, but the moments leading up to that climax made it necessary. Walter had reacted out of fear. Out of desperation. Had he not reacted, Mae and Cecil Pigg would have lost two sons that day instead of one.

Mildred had gone upstairs to get Jackson ready for school. The three of them always had breakfast together at the kitchen table. On Wednesdays Walter usually got an early start so he could enjoy the paper with a cup of coffee. Since becoming mayor, *enjoy* was a mischaracterization of the time he spent with the Beacon unfolded before his eyes.

He heard Mildred enter the room at his back and looked around to see her alone. "Where's Jackson?"

"Upstairs brushing his teeth," she said. "What's wrong?"

"Listen to this."

According to Hayes Police Chief Glenn Ball, Mayor Pigg is being investigated for a forty-two-year-old murder. "What began as a routine traffic stop last year has turned into something none of us expected," Ball said in an interview on Monday. On December 22, 2018, police stopped the Lincoln Town Car belonging to the mayor for erratic driving. Thinking they were dealing with the mayor, the officer contacted Chief Benson for direction. "Benson told him to play it by the book," Ball stated. "That's how he ran the department and that's how it'll be run under me. Everybody gets the same fair shake."

That late-night traffic stop culminated in the arrest of Roger Pigg — the mayor's brother — when the officer found a large amount of cocaine underneath the driver's seat. According to the police report, Roger Pigg denied knowledge of the drugs and no drugs were found in his system. "That's how the law is," Ball said. "You borrow someone's car, you'd better check under the seat."

Walter paused and looked up. Mildred stood slack-jawed, halfway between the table and stove, frozen in place with a plate of eggs and sausage in one hand and a bowl of biscuits in the other. "Can they get away with that?"

Walter continued.

After the arrest of his brother, Mayor Pigg ramped up his efforts to fire Police Chief Benson. According to a source within the department, the mayor's attack on Benson crossed the line. Ball echoed the sentiment. "One of the hardest parts of my job now is dealing with the sense of betrayal within the ranks. I tell them what Benson would've told them: Keep your chin up and do your job."

Mildred slammed the plate and bowl down on the table. A biscuit bounced free and rolled toward the salt and pepper shakers. "That's ridiculous! We'll sue!"

"He's not finished," Walter said.

Mayor Pigg denied knowledge of the drugs found in his car during the traffic stop, but his brother had an angel looking over his shoulder. Because he was indigent, the court appointed attorney Tipton Palo to represent him. "The irony is glaring," Palo told us. "At first I considered asking the judge to remove me and pick someone else, given the election and all, but after discussing it with my law partner, I decided that I would move forward with it and do the best I could."

Tipton Palo's best proved to be good enough for his client and perhaps for another brother as well. Mark Pigg drowned in a gravel pit when he was fifteen. "Authorities were perhaps a little quick to rule it an accident because Mark had a broken arm and the only witness was his younger brother Walter," Palo said. Walter Pigg was ten years old when his brother drowned. According to newspaper reports from the time, Walter tried to save his brother but lost him in the murky water. "My client said the mayor told him quite a different story when he came to visit back in December," Palo said. According to his client, Mayor Pigg admitted to forcing their brother's head under water until he drowned. There is no statute of limitations on murder.

At that point Walter stopped. Tears flooded his eyes and blurred the words. There's no statute of limitations on guilt, either, but the article didn't go that far. Mildred reached across the table and patted the back of his hand. His voice cracked when he folded the paper and slid it toward her, suggesting she read the rest for herself.

"The last paragraph talks about Amy," he said, then he heard the familiar creak of the stairs and knew his grandson was bounding down them. So much energy so early in the morning. He was glad the boy wasn't old enough to read the newspaper.

"Of course they had to drag her into it," Mildred said. Her lips moved as her eyes scanned the words of the last paragraph. Jackson bolted into the room and threw himself into his chair. "You act like you're starving," Mildred said, breaking from the article long enough to spoon eggs and a sausage patty onto his plate. Jackson didn't usually eat biscuits unless there was gravy, which there wasn't.

"Did you catch the part where I declined comment? That Holiday galoot called me Monday and asked if I had any comment on Roger's drug arrest. I told him to go fly a kite. I'm surprised they didn't quote me."

"It's time we get a lawyer of our own," Mildred said. "Sue their pants off."

Walter ticked off the household budget in his head. A lawyer of any caliber was out of the question. She was letting her emotions get the better of her. Women tend to do that sort of thing. It's probably why they're better at childrearing than men. The emotional side. Fathers play a different role, though sometimes Walter struggled to know what his role was. He had certainly fallen short. His father had made it look so easy. So natural. When Amy came along Walter thought it would come to him but it didn't, and now she was in prison for killing her husband because her father didn't protect her.

* * *

Tipton's spirits soared as he read the newspaper over orange juice and light toast. Dexter Mann had outdone himself except for leaving out the part about Walter's gambling addiction. It was a glaring omission. He read the article twice while draining the last bit of orange juice from his glass. The last swallow was almost pure pulp. You don't get pulp in that artificially flavored stuff.

"See, you can eat a healthy breakfast and still smile," Autumn said as he rolled up the newspaper and clamped it underneath his arm.

He rose from the table and gave her a peck on the forehead. "That's not why I'm smiling," he said, "and I wouldn't call that breakfast, but thanks for trying."

She twisted her face into a fake pout and for a brief instant reminded him how attractive she had once been. He slapped her backside and told her to have fun at school, then he was out the door. Mann didn't answer when he called. With a full week before his next deadline, the lazy bum was probably still in bed. What a life. He wasn't rich though, and newspapers were becoming obsolete. Dinosaurs. The internet was their ice age, but in small towns such as Hayes they still served a purpose. Hayes hadn't spawned anything newsworthy since the Piggs were abducted by that psycho from

California. Too bad the psycho hadn't planned better. Tipton would be mayor and Walter Pigg would be decomposing in a shallow grave someplace remote. Coyotes would eventually sniff him out and dig a little and finish the job. No one would know or care.

The office was locked up tight when he arrived. It wasn't like Candice to be late. He couldn't remember the last time it happened. It only mattered because he had to make the coffee and he couldn't remember if it was two scoops or three.

He hung his coat in his office and went to the break room and found the coffee in a cabinet underneath the counter directly below the coffeemaker. Years ago they had splurged for one of those commercial jobs that has two burners so they could impress clients by always having a pot at the ready. Important clients appreciate the extra effort that goes into keeping coffee fresh, even if it means dumping out a full pot and starting over because it sat on the burner too long. Candice was very conscientious about it. Very attractive, too, but why had that crossed his mind?

Half an hour passed and still no Candice. He checked his calendar and saw no mention of her taking a vacation day. It occurred to him that something might have happened to her but surely someone would have called. She had people, he supposed.

He tried Dexter Mann again with the same result. Lazy bastard probably slept till noon on Wednesdays. Probably rolled out of bed for lunch then went to the country club hoping to latch onto some doctor or lawyer or businessman for a free round of golf. Mann was a tick, and he needed a host to survive. Someone to latch onto and suck the blood from because there's only so much news in Hayes. Most weeks the paper consisted of recycled features on local businesses that purchase advertising space, or on the people who invite him to parties. Soft pieces to make them feel good, so they'll continue to let him rub elbows and drink their brandy.

* * *

By nine o'clock the calls had begun trickling into the office. Mildred fielded them, telling anyone she didn't recognize that the mayor was in a meeting, or that he was currently out of the office. It was too early to know the full extent of the damage, but he expected the worst. Mildred had cautioned him not to over react, but how does one not react to such a blatant lie? His Facebook page had nothing. Too early for that crowd, he supposed, so he decided to launch a preemptive strike with a post.

This morning I read with trepidation the hit piece that adorns the front page of the Hayes Beacon. The implication that I am responsible for my brother's death is reprehensible. Mark was fifteen and I was ten. I followed him to a gravel pit where we liked to swim. Our parents forbade us to go near it, but it was a brisk walk from the house and Mark was supposed to meet a girl there (though he never told me outright) but she didn't show. It was the Fourth of July, 1976. Our nation's bicentennial. There was an all day celebration at the park and that's probably why she didn't come.

Mark was standing in water up to his knees and I was playing at the water's edge. He wouldn't let me in the water because he knew it was dangerous. I'll never forget the moment the gravel shifted. My brother disappeared as though the earth opened up and swallowed him. In essence, that's exactly what happened. The gravel shifted and created a vacuum and my brother filled it, but only for a moment. He popped back up but the water that had been to his knees was now over his head and his arm was in a cast and he struggled to keep his head above water. I jumped in and did everything I could, but it was not enough. He was so much bigger than me. I was small for my age back then. I barely managed to save myself.

Not a day has gone by that I haven't thought of Mark. He had so much promise. Many times I have wished it had been me instead of him because he would have made something of himself where I have failed. This morning, when I read the horrible lies in that wretched rag they call a newspaper, I caught myself thanking God my parents are not around to see it. It would have devastated them.

Shame on Dexter Mann. Shame on the Hayes Beacon. Shame on the ones of you who have been calling my office all morning upsetting my wife with the nasty things you've said. I've always heard politics is a nasty business, but I never imagined how nasty. I'm being skewered by the friends of my former opponent. My brother Roger was arrested under false pretenses. The investigating detective found proof that the drugs were planted in my car. He had fingerprints. It was the same man who had previously slaughtered a horse and left the head on my back porch. Once that detective was elevated to Acting Police Chief, Assistant Chief Ball took the case and as if by magic the fingerprint evidence disappeared. Poof! They squeezed my brother. Threatened him with prison unless he gave them something on me. I have no idea where he is or if he's safe. None of my siblings have heard from him. Someone claiming to be Detective Gant called my three sisters and upset them. Detective Gant called one of my sisters in my presence and she assured me the man who had called her was older. Is it that difficult to make the connection between the vanishing fingerprint evidence and a man not Gant calling my sisters claiming to be him? I'm certain all this would go away if I resign my office, but that won't happen. Hayes is in the clutches of evil and I won't stand for it. The puppets and their puppet master have unleashed a dog that not only won't hunt, it will spin around and devour them. I know who you are. You can't hide.

He leaned back and squeezed his eyes shut, then he opened them and read what he had written from start to finish, then he clicked Publish.

* * *

Candice showed up around nine thirty, slamming her purse on her desk and casting foul looks toward Tipton, who watched her with curiosity through his open door. Something had her in a mood. After a few minutes of her not coming to him, he went to her.

"Flat tire?"

She glared up at him.

"Car trouble?"

"How can you be so coldhearted?"

Suddenly he remembered. Rance. "Oh my God, I forgot."

"You're supposed to be his friend."

"I was at the hospital last night," he said. "I didn't see you there."

"Because you didn't call and tell me."

"I didn't call you this morning, either."

"I was on my way to work when he texted me."

"Good, he must be doing better. When are they doing his stents?"

"They finished an hour ago," she said.

He felt bad, but it wasn't his fault. The newspaper article had distracted him, and Rance could have texted him, too. Explaining that to Candice hit a wall. She was at that stage of female anger where anything he said would be used against him. She snapped about the article, too, saying it was disgusting and libelous.

"Don't throw law at me," he said. Who did she think she was?

She slammed her bottom left drawer and completed the ruse of arranging some papers on her desk. Knowing he wasn't going to get anything more submissive out of her, and realizing how difficult she would be to replace, he retreated to his office and locked away some case files, then he put on his coat and started out again. "I'll be at the hospital," he said as he passed her desk.

On the way to the hospital he tried Dexter Mann again. This time Mann answered. "Why didn't you mention Pigg's history with gambling?"

"You're welcome," Mann said. "I think it was a great piece too."

Apparently it was going to be one of those days when everyone decides to be difficult. "Great, except for that glaring omission," he said. "Everything else was brilliant." Using the word brilliant in conjunction with Mann bordered on malpractice, but he thought it easier to talk him up a tree than down. "The best time to kick a man is when he's down. Remember that next week."

"Stubbs told me to lose that part."

"Which part?"

"The gambling part."

"You ran it by Stubbs? Why the hell would you do that?"

"He called me up out of the blue and told me not to write anything else about the mayor's gambling."

Tipton slammed his brakes to keep from blowing through a stop sign. A man in a pickup truck blew his horn. "And you didn't think you should tell me?"

"I assumed you knew," Mann said. "The guy scares the shit out of me."

* * *

"I had some things to take care of at the office," Tipton said to Rance, who was lying flat of his back with tubes coming out of his nose and an IV in his arm. He barely turned his head at the sound of Tipton's voice. The nurses had confiscated his toupee, apparently, and he wondered what Candice thought when she saw him without hair. Maybe it wasn't the first time, come to think of it.

He crossed the room and sat in a chair by the window. The view was the roof of an adjacent building. A pigeon roosted on the far ledge. "You'd think with the prices they charge they could give you a room with a view."

"What things?"

"What?

Rance looked at him for the first time. "You said you had things to take care of at the office," he said. "What things?"

"What difference does it make?"

"I'm your partner," Rance said. "I'm lying here dying and you can't even come visit me?"

"I came last night," Tipton said. "I got my ass up out of bed in the middle of the night and waited down the hall with your deaf girlfriend until the doctor said you weren't going to die."

Rance's grinned. "Long black hair?"

"Yeah, sure, I guess," Tipton said. "How many deaf girls are you dating?"

"Dating's a strong word," Rance said, then he coughed when he tried to laugh.

"At first I thought she was just rude."

"It's an act," Rance said. "She just likes freaking people out."

"What? You mean she's not deaf?" He tried to recall if he had said anything that might come back on him.

"Nah, she's deaf," Rance said. He grinned again. "I had you though, didn't I?" At least he was in a better mood.

Tipton was eager to get back to the office. Hospitals made him nervous. "So we're good?"

Rance nodded. "Go make us some money."

CHAPTER 25

By Thursday afternoon, Mildred and Kelsey had logged over two hundred calls. They kept tabs on paper using the crude but effective method of vertical and slanted lines. Four straight and one slant make five, and the column headed AGAINST carried the FOR column three to one. Mildred suggested that people don't call when they're happy. Anger is what drives someone to pick up the telephone and call City Hall. No one ever calls to say they had *not* hit a pothole on the way home from work.

He appreciated her efforts but the damage was done. Even his heartfelt rebuttal on his official mayoral page had yielded mixed results. The comments broke against him by a slight margin. Some were brutal. A handful called him a racist. One comment from a woman calling herself Unique Monique said someone should hold *his* head underwater until *he* drowned.

"You should report this Unique Monique to the police," Mildred told him over lunch. She had sent Kelsey down the street to the diner for plate lunches. The Thursday special was meatloaf with green beans, new potatoes, and a roll. He preferred cornbread but didn't complain lest he alienate the only two people in the world who truly had his back. The tiny break room had a microwave and a mini-fridge and four feet of counter space that went mostly unused. Someone had painted the walls white instead of beige like the rest of the building.

"I checked out her profile," Kelsey said, "and she's all about peace and love."

"Peace and love my foot," Mildred said. "She should be locked up."

"I'm a public official," Walter said. "People can say anything they want about me whether it's true or not."

"Well they can't threaten your life."

"I think Unique Monique was speaking figuratively," he said. "At least I hope she was. I'll be sure to keep my eye out when I walk past Tranquility Fountain." In the middle of the court square was a fountain that blasted water ten feet into the air in various choreographed patterns with LED lights that changed colors, making it a beautiful place to sit and find peace, except during high school graduation month when someone always managed to fill it with soap.

"Well it wouldn't hurt to report it just in case," Mildred said.

"She's right," said Kelsey. "The world's full of crazies."

"I'm not very popular over there at the moment," he said, meaning the police station. "If they hung my picture on the wall a dart game might break out."

Kelsey was something of an enigma to Walter. She was polite and efficient and a great help to Mildred. She seemed intelligent and stable and considerate of others, then there was her red and purple hair. The red looked natural enough, but the purple varied from streaks to dominance depending on her mood, or perhaps it was the odd coloring that dictated her mood. And it wasn't just the hair. Her eye color varied too. Some days they were green, some days blue. Until Mildred explained color contacts, he had thought she had a medical condition and had been careful not to let her catch him looking.

"Do you like my hair?"

His embarrassment was as quick as it was thorough. Walter had been raised to consider staring impolite, yet here he was gawking like a toddler over a restaurant seat back. He looked to Mildred for rescue but she averted her eyes and bit her lip to keep from smiling. He was on his own.

"Would you believe me if I said yes?"

"No."

"Whatever you're rebelling against must be important to you."

She laughed and his embarrassment eased. "At least you're honest."

"I think my husband is trying to change the subject," Mildred said.

Walter was all for changing it back. "Imagine how the Hayes Beacon would spin it if I reported a Facebook post to the police." He forked a potato and flopped it into his mouth.

"Don't talk with your mouth full," Mildred said.

Walter chewed and swallowed. "I talked then filled my mouth." He forked another potato and wagged it at the two women. "I'm not afraid of Monique, no matter how unique she is."

"Who says it's a woman?" Kelsey said.

"Good point," Walter said, talking between swallows. "Monique might be transgender. Maybe that's what makes her — it — unique."

Mildred frowned. "Don't you dare say that online."

"I didn't say it online. I said it here, in our private break room, over our private lunch."

"It's offensive," Kelsey said.

"You're young," Walter said. "Everything offends you."

"He didn't mean anything by it," Mildred said. "Walter's fifty-five going on eighty."

Walter finished his green beans while staring at the young assistant. "Detective Gant took a shine to you I think," he said. "Maybe you want me to report Unique Monique so he'll come by again."

She blushed. "He was only being polite."

"He could've been polite to Mildred," Walter said.

"Stop teasing her, Walter."

"He's not bothering me, Mrs. Pigg," Kelsey said. "Detective Gant's cute."

"Well don't tell him that," Mildred said. "Men don't like being called cute."

"Who says we don't?"

Mildred ignored him. "Men are supposed to be handsome, not cute," she said to Kelsey.

"He's not handsome," Kelsey said, "but he is cute."

"Well for heaven sake don't tell him *that*," Mildred said.

Walter winked at the girl. "I'll tell him for you."

"Don't you dare!"

Walter and Mildred laughed, then Kelsey smiled and repeated that he *was* cute.

"I've just had an epiphany," Walter said, looking at Kelsey. "You said it's easy to make fake profiles and comment without anyone knowing who you are."

"Did I?"

"Well, is it or is it not?"

"Sure, I guess."

"It just dawned on me that if you did that and went on my page, you might turn the tide in my favor."

"That's dishonest," Mildred said. "And it didn't just dawn on you because you —."

"It's not dishonest if what she posts is true," he said. "All I need is someone taking up for me, and it has to be someone not connected to me. It has to be a stranger." He winked at the young assistant. "Or someone pretending to be a stranger."

"Maybe I could post something," she said.

Mildred opened her mouth to protest but was interrupted by a deliveryman with a large manila envelope with the word CONFIDENTIAL stamped above the address in large red letters. It was addressed to Walter and it had clear tape over the metal clasp at one end.

"Whoever sent this didn't want anything falling out," he said after the deliveryman left. Kelsey retrieved a paring knife from a drawer behind her and Walter used it to defeat the tape, then he straightened the clasp and opened the flap.

"Should I leave?" Kelsey asked.

"No need," Walter said, then he dumped the contents onto the table. It was an 8x10 glossy of Amy. His heart stopped when he saw her battered face. Mildred gasped. Kelsey grabbed Mildred's hand and asked who it was.

"It's our daughter," Mildred said, barely able to get the words out. Then, "Is there a note?"

Walter looked and said there wasn't, then he flipped the photograph over and saw something written across the back with a Sharpie. *RESIGN.*

Mildred burst into tears. "Who could do such a thing?"

"I don't know," Walter said, but he was lying. He recognized the handwriting.

* * *

Walter lied to Mildred twice. First by saying he didn't know who sent the photograph, then again when he told her he was going to the police station to talk to Detective Gant. He was certain the handwriting belonged to Stubbs, and he was just as certain that going to the police would be a fool's errand. Even if Gant wanted to help there was little he could do. Stubbs wasn't dumb enough not to cover his tracks, so Walter decided to answer threat with threat.

Mildred's anguished cries still rang in his ears as he parked the city Impala on the street in front of the pawnshop where Perry Stubbs kept his lair. From the sidewalk the business looked innocuous enough. It was a place where someone down on his luck could pawn anything for a fraction of its value in hopes he might be able to return before the deadline and buy it back. It was also a place where thieves looked to turn a quick buck by offloading stolen goods, and where people looking for a quick deal might purchase someone's misery at a discount. Unadvertised to passersby, the place had a back room where lurked a miserable creature willing to give odds on almost anything. The small back room was dingy and dark and smelled of cigarette smoke and was almost always accessed from the alley. Stubbs was there because Walter had circled the block and had seen his truck parked near the alley door. Many times Walter had come and gone through the back. Deeper in the hole with each exit. More desperate. Looking back he wondered why he hadn't simply stopped, but there is nothing simple about addiction.

Climbing the three steps from the street to the sidewalk took effort without a handrail. The handicap ramps were at either end of the block, so the net pain would have been the same either way. Before driving to the pawnshop he had raced home and up the stairs to the steel lockbox on the shelf in his bedroom closet where he kept his handgun locked away.

He pushed open the heavy glass door and heard a chime. A large man sat behind the counter against the back wall watching television. When he saw Walter he muted the TV and stood. He was tall, with a shaved head and a thick patch of dark hair surrounding his mouth and pulled to a point about an inch below his chin. He wore a denim vest with a lot of patches that probably meant something to the underworld. Somewhere amongst his belongings was a motorcycle, Walter imagined. A Harley Davidson with loud pipes and handlebars extended to a preposterous height. He had a menacing look about him that sent a chill up Walter's spine and almost caused him to turn around and leave.

"Well if it ain't the mayor," the man said with a toothy grin. "Shouldn't you be using the back door?"

Walter kept walking.

"I heard you had a pretty bad limp but damn, shouldn't you be using a cane or something?"

Walter focused on the image of Amy in his head and pressed on. The man was a walking billboard for bad tattoos. The skull and crossbones on the back of his left hand looked to have been scratched on with a rusty nail. Both arms were covered from wrist to his elbow with green ink. If there was a pattern, Walter couldn't see it. Above his left elbow was a heart with an arrow piercing the word LOVE. On his right bicep was a rattlesnake with its tail in the air and venom dripping from its fangs.

Walter was two steps from the counter and the man's smile had begun to droop.

"What's the matter? You a damned mute or something?"

Walter pulled the gun from the belt clip underneath his coat and placed it on the counter with the barrel carelessly pointed at the man's abdomen.

"Springfield XD-9," the clerk said without touching it. "That's a lot of gun for a little guy." He picked it up and examined it. "You looking to pawn or sell?" He grasped the slide with his left hand and pulled it back. A bullet leapt from the chamber and bounced off the glass countertop and onto the floor. "What the hell!" He dumped the magazine into his hand then quickly ejected the newly chambered round. It missed the counter and hit the floor somewhere inside the man's workspace. He slapped the gun on the counter and shook the magazine at Walter. "That's a good way to get somebody's head blowed off!" He thumbed the magazine empty and swatted the unspent shells off the counter and sent them clattering across the floor, then he dropped the magazine onto the counter and cleared his throat. "People get killed with that careless shit," he said. "Now you pawning or selling?"

"Warning," Walter said, then he took the gun with his left hand while at the same time pulling a second magazine from his coat pocket. He shoved the magazine into the handle and chambered a round.

The clerk didn't know whether to fight or run. "What the hell?"

"Tell Stubbs I got his message," Walter said, then he slowly returned the gun to its holster and retrieved the empty magazine from the counter. "Next time I'll use the back door."

* * *

Stubbs sounded irate, screaming into the phone how he was going to burn Pigg's house down with everyone inside, then he was going to break both his legs, then he cursed a while about how spineless their new police chief was. Somewhere around the two-minute mark Tipton heard the part about Pigg going into his pawnshop and threatening his clerk with a gun.

Sounded easy enough to prosecute, but there was more. Stubbs had sent Pigg a photograph of his daughter. Tipton stopped him. Don't say another word. All sorts of images swirled inside his head. Pigg's daughter was attractive, if memory served. Her pictures had been all over the news two years ago when she went to prison, but not *that* kind of picture. Then Stubbs said something about bruises and a busted lip and Tipton stopped him again.

"Don't say anything else about what you sent Pigg. The less I know the better."

"Stop talking like a damned lawyer and light a fire under your police chief," Stubbs said.

"He's not my police chief."

"Well he damned sure ain't mine!"

That was the trouble with Ball, it was impossible to know whether he was in the pocket or out. They had dispatched Benson without a long-term plan. Now they had a mess on their hands. Either they let Pigg have his way and install an honest man, or they throw their weight behind Ball and hope for the best.

"I'll talk to him," Tipton said, and he didn't have to wait long because the chief beeped in. Tipton ended one call and fielded another. "I was just about to —.""

"Pigg's been in with Gant for almost an hour," Ball said.

"So?"

"They're plotting against me."

"What difference does it make? The board's already voted."

"Well I don't like it!"

"Then do something about it," Tipton said. "You're the man's boss. Break up the meeting and send him someplace. Just don't send him anywhere near Pigg's brother. I've got that case right where I want it."

"I don't trust Brad Stovall," Ball said.

"If it wasn't for Brad Stovall, you'd be pounding the streets looking for a job."

"He didn't do it for me."

"What difference does it make who he did it for? It's done. Stubbs is pretty pissed at you, you know."

"Stubbs can kiss my ass."

Tipton groaned. If the man knew how close Stubbs was to driving him down a logging road and putting a bullet in the back of his head he'd be more careful what he said, and who he said it to. "Next time Stubbs calls you, tell him you're looking into it."

"Into what?"

"Whatever it is he calls you about. Damn, do I have to spell it out in block letters?"

Ball hung up. Tipton let his phone slip from his hand and bounce against the desk, then he buried his face in his hands and cursed Walter Pigg under his breath.

CHAPTER 26

The weekend brought a small degree of calm for Walter after he locked his Facebook page against comments on Friday morning then reversed the decision that same afternoon. He had promised transparency and shutting down the conversation violated his own principles. Mildred agreed, though she continued to oppose the page in general.

Brant Haskell no longer took his calls.

Roger was holed up somewhere on Tipton Palo's dime, waiting for the opportunity to tell his story to a grand jury. Gant had told Walter as much, with a warning not to spread it around. Ball had told Gant his mayor would soon be wearing stripes, but the detective didn't think the case had legs, though he admitted to not being privy to the evidence.

Jackson came out onto the back porch where Walter had taken his lunch and climbed into his lap. He had his mother's eyes — shape, not color — and her ability to soothe him whenever he felt stressed. Walter pulled him tight and asked if he was warm enough. The boy said he was. The temperature hovered in the low fifties so it wasn't cold. Winters in the South are hit or miss. Usually the bitter cold doesn't come until February, if it comes at all. Some years March is colder than December. Hit or miss.

"What are you doing out here, Papaw?"

"Thinking, son. Just thinking."

"Thinking about what?"

An itemized list sprang to mind, but the boy was too young to carry that burden, so Walter squeezed his grandson's knee and told him he was thinking about how much he wanted to go fishing when spring came. Walter never had been much of a fisherman, and it occurred to him he had let his grandson down in that regard, fatherless as he was. His recent trip with Roger had been more reconnection than leisure. A huge mistake he vowed never to repeat.

"When is Momma coming home?"

"Soon," Walter lied. For now they could get away with reflex answers, but their grandson was maturing by leaps and bounds and soon he'd demand answers. Real answers. Answers he would deserve.

"Momma killed Peter."

Walter patted the boy's leg. "Someday I'll explain all that to you. Don't be mad at her."

"I'm not mad," Jackson said. "Peter was mean."

Tears soaked Walter's eyes as he thought about his daughter going through so much pain and probably never once thinking to call him for help.

"Peter won't ever hurt you again," Walter said. "Nobody will. I'll see to that." It was an empty promise, but at the moment he meant it. Nobody makes it through life without bumps and bruises. The boy hugged his grandfather then slipped off his lap and scurried back inside. A few minutes later, Mildred came out.

"I finally got to talk to somebody at the prison," she said.

"And?"

"They said she's all right."

"That's it?"

"That's the only information they would give me," she said. "I think I'll fly out and see her in person."

"When?"

"Now. As soon as I can get a flight. The lady said if I'm there tomorrow, I can visit her between two and four."

"We'll all go," Walter said.

"Can we afford it?"

"No, but we're going."

* * *

Walter sat with Mildred and Jackson at a small round table in a large white room with a diverse mix of inmates and visitors, wondering if Amy had refused to see them because of her battered face. The ten minute wait seemed like twenty. Mildred's face tightened with each passing minute, until she looked as though she might burst into tears at the slightest provocation. It was Walter's cue to remain silent lest anything he say be used against him during the flight home.

Cell phones weren't allowed so they had to pass time the old fashioned way. Walter counted floor tiles and determined the room to be 40 x 30. The tables were spaced far enough apart to give each family some semblance of privacy.

"It's very clean," he said, afraid if he didn't say something he might explode. Mildred acknowledged him with a quick glance up from her hands which were on the table and white from wringing.

"Where's Momma?"

Mildred patted the boy on the head and told him she would be out any minute.

"My private parts are still numb from being groped," Walter said, still recovering from the indignity of being thoroughly searched and patted in the adjoining room.

Just as Mildred opened her mouth to scold him, the door opened and in walked Amy. Walter's first thought was how good she looked. Not a mark on her that he could see, and she didn't appear to be wearing makeup to cover the bruises.

Jackson flew from the table and rushed into his mother's arms. She scooped him up and gave him a tremendous hug.

Mildred reached across and grasped Walter's hand and hung on for dear life.

"She looks good," Mildred said, mirroring Walter's thoughts. She was three feet away now and still he saw no visible signs of the brutal beating she had suffered.

She reached the table with Jackson in her arms. "It scared me when they told me you were here. I thought something terrible had happened." She cut her eyes to her son, then she sat down and kept him in her lap. "Is anything wrong?"

"You tell us," Walter said.

Amy looked confused. Mildred placed her hand on Amy's forearm. "You must be terrified," she said. "Being here in this awful place."

"I'm used to it."

Besides the other inmates and their visitors, there were three guards standing against three walls. Watching. Listening. The tables seemed closer now that Amy was there and they had things to say. Walter knew she was putting up a front for her son when all she wanted to do was break down. To come apart at the seams and let someone hold her and tell her to pull herself together. Walter had felt that way too, back when his life was coming apart. Mildred had stuck by him, and Amy. She put up the money so they could keep the house and so he could keep what little crumb of dignity he had left. He owed her so much and he wished it were the other way around.

"Jackson's been doing well in school," Walter said. "Show her your report card." The boy pulled a slip of paper from his pocket and handed it to his mother. It had been Walter's idea to bring it. Give the boy something to show his mother because they had something to show her, too.

She smiled. "All A's and B's," she said, then she gushed about how proud she was of him.

"It ain't nothing," Jackson said.

"They don't give marks on grammar at his age," Walter said.

"Oh, Daddy, you haven't changed a bit."

"Your father's changed a lot," Mildred said. "You'd be proud of him."

"I've always been proud of him, Momma."

Mildred patted her arm. "How are you really?"

"It's not easy, but I'm making it. I've made a friend so I'm not completely alone. She's a lifer so I don't have to worry about her leaving me." She frowned. "I suppose that's selfish of me."

They chatted until their time was almost up, then Mildred told Jackson to kiss his mother goodbye and she escorted him out, leaving Walter and Amy alone so he could show her the picture. Jackson hadn't seen it and hopefully never would.

Walter waited until they were gone. Amy had watched Jackson until the door closed behind him. When Walter looked back at her he saw the tears in her eyes and felt a cool burn in his chest, like a red-hot branding iron quenched in ice water. "Tell me how it happened."

"We've been through it already, Daddy," she said. "Do we really have to do this now?"

"Not Peter," he said. "I'm talking about you being attacked."

"Attacked?"

"Stop being tougher than you are," he said, then he pulled the photograph from his shirt pocket and unfolded it. The guards almost hadn't let him bring it in, but he was nothing if not persistent.

"Where did you get that?"

"It was mailed to me."

"By who?"

"It doesn't matter who," he said, though it did matter some. "One of the guards, probably. Or an inmate. I would think they check the mail and wouldn't let a thing like this go out."

"Daddy, I don't know what you're talking about. Where did you *really* get this?"

"I know who's behind it," he said. "What I want to know is who did it. It's important you tell me."

"Peter did it, Daddy," she said. "Why are you bringing this up now?"

"Stop playing games," Walter said. "Perry Stubbs has to be stopped."

"Daddy, that's an old picture. Look how young I was."

Walter studied the photograph again. She didn't look younger at all. If anything she looked older. "Where was this taken?"

"At the hospital."

"When?"

She looked down and her voice took on the weight of the world. "It could've been any number of times."

Walter slammed the table with his fist. The guard nearest them took a step forward then stopped. "How could you let him do this to you?"

"There's a million reasons why, Daddy. Is this why you came? Why didn't you call and ask me?"

Walter folded the photograph back into his pocket. "Are you telling me the truth?"

"Yes."

"No one here has hurt you?"

"No."

"No one has threatened you?"

"I'm in prison, Daddy."

He deflated. His daughter's life was hell and he was powerless to help her. "Sometimes I can't sleep at night thinking about you in here."

"Don't, Daddy. It's hard enough."

"I stare up at the ceiling and wonder if you're being beaten, or worse … then I get this." He tapped the pocket that held the picture.

"Somebody's trying to upset you, Daddy."

"Who had access to this photo?"

She shrugged. "The cops. People at the hospital. I don't know."

A guard barked a two-minute warning. They spent the remainder of their time talking about Jackson, and about how good things were going to be when she got out. They both made promises they couldn't keep, such as promising not to worry. She promised to stay in Hayes for a while after she got out. Long enough for Jackson to grow up. Walter watched her eyes flood with tears but she didn't cry. In all likelihood Jackson would be grown by then.

* * *

Walter complained of jet lag all morning and into the afternoon. He was cranky and the women gave him a wide berth, allowing him to eat lunch at his desk without nagging him to join them in the break room. They had spent Sunday night in California after visiting Amy and had arrived back in Memphis on the early flight.

Lunch was a bowl of chicken noodle soup he had found in the break room and heated in the microwave. When he finished, he patted the plastic bowl dry with a napkin and returned it to his desk drawer, then he wiped his desk clean of spots where he had dribbled.

Mildred appeared in the doorway with a strange look on her face. "You won't believe who's on line one," she said, expecting him to guess, he supposed, instead of telling him outright. "I'm not sure you should take it."

"Then why tell me about it, Mildred?"

"Well you don't have to bite my head off."

He apologized, not because he was sorry but because he didn't want to spend the rest of the day tiptoeing around her. She was right, though. He never would have guessed.

The first two words out of Rance West's mouth were his name, then he said the call was off the record as though speaking the phrase bound Walter to some solemn oath not to repeat what he was about to hear.

"I hang up in five seconds," Walter said. He couldn't imagine anything Rance West had to say that would interest him.

"You need to watch your back," West said.

"Are you threatening me?"

Mildred's eyes grew big.

"Just the opposite," West said. "I'm warning you to be careful. You've made some powerful enemies since the election."

"You being one of them?"

"Not me, Mister Pigg. I —."

"Mayor Pigg," Walter corrected him. If Tipton Palo was going to send his lapdog to bark he was at least going to respect the office. He heard an audible sigh through the phone.

"I'm neither powerful nor your enemy, Mayor Pigg."

"Ha!"

"Believe what you will," West said. "My conscious is clear now."

"Why? Because you've told me what I already know?"

"Do you know that the police chief is planning to arrest you?"

"That's absurd! On what grounds?"

"Manslaughter would be my guess," West said. "Murder if they think they can make it stick."

"They being your law partner?"

"I don't know about that. Tipton doesn't talk to me about that stuff."

"Why should I believe you?"

"Don't," West said. "I have no idea whether or not my partner is involved, but it wouldn't surprise me."

"Did he have anything to do with sending me that horrible picture of my daughter and scaring my wife half to death?"

"I don't —."

"Or hanging the horse head on my back porch?"

"Maybe. I like to think not but I don't know anymore. I've suspected him of being involved with Perry Stubbs for a while now but I can't prove anything."

"You're the one representing his henchman."

"I'm a lawyer, Mayor Pigg. That's what I do."

Walter's anger had begun to abate but he wasn't ready to trust the man. Tipton Palo was a snake and Rance West traveled in the same grass. "Why are you telling me all this?"

"Have you ever had a near death experience, Mayor Pigg?"

Walter remembered hearing about West having a heart attack but he hadn't known how serious it was. Hadn't cared, either, to be honest. "I think you already know I have."

"It changes a man's perspective."

The admission struck a chord with Walter. Rance West was either being genuine or he was a very good liar. "Does your partner want this job that badly?"

"More than you can possibly imagine."

"Why?"

"Power."

"There's very little of that."

"Prestige."

"If he wasn't trying so hard to take it from me, I might give it to him."

"Don't expect anything else out of me," West said. "This conversation never happened."

CHAPTER 27

Glenn Ball had the investigative skills of a gerbil and here he was chomping at the bit to arrest Pigg for murder. Tipton was tired of micromanaging him.

"Why do you have to resist everything I tell you to do?"

"For one thing I don't take orders from you," Ball said.

"The hell you don't. One phone call from me and you'll be driving a patrol car again."

Ball muttered something unintelligible, then he broke the news that Roger Pigg was in the wind.

"What's that supposed to mean?"

"He's gone," Ball said. "Absconded. The pigpen is empty."

Obscenities hit Tipton's brain like pellets from a scattergun. It took every ounce of restraint he could muster not to scream them into the phone. "I thought you had a man on him, you idiot!"

"You said protect him, not keep him from running away."

"You're useless."

"My man was in the john," the chief said, sounding contrite all of a sudden. "When he came out Pigg was gone. He feels real bad about it."

"Find him," Tipton said.

"We're doing everything we can."

"You've got twenty-four hours."

"That may not be enough time."

Tipton hung up and called Stubbs. The old man didn't take it as hard as he had expected. All he said was there was more than one way to skin a cat, and that he had himself a brand new cat skinner by the name of Jonce Nash. The name meant nothing to Tipton, but Stubbs said he was fresh out of the pen and came highly recommended. A real mean bastard who liked getting his hands dirty. Tipton didn't like the idea of bringing in somebody new but he kept his objections to himself. Stubbs would do what Stubbs wanted to do, with or without consent. He fancied himself the top dog and for the time being it had to be that way. For the time being.

"Maybe I'll have him take Pickle for a little ride out in the country," Stubbs said, and that was that. Tipton sat for a long time after the call ended wondering if the feds had just planted their spy.

* * *

Judge Kilfiche was two minutes into reliving an old case involving a county supervisor who had been caught red-handed accepting kickbacks from everyone from the gravel supplier to the local tire store when Mildred buzzed and told Walter he had an important call on line two.

"I've overstayed my welcome," Kilfiche said, looking more amused than offended. Walter waved him off and told him to keep his seat, then he picked up the phone and heard Roger begging him not to hang up. He frowned and rolled his eyes at the judge, then an idea struck him and he put the call on speaker.

"We've been worried sick," he said, eye-locked with the old judge. "Where are you?"

"You got me on speaker?"

"Must be a bad connection. Are you on a cell?"

"They took my cellphone," Roger said. "I'm calling from a pay phone at the hospital."

A myriad of reasons why Roger might be in the hospital sprang to mind. He broke eye contact with the judge.

"What happened?"

"I got away."

"Got away from what? Why are you in the hospital?"

"I'm not *in* the hospital," Roger said. "I'm *at* the hospital. It's the only place I could think of that's still got pay phones."

"Who took your phone?"

"That cop they assigned to protect me. I've felt more protected in a homeless shelter."

"You've been in a homeless shelter?"

"Never mind that," Roger said. "All I wanted to say was ... that stuff they printed in the paper ... I didn't say it exactly that way. I know you didn't drown Mark on purpose."

The judge raised his eyebrows. He probably thought it was staged. Too perfectly executed to be exactly what it was — good timing. Putting his brother on speaker had been a gamble. Any interaction with Roger could break either way.

"I may be in a lot of trouble because of you," Walter said.

"My lawyer told me you put that detective up to destroying the fingerprint evidence he could've used to clear me."

"That's a lie!"

"I know that now. At least I think I do. Me and you ain't ever been at odds like this, Walter, and I don't like it."

Walter wanted to reach through the phone and snatch his brother's head off. "The evidence disappeared when Chief Ball took over the case. Check the timeline."

"All I did was borrow your car, man, and now I'm facing ten years. He said if I gave the cops something on you they might go easy on me."

"Who said that?"

"My lawyer. He said the jury won't hear about the fingerprints because the evidence was tainted."

"That's ridiculous," Walter said. The judge nodded and mouthed that what Roger said was true. "You need another lawyer. Palo's using you to get to me."

"You sure I'm not on speaker? Sounds like I'm on speaker."

"No," Walter said. "It's the connection. It sounds the same on this end." He hated lying but his brother had boxed him into a corner. His only hope was to pull Kilfiche over to his side and hope Sharp would follow suit. A tie wouldn't get rid of Ball but it would hamstring Brad Stovall.

"If you've got Mildred listening that's fine, but I don't want you setting me up. I know you think you've got reason, but it ain't right I'm caught up in this. All I did was borrow your car."

"Mildred's not listening," Walter said. "And I'm not setting you up. How would I set you up when you're the one who called me?"

"I'm paranoid," Roger said. "I need a drink."

"Don't drink. The last thing either of us needs is for you to get drunk and do something stupid."

"I didn't mean for any of this to happen."

"Sit tight," Walter said. "I'm on my —."

Roger hung up.

"He'll run like a rabbit," the judge said.

"My brother's been running since the day he was born."

"Since he was born, or since the drowning?"

Good question. The problem was, Walter didn't know the answer. He couldn't remember exactly. Everything before the gravel pit seemed distant, like a movie he had seen as a child and now all the scenes didn't quite fit together. There were gaps and inconsistencies. Truth and fiction. Years of dreams and nightmares had blurred the line between reality and imagination.

"I don't know," Walter said. "It was such a long time ago."

"What really happened that day?"

"Mark drowned," Walter said, staring now at something decades beyond the wall his eyes were fixed on. "I posted the truth about it on my Facebook page."

The judge scoffed. "Nobody posts the truth about anything on Facebook."

"I posted the truth as I know it," Walter said. "The way I remember it. Sometimes … I wonder … I wish there had been a witness. An impartial witness who could either clear my conscious or damn me."

"Well it won't go anywhere in court," Kilfiche said. "No judge worth his salt would let a thing like that go to trial, and Judge Bishop is worth his salt. I can vouch for that."

"Tipton Palo's got a long reach," Walter said.

"Not that long of a reach. Bishop's too honest for that ambulance chaser to corrupt."

"I hope you're right," Walter said. "I wish I'd never let Haskell talk me into this. Neither one of us thought I could win, you know. I wasn't supposed to win."

The judge laughed. "It wouldn't surprise me to see you run again."

"That'll be the day. No one in their right mind would vote for me a second time."

"I didn't say you'd win."

For a split second Walter felt offended, then he laughed. "These next two years can't go by fast enough to suit me."

"A lot can change in two years. You're trying to clean up this town when most people don't even know it needs cleaning up. If they ever find out the truth, they may never let you leave office." It seemed an odd thing for the judge to say after the stand he took on Ball, but Walter needed all the help he could get so he kept the thought to himself.

"All I care about is taking down Perry Stubbs."

"Take down Perry Stubbs and you've cleaned up the town, Walter. Do you have any idea how many people he'll take down with him?"

"He's the only one I'm interested in," Walter said. He sighed and leaned back in his chair. "I guess it doesn't matter now that Ball's chief."

"The mayor has a certain authority over the police department … within oversight of the board, of course."

"Meaning?"

"For all practical purposes, Ball answers to you."

Walter leaned forward again. Interested. "Go on."

"You can't order him to do something, but a wise department head knows how to take suggestions from his mayor."

"That leaves Ball out," Walter said. "He's dumb as a rock and he hates my guts."

"Not so dumb, maybe," Kilfiche said. "Give him a little time to soak."

Walter decided to take his shot. "After the other day he knows the board's against me. I can't touch him."

"There might be something," Kilfiche said.

"I'm listening."

"If Palo's not in bed with Stubbs then I'm a monkey's uncle," Kilfiche said. "Maybe the reason he's fighting you so hard is because he's afraid of you."

Walter had suspected Palo and Stubbs but had no idea the judge felt that way too. "What makes you think they're connected?"

"I remember when Tipton Palo was just another lawyer with a shingle. He had talent, mind you. I knew the first time he stood in my courtroom he was above average. He didn't have money, though. Not real money. That didn't come until he started representing Stubbs."

"Can you prove it?"

"Nope. They're both as slick as goose shit."

Walter sighed. "So what you're saying is that I should give up?"

"On the contrary," Kilfiche said. "I think you should contact the IRS." He stood to leave. "That's how they got Capone, you know."

* * *

Wednesday's paper disappointed Tipton again. Nothing new on Pigg except a Section B story on how street maintenance had declined since the mayor took office. Tipton wadded it up, sale papers and all, and shoved it into the trashcan beside his desk. Mann had no initiative. Instead of punch and jab, he was punch and wait.

At eleven o'clock he called Autumn and offered to pick up something and meet her at school for lunch. She declined. Too much hassle getting him in and out because of all the new security, plus she had a class from eleven to twelve on Wednesdays and only got twenty minutes. He bristled. "This is the second time you've blown me off."

"You're not the only one with a job."

Rance was still in the wind. Recuperating, or getting drunk. Maybe he was testing his stents with the deaf girl. He called Ball to make sure he was still on his chain but the chief didn't answer. He slammed the desk with his fist and Candice rushed in and asked if he was okay.

"It's nothing," he said. She was wearing a red top with white lace along a plunging neckline and he struggled to keep his eyes on her face.

"With Rance having his heart attack I've been jumpy," she said. Did she think he was as old as Rance? He had put on a few pounds but he wasn't fat.

She returned to her desk and he tried Ball again. Still no answer. It was noon and he had skipped breakfast so he grabbed his jacket and headed out. As he passed Candice's desk he stole a look at her cleavage but kept walking, then he stopped and turned back. "Come to lunch with me. There's this new —."

"No."

"We'll discuss cases," he said. "Strictly business. I'll even write it off."

"I'm not interested."

"Just like that?"

"Just like that," she said, gathering the lace at her throat without looking up. "Since when do you discuss cases with me?"

He forced a laugh to hide the anger growing in the pit of his stomach. Who did she think she was? "Fine," he said. "I was just trying to be polite."

"You were trying to look at my breasts," she said. "And you're making me very uncomfortable."

He stormed out without answering her charge. His legal mind conjured a sexual harassment lawsuit with her taking the firm for a million plus. The scandal would wreck his career and his marriage. Rance would side with her. Probably represent her.

By the time he returned he had hammered out a path forward. "I apologize for my behavior," he said, stopping at her desk and trying his best to sound contrite. "You're a very attractive woman and I overstepped."

"It's okay," she said.

"For what it's worth, I've never cheated on my wife." Looking wasn't cheating. Looking was curiosity. Comparing apples to apples, or in the case of Candice and Autumn, grapefruits to apples, not that there was anything wrong with apples. Women play games. The prettier the woman, the more complicated the game.

"I'm sure she appreciates that," she said. He couldn't tell if she was being sarcastic or not so he abandoned his efforts and shut himself up in his office. Ball answered when he called this time. The hunt for Roger Pigg was a dead end. The Pigg sisters were onto him and no longer took his calls. He had no clue where to look. Gant was still asking questions, demanding to know what happened to evidence in a case that was none of his business.

"If I arrest the mayor he'll resign by the end of the day," Ball said.

"Arrest Pigg and the aldermen will hang you from a lamppost."

* * *

Walter sat in his car behind the burned out ruins of Jerry's Muffler and Glass, waiting for a man who promised Perry Stubbs on a platter. The man had called Walter's cell while Mildred was out getting their lunch. He left without telling Kelsey where he was going.

The man on the phone sounded nervous. Walter was nervous too. From his vantage point he could hear the occasional traffic on the street but couldn't see it. He also heard the noise of children playing on the playground of the elementary school two blocks behind him. The sky was overcast and he felt a knot forming in his gut. The longer he waited, the bigger the knot grew until his palms began to sweat and his throat shrank to the size of a drinking straw. If something didn't break soon he knew he would run. Walter had spent a lifetime running.

His phone vibrated in the console and Mildred's name appeared on the screen. Then she texted. Seconds later a tone told him she had left a voicemail. It occurred to him that the meeting might be a ruse to get him out of the office. Maybe Mildred was the real target, or Jackson. For all the talk of security, he knew practically anyone could walk into the school and pick up his grandson.

He grasped the ignition and the passenger door opened. He jerked his hand away and looked. His heart did somersaults in his chest. A man plopped down in the passenger seat and told him to keep his hands where he could see them. Walter recognized the voice from the phone call but the face was covered with a green ski mask.

Walter tried to think of something manly to say but all that came out of his mouth were grunts and groans. What a pathetic specimen he was.

The man pulled a gun from his coat and jammed it into Walter's ribs. "Drive." Vomit washed up into Walter's throat but he managed to swallow it back down.

"Now!"

Walter knew if he drove away he was a dead man. His only chance was for the plan to work. His eyes searched the rearview mirror, then the outside mirrors. Where was Detective Gant? Had Stubbs bought him off? He moved his left hand toward the door handle, trying to be discreet, hoping the man was a bad shot, then the passenger door flew open again and a struggle ensued. Gant pulled the man out of the car and threw him to the ground as Walter rolled out the other side and landed on his hands and knees, then he puked. Afterwards he heard a garble of voices, then realized the detective was asking if he was okay. Define okay, Walter said under his breath, then he pushed himself to his feet and wobbled around the car to see who had almost killed him. Gant had his assailant face down with a knee between his shoulder blades. As soon as he had the handcuffs secure, he rolled him over and sat him up.

"Corey Pickle," Walter said, surprising himself that the words came out. His breath came in rapid spurts and he thought he might pass out.

Pickle looked up at Walter and grinned. "I'll be out in an hour," he said, and he was probably right. Walter glared at him, then he kicked him in the face.

CHAPTER 28

What disturbed Tipton more than Corey Pickle's arrest was the fact that it took almost twenty-four hours for him to hear about it. Mid-morning Thursday he was walking across the court square toward the courthouse when Chief Ball pulled his car to the curb and lowered his window with the news.

"Why didn't you call me?"

Ball dripped his arm out the window and drummed his fingertips against the door. "I figured Stubbs told you."

"Keep that detective away from him," Tipton said. "I'll be over as soon as I get out of court. Tell him to keep his mouth shut."

"He's already got a lawyer."

"Who?"

"Banks."

"Ernie Banks? How the hell did that happen?" Ernie Banks was a lawyer Stubbs sometimes used to write up business contracts. He hadn't tried a criminal case in years.

"Beats me," the chief said, about as unconcerned as a man could be. "Stubbs sent him over I reckon."

"You reckon?"

"Banks showed up and said Stubbs sent him to clean up after his man, so I reckon that's what happened."

"Pickle went along with it?"

"Pickle's not in much of a position to be choosy," Ball said. "I guess you could say he's in a pickle." He snickered at his funny. Tipton wanted to yank him out of the car and stomp his face but they were on a public street. "Don't get your back up," the chief said, suddenly defensive. "I was just making a joke."

"Nobody talks to Pickle until I get this cleared up," Tipton said. "Got it?"

"Too late for that. Gant got it all on video. I couldn't shut it down now if

I wanted to."

"If you were doing your job it wouldn't have happened in the first place."

"Ain't on me," Ball said. "I can't be everywhere at one time. Besides, so what if Pickle takes a ride? The way I hear it, Stubbs already replaced him anyway. Some ex-con fresh out."

Tipton balled his fists and gritted his teeth. Ball was too dumb to comprehend the damage if Pickle talked. He couldn't figure Stubbs, either, sending a pencil-pusher like Banks over to clean up his mess. It was almost as if he wanted Pickle to talk.

* * *

MAYOR PIGG CAUGHT ON POLICE SURVEILLANCE TALKING TO HITMAN was the headline Walter conjured inside his head as he meticulously guided his three-bladed razor from collar bone to jaw, plowing off a thick layer of white foam with each stroke then rinsing the razor clean under the faucet. His hands no longer trembled but he still had a twitch in his left cheek near the corner of his mouth. Nervous residue from yesterday's near brush with death. He could still feel the press of Corey Pickle's gun in his ribs.

Mildred didn't know. She knew Detective Gant had used him for bait in a sting operation that took Pickle off the streets, but she didn't know how close the bait had come to getting swallowed, and if Walter had any say in the matter she never would. She was mad enough as it was.

It had been a good plan foolishly executed. That's how the detective had phrased it, taking all the blame onto himself like a good soldier even though the operation had been Walter's idea. Neither of them had expected Pickle to pull his gun before Walter had time to lay out the terms of the deal.

He heard a noise downstairs and shut off the faucet. Mildred had taken Jackson to school in the Town Car (the cops had released it back to him) and was probably at the office helping Kelsey field calls from the angry mob that was forming against him. His heart beat in his ears as he strained to listen. Had it been a real noise or only his imagination? He mentally calculated the steps to the closet where his handgun was safely locked away in a steel box on the shelf. Cecil Pigg had left guns lying around but his sons and daughters knew better than to touch them without his permission. Things were different then. People were different.

Half a minute slugged past without any noise in the house whatsoever. Corey Pickle was in jail for the long haul according to Gant. Judges frown on people who commit felonies while out on bail for a felony. Walter stroked his throat with the razor again. Not even a ghost could get up the staircase without at least one stair creaking. He put down his razor and wiped his face clean with a towel, then rushed the process of getting dressed and out of the house. When he opened the side door and stepped into the garage he stopped and waited for his eyes to adjust to the darkness. If somebody was lying in wait for him he didn't want to throw on the light and make it easy for him.

He decided to call out. "I've got a gun," he said. "I'll blow your head off." No reply. He should have cursed. A man ready to blow off another man's head would probably curse. He was lying of course, about the gun. Mildred would hit the roof if she caught him carrying a loaded gun in his pocket.

When his eyes adjusted he realized he was alone, but that didn't mean no one had been there. Maybe Stubbs had another man besides Pickle, and maybe instead of killing horses he rigged explosives. There was only one way to know for sure and that was to get in and turn the key. It wasn't bravery. Necessity made him open the car door and get in. He couldn't very well skip work without explaining why to Mildred. Besides, if he was going to blow himself up he wanted to do it without his wife and grandson around. He had that much decency about him at least.

The car didn't explode when he turned the key. It didn't explode when he raised the garage door, nor when he backed down the driveway. By the time he reached the office all that fear had turned to anger. Being a coward is a frustrating business.

Mildred was at her desk when he waked in. "What's wrong with you?"

"Nothing."

He felt her eyes on his back as he lumbered toward his office. As he closed the door he heard Mildred tell Kelsey that husbands are harder to raise than children. A few seconds later she buzzed him and told him Alderman Sharp had already stopped by twice, then he heard Kelsey say three times, then he heard the alderman's voice. Walter told her to send him in.

"Looks important," Walter said when the door opened and he saw the alderman's dour expression. It had to be important for him to stop by three times without calling.

"Too important for the telephone," the alderman said.

Walter invited him to sit. Sharp settled himself into Walter's guest chair and searched the floor for the words he needed to say. "I may as well come out with it." He cleared his throat. "Stovall's planning to ask for your resignation at the next board meeting."

Brad Stovall was the least of his worries. Stubbs wanted him dead and Stovall wanted him to resign. "I guess you've been promoted to messenger boy?"

"I ain't nobody's *boy*," Sharp said. "I came because I thought I owed it to you."

Walter didn't mean boy in the way the alderman took it. People were too sensitive these days. It was getting so a man couldn't say anything without offending someone. He thought about apologizing but decided against it considering the nature of the visit. "Judging by the look on your face I'm assuming you agree with him?"

"He laid out a convincing argument."

Walter didn't say any of the things that crossed his mind, such as what a backstabbing underhanded dirty dealer the preacher was, or how quick he was to sell his soul to the devil, or —.

"Judge Kilfiche is on the fence too."

"I see," Walter said. "Just like that, huh?"

"We've got to think of the town," Sharp said. "I've never seen so much turmoil."

Walter stared at a defect in his desk. A small crack in the wood about an inch from the edge. It had been filled with something artificial and smoothed over so that it was barely visible. It was a good patch job. He hadn't noticed it until the second week. Now he couldn't keep his eyes off it. It annoyed him to the point that he considered tossing the desk out and bringing in something new, but the board had to approve expenditures and would probably make a public spectacle out of denying him even that. "There aren't words to express how very much I'd like to wake up in the morning and be plain ole Walter again. I'd gladly hand this town back over to you fine folks on the board, if only —." He rocked back and forth in his chair, ignoring the stabbing pain that ran deep into his left thigh, trying to look inside the alderman's soul to see what kind of man he was underneath all the trappings of his position. Not his position on the board, but his position in the community. In his church. "Can the board force me to resign?"

"No."

"Then you have my answer."

"You've lost the confidence of the people."

"Of the board you mean."

"That too."

Walter leaned forward and folded his arms on his desk. "Since the day I took office that hack over at the newspaper office has been skewering me with lies and innuendo. No, I take it back. Since before I took office. Remember the headline that Wednesday after the election?"

"I remember."

"But that's okay with the board," Walter said. "The board doesn't care about any of that. All the board cares about is —." He stopped and tried to think of what the board cared about and drew a blank. "Tell me, Alderman Sharp, what *does* the board care about?"

"I understand you being upset, but —."

"No, Alderman, I'm not upset. I'm not upset at all. I'm happy as a lark. I'm downright giddy. Finally, after two months of spineless inaction, the board of aldermen has taken a stand on something! Good for you!"

"I expected you to get upset," Sharp said. "Of course the board can't make you resign but without our support you'll be —."

"Useless?"

"Powerless … is what I was going to say."

"And after I'm gone?"

"The board will appoint an interim mayor."

"Tipton Palo?"

Sharp couldn't look him in the eyes. "We haven't discussed that far into the future."

"But it will be whoever Brad Stovall wants because he has the votes, and you and the good judge will go along for the sake of unity."

"I would oppose Tipton Palo."

"Of course you will," Walter said. "Right up until the moment you say aye."

Sharp looked up. Walter thought he looked like the hangman who had his hand on the lever but couldn't bring himself to throw it, and he saw himself looking like the man with his neck in the noose wondering why the hangman was taking so long.

"I want time to finish what I've started," he said.

"I don't think Brad —."

"One month."

"I don't see what difference a month will make."

"It's a deal then," Walter said. "The board gives me one month and if the people of this town still want my head I'll give it to them."

"That's not what —."

"Good day, Alderman Sharp."

* * *

Friday afternoon was a light day at the courthouse. Tipton was in at one and out again at two. His case was over before it began due to some family emergency with the prosecutor. Probably something cooked up in the judge's chamber because the two men were avid deer hunters with memberships in the same club. Tipton didn't understand hunting. He wasn't raised around guns the way most southern men are. Rance was a hunter, but it didn't consume him. It wasn't a disease with Rance.

Stovall wouldn't answer his phone when Tipton called, so he borrowed Candice's phone and tried again. He answered. "Stop dodging me," Tipton said. "You're going back on our deal." He was angry and he had a right to be. Wayne Toms had given him a heads up the night before but Tipton hadn't believed him. Hadn't wanted to, anyway. Believing or not believing is an involuntary reflex.

Stovall cursed Toms. Called him a nobody. A useful idiot. More idiot than useful. Tipton shared his opinion, but reminded him that without Toms, he wouldn't control the board. Throw in the mayor, and the worst he could do was a tie. Sharp and Kilfiche would always be elusive.

"It was a mistake getting rid of Tom Sherman," Stovall said. "Now we've got ourselves a mayor we can't control."

"You couldn't control Sherman."

"Maybe not, but at least he wasn't a nut."

Stovall explained how Sharp and Kilfiche had decided between the two of them that Pigg deserved another chance. A month. "What can I do?"

"You do what I tell you to do," Tipton said. "Stick to the plan."

"Stick your plan up your ass," Stovall said. "I'm getting tired of you anyway."

* * *

Walter spoke to a Mr. Greeley with the Internal Revenue Service. Twice he had to ask him if he was still on the line. After five minutes Greeley said it sounded to him like a state matter. Walter persisted. Greeley said he'd look into it.

So much for that.

Gant said he doubted Palo or Stubbs had their hooks into anybody at that level. On the bright side, Pickle was agreeable to a deal if the terms were right.

"What sort of terms?"

"Full immunity."

"Give it to him."

"It's not your call. Or mine."

"It was me he tried to kill," Walter said.

"That ain't how it works."

Walter said he'd speak to the DA. Gant told him not to get his hopes up. Walter asked if he thought the DA was protecting Stubbs.

"Just lazy," Gant said, though he admitted it was a guess.

"If he takes down Stubbs and Palo he can run for the state legislature," Walter said. "Or congress."

"Maybe he doesn't want that."

During the ride home Walter told Mildred about his strikeout with the IRS. Even she was surprised. They're supposed to be ruthless. Jackson asked from the back seat what the IRS was and Walter told him he'd find out soon enough.

"They collect taxes for the government," Mildred said.

The boy said oh, as though he suddenly understood.

Walter turned onto their street and rolled into view of their house. He saw Ball's car in their driveway at the same moment Mildred asked who it could be. "It's Ball," Walter said. "This should be fun."

The chief was parked in the middle of the driveway, blocking Walter's access to the garage unless he swung around through the grass. Walter wasn't one to abuse his lawn, so he parked behind him. Ball's car door opened and he got out and met Walter between their respective bumpers. Mildred and the boy stayed put because Walter told them to.

"Looking for stray dogs?"

"You're under arrest," Ball said.

"You've lost your mind!"

"I need you to turn around and put your hands behind your back."

"On what charge?"

"Murder. Your brother made some pretty damning statements against you."

"Did my sisters back up his story when you called them pretending to be Detective Gant?"

Ball's face reddened.

"You think I didn't know?"

"It's nothing personal," the chief said. "Nobody's above the law."

"You've got a lot of nerve."

Ball shifted from left foot to right. "I can call a patrol car if you won't go quietly."

"Call two," Walter said. "Call every car you've got and I still won't go quietly. I'll go loudly. I'll blow the roof off you and your band of devils!"

"This is unnecessary," Ball said. "Think of your wife and grandson."

Walter took a step toward the chief. "Lay one hand on me and I'll give you a real charge to arrest me on, only you'll be lying on the ground looking up!"

Ball stumbled backward against his car. "Now you see here!"

"Go back and tell your handlers they made a big mistake sending Corey Pickle after me. He's singing like a bird. Chirping his little head off. We know about Benson too. Tell Palo and Stubbs we know what they did to Benson!"

Ball inched backward to the corner of the car then turned and darted for the door. Walter's chest rose and fell with a heavy rhythm as the chief wheeled the car around and made his escape through the grass. Mildred rushed to his side and grabbed his elbow. He felt seven feet tall and bulletproof and his woman was there to witness it. Walter Pigg, kicker of ass, except he hadn't kicked. He had only threatened. The real work was ahead of him. Corey Pickle had to sing.

CHAPTER 29

Walter opened the meeting and sat in stoic silence while the minutes were read. Sharp had assured him Stovall wouldn't call for his resignation, but he had his doubts. Sharp had burned him before. The meeting dragged on with half the seats in the room filled. A big turnout for any other mayor, but Walter had been packing the house on a regular basis. Every time he made eye contact with Stovall, the normally belligerent alderman looked away. He lacked the confidence to bring his ultimatum to a vote.

For now.

The last order of business was the spring convention of mayors in Biloxi. The board approved the expenditure over Walter's objections, even after he vowed not to attend.

"I refuse to go."

"It's the mayor's duty to go," Stovall said. "Whoever that may be."

"I refuse to waste taxpayer money on a beach vacation," Walter said, ignoring the alderman's dig. He knew they weren't approving the expenditure for him.

"Someone needs to represent Hayes," Kilfiche said.

"Tom Sherman always went," said Sharp.

"Maybe he's afraid of casinos," Wayne Toms said to the amusement of half the audience. The other half shook their heads and mumbled against Toms. The low blow angered Walter, but he took the pulse of the room and allowed the comment to stand on its own. He was learning.

Before gaveling the meeting closed, he looked out at those assembled and told them to be sure to attend the next meeting because it was going to be a humdinger. "Bring your friends and watch the show," he said, then he swung the gavel.

Everyone filed out except Walter and Mildred. She stayed because he stayed, and he stayed because he didn't want to walk into an ambush. He didn't want to be cursed at and called names by those who laughed when

Toms said he might be afraid of casinos. He lingered because he had seen the nastiness in their faces. He lingered, in part, because he was going to miss the place after they pushed him out.

* * *

The front-page story should have been about the board's call for Pigg to resign, but thanks to Stovall's bungling, it was a puff piece about a furniture factory donating five hundred dollars to the county library. Mann had also buried the story about Corey Pickle on page six underneath the church directory, beside an advertisement for ABC Daycare. At least he had the good sense to do that.

Ball had become elusive all of a sudden, but Tipton had clients in jail who overheard things and reported back to him because he put a little something in their commissary accounts, so he knew Pickle had been running his mouth about Stubbs hanging him out to dry.

He called Stubbs to warn him, but first he wanted to know why he had sent Ernie Banks instead of calling him.

"Since when do I have to explain myself to you?"

"If you had called me he'd be out on bail right now instead of singing his guts out," Tipton said.

"Maybe he's where I want him to be."

The attitude befuddled him. Stubbs was stubborn as a mule but he wasn't dumb. He had to know that leaving a man like Corey Pickle in jail was asking for trouble. "Just what is it you're after?"

Stubbs hung up. Tipton called back three times and all three times it went to voice mail. He slammed the phone down and saw Rance standing in his doorway. "What the hell do you want?"

"Good morning to you too," Rance said.

Tipton apologized. "It's been a rough morning."

"Well it's about to get a lot rougher," Rance said. He was at Tipton's desk now but he didn't sit. "I just left your place and I think you'd better get home."

"What the hell do you mean you just left my place?"

"She called me."

Tipton shot to his feet and balled his fists. Rance held up both hands and stepped back. "Hold on, pal, it ain't like that. She's leaving you."

"Get out!"

"If you hurry you might catch her."

Tipton felt the world crashing down around his shoulders. Autumn couldn't be leaving. She hadn't given him any warning. Everything was fine. "You're lying."

"Go see for yourself."

Tipton's knees trembled. He wanted to scream, laugh, and cry all at the same time. A wave of nausea scalded his stomach and pushed up into his throat. He felt the room spin. Not knowing what else to do he lunged across the desk and grabbed Rance by the front of the shirt. Rance jumped back and sent buttons flying. Tipton lost his footing and fell across the desk. Rance stumbled backward with his shirt open, then Candice rushed into the room and threw herself between them.

"What the hell's wrong with you two?"

Tipton climbed over the desk and made another grab but it was too late. He couldn't get to Rance without going through Candice and as mad as he was he wasn't mad enough to hit a woman.

"You'll kill him!"

"Get him out of here!"

"I'm trying to help you," Rance said over her head. He looked scared. Rattled. Candice was mad. She put her hand on Tipton's chest and told him to back the hell off. "She called me and said she was leaving you," Rance said. "I went over to talk her out of it."

"She wouldn't call you!"

Rance told Candice to go back to her desk.

"He'll kill you."

"Go back to your desk!"

She left.

"If you're having an affair with my wife I'll kill you."

"She thinks you're having an affair with Candice," Rance said. "She called me to ask me if I knew."

"You're a liar."

"Autumn told me you said Candice's name in your sleep last night."

Tipton remembered the dream. He and Candice were alone in the office and she came onto him. She opened her shirt and asked him if he liked what he saw and he said he did. He liked it very much. Then he said her name over and over as she pleasured him, but it was a dream. He had to catch her and tell her it was just a dream. A man can't help what he dreams. "I didn't dream anything," he said. "She dreamed it herself."

"Go," Rance said. "I'm not the one you have to convince."

* * *

Tipton ran from room to room calling Autumn's name like a madman even though he knew she was gone. The garage was empty so of course she was gone. Her car didn't drive itself away. Desperate minds cling to impossibilities.

His search ended in the bedroom where he collapsed on the bed and stared up at the ceiling. How many times had he stared up at that very ceiling with her head on his arm and her body pressed against his? He had to find her and bring her back. If not on her own then by force. She belonged to him. He had given her everything. His desperation morphed into anger. Mild at first, then seething. He had given her everything and she had betrayed him. He had spoiled her, hadn't he? Had their marriage been a lie? Was it not the way he knew it?

Every man is entitled to his own truth. His third year law professor had told him that. Told *him*, not the class. They were in a coffee shop off campus. It was Sunday. Why or how they bumped into each other he couldn't remember, but he would never forget the conversation. It was the first time anyone had ever told him he had a gift. Lots of people had told him he was intelligent. One or two had told him he was brilliant, but no one had ever told him he had a gift. A gift is something unique. It's something placed inside a man by the hand of God.

Every man is entitled to his own truth, and your job is to sell your client's truth to the jury. To the world if need be, but to the jury especially.

But what if his truth isn't true?

It's true because he believes it and because you make others believe it. That's all truth is.

But what if he doesn't really believe it? What if he's lying to save his own skin? What if I know he's lying?

Doesn't a man have a right to save his own skin?

Autumn was denying him the right to save his own skin. She was flushing their marriage down the drain because of a stupid dream. Not because of a dream, but because she imagined a dream. She dreamed a dream. It was his truth, damn it, not hers. His truth. There had to be more to it than a dream. Imagined or real, one dream doesn't rip apart a marriage. Over the course of the next several minutes it occurred to him — she wasn't jealous of Candice, she was jealous of him. Of his success. He had made something of himself. He was respected. He rubbed elbows with important people, and what was she? A schoolteacher. She lived above her station because of him. His efforts. His talents. She had reaped *his* fruits.

He shot up from the bed and grabbed his phone. She had taken a lover. Probably one of her students. Some young stud infatuated with his teacher. It happens all the time. High school boys have so much testosterone it blinds them. They don't care about age. They don't care that a woman is in her forties and married. They don't care that she's plain.

He rushed downstairs and filled a tumbler to the lip with bourbon. It was early but he had an excuse. Who could blame him? Then he called Ball. What good was having a police chief in your pocket if you didn't use him? Feckless as he was, surely he could find a woman who didn't know anything about running.

"It's not my job to keep track of your wife," Ball said. Tipton could hear the sneering grin through the phone.

"She's run off with one of her students. That makes it a crime."

"What's this student's name?"

"How should I know?"

Ball probably didn't mean to laugh. Tipton wasn't so unreasonable that he couldn't give him the benefit of the doubt in that regard. "When you find her I want it kept quiet," Tipton said. "Bring her home and let me handle it."

"Don't you have an investigator of your own? This sounds like a —."

"I don't trust him," Tipton said. Clarence Fine was Rance's man and lately he didn't know how much he trusted Rance.

"I'll see what I can do," Ball said. Tipton knew he was lying. He didn't trust Ball either.

* * *

Walter paced the outer office like a cat, much to his wife's dismay. She scolded him, then threatened him, then begged him to please stop before he drove her insane.

He stopped. "You should be happy to see me walking."

Mildred rolled her eyes. "You weren't so annoying when you were in your wheelchair," she said. He knew she was teasing, but Kelsey's eyes flashed big. Walter didn't know how much Mildred had told her about their ordeal with the demon.

"I saved her life you know," he said to Kelsey. "Did she tell you that?"

"He saved all our lives," Mildred said. "Me, Jackson, the Bradfords."

"Don't bring *them* up," Walter said, meaning the Bradfords. What a miserable couple those two were. "My only regret is that I pushed the demon out the door before he had a chance to throw Mrs. Bradford out."

"We were in an RV," Mildred said. "Doing eighty down the interstate."

"More like seventy," Walter said.

Kelsey said she remembered seeing it on the news when it happened.

"I'm a hero," Walter said. "And my wife won't let me pace."

"You should let him pace, Mrs. Pigg."

"I saw you wink," he said. The women laughed. Walter started pacing again. He made three circuits then stopped. "I'm mayor of this town and can't even get my name in the paper unless I'm being skewered."

"Take me to lunch," Mildred said. "I'm tired of eating in."

Walter tried to talk her out of it but she insisted. She was going down the street to the diner even if she had to go alone, so he relented. The place was crowded but the waitress found a table for them against the wall, telling him she remembered he didn't like being walked around and bumped into while he ate. Behind them sat two men swapping biggest buck stories.

Mildred ticked down the menu, dismissing each item one by one. Walter watched her with unease, afraid she might still be undecided when the waitress came back to take their orders, thus delaying his agony.

He suggested the pea soup. She had mentioned before how much she liked it. She said she might try the chicken sandwich instead. Wonderful. Then she saw a waiter deliver a plate of spaghetti with garlic toast to a nearby table.

"That looks good."

"Smells good too," he said.

When the waitress came, Mildred ordered pea soup. The deer hunters at the table behind them broke camp and left. Walter was glad for the extra space. They ate without incident, then the waitress brought the check and placed it on the table. Walter reached for it but another hand grabbed it. He looked up and saw a face he didn't recognize, and for a moment he expected trouble.

"Lunch is on me," the man said.

Walter was taken aback and reached for the ticket that was already in the man's hand. "That's not necessary."

The man pulled the ticket away. "I've been hoping to bump into you," he said. "I think you're doing a great job."

"Thank you," Walter said, his brain scrambling for some intelligent response. He didn't fare well in close quarters. "I don't get out much," he said. "I'm always afraid of getting mobbed."

The man laughed. "Like Elvis?"

"No, like Mussolini. They hung him in the street." Mildred kicked him in the shin. He looked at her. "They hung his wife, too."

The man laughed again, then told Walter he admired the way he stood up for the little guy. At first Walter thought he meant Jackson, then he realized he meant the people. Ordinary everyday people who are tired of getting stepped on or over by the Palos and Manns and Stovalls.

"They treat you worse than anything I've ever seen. I hope you clear the whole lot of them out."

"I hope so too," Walter said. He thanked the man again and meant it. The man left them and he realized he hadn't thought to ask his name. "I should've asked his name," he said to Mildred. "I'm not very good at this you know." Mildred looked as proud as he had ever seen her look. He folded his napkin across his plate and lost himself in her eyes. "Well at least there's one," he said.

"Two," Mildred said. "Soon it'll be the whole town."

CHAPTER 30

Once every four years the people get a say in things. Between elections they are held hostage by the people they elect. Between elections they have no recourse except to lodge complaints. Every four years it's the same pool of people to choose from. We elect them to different offices, or to the same office ad nauseam. Week after week we read the same names in the Hayes Beacon. Anything they do is ordained to be news. Anything we do is passed over as ordinary, because we are ordinary. My name is Walter Pigg, and I somehow stumbled my way into position as your mayor. Your mayor. My goal is to be a mayor for the people, but I am out of my element. I'm a fish out of water. I feel as though I have accidentally walked into the banquet room at the country club wearing pajamas with a hole in the seat. By electing me you have upset the status quo. You have infuriated the powers that be. You have riled the editor of the Hayes Beacon. You have turned the Board of Alderman on its ear. My character is under attack because the Tipton Palos and the Dexter Manns don't want me upsetting their apple cart. They know if I stay in office I will do everything in my power to rid this town of the corruption they fight so hard to protect. I am a flawed man. Deeply flawed. The board has threatened to demand my resignation at the next meeting. They can't force me out, but I will resign if I don't have your support. A mayor without the support of the people is an empty suit. Will you help me take back our town?

He read the paragraph three times before publishing it to his Facebook page, then he buzzed Mildred and asked her to read it. She already had. She must've been sitting at her computer waiting for him to click the button, knowing he was up to something because of how quiet he was inside his office, or simply because wives always know what their husbands are up to.

"If you wanted my opinion you should've asked before you posted it."

"I want your opinion of the content," he said, "not your permission to post it."

She planted her hands on her hips and glared at him from his office doorway. It seemed a very long time before she spoke again. "I think it sounds desperate."

"I thought it was very candid," he said. "I was talking to the voters, not to the Palos and the Manns."

"Maybe you should try to get your old job back."

"That's a vote of confidence."

"If you resign I'll lose my job too. Did you consider that when you made your deal with the board?"

"I have no intention of resigning," he said. "You can't fight bullies by being kind."

* * *

Tipton took lunch at home. Four shots of brandy with a bourbon chaser. Something to settle his nerves. Candice had cleared his calendar without being asked to, unless Rance had ordered it done, in which case Rance might be trying to push him out and take over the firm. A bold move, especially for Rance. Too bold, come to think of it. At any other firm Rance would do good to make junior partner, but inferior people often overrate themselves. He wasn't much better at commanding a courtroom than he was at running a campaign.

He did need the break. Regardless whose idea it had been, going into the courtroom with his head in such a spin was a terrible idea. Mood affects performance in any profession. Same for doctors, he supposed, which reminded him to ask his doctor how things were going with the wife next time he had a procedure done.

He downed another drink. His head felt woozy because he chugged them too fast. The secret to day drinking is pacing. Think marathon not sprint. Thoughts came at him like pellets from a shotgun. Every kind of thought.

Autumn was having a mid-life crisis. She was too young for menopause and too old to feel attractive. Some young punk had told her she was beautiful and she lost her head. What else could it be? Who else in Hayes could give her what he could? All the wealthy men had wives of their own to worry about, and if any of them wanted a mistress there were plenty of younger women to choose from, like Candice Bey. Why had her name popped up? He considered calling her — Candice, not Autumn. He had called Autumn a thousand times but she refused to answer, so why not call Candice? If Autumn could cheat so could he. He picked up his phone and hovered his finger over her name, thinking how humiliating it would be if she turned him down. The first thing she would do would be to call Rance and they would both have a laugh together. His throat felt suddenly dry, and he remembered the first time he called Autumn all those years ago. He remembered all the times he picked up the phone and chickened out, then that one time when he didn't.

He put the phone down then picked it up again. Maybe he couldn't call Candice but he could call Autumn. A thousand times he had hung up when her recorded voice told him to leave a message. A thousand times he had chickened out. She would listen if he left a message. How could she not?

The phone rang. Her voice told him to leave a message.

"Call me. Please."

He downed another drink then called again.

"Why won't you call me? Where the hell are you?"

The pain swelled inside him until he couldn't hold it anymore. In his drunken stupor he couldn't restrain himself so he called again. As the phone rang his pain turned to anger. The sound of her voice made him furious. "You won't get a cent you miserable bitch!"

* * *

Gant had good news for a change. The FBI had sent an agent to talk to Corey Pickle. Ball was furious, of course, which suited Walter more than it suited the detective, Ball being his boss and all. As much as Walter wanted to reassure him it was temporary, he knew better. They both knew who was temporary. Everyone knew. Walter felt it in the air like some static electrical charge building until it takes off a fingernail. Walter was that fingernail. His mayoral career would forever be stained with an asterisk. Two asterisks, because the first one already existed. *Elected by special election to fill the unexpired term of Mayor Tom George.* Maybe it didn't read exactly that way, but something in the ballpark. Walter hadn't seen it written anywhere yet. Maybe they would put it on his tombstone.

Corey Pickle was temporary too. Minus an angel on his shoulder he was as good as dead. Walter had little faith in the FBI's ability to protect Pickle from Stubbs. Less faith in their willingness to because according to Gant, Pickle was still being held in general population. The sheriff ran the jail and without credible evidence of a threat he refused to move him, leading Walter to believe he was as crooked as Ball. More so, perhaps, since he had been in power longer. In some odd way, Walter felt sorry for Pickle. Who could know what the man was before Stubbs sank his teeth into him?

"What kind of man is he?"

Gant had been saying something but Walter hadn't been listening. It was an unfortunate condition he had where his mind wandered while someone was talking to him. Not always, but sometimes, and it didn't seem to matter how important the thing being said was. It had dogged him all his life, especially in school.

"The agent? I don't know, but he —."

"No, Pickle," Walter said. "What kind of man is Corey Pickle?"

Gant hesitated, seeming to grapple with the question as though Walter had just asked him to solve the square root of infinity. "Uh … well, he's your typical lowlife, I guess. Multiple priors but nothing ever stuck. He did nine months for aggravated assault a few years back."

"Never mind," Walter said. They were in Walter's office with the door closed. Gant had taken a big chance calling in the feds against Ball's orders. He looked nervous but not panicked. "I believe you to be a man of honor."

"I try to be," the detective said.

"You may lose your job over this."

Gant nodded. "I took an oath to uphold the law."

"I'll do everything I can."

"I'll land on my feet."

"There's not much time," Walter said. "How quickly will they move?"

"Not fast enough I'm afraid. The FBI doesn't arrest until they have enough for a conviction."

"All they have to do is get a search warrant and find his book," Walter said. "I can tell them exactly where he keeps it. He's too arrogant to move it."

"It's more complicated than that."

Walter's mind began to race. "Stubbs considers himself untouchable. If he knows the FBI is here he might move it. He might even destroy it. It's important to make this agent understand the consequences of underestimating him."

"You're asking me to light a fire under the federal government."

Walter nodded. Of course he was asking the impossible. The federal government is an unwieldy beast. "Please do what you can." Gant had stuck his neck out by going to the federal authorities when the investigation should by all rights be a state matter. How he pulled it off was unimportant to Walter. He pondered the probability that the FBI would throw it back to the state without a real investigation. Pondering was his thing, the way cooking is someone else's thing, or crocheting socks and baby blankets. Everyone has a talent and Walter's was thinking, not that he considered himself overly intelligent. Thinking isn't necessarily solving, and his talent was thinking.

"Suppose a little bird tells Stubbs the FBI is talking to Pickle?"

"I'm sure he already knows," Gant said.

"But what if he doesn't? Pickle has to know he's being hung out to dry."

"Or he's dumb enough to think Stubbs has something up his sleeve."

Walter grunted. "What Stubbs has up his sleeve will probably get Pickle dead."

CHAPTER 31

AUTUMN: *I'm not coming back*

Her text caught him by surprise. He was on the balcony nursing a hangover Saturday morning with black coffee and dry toast. The sun sat high enough to erase the shadow cast by his rooftop and melt away the last remnants of frost from the grass. The morning air felt brisk against his pajamas and socked feet as he cradled the warm mug between his hands an inch below his chin. He jumped at the ding of the incoming message and sloshed coffee down the front of his shirt. His insides churned as he read the words.

TIPTON: *we need to talk*

AUTUMN: *talk to my attorney*

He flung the mug over the railing, splashing himself and everything around him with coffee.

TIPTON: *how dare you talk to me that way*

His chest heaved as he stared at the screen.

TIPTON: *please*

AUTUMN: *it's over*

TIPTON: *how can you say that*

TIPTON: *where are you*

TIPTON: *what's wrong with you*

TIPTON: bitch!!!

He dropped the phone onto the little metal table and closed his eyes. His head spun and his stomach churned, then he rushed to the railing and vomited onto the ground below. Everything he had worked for was about to be gone. Who did she think she was? His emotions sloshed between hating her and wanting her back, like water in a tub being tilted one way then the other. The part of him that hated her wanted to hurt her, and the part of him that wanted her back felt small. Tiny, because he couldn't control himself. Insignificant, which is the worst thing a man can feel. Worse than hopeless, because insignificance is hopelessness that doesn't matter because no one cares. He needed to cry, but that's what she wanted him to do. She wanted to destroy him. The tub tilted again. The water sloshed.

TIPTON: *I'll find out who he is and destroy him*

TIPTON: *I'll make you wish you'd never been born*

TIPTON: *Both of you!!*

Nothing from her. Silence is a powerful weapon in an argument. It turns an argument into a one-sided rant. The ravings of a lunatic. It demonstrates with damning conclusion who has control. The lawyer in him knew that every message he sent would be thrown back in his face by her attorney, but the husband in him couldn't stop.

TIPTON: *answer me whore*

Of course she didn't answer. She was probably holding the phone so her lover could see — so they could laugh together at how he was coming apart at the seams. He could see them sitting on the edge of the bed, him leaning in so that their naked shoulders touched as they read the messages and giggled. Tears flooded his eyes and he buried his face in his hands and cried like a baby.

Crying numbed him. Two could play her game. He grabbed his phone again and called Candice without giving himself time to chicken out. She flaunted herself didn't she? She wore revealing blouses and tight skirts and was always leaning over his desk daring him to look.

The phone rang once, twice, then three times. He was in her contacts so it was too late to back out now. A lump formed in his throat as he visualized her unbuttoning her blouse and dropping it to the floor.

"Hello?"

The lump in his throat doubled in size. He tried to swallow but it refused to go down.

"Tipton?"

"Are you busy?" What a stupid thing to say. He sounded like a schoolboy calling a girl for the first time.

"No, why?"

He cleared his throat. There was nothing readable in her voice. "How would you like to come over?"

She hung up. No goodbye. No I can't. Nothing. The image of her naked vanished and in its place he saw her sneering at him. She was probably calling Rance so they could laugh behind his back, or maybe Rance was there. Maybe she hung up because he had interrupted something. He replayed the call again except this time Rance answered, and instead of saying hello he laughed.

* * *

"I know what I know," Walter said to Special Agent Casper after spending the better part of an hour trying to convince him not to hand the case back over to state authorities. "I'll testify to the names I saw in Stubbs's book."

Unfortunately none of the names he remembered seeing belonged to anyone within the Mississippi Bureau of Investigations. They were sitting on Walter's back porch because Walter had insisted they not talk in front of Mildred and the boy.

"See that rafter there," Walter said, pointing toward the part of the roof that overhung the porch steps. "That's where Pickle tied the rope when he hung up that horse head."

"I understand, and I'm sure it must've been —."

"My wife and grandson discovered it. My grandson has already seen more than his share of trauma. My wife, too, thanks to me getting in over my head with Stubbs. The man's worse than you think he is."

"You have my sympathies, but I —."

"He's more than just a bookie. He's a monster."

"Mayor Pigg, I have no doubt that everything you're telling me is true, but it doesn't change the fact that nothing I've seen rises to the level of a federal crime. If it makes you feel any better I'll express your concerns to the state attorney general."

"That's not good enough," Walter said.

"I'm afraid it'll have to be."

They had reached an impasse. Mildred stuck her head out the back door and asked if they were ready for lunch. Special Agent Casper declined, saying he had another interview to conduct, not divulging who the interviewee was, even when Walter asked. Mildred retreated. Walter felt a glimmer of hope, then not. Why would a man declare a case dead before conducting all his interviews? Unless, of course, the interview had nothing to do with Stubbs. Had he found something else? For a split second Walter wondered if he might be the new target. Had Roger convinced him to look into Mark's drowning? Could that somehow be federal? He didn't think so, but the mere mention of interviewing someone else after he had declared the case closed sent his brain tripping over itself.

Special Agent Casper stood. He represented average in its truest form. Average build, average height, average weight, average age, yet nine out of ten people would spot him for a government man at first glance because of the clothes he wore and the blacked out car he drove. He gave Walter a card from his pocket with his name and phone number and the official seal of the Federal Bureau of Investigations. Hoover's men. J. Edger's, not Herbert's.

"I'm curious," Walter said, "if it's not classified. What was your impression of Stubbs?"

"I didn't interview Stubbs."

"What? Why not?"

"We've been over it already," the agent said. "My reason for coming here was to determine if a federal crime has been committed."

"Would it hurt to talk to him?"

"There's no reason to."

"Maybe it would throw a scare into him."

"That's not how the FBI operates."

"Hogwash! You scare me and I haven't done anything," Walter said.

Casper smiled. "Well I certainly didn't mean to scare you, Mayor Pigg."

"You know what I mean. Fear's a useful tool. Maybe if he thought he was being investigated he might overplay his hand. The attorney general might appreciate it."

Casper checked his watch. "Tell you what I'll do, Mayor. I've got a little time to spare. I'll talk to Perry Stubbs."

Walter's hopes soared. "Be sure to mention the book."

They shook hands. "But I'm still leaving town."

* * *

Mildred shattered the peace and quiet of Sunday morning with a blood-curdling scream. Walter had just descended the stairs and immediately the image of another horse head swinging from a rope popped into his head. He rushed into the kitchen and halfway to the back door before his grandson popped through from the outside with Mildred pushing him.

"This has got to stop," she said. "It's got to stop!"

Walter lunged and wrapped his arms around her and guided her to the table, guiding his grandson too because Mildred had a death grip on the boy's arm. He pushed her down into a chair and she pulled Jackson into her lap, as though one movement forced the other. Whatever she had seen outside had scared her more than the horse head. Jackson began to sob.

"See what it's done to him? Do you see, Walter?"

He saw the effect but not the cause, so he ordered them to stay put then went outside, bracing himself but not enough. It looked to be some type of animal skinned and hung up like a side of beef. A pig, perhaps, or a large dog. The sight of it nauseated him. He called 9-1-1 and retreated back inside. Special Agent Casper had kept his word and talked to Stubbs. No doubt about that.

The police arrived like swooping buzzards. The first officer on the scene said it looked to be a German shepherd, or some breed of husky. The second cop guessed coyote.

"Get on your radio and tell them to stop coming," Walter said, not wanting his lawn to become a circus like last time. "It's not human, this time at least." He looked at their faces and wondered if they wished it were him. "Cut that thing down and get it out of here."

"Shouldn't we wait for the chief?"

"No. Deny him the satisfaction."

The younger of the two officers climbed the steps and pulled his knife to slice the rope. Walter stopped him and took a picture with his phone, then nodded. The animal hit the ground with a sickening thud.

"What do we do with it?"

"Haul it away," Walter said. "Put it on your chief's desk."

The older officer said they would call someone from the city maintenance crew to come get it with a truck.

"Next time it may be me you're cutting down," Walter said. "But don't get your hopes up."

"Most of us appreciate what you're trying to do," the younger officer said. At first Walter thought he was being sarcastic, then he believed him. The older officer agreed with a nod. "We think it's a shame how they treat you."

Walter felt a lump in his throat. "Thank you," he said, trying not to get emotional. Hearing it from his cops meant more than all the social media posts combined. "How do you feel about your chief?"

They dummied up. It was a stupid thing to ask. "Never mind," he said, then he went back inside and texted the picture to Special Agent Casper.

* * *

Tipton sat outside the Marriott in Memphis waiting for Autumn and her lover to show themselves. She had used her credit card to pay for the room and he had thought to check. He found her white Land Rover parked near a side entrance beside a red Mustang with a Union County tag.

He groped his jacket pocket and felt the bulk of the .38 revolver he had given her for protection. Bringing it — using it — seemed fitting. Just. The best he could hope for was to plead temporary insanity. A crime of passion — another reason to use her gun. He surprises her in her room and she pulls her gun and he wrestles it away and it goes off. Explained the right way, he might do no time at all. Of course there was the problem of the lover. Killing him would be the temporarily insane part of the plan.

His mind stumbled over the legal technicalities because he was drunk. If not drunk then sufficiently lubricated. There would be plenty of time afterwards for constructing a defense. It would be his word against physical evidence, and evidence can always be compromised. Almost always. Throw enough money at a thing and it moves.

It was the middle of the afternoon and the parking lot was practically empty. As he walked past the Mustang he resisted the urge to drag his key down the side. Keying the lover's car suggested intent.

Entry through the side door required a key card so he walked around the building and entered through the front. The nice lady at the desk didn't hesitate to give him a room key when he told her he was meeting his wife. The elevator lifted him to the fifth floor and spat him out into the plush corridor against the noise of a vacuum whirring down the hall. Perfect cover, he thought, as he followed the arrowed sign toward room 512 where his wife and her lover writhed together in ecstasy, unaware of the danger outside the door, then standing in the doorway. Watching. Seeing their naked bodies slick with sweat. Her on top and he didn't even know she liked it that way. Autumn was full of surprises.

Her lover saw him first. Too old to be a student, which would make the temporary insanity angle easier to sell. Killing a high school kid probably wouldn't sit well with a jury. They locked eyes. Tipton didn't know him at least. It wasn't one friend going behind another's back.

Lover boy's eyes were big as half dollars. It was a delayed reaction. Three seconds exactly. Tipton counted them off inside his head. One Mississippi, two Mississippi, three Mississippi. Autumn kept moving. Didn't break her rhythm, then she did. She sensed something was wrong and stopped. Her body went stiff. Too bad he couldn't see her face at that exact moment. He pulled the gun from his coat pocket. It was his best black suit. Navy, actually. The suit he wore when he won his biggest case. Lora-Lee Pickle (no relation to Cory Pickle) killed her husband in cold blood and Tipton got her off. It didn't hurt that she was twenty-six and gorgeous, or that the husband was twenty years her senior and wealthy. Instead of letting the prosecutor paint her as a gold digger, Tipton painted the dead husband as a dirty old man.

Autumn twisted at the waist to see what had her lover's attention. Her jaw dropped and she looked desperate to say something. Anything. Something clever that might save her life, but she was struck dumb.

He raised the gun and aimed at her face but he couldn't pull the trigger. His hand trembled. "Get your clothes on," he said, hearing himself speak as though he were a bystander. He really had meant to kill them both.

"What are you doing?"

"Get dressed!"

She leapt off her lover and pawed at the floor for her clothes. Tipton swung the gun toward the man's chest and told him to get out. He rolled off the bed and grabbed a pair of jeans.

"Leave it," Tipton said. "You've got two seconds before I pull this trigger." He stepped aside as the naked man ran past him into the hallway. Autumn watched in horror. Her life had suddenly become a nightmare.

CHAPTER 32

The television blared from the bedroom. Putting a television in the bedroom was the worst decision Tipton and Autumn ever made. Their relationship changed that day. Their lives changed. In one fell swoop, the bedroom became an extension of the living room. Movies and sitcoms that began in one room ended in another. They made love less often, then hardly ever. It was more him than her. She tried. He realized that now. She really did try.

"He doesn't mean anything to you," he said to her as she lay on the bed, puffy-eyed and sobbing. She hadn't stopped crying since he brought her home. He passed through on his way to the bathroom to brush his teeth and get ready for bed. She didn't answer. Halfway through brushing his teeth he looked out at her, toothbrush in hand. "Well, say something," he said. Anything was better than silence.

She drilled him with bloodshot eyes but said nothing.

"I could've killed you both and walked away scot-free," he said. "Temporary insanity. It's a thing, you know."

"Why didn't you?"

Good question.

He turned off the light and stepped out. Her eyes were aimed at him but her head was someplace else. With *him*. "I wish I hadn't seen it," he said. "Why couldn't you have been more careful about it?" Maybe she had been careful. "How long has it been going on?"

She looked away again.

"Until today I'd never heard of Eli Dobine. Where'd you meet this guy?"

"Do we have to do this?" Her voice barely crossed the room. A fresh tear rolled down her cheek.

"Yes we do," he said. "If you expect me to forgive you then you have to at least pretend to be contrite." He stripped off his pants and shirt and climbed into bed. "Do you love him?"

She took too long to answer. An invisible fist clamped his heart and made it impossible to breathe. For a moment he thought he was having a heart attack. If he collapsed to the floor would she call an ambulance or let him die? A week ago it would have been a ridiculous question, now he didn't know.

"I don't know," she said.

"What about me? Do you still love me?"

"Yes, but —."

"Don't," he said. But erases the before and excuses the after. He reached for the lamp on his nightstand and extinguished the room. Pain flourishes in darkness. He stopped fearing a heart attack and began praying for one. Tears spilled out of his eyes and ran down both cheeks as he lay on his back and stared up at the dark ceiling. Autumn's shell lay beside him, within reach yet untouchable. She had shed her body the way a snake sheds its skin and left it on the sheet beside him.

"Two weeks," she said, barely audible.

"What?"

"You asked me how long."

Two weeks and she was ready to turn her back on a life. Her life. Their life. "You'll forget about him."

She didn't answer. He would never look at her again without seeing Eli Dobine's face.

* * *

All day Mildred had been asking Walter who could do such a horrible thing to a dog. Skin it and hang it on a man's porch as a warning not to … what? What was Stubbs warning him not to do? The man had the police chief and half the board in his pocket. What could Walter do to him? The IRS didn't want him. The FBI couldn't touch him. He had beaten Walter at every turn. What was it he needed to warn Walter not to do?

"Do you think it'll scar him," Mildred asked after they were in bed. "For life I mean?"

It took Walter a moment to piece together that the *him* was their grandson and the *it* was his seeing the unfortunate animal without its skin. "He'll probably brag about it at school."

"I'll tan his hide if he does!"

"Boys will be boys is not just a slogan, Mildred. It's a fundamental law of nature."

She exhausted her lungs toward the ceiling. "First the head, now this. Amy would be so disappointed in us."

"I know a thing or two about childhood trauma. He'll be fine."

Mildred switched off the lamp. "You don't know that. Just because you overcame something terrible doesn't mean everyone does."

Enough said. If Mildred wanted to worry about their grandson, then so be it. Walter wasn't about to lose a night's sleep being lectured to. He lay there in the darkness staring up at a ceiling he couldn't see, thinking about Mark then forcing himself not to. The bedroom was dark as a cave, thanks to the piece of electrical tape he had stuck over the little green light on the smoke detector over the bed — the one Mildred had made him install just in case the several others throughout the house failed to wake them if the house caught fire, and hotel curtains with backing that blocked light, and no clock with big red numerals. His inability to sleep unless the room was totally dark had driven her crazy for the first few years of their marriage, then she got used to it and stopped complaining. It occurred to him that it was always her adapting to his needs and not the other way around.

"Am I selfish?"

"Yes."

He hadn't expected an answer so quickly. His follow-up question no longer applied, so he thought of another one. "Am I vengeful?"

"No."

"I have a tendency to carry grudges."

"Where's this going, Walter? I'm tired."

"Why am I the only one who thinks Stubbs is a threat to this community?"

"I want him in jail as much as you do."

His spirits lifted. "So you think I should keep trying?"

"Yes."

"Even if everyone thinks I'm just trying to get back at him for my gambling?"

"You don't need anyone's permission to do the right thing, Walter."

* * *

Tipton stepped out of the bathroom with shaving cream on his chin, razor in hand, and asked Autumn if he let her go to work would she promise to come home. It seemed a perfectly logical question.

"If you *let* me go to work? Seriously?"

The bedroom was dark enough that he had to strain to see the features of her face as his eyes adjusted to the light-dark transition. He pulled the towel from his shoulder and wiped his face. Anger dripped from her voice like venom from the fangs of a viper. Whatever had come over her had her fully engulfed. It crossed his mind that it might be drugs. Something upscale, he hoped, if it had to be that. Watching her teeth rot and her face go sallow from meth would be more than he could stand. If anyone asked, not that polite people do, he might blame her doctor for overprescribing painkillers and getting her hooked. Of course he would have to invent some underlying reason for the pain, but that would be easy enough. Anyone can have pain. There could be no excuse for Eli Dobine, though. He'd have to keep that one under wraps.

He retreated into the bathroom and checked his face in the mirror, then tossed the towel onto the counter. "You don't have a car," he said loudly.

Hers was still parked at the hotel in Memphis because he had brought her home by force. "I see no reason to rehash this every morning. I'll send someone for your car today. Behave yourself and you might get the keys back." He stepped out of the bathroom in time to see her throw back the covers and fly out of bed. At first he mistook her dash to the bathroom as aggression, then she stomped past him and slammed the door. He heard the shower come on and knew he had time to get dressed before she came out again.

A few minutes later he heard the shower go off then the picking up and putting down of the various bottles and brushes and tubes that littered their bathroom counter. When the door opened she stepped out naked, then stopped abruptly when she saw him standing near the bed looking at her.

"Afraid I'd climb out the window?"

"It crossed my mind." She looked good naked. Better than she had looked in a long time. His desire made him angry. Worse because she knew. Women always know.

She moved to the dresser and took her time getting dressed.

"If you don't hurry you'll be late."

She applied an earring to her right ear, then reversed the angle of her head and applied the left. "So how do we do this? You drop me off and pick me up in the car-rider line with the other children since the school doesn't have a whore line?"

"I thought I'd drop you off in the back where you usually park."

"So the other teachers can see how charitable you are?"

"Only if they know," he said. "Do they?"

She sighed. "No. Not yet."

"There's no reason for this to get out," he said.

"It always does."

* * *

Walter entered the diner and saw all four county supervisors sitting as a group at a table against the back wall. He knew they would be there because they always ate breakfast together on Mondays, probably discussing new ways to turn a personal profit from their public service jobs. Their jovial conversation evaporated as he approached the table. The two with their backs to him twisted their necks, then their faces followed him as he pulled an empty chair from the table behind them and waited for them to shuffle themselves this way and that to make room.

"Just in time for the check," Chance Collins said with an energetic laugh that very quickly infected the group. They all had bellies. All were better than fifty. Three of them wore beards. Collins had the shadow of a mustache on his lip but was otherwise scraped clean. Most voters have no clue what a supervisor does — how much power he has — so they elect farmers and production line supervisors and, in the case of Collins, the grandson of a man who held the office for thirty years before landing in the federal pen for taking bribes and kickbacks and strong-arming contractors. Barker Collins served five years then died two months after his release in March of eighty-four. He won his first election from a doublewide and his second from a brick three-bedroom flat. Halfway through his fourth term he built himself a mansion.

Walter glanced back toward the door, then leaned in and said at a whisper, "You might want to pick up your own tabs for a while."

The waitress came and asked Walter if he'd like to order and he politely declined. Mildred had fed him before he left the house. Her interruption gave his targets time to exchange puzzled looks and shrugs. Andrew Gerhardt asked the million dollar question. He wore red suspenders, probably because a belt buckle would have ripped into the overhang of his gut. "What's that supposed to mean?"

"Nothing," Walter said, feigning a sudden disinterest that stuck out like a sore thumb. "If you guys are comfortable with it."

"Comfortable with what?"

"When I approached you men on Brad Stovall's behalf," he said, pausing for effect, continuing only after looking each man in the eye and seeing alarm, "I was unaware of certain things."

"What things?"

"My intentions were completely above board," he said. "If anyone asks you tell them that, okay?"

"Stop grandstanding," Collins said. "If you've got something to say, say it."

"I just did," Walter said. He folded his hands. "I'm afraid I can't say anything more. I've been warned."

"Warned by who? Spit it out, Pigg." Collins lived up to his hype of being easily agitated. Drop a hint to a man like Collins and his brain will work itself to death. Stubbs had taught him that, though not on purpose.

Walter made a show of looking around to see if anyone might be listening. "I'm sure you know the FBI's in town."

"I thought he left," Gerhardt said. He looked around the table, searching for confirmation.

"What's that got to do with us?" Collins said. "We ain't done nothing."

Walter faked a sigh of relief. "Good. Glad to hear it." He stood. "I figured Stovall was bluffing."

CHAPTER 33

Brad Stovall sounded out of breath. In a panic. Borderline suicidal. Tipton had almost sent the call to voicemail because talking to Brad could be taxing. "I've got the damned FBI breathing down my neck and you'd better do something!"

Tipton smelled a set up. The FBI had something on Stovall and they wanted to trade him for a bigger fish. His brain raced in a dozen different directions at once. How could the FBI know anything unless someone told them? Not Stovall because he didn't know anything damning enough to involve the feds. Or maybe it wasn't the feds. Maybe it was the state. That state investigator — Snapper — had wrapped up the Benson investigation and left town, or had he? But why Stovall? The only person who didn't believe the suicide angle was Pigg. Had he finally found someone to believe him?

"Did you hear what I said?"

Think man, think. If the FBI or the MBI or — Gant. The detective was after his chief and Pigg had convinced him that Stovall was the back door. Back door to what? Had Pigg figured out —?

"Dammit Palo, either you talk to me or I'll come down there and make you talk! I'm not going down by myself."

"Calm down," Tipton said, his brain racing a mile a minute. Then it hit him — Corey Pickle. Of course. Pickle knew too much. Stubbs should've known what would happen when he railroaded him with a low-IQ attorney like Banks. His brain reached down and grabbed another gear. Was Stubbs setting him up?

"Don't tell me to calm down you son of a bitch," Stovall said.

"Come by my office and we'll sort it all out. I'm sure it's not as bad as you're making it sound."

"How would you like the FBI looking up your skirt?"

"Drop by this afternoon," Tipton said, certain now the conversation was being recorded. "You're obviously upset. I'll clear a spot on my schedule."

* * *

Alderman Kilfiche showed up at Walter's office with two white paper bags and two Cokes in glass bottles. Kelsey followed him as far as the doorway and gave Walter a shrug. What could she do? Wrestle the old man to the ground?

Walter dismissed her with a wave. She closed the door.

"You refused to meet me for lunch so I'm bringing lunch to you," Kilfiche said.

"Refuse isn't exactly the word I'd use," Walter said. As he recalled, the alderman asked him to lunch and he politely declined. Public resentment of him had receded somewhat, but he still ran the risk of being humiliated by some bully. People take unearned liberties with elected officials, and harassing them as they took their meals had become all the rage, if not in Hayes, then elsewhere across the nation so why take the risk? Some of the comments on Facebook had been downright nasty.

The octogenarian emptied the bags onto Walter's desk. Two cheeseburgers, two fries, and little packets of ketchup and salt. "You practically have to threaten to sue to get ketchup through the window these days." He frowned. "No napkins I'm afraid. The little imp probably left them out on purpose. Retaliation for having to hand over the ketchup." He placed one cheeseburger and a box of fries in front of Walter and the other on his side of the desk, then he passed Walter a bottle. "Coke tastes better out of glass bottles," he said. "Don't you think?"

"I've never noticed," Walter said.

"Plastic leaves a residue that causes cancer. Did you know that?"

"I didn't know," Walter said. "Hamburgers clog your arteries, though. If you don't believe me, ask my wife."

The old man took a conservative bite and chewed slowly. "Your conversation with the supervisors this morning," he said, violating the most basic rule of conversation during meals by talking with food in his mouth. "What did you expect to come of it?"

"News travels fast," Walter said. "I suppose you've come to lecture me?"

"On the contrary, Mayor Pigg, I'm here to bow to the master." He laughed as he took another bite. "You threw quite a scare into those boys and let me tell you they deserve it. A more crooked bunch I've never seen. Dirty bastards every one, pardon my French."

"All I did was stop by to say good morning."

Kilfiche laughed. Walter had never seen him so animated. "Right now they're probably at home throwing stuff out the back door."

"Stuff?"

"Big screen TVs, grandfather clocks. Whatever gifts contractors and suppliers pass under the table these days."

"I'm surprised I haven't heard from Brad."

"They threw him out first," the judge said, laughing and chewing. "Out the back door like piss from a bucket. Canceled all their contracts and told him he was finished."

The plan had worked better than Walter had hoped. "The next board meeting should be interesting."

"Theirs or ours?"

"Ours," Walter said. "I may as well tell you now, I'm not resigning. Brad Stovall can threaten all he wants but —."

"You don't know?"

"Know what?"

The judge stopped chewing and grinned. "Stovall resigned."

"No."

"About an hour ago. I thought surely you knew."

Walter had expected to rattle his cage, but not this. The three man alliance was broken. "Effective when?"

"Immediately. He's out. No more Brad."

"What happens to his seat?"

"We'll have a special election. Don't be surprised if Palo runs for it."

"Not as long as I'm mayor," Walter said. "He's too proud."

Kilfiche smiled. "You know, I think you're right." He slapped the table with the flat of his hand. "By golly Walter you may be a mayor yet!"

* * *

Tipton heard it from Dexter Mann. Brad Stovall had gone off the deep end and resigned his seat. He didn't know if Mann was fishing for a quote he might use in Wednesday's paper or if he was genuinely concerned.

"Just write the damned article and leave me out of it," Tipton said after listening to Mann's drivel.

"Which way should I go with it?"

"You're the writer. Write." Tipton knew what he meant. He could cover for Stovall or skewer him. Say he resigned to spend more time with his family, or tell the truth. Leave some skin on him so he could run again someday, or flay him. Mann's problem was that he couldn't make a decision for himself. He needed someone to tell him what to do. What to write. "Ask him why he resigned then write what he says."

"What's eating you?" Mann asked. Tipton dropped the phone into the cradle, Candice stuck her head through the door and asked if he was all right, claiming she had heard him yelling but he was certain he hadn't raised his voice. She'd been lurking outside his door, eavesdropping, or waiting for an opportunity to come in and make sure he noticed she was wearing the blouse with the low button again. Maybe she regretted blowing him off when he called Saturday morning.

"Get out and close the door."

She told him he had a one o'clock.

"Cancel it. Clear my calendar for the afternoon."

"But he's already here."

"Out!"

She slammed the door. Tipton flipped through the calendar in his brain, trying to remember who his one o'clock was. Tolbin something. Richard. No, Ralph. Who names their kid Ralph anymore? Ralph Tolbin, the old man who slipped and fell in the Piggly Wiggly. Had he fallen in Walmart or Walgreens it might be a case worth his time. Maybe he could push him off on Rance.

He called Stovall. "What the hell do you mean resigning without asking me first?"

"I don't work for you," Stovall said.

Tipton could tell he'd been drinking. Washing down the bile of kneeling before the great Walter Pigg. "Withdraw it. Take a few days off and think it through. Take the wife to the beach."

"My wife hates the beach."

"Nobody hates the beach," Tipton said. "Ask her and see what she says."

"It's January."

"All the more reason to go. You'll have the place to yourself so you can get your head on straight."

"You got yours on straight?"

"Don't worry about me. You get your ass back on that board and do your job."

"I am doing my job," Stovall said. "Hauling dirt and gravel's my job. The only reason I ran for alderman was to get more business and now look at me. I'll probably go bankrupt but it won't matter because I'll be in prison."

"Nobody's going to prison," Tipton said, then he slammed the phone down and pinched the bridge of his nose between his thumb and forefinger to stop the room from spinning. Everything was coming apart and all he could think about was that in three hours he'd be picking Autumn up at school and her friends would be staring at him. *There he is. The loser husband. The man who's not Eli Naked Dobine.* Where do they get off? What right do they have whispering about him behind his back? It's her they should be talking about. She's the one who broke the trust.

That was the nut of it. Trust. Tipton had never trusted anyone except Autumn. Not his mother. Not his father. Not Rance. Not any of his teachers or his pastor or —.

Tears welled in his eyes and would have spilled over had he not wiped them with the cuff of his shirt. At least the door was closed. Candice might barge in. She'd been known to. She took liberties with the lack of employee discipline. Blame that one on Rance.

He tried to push Candice out of his head. The last thing he needed was another complication. That's all it was — a complication. One tiny span of time in a lifetime of spans that would barely be a wrinkle after all was said and done. Not true. Autumn *was* his life. Everything he had built was for her. For them. He hadn't realized it until he stood in the doorway of that hotel room in Memphis and saw her riding Eli Dobine. Room 512. They were alive because killing her would have meant killing himself. Two lives with one bullet. Three lives with two bullets, actually, because Eli Dobine was there, and wretched or not, he amounted to a life. All lives have some value. Most lives. With a violent swipe of his arm he cleared the desk. Everything went flying. His stapler hit the floor and broke open at the hinge. Paperclips scattered. Ink pens and paper tumbled and bounced. Only his nameplate remained. Tipton Palo against the world.

The door opened and there stood Candice again.

"Get out!"

CHAPTER 34

Dexter Mann's treatment of Brad Stovall's resignation in Wednesday's paper began and ended on page two. The article was short and to the point: Alderman Brad Stovall tendered his resignation amid a cloud of suspicion. There was more, but not much more. Mann left readers with the impression that Stovall was somehow afoul of the law and would soon be dealt with.

"This is where they eat their own," Brant Haskell said to Walter as he strode into his office uninvited. All of a sudden he was taking Walter's calls again and Walter hadn't even called. "I've seen this sort of thing before." He tossed a rolled-up copy of the Hayes Beacon onto Walter's desk, then sat without being asked. Haskell was a man accustomed to getting his way. The kind of man Walter typically avoided, yet here they were, entangled, because one had talked the other into running for mayor.

"By all means, have a seat," Walter said. He pushed the newspaper aside without unrolling it. "I've seen it already."

"Brad Stovall froze me out of the city's fuel business two years ago and I want it back." Walter opened his mouth to speak but Haskell raised his hand and cut him off. "I'm not here asking for favors. I'm demanding what's due me."

"Due you?"

"I turned in low bids every single time and Stovall threw them out because he said I wasn't big enough to handle demand."

"I didn't know he had that kind of power," Walter said.

"Him and his two clowns -- Lyle Townsend and Wayne Toms. They've cost me a lot of money. I had to lay off two drivers. Jobs that went to Tupelo."

"I won't use my influence for your personal gain," Walter said.

"I put you in that seat."

"Here it comes," Walter said. "I've been wondering when you'd get around to it."

Haskell hammered the desk with his fist. "How much money do you think the city spends at Lyle Townsend's feed store?"

"I wouldn't know."

"Twenty thousand dollars last year. All I want is my share of the city's fuel business. Give me Water and Light and I'll be happy."

"It's not my call."

"Remember when the city built the sports complex? Care to guess who hauled in all that dirt?"

"You don't have to worry about Stovall anymore."

"Exactly one month after Stovall led the charge to switch the city's seed business to his buddy Townsend. Quid pro quo."

Walter understood his anger but there really wasn't anything he could do.

"Easter's coming up," Haskell said. "Wayne Toms supplies the eggs."

"His supermarket," Walter said. He sighed. "Of course."

"And the Fourth of July picnic in the park? Bet you can't guess when the city started handing out free bottled water to the public."

"With the city buying the water from Toms?"

"Now you're catching on," Haskell said. "Every dollar that passes through this town gets squeezed by somebody."

Walter wondered about Sharp and Kilfiche. Suddenly no one was above suspicion. "I'll see what I can do," he said. "As long as it's legal."

* * *

Autumn took it upon herself to move into the guest bedroom. Rance would handle the divorce for Tipton if it came to it, though he still hoped he could salvage his marriage. Losing her to another man made him realize how much he wanted her, or it made him want her more than he ever had. He couldn't be sure which. Feelings are slippery things. For the entirety of their marriage Tipton had been in control. He had called the shots. Until now he hadn't realized she minded. He was happy, so he naturally thought she was too. Content, now that he thought about it. Satisfied. Happiness exists on another level, out of reach for most people. Happiness is a pipe dream. A charade. A farce. No one is really happy. How can they be? It goes against human nature to be happy.

He barely read the newspaper. Stovall meant nothing to him. Let him go back to trucking dirt and gravel. Tipton had covered his tracks where Stovall was concerned. He wasn't worried. Autumn had thrown his life back into perspective. She wanted them to go see a counselor, as though he had done something wrong instead of her, or something as wrong as what she did. As though a counselor had some magic wand to wave and make Eli Dobine go away. Clothe him and flush him from Tipton's memory. Whoever said life isn't fair hit the nail on the head. Somebody should give that person a medal. Fair would be him taking Candice to a hotel to even the score. Everyone would suspect him of it anyway so why not do it? Rich young attorney with an attractive secretary in his employ. Dexter Mann could splash Autumn's affair on the front page of the Hayes Beacon every week for a month and people would still blame him for offending first. Why hadn't he?

Candice came into his office with some papers. When she stopped, her scent washed across his desk and enveloped him. "What perfume is that?"

"I don't wear perfume."

"You're wearing something."

She smiled. A woman can't help but smile when she's being flattered. It didn't mean anything. "Probably my lotion," she said, then she probably told him what brand she used but his eyes were unfastening the buttons on her blouse and he didn't process the information. She noticed because her hand instinctively went to her neck and gathered the collar that was already gathered. She asked him if he was feeling better, but she didn't really care if he was or wasn't. Her tone betrayed her. Tone is the layman's lie detector. Tone and the eyes. No one can control both at the same time. Her eyes betrayed her discomfort and her tone betrayed her lack of concern.

"If you'll sign these papers I'll take them to the courthouse," she said.

"You've heard about my marriage," he said without meaning to. Something in the moment drew the words out without his brain's permission. He was on the verge of flirting with her and he hadn't flirted in years. Not since he dated Autumn. Perhaps that's why his marriage went sour -- they stopped flirting. He stopped first. The entirety of his married life flashed before his eyes and he felt himself wanting to confide in someone. In Candice, either because she was there or because she looked like a soft place for a man with troubles to land.

"Yes," she said. "I'm sorry."

"We're trying to work things out."

"That's good," she said, but he didn't believe her.

He stopped signing and looked at her. "You say that but you don't mean it."

"Of course I do."

"I read people for a living," he said. "Go ahead and say what's on your mind."

"It's none of my —."

"I could use a good dose of honesty."

She straightened herself and exhaled. "Okay. Can you can forgive her for what she did?"

The Christian answer was yes, but he had asked for honesty so he gave it in return. "I don't know."

"You can't work things out if you can't forgive her."

"She betrayed me. She'll have to accept certain conditions."

"Such as?"

"Me knowing where she is at all times. Access to her phone."

"Sounds like probation."

"She deserves it."

"Do you?"

"I don't understand."

"You can't make her miserable without being miserable yourself."

He hadn't thought of it that way. She was right, but what choice did he have? Divorce would mean financial disaster for him and a windfall for her. It wouldn't matter that she cheated. He finished signing the papers and offered them back, gripping them as she took hold. "This is all her fault you know."

"Is it?"

"What's that supposed to mean?"

She pulled the papers from his hand. "There's always blame on both sides."

"She cheated on me."

"Rance told me one time that you control a courtroom like no one he's ever seen."

"He said that?"

"Marriage isn't a courtroom."

* * *

Walter made good on his promise to Brant Haskell and had lunch with Will Denver, the superintendent of public works. Like so many men in appointed positions, Denver had held the position for decades. They exhausted the noon hour over burgers at the diner with Denver proclaiming that he didn't normally have lunch with mayors. Walter thought it best to talk to him directly before approaching the aldermen, and he was soon glad he had because the superintendent seemed very open to the idea of doing business with Haskell.

"Ain't right the way they pushed him out," Denver said. "Local businessman just trying to make a living. Now I'm forced to buy fuel out of Tupelo, and my equipment don't run a bit better on Prater fuel than Haskell fuel."

They talked about the bidding process and how corrupt it was. Worse than Walter had ever imagined. Mayors and aldermen and supervisors oversee a lot of money, and stand to make a lot if they play their cards right. Kilfiche and Sharp were straight shooters, at least as far as Denver knew. Mayor Sherman had been too, though there had been rumors near the end. Nothing substantiated, and nothing Denver believed. A damned lie, was how he phrased it. Something Tipton Palo was behind because he wanted to be mayor so bad he could taste it.

"You sure did knock the wheels off his wagon," Denver said, laughing as though remembering some highlight of his life. At that moment Walter felt as though he could ask for anything and the superintendent would break his neck trying to deliver. Instead, he asked only that Denver speak favorably if the aldermen asked his opinion on the fuel contracts. Denver went a step further and promised to contact them instead. If the mayor could stand up, so could he. The meeting ended with a firm handshake and Will Denver's exuberant endorsement of Walter as the town's mayor. "The town needs a man who's not afraid to buck the system," Denver said. "Needs it bad."

* * *

Matt Harper didn't do lawn work himself, but he oversaw the crew that kept Tipton's lawn immaculate. Harper owed his business survival to Palo, and he rarely missed an opportunity to kiss his ass. Less than an hour ago he was having lunch at the diner and overheard snatches of a conversation between the mayor and the city superintendent. Now he was in the outer office trying to bulldoze his way past Candice.

Tipton heard the commotion and recognized Harper's voice immediately. Something about Pigg, and he heard him say Mister Denver. He told Candice over the intercom to let the boy back. Five seconds later the twenty-something-year-old entrepreneur stood two feet from Tipton's desk saying he heard Mayor Pigg talking to Will Denver about giving fuel contracts to Brant Haskell. They talked about Brad Stovall, too, but he only heard bits and pieces.

"Mister Denver told the mayor he was glad to see somebody finally stand up to you, Mister Palo."

"Stand up to me?"

"He said you were behind something, but I couldn't make out what. It sounded like he was really coming after you."

"Denver?"

"No sir. The mayor."

Tipton fixated on the young man, tapping his fingertips together, wondering what kind of man Will Denver was and how much Stovall had told him. Stovall had a big mouth, and now that he had resigned there would probably be more Will Denvers popping up.

"Why bring this to me?"

Harper grinned like a bellhop who had lugged up the heavy bag. "I — uh —."

"I'm not in the fuel business," Tipton said.

"He … Mr. Denver … said you were the reason he —."

"Whatever scheme Will Denver and Brad Stovall hatched didn't involve me," Tipton said. It was true, too. Denver was mad at Haskell because he either didn't get a kickback or didn't get as much as he felt he deserved. Tipton remembered only because Stovall had come to him for advice. He owed one of the other aldermen a favor but he didn't want to land in jail over a corruption charge. Tipton sent him away with a warning to keep his mouth shut and stop advertising it and he would be fine. Kickbacks are as much a part of government contracts as the bids themselves. More, perhaps, because a bid takes a lot of paperwork and a kickback only takes an understanding.

Matt Harper couldn't keep his hands still. Didn't know quite what to do with them. He was on the witness stand and his story had just come apart and everyone was looking at him, wondering what next. Tipton enjoyed the boy's discomfort. He used discomfort as a tool. A means to an end.

"Forget what you heard," Tipton said, "or *think* you heard." He shooed him away, then told him not to go around repeating his nonsense because somebody might believe it.

"Yes sir," the boy said. He had just dropped his lollipop in the sand and he didn't know whether to pick it up or cry.

"Go! I'm busy!"

He bolted. Tipton watched him dart away like a frightened rabbit, then he buzzed Candice and told her to do her job next time. Seconds later he felt Rance's presence in the doorway but pretended not to. One rabbit taking the place of another. He wasn't in the mood.

"What was that about?"

"Nothing," Tipton said without looking up.

Rance came in and plopped down and threw his leg over the arm of the chair as was his habit.

"I'm busy, Rance."

"The trouble with you, Tip, is that you look down on people."

He ignored the shortening of his name this time. Rance was trying to get under his skin. Trying to prod him into another fight. Why, he didn't know, but Rance was … well, Rance. "Go away."

"You're brooding," Rance said. "You're bringing your personal life to work with you and it's bad for business."

Tipton looked him square in the eyes and told him to get out. Rance laughed it off. "The trouble with me is, I don't mind your grouchy disposition. That's why we can be partners without ripping each other's throats out. Well, almost without ripping each other's throats out."

"You're about two seconds from testing that theory," Tipton said.

"Don't you have court this morning?"

"All the more reason for you to get out."

"I heard a nasty rumor," Rance said. "Something about you going into court drunk."

"I wasn't drunk."

"Drinking then," Rance said. "People are starting to talk."

Tipton slammed the desk with his fist. "Get out!"

Rance unhitched his leg from the chair. "You get a mulligan because you're going through a rough patch," he said. "Don't push it too far. You don't have that many friends left."

"I'm finding out who my real friends are," Tipton said. He felt a sudden urge to punch Rance in the face.

"And your real friends are finding out who you are."

Tipton closed his eyes and squeezed the bridge of nose, hoping that when he opened them again Rance would be gone. "Thank you for your concern," he said, trying hard to sound sincere. Rance had come in to see if he'd been drinking. The entire visit had been a sobriety test.

"Take it easy on Candice," Rance said. "She doesn't know how to take you sometimes."

Tipton sat with his fists clenched and watched his partner leave. Candice had probably told him everything. More than everything, and Rance probably gobbled it up. People believe what they want to believe. Who else had she told? He pulled open his bottom drawer and lifted out a bottle. Vodka. Something Judge Bishop couldn't smell.

CHAPTER 35

"I want Pigg dead."

Stubbs looked down from the seat of his Dodge pickup with unmistakable amusement. For a moment Tipton thought he might laugh. He didn't like sitting low in his car like an underling to the high and mighty Stubbs, but the man refused to get out and talk face to face. People pass by and see two men talking and yada yada yada.

They were parked in the lot of an abandoned factory. One of several abandoned factories in the town's only industrial park. It was a clear day. The sky was solid blue without a cloud in sight, and Tipton wished he could wad it into a ball and hurl it into space. "Didn't you hear what I said? I want Pigg dead."

"I heard you."

"Walter, not his dim-witted brother."

Stubbs pulled the cigar from his left check then shoved it back into the right. Wet and slick and nasty. "I got no clue what you're talking about," he said. "Now if you need something pawned, say, your wedding ring for instance, then just stop by the shop and see my man. He'll give you top dollar. Tell him I said so."

"Drop the bullshit," Tipton said. "And leave my marriage out of this."

"I only agreed to meet because you sounded desperate on the phone. You in some kind of trouble?"

"You think I'm wearing a wire? Is that where we are now?"

"Makes no difference to me if you are or not," Stubbs said. "I got nothing to hide." He grinned and showed bits of cigar on his teeth. Disgusting.

"Look," Tipton said, "I've got as much to lose as you do, maybe more, so drop the gangster routine. This new man you've got — is he as good as you say he is?"

"What man?"

"Let him take care of it."

"Is that band solid gold, or just gold plated?"

"Stop jerking me around! Tell me the man's name and I'll talk to him myself!"

Stubbs chomped his cigar and grinned again. "I think the name I heard was Eli Dobine."

Tipton jerked the car into gear and lunged forward, then he stomped the brake and backed up again. "How do you know about Dobine?"

Stubbs grinned with his entire face this time. He pulled the cigar from his jaw and held it soggy end up, examining it, talking to Tipton but looking at the cigar. "I know Dobine." He laughed. "Hell, I know everybody."

Tipton gripped the steering wheel until his knuckles turned white. If he'd had a gun he would've shot Stubbs dead. "Did you send Dobine after my wife?"

Stubbs tucked the cigar back into his mouth, still grinning. Grinning like an opossum. "Shit, Palo, what I hear about your wife ... nobody has to go sending anybody."

Tipton stomped the accelerator and sped away. If Stubbs sent Dobine to steal his wife he'd kill him. Both of them. Stubbs and Dobine dead together. He turned into the street without looking and pushed his foot all the way to the floor. The car's engine whined and his head jerked every time the transmission shifted. Four times, then he had to let off and go hard on the brakes because the street T'd and there was nothing straight ahead but fence and the back side of a foam plant.

What I hear about your wife ...

He turned left and took his foot off the pedals and let the car coast. What had Stubbs heard about Autumn? His life was upside down and he didn't know how to set it right again.

* * *

Walter's euphoric rise from the ashes of public ridicule ended when Mildred called him to the front window because a white Dodge truck was sitting in their driveway. Walter recognized the truck immediately. He ordered Mildred upstairs to get his gun from the closet. Giving her orders wasn't something Walter took lightly, but he knew she would go and not argue. She trotted upstairs without asking who or why. Fear has a way of motivating people.

He fingered a slat in the blinds and peered out. Stubbs was ten feet from the front step. Walter looked back at the empty staircase and yelled up for Mildred to stay put. Don't come down. She didn't know how to fire a gun, let alone shoot a man. She could point it and threaten, though, if Stubbs made it upstairs and went after her. Stubbs didn't know she couldn't shoot.

Stubbs pounded on the door instead of ringing the bell. The man had probably never rang a doorbell in his life. Ringing a doorbell is too feminine. Too girly for a man like Stubbs. Walter's blood ran cold. He regretted going to the pawnshop and puffing his chest out like some television gangster.

"Open up, Pigg! I know you're home."

Mildred had probably already dialed 9-1 and stood ready with her finger hovering to complete the call. "My wife's already called the police."

"You'll want to call that off," Stubbs said through the door. "This is a friendly visit."

Walter opened the door. Stubbs held a packet in his hand. A manila envelope large enough to contain letters unfolded, or more photographs of beaten daughters. The envelope bulged against the brass-colored clasp. "You've got balls, Pigg," he said. "Damn me if you didn't used to be the sorriest excuse for a man I'd ever seen." He pushed the envelope into Walter's chest.

"What's this?"

"Tipton Palo."

Walter clutched the envelope without meaning to. Stubbs looked older than he remembered. "I don't understand."

"You will," Stubbs said, then he turned and walked back to his truck.

* * *

Tipton noticed the portrait of himself hanging cocked on the wall. He straightened it, then he stepped back to admire it, remembering when Autumn surprised him with the artist on his fortieth birthday. The thing had taken a week because he refused to sit still for more than an hour at a time, but the piece came out perfect. From the moment the paint dried it had stood guard over his wall safe. Now something had cocked it.

Autumn had been home alone all day, or had she? Maybe she had called Eli Dobine over and they had tried to hack his combination, or maybe it wasn't Dobine. If Stubbs was right, it might have been any man in town. Any man at all. He thought about Matt Harper — the yard man — and all sorts of nasty things raced through his mind. Young man, older woman. Maybe Harper had been a student of hers back when she had looked better. Maybe Harper didn't care how she looked because she looked good enough for an afternoon romp. First the wife, then the lawn. How many times had it happened?

He slapped the portrait off the wall and sent it tumbling across the floor, then his heart stopped. They hadn't guessed the combination — they had blown the safe open with a torch.

"Autumn!" He bellowed to the top of his lungs. Bellowed so hard his throat hurt. Her car was in the garage so he knew she was home, unless —. "AUTUMN!"

Something crunched beneath his feet and he looked down. Tiny fragments of something hard. Metal. Bits of safe heated and splattered by the torch. The door of the safe stood ajar with a hole blown through where the locking mechanism had been. Only one hole so somebody knew their safes. Autumn hadn't done it alone. She probably wouldn't know which end of a torch to light, but she knew where the safe was. Nobody else knew that but her. Everybody probably assumed he had one, but nobody but Autumn *knew*.

His throat felt like a two-day hangover when he pulled the door open. Of course the money was gone but that wasn't what concerned him. The documents were gone too. Damning, detailed documents. Only Autumn's car keys remained. Was that some kind of hidden message? "Autumn! Get your ass down here!" He had locked them away until she learned to behave herself, now she was gone and his life was over. Really over, not just lovesick over. The documents had been his insurance policy against Stubbs. Against other people too, but especially against Stubbs. Now Autumn would use them to blackmail him. By now she knew everything. All the ugliness he had shielded her from so she could live like royalty.

He leaned his head against the wall and wept. Tears flowed down his cheeks as he sobbed uncontrollably. A hand touched his shoulder. His first thought was that he was about to be executed, but the hand was gentle, not firm. Familiar. He turned and saw Autumn. Her left eye was swollen shut and her bottom lip was fat and crusted with blood. He grabbed her by the shoulders and shook her. "Who did this?"

She looked away.

"Was it Dobine?"

Her eyes flew wide. He knew without her saying that it wasn't Dobine. "Some man," she said, as though she were caught in a nightmare she couldn't escape, like Dorothy getting spun away by the tornado in the Wizard of Oz.

"Old or young?" He shook her and told her to think. "Was it Perry Stubbs?" She shook her head. If not Stubbs then who? "Do you know his name? Talk to me damn it!"

Her lips quivered and she started to cry. "He raped me."

* * *

Walter opened the envelope and dumped the contents onto the kitchen table with Mildred videoing it with her phone. Videoing had been her idea. An excellent one, considering all Walter knew about Stubbs. She stood across the table from him and he kept having to remind her to point her phone at the envelope instead of his face.

The envelope contained papers. Hand-scribbled notes and typed pages with dates and times and dollar amounts, all with names attached, and brief descriptions. Many of the names Walter recognized, some he didn't. What was Stubbs's angle?

"He's given me Tipton Palo with a big bow tied around him," he said to Mildred. "But I don't know why." He examined a document then held it up for her to see. "Remember that lawsuit a few years ago against Drucker Industries? Palo raked in almost a million dollars." He held the paper straight with both hands so she could video it. "This is a list of jurors. He bribed Randal Kemp, Joliene Mercer, and Charles Beal."

Mildred gasped. "Charles goes to our church."

He held up another paper. "This scribble is hard to read but it shows a payment of twenty thousand dollars to W. A. Benson two weeks before he died." The board would eat crow on that one, he thought, as he returned it to the pile. There was nothing on Stubbs, though, which didn't surprise him considering the source.

* * *

First Tipton had a drink to steady his nerves, then he had another. Three hours later he woke up on the sofa in the living room with an empty whiskey bottle on the floor two inches from his hand. His head throbbed and his vision was blurred and his mouth felt like cotton. It only took a few seconds for him to remember the safe, but it took a full minute to sort out whether or not he had confronted Stubbs. He hadn't. The only thing he had confronted was a bottle of Wild Turkey.

He pushed himself up and staggered upstairs and out onto the balcony. It was dark and cold. The wind was out of the north and it whipped up the tail of his shirt as he stood at the rail and stared out across the golf course and saw snatches of brown grass that would be green in two months. Autumn was in bed asleep or pretending to be. Tears seeped into his eyes but didn't spill over. He had cried himself out. Whoever had his records held his life in his hands. The police would have used a search warrant, not a torch, and they wouldn't have raped his wife. It had to be Stubbs — his new man. If Stubbs had the documents then there was a glimmer of hope. Stubbs couldn't go to the police. It went against every wretched thing the man stood for, not to mention the fact that he would be sending himself to prison. They had themselves a cold war, protected from each other by the threat of mutual destruction. So why had Stubbs betrayed him?

The ground looked farther away than it actually was because the lack of light played tricks on his eyes. If he jumped it might break his neck, or it might break everything else and leave him helpless. Suffering. It was the first time in his life he had thought of committing suicide and it was a fleeting thought, replaced almost immediately by an overpowering urge to destroy everyone who came against him. Pigg became an afterthought. Stubbs had pushed Pigg to the back burner. Revenge took a back seat to survival.

Stubbs was smug when he answered. Tipton knew without asking that he was responsible. "I want my papers back," Tipton said in his sternest voice. Stern laced with alcohol.

"I don't have them."

"The hell you don't," Tipton said. "And you tell that new man of yours he's dead for what he did to my wife."

Stubbs laughed. "You're drunk."

"And I want my ten thousand dollars back."

"I don't have that either," Stubbs said.

"Jonce Nash," Tipton said, suddenly remembering the man's name. It was an odd name, Jonce. One he should've remembered. "You tell Jonce Nash he's dead."

"Tell him yourself," Stubbs said, "but I'd advise you to be careful. He scares me a little." He laughed. Nobody scared Stubbs, not even a little.

"You can't use any of it," Tipton said, meaning the papers. "If I go down, you go down. That's how this plays out. You've got your ledger and I've got my papers."

"Except you don't have your papers anymore," Stubbs said. "And I've still got my ledger."

"You'd be a fool to use it."

"I don't intend to," Stubbs said. "And I don't have your papers. Well, I have some — everything with my name on it — but the rest I gave to Pigg."

Tipton felt himself choking. Literally choking. Unable to breathe. A gurgling sound rose up from his throat then the dam burst and he exhausted himself into the phone.

Stubbs laughed. He wouldn't stop laughing.

"You're lying," Tipton said. "You'd be stupid to —."

"You're finished," Stubbs said, no longer laughing. His voice came across the line hard and cold, like steel pulled across silk. "You've become a liability."

"Pigg hates you."

"And now he owes me a favor. Two birds with one stone."

"I'll tell everything I know."

"You won't talk," Stubbs said.

"Like hell I won't."

"You've got a wife to think about," Stubbs said. "Be a shame if something bad happened to her. Something really, terribly bad."

Tipton tried to say nice try, that she had cheated on him and he didn't care, but his voice cracked and he couldn't say it even to save himself.

"And your momma," Stubbs said. "Don't forget about momma."

"Okay," Tipton said, barely audible. "Okay."

CHAPTER 36

Walter went to Tipton Palo's law office with a large manila envelope clutched against his side. The young lady at the reception desk didn't know quite what to do with herself when she looked up and saw him. When he politely asked to see Tipton Palo, she hesitated, as if unable to completely process the request, then she left her desk and disappeared into an office with Palo's name on the door. After a moment the door opened again and the woman stepped out looking somewhat more relaxed. She waited until she reached her desk and sat again before telling him he could go in.

The office was grand compared to Walter's. Expensive furniture, paintings signed by artists he had never heard of, a gigantic desk that probably cost more than all the furnishings in City Hall combined. Palo wore a perfectly pressed white shirt with a blue tie loose at the neck, but his hair was sloppy, as though it had been combed in the dark, and he had dark circles underneath his eyes.

Palo didn't ask him to sit. His eyes followed the package Walter carried.

"May I sit down?"

"Yes," Palo said, straightening himself. "Can I get you a drink? Coffee?"

"No," Walter said. "I'll only be a minute. I know you're busy." He patted the envelope. "Extremely busy." He took his time sitting, partly because of the pain but mostly to draw the thing out. Palo deserved to suffer.

Palo's Adam's apple stroked his throat. "You're the last person in the world I expected."

"Am I? Perhaps you expected someone more official — someone like Detective Gant, or maybe Sergeant Snapper?"

Palo's eyes searched for the envelope that was now hidden by the desk. Walter lifted it and placed it between them. Palo wanted to grab it — to snatch it away and run with it, but he was too smart for that. He hadn't gotten where he was by being rash.

"Someone delivered this to me last night," Walter said. "Go ahead, take it.

You already know what's in it?"

Of course he knew. Every twitch of his body said he knew, but still he couldn't resist fingering open the clasp and making sure. A man who makes his living dealing in facts can't take someone's word for something so monumental.

"Photocopies," Walter said.

Palo's Adam's apple stroked his throat again. "And the originals?"

"Someplace safe," Walter said. "Safer than where you kept them."

"In your possession?"

"I haven't shown them to the police, if that's what you mean," Walter said. The effect was immediate on Palo's face. A glimmer of hope, then something devious. "If you're thinking you can kill me and no one will know, don't. I've made arrangements should that happen." Walter had no such arrangements other than Mildred also knowing, but he felt the need to throw it in.

"How much?"

Walter had expected him to try and buy his way out. One private transaction and he and Mildred could retire in comfort. He could resign his office and put all the fuss and worry of trying to please the un-pleasable behind him. Curiosity tempted him to throw out some ridiculous figure, but he refrained. Better to stick to the plan he had rehearsed in the car on the way over. "They're not for sale."

"Then why are you here?"

"I want you to tell me what's missing," Walter said.

"What's missing?"

"I know you and Stubbs have some kind of racket going, but nothing in any of these documents implicates him."

"I don't know what you're talking about," Palo said. "I hardly know Stubbs."

Walter stood without noticing the pain in his back. He would feel it later, after the adrenaline was gone, but at that moment he felt nothing but impending victory. "You have twenty-four hours to give me Stubbs or I'll turn everything over to the police." He waited for Palo to absorb the ultimatum. "Ball can't fix this one for you." He tapped the envelope with a finger. There wasn't much on Ball, but there was enough to keep him from interfering.

* * *

It took all morning for Tipton to locate Jonce Nash and arrange a secret meeting. He was brash and conceited and showed absolutely no hint of loyalty to Perry Stubbs or anyone else on earth. He said he had a wife who was dead and a boy who had run off to Mexico with two tramps -- a hobo and a whore, and they were pretending to be a family and they had no idea he knew where to find them. All he needed was money, and Stubbs paid better than the job he had at the feed store lumping fifty-pound sacks of who-cares-what with a bunch of Mexicans whose only English is nod and grin.

"I'll make you rich," Tipton said.

"I ain't no hired killer," Nash said. "I ain't dying strapped to a gurney with a plug in my ass."

"We'll get to the details in a minute," Tipton said. "First I need some answers."

"First you give me the ten grand you promised," Nash said. They were sitting in Tipton's car inside an abandoned warehouse behind a furniture factory that had burned three times. It was dark except for the light that spilled in through the roll-up door Tipton had left up. His car was running and he wondered how Nash got there because there was no other vehicle in sight. It occurred to him that Stubbs may have dropped him off and he felt suddenly foolish. The gun in his waistband was useless with the man sitting so close. He should have put it underneath his leg, or in the pocket of his door.

"Why don't we get out so we're not so cramped," Tipton said, opening his door and flooding the car with light.

"Why don't we stay put and you give me the ten grand?"

Tipton pulled the door closed, extinguishing the light, unsure if Nash scared him more in color or in grayscale. The man's eyes were intense, as though a fire burned him up inside. He'd seen that look in clients high on narcotics, but Nash didn't give off the vibe of someone using. "You took more than ten thousand from my safe," he said, then he flinched when Nash grabbed him by the collar and shook him. The man was quick as a cat. Unbelievably fast. The gun in Tipton's belt was a joke. "Ten thousand's a drop in the bucket," Tipton stammered through the knot in his throat. The moment it took for Nash to release him and shrink to his side of the car seemed an eternity, then they both relaxed a bit. Tipton regained some self-control. Nash seemed the kind of man who would do anything for money. Anything but murder, if one believed him, which Tipton didn't.

"I'll listen," Nash said. "But you better know I tote me a big bucket."

"Fifty thousand," Tipton said. He was prepared to double it, but a man doesn't start with his best offer on the table. "And all you have to do is bring me the papers Stubbs took out of that envelope you stole from my safe."

"Two hundred grand and I won't beat you until blood runs out your ears."

"Beat me and you get nothing," Tipton said. He wasn't so scared anymore. Not the way he had been. The jolt of being grabbed by the throat had raised the bar. "He keeps an old ledger in the safe behind his desk. Bring me that too and I'll double it."

Nash hesitated too long not to be hooked, then he said one-fifty. Tipton refused to budge. "A man can do a lot in Mexico with that kind of money."

"He can do more with one-fifty."

"Corey Pickle will do it for fifty," Tipton said. "Probably less, and he has better access."

Nash grinned, showing a full set of incredibly white teeth that stood out against his scruffy features. "You seen Corey Pickle lately?"

A chill shot up Tipton's spine. "You said you don't do murder."

"I'm the damnedest liar you ever knowed," Nash said. "One hundred grand and if you cheat me I'll cut you up so slow it'll make the devil shit down his leg."

* * *

The clock was ticking for Palo. It had been almost twenty-four hours and Walter hadn't heard a peep. Trying to purchase dirt on Stubbs had been a long shot but one he had to take. Mildred knew nothing about their meeting. In twenty-three minutes and fourteen seconds he would make a phone call to Gant and hope he could shake something loose.

Palo burned up another four minutes and change. Walter allowed his cell phone to ring three times before he answered. Little things matter when you deal with unscrupulous men.

"How do I know you won't turn everything over to the cops after I give you what you want?"

"Do you have what I want?"

"That and more," Palo said. "I'll give you his ledger as a token of my good will."

"And I'll give you your documents back," Walter said.

"I'm supposed to take your word for it?"

"Unless you can think of a better way," Walter said. "Keeping in mind that having me killed sets off a process you can't possibly stop."

"I want everything," Palo said. "Including the copies. I won't have you holding this over my head."

"I've scanned everything into a PDF," Walter said. "Upon my death that copy gets emailed to the authorities. It's an automated service I found on the internet. It's amazing the things they do with technology these days. You can't possibly stop it, so you'd better make sure I stay alive." He really had found such a service on the internet.

"No deal," Palo said. "I won't live the rest of my life wondering when you'll drop dead and send me to prison."

"Better than spending it living in prison waiting to get out," Walter said. "Besides, I have a mechanism in place to protect you if I die a natural death." Mildred was that mechanism, though she didn't know it yet. No need worrying her with details until he knew the deal was solid. "And I suppose there's a statute of limitations with this sort of thing so you won't have to worry forever."

"And I'm supposed to take your word for all of this? I'm supposed to believe you'll let me go free when all you have to do is send an email?"

"You lawyers do this sort of thing all the time," Walter said. He had rehearsed it until the words flowed off his tongue without effort, as though they were true. As though he wouldn't turn everything over to Gant the moment he had the goods on Stubbs. Let God judge him for his dishonesty. Sin heaped on top of sin. "Little fish gives up the big fish in exchange for his freedom. Isn't that how it goes?"

"I'll send the package to you via my personal courier," Palo said. Walter was impressed that he had a personal courier but responded with a simple *that's fine*. Now the question was how long did he have to wait, and how was he going to break the news to Mildred?

* * *

Tipton sealed the documents and tattered ledger into a box with enough tape to survive a tornado, then dispatched his courier to the mayor's office with instructions to deliver it to the mayor and no one else. No exceptions. The boy he used was reliable and wouldn't be cowed by the mayor's wife. What Pigg shared with her was his business, but the boy was not to give her the package. He nodded that he understood then took off with the urgency his mission required.

He checked the tracking app on his phone to make sure Autumn was at school, or at least that her phone was at school. Tracking her whereabouts would be part of his daily routine now, like checking his email. Her sins were now his burden. His cross to bear. Being raped, if it actually happened that way, didn't erase her infidelity. Sometimes he called her between classes to make sure she didn't leave the phone with a friend. Text messages weren't enough, he had to verify her location and identity and she had to submit to it if she wanted to stay. Intended, not wanted. She'd made it clear she didn't want to stay, though she had agreed to try. Until he said otherwise, her phone was her ankle bracelet.

With the boy gone and Pigg on hold, Tipton called Jonce Nash and told him to meet him at the same warehouse in half an hour. Nash sounded eager. Tipton hoped he had the stomach for his next job. A man can do a lot with one hundred thousand American dollars in Mexico, but he can do a lot more with half a million.

CHAPTER 37

A courier arrived with a package for Walter. Mildred let him through because she had been told it was coming and what it contained. Walter had confided his plan to her and she was understandably terrified. He began to second-guess himself. As long as he withheld the information on Palo, he was guaranteed some degree of safety. Not only could Palo not touch him, but he had every incentive in the world to protect him from Stubbs. They shared a common interest, so to speak. Double-cross Palo and he might never feel safe again.

Mildred urged him to stick to his deal with Palo. Stubbs was his target. Without Palo's help Stubbs might find some loophole in the system and go free. Besides, Stubbs might not be the only one Walter needed protection from. Those documents, and that ledger, implicated a lot of important people. A lot of very powerful people. Walter would have a very large target on his back. So would everyone he loved.

On top of the stack of papers was a note. *Hold Off. You'll know when.*

* * *

Tipton sat in his car with his cell phone cradled in his hands, staring at the picture of Eli Dobine's bloody face. Blood from a gash below his right eye washed his entire cheek red. The eye was swollen shut. His nose bent leftward with cakes of blood and snot hanging over and into his open mouth. Two front teeth were missing and a third was broken halfway to the gum. The left eye looked full of misery and understanding. He wouldn't go near Autumn again. Nash had sent him the picture as a bonus — a thank you for your business kind of thing. Jonce Nash was a valuable asset, but he scared the hell out of Tipton because he had no discernible conscience. No soul. He was the kind of man put on earth for the sole purpose of bringing misery to others. Tipton put the phone down and lifted his foot off the brake and eased out of the parking lot and into the street. Five minutes later he got out and raised the steel door and pulled his car into the warehouse and waited. Nash was late. Every creak of the old structure made Tipton jump. He was sitting in his car in a dark warehouse with a briefcase full of cut up newspapers and a gun in his hand. The gun was untraceable back to him. Chief Benson had given it to him as a present over a decade ago. It was the only piece of physical evidence that tied his client to the murder of a liquor store clerk. Benson had been in his pocket ever since. It was Benson who introduced him to Stubbs, and Stubbs who introduced him to money. Real money.

He saw Nash walk through the roll-up door as though he were going to a picnic, as unaware of his fate as a cow riding the conveyor belt at a slaughterhouse. Content in his ignorance. Tipton couldn't possibly let him live. It wasn't just about the money anymore. It was simple cause and effect. Pigg was a conundrum to be dealt with in time.

Tipton pushed open his door and got out. He couldn't have blood in his car, plus he needed the freedom to move. He slipped the gun into his right front pocket with the butt partially exposed for easy access but not visible because it was dark. He wondered if Nash could see him at all, walking as he was with his back to the only source of light. The briefcase hung from Tipton's left hand, leaving the right free.

"Is he dead?"

Nash closed half the distance between them before responding. "Can a cat lick its ass?"

"You have a peculiar way with words."

"How'd you like that picture I sent over?"

"Touching," Tipton said. "How'd you know about Dobine?"

Nash laughed. "Hell, everybody knows about that. You got my money?"

"How do I know Stubbs is dead?"

"I slit his throat ear to ear," Nash said. "Whispering in his ear that you sent me as he drew his dying breath. Ain't that how you wanted it?"

Tipton hadn't dictated the method, but he approved. He tossed the briefcase at him, then raised the gun and fired. Nash batted the briefcase away and stumbled backward, then he fell to one knee and a hand. Tipton fired again. Nash scrambled to his feet and ran. Tipton emptied the gun at his back but Nash kept going. His ears rang and his heart raced. He fished his phone from his pocket and turned on the light and found the briefcase. There was blood on the floor. Not much but at least Nash was hit. Think, man, think. What if he goes to the cops? Or to the hospital and they call the cops? Calm down. Think. He tossed the gun and briefcase into the trunk and put his hands over his ears to stop the ringing. Maybe Stubbs wasn't really dead. Nash had sent a picture of Eli Dobine battered and bloody but not one of Stubbs. He called Stubbs's cell phone, then his office, already thinking alibi. Why would he call a man he thought was dead? It's not what they suspect, or even what they know. It's what they can prove, and nobody worked a jury like Tipton Palo.

* * *

Walter didn't have to wait long to know it was time. The news of Stubbs's death hit the town like a clap of thunder. Walter heard it directly from Gant, then social media exploded. The aldermen called him one-by-one in rapid succession, as did dozens of other officials and citizens wondering if he'd heard the news. Mildred screened the calls and eventually stopped letting them through altogether. Walter left his office and went to the police station with a box of documents in his hands that implicated Stubbs and a thumb drive in his pocket that implicated Palo. Stubbs's murder hadn't been part of the deal, and Walter wondered if he and Mildred were next.

A uniformed officer picked Jackson up from school and whisked him to City Hall and stood guard while Walter went out against the officer's advice. Tipton wouldn't dare gun him down in broad daylight on Main Street. For the first time since taking office, Walter entered the police station with the full authority of his position clearing his way. Gant waved him into his office and closed the door. Walter had told him over the phone what he had, now he would deliver the goods. Chief Ball tried to push his way in but Walter ordered him out. Ordered, not asked. Ball retreated. His hours were numbered. Walter had already called an emergency meeting of the board to remove the men named in the documents. Replacing them would be a monumental task that threatened to deplete the pool of human resources immediately available within each department. The reach of the evidence was so vast that Walter had considered keeping it to himself because of the damage it would do to the community and to the scores of people whose names were in the ledger. He felt sympathy for those who would be collateral damage, but keeping quiet would amount to complicity, so here he was, handing the box to the detective who would soon be chief.

"I want my family protected."

"You've got my word on that," Gant said.

Walter stared at him long enough to take his measure, then tossed the thumb drive into the box, ridding the town of more evil than an honest man could fathom.

www.ingramcontent.com/pod-product-compliance
Lightning Source LLC
Chambersburg PA
CBHW021103110726
47900CB00007B/2004